SAILING ON THE ICE

and Other Stories from the Old Squire's Farm

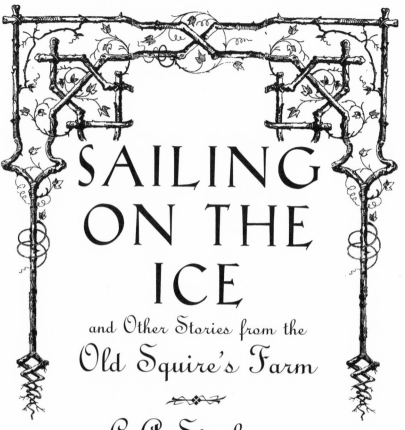

SAILING ON THE ICE

and Other Stories from the
Old Squire's Farm

C. A. Stephens

COMPILED AND EDITED BY
Charles G. Waugh and Larry Glatz

RUTLEDGE HILL PRESS
Nashville, Tennessee

Published in Nashville, Tennessee, by Rutledge Hill Press, 211 Seventh Avenue North,
Nashville, Tennessee 37219. Distributed in Canada by H. B. Fenn & Co., Ltd.,
34 Nixon Road, Bolton, Ontario L7E 1W2. Distributed in Australia by Millennium
Books, 33 Maddox Street, Alexandria NSW 2015. Distributed in New Zealand by
Tandem Press, 2 Rugby Road, Birkenhead, Auckland 10. Distributed in the United
Kingdom by Verulam Press, Ltd., 152a Park Street Lane, Park Street, St. Albans,
Hertfordshire AL2 2AU.

Typography by D&T/Bailey Typesetting, Inc., Nashville, Tennessee

Library of Congress Cataloging-in-Publication Data

Stephens, C. A. (Charles Asbury), 1844–1931.
    Sailing on the ice and other stories from the old squire's farm /
C. A. Stephens ; compiled and edited by Charles G. Waugh and Larry
Glatz.
        p.   cm.
    ISBN 1-55853-424-5
    1. Maine—Social life and customs—Fiction.   2. Grandparents—
Maine—Fiction.   3. Domestic fiction, American.   4. Farm life—
Maine—Fiction.   5. Children—Maine—Fiction.   6. Orphans—Maine—
Fiction.   7. Family—Maine—Fiction.   I. Waugh, Charles.
II. Glatz, Larry.   III. Title.
PS3537.T3533S75   1996
813'.52—dc20   96-30306
                                                                                   CIP

Printed in the United States of America
1 2 3 4 5 6 7 8 9 — 99 98 97 96

CONTENTS

INTRODUCTION

'TWAS JUST AFTER NEW YEAR'S DAY, 1870, THAT THE present writer, then a youth just emerging from his teens, climbed the two long flights of stairs at 151 Washington Street, Boston, and knocked at the door of the then unpretentious office of *The Youth's Companion* magazine. In my pocket, well out of sight, was an envelope containing two stories for which I was in bashful quest of a publisher. Less than a year previously, I had made the brave resolve to live by the use of a pen, but felt like putting it as modestly as possible.

In response to a knock that was so discreet that I had to repeat it, a low, gentle voice said, "Come in." On entering I saw sitting at a little table at the far end of the room with a single window—just beyond a tall coal stove in active operation, for it was a cold winter's morning—a spare, alert, neatly dressed man with black hair and a short, trim, dark beard busily correcting what looked to be a printer's "proof."

This was the publisher of *The Companion*, Mr. Daniel S. Ford, afterwards so widely known for his many charities, benevolences, and social works in Boston. At that time he had lately come into possession of *The Youth's Companion*, previously a child's periodical, and was working hard, conscientiously and painstakingly, to establish it as a safe, clean, and interesting journal for young people and the home circle. To this end, and with this purpose steadily in view, the entire energies of his life were devoted.

Something of this high purpose impressed itself upon his stray visitor on that first morning of our meeting. It was in his entire manner and in the reserved yet kindly smile with which he listened to the object of my call and the hope I expressed of becoming a contributor to the paper.

"You may leave your two stories with me," he said at length. "I will read them and tell you if I can use them. Come in again day after tomorrow."

On the occasion of my second call, Mr. Ford's manner was slightly less reserved. He asked me where I hailed from and where I was stopping in the city.

"I think I can use your two stories," he said. "What do you expect to get for them?"

I replied that I would be glad to receive whatever he was willing to pay.

"Will seven dollars satisfy you?" he asked. I said it would; though I had secretly hoped to receive ten. Secretly, too, I had hoped for a word of praise, but doubtless that was undeserved; I was only too well content to have the stories accepted and paid for.

"If you see fit, you may let me read two more of your stories," he said, and meantime wrote a few words on a slip of paper which he bade me hand to the lady I would find sitting at a desk in the back room down one flight of stairs on my way to the street. "That lady is Miss Gorham," he added. "She will pay you fourteen dollars."

That little dark room was then the business office of the paper, and it was at the hands of Miss Gorham that I received my first earnings as an author—two five-dollar bills and four ones—from *The Youth's Companion.*

The week following found me again ascending the stairs at 151 Washington Street, this time with two more efforts in the story line. These in due course were accepted and ten days later, two others. I was also much exhilarated by an increase in the price. "I shall pay you ten dollars a piece for these last stories," Mr. Ford had said.

During the following years, and even when *The Companion* became itself more prosperous, adding several hundred thousand names to its subscription list and moving to better quarters at 41 Temple Place, Mr. Ford himself was nearly always to be found in a small narrow office at the head of the first flight of stairs from the street, sitting at a little work table, changed as time passed for a small rolltop desk—a desk which at the time of his death in 1899, came into the writer's possession and is still a treasured memento.

In those early years with *The Companion*, it had been part of my services while traveling to collect materials for stories, to talk with boys and girls who read *The Companion*, as well as with their parents, and to learn from them what had pleased them best and what they would like in the future. During the first hour after returning to *The Companion* office from these trips, I talked over anything new I had learned in this respect with Mr. Ford, with a view to shaping my stories and articles in accord with the glimpses I had gained of popular taste.

One fact had long impressed me as a result of hundreds of conversations with young folks, namely, their desire to know whether this or that story published in the paper was really true and whether the characters portrayed in them were now living and if so, what they were doing at present. I discovered, if I were obliged to confess that the tale in which they had become interested was fiction, they appeared to be disappointed. Sometimes even, they did not scruple to find fault because they had been told an untruth.

Older people who read novels and other works of imagination, rarely asked such questions. They do not expect them to be true; they know that all such writing is of the author's invention. If the characters depicted are well drawn and lifelike, they do not inquire further.

With the young, however, that is not so. There is, I find, in our boys and girls an innate and still unvitiated desire for truth; they want to think that the stories they read and like are of actual occurrence.

In conversation with Mr. Ford I had several times mentioned this desire on the part of our younger readers, and I recall he replied, "That is a natural and healthy instinct. All fiction is in reality falsehood; the young distrust it; they desire truth."

Evidently this idea lingered in his mind, since some months later he suddenly asked me if it would be possible to satisfy this normal taste for true stories.

Not an easy question to answer, as stories were then and are now prepared. For a year or more I pondered it at odd moments: how to give young people which we could assure them were true and yet make them as graphic, dramatic, and generally entertaining as those tales of the imagination which authors were sending us.

Some progress was made by offering prizes to amateur writers of stories, but this effort demonstrated clearly that stories of actual experiences, by unskilled writers, are as a rule dull and lacking in interest. A good story, whether fact or fiction, requires skill in narration, and some literary gift on the part of the author. Yet there are thousands of experiences and adventures, lying latent and unrecorded in the memories of our people, which would make good stories if told with literary ability. How could these be obtained and put into print?

To this end the following plan was at length contrived. An envoy of *The Companion*—myself or someone else—was to make it their business to travel about and interview the readers of the paper, with a view to collecting incidents and adventures from their experiences in life and to gain permission to put these in story form. Merely the facts, details, and local "atmosphere" were to be obtained. This material was then to be brought to *The Companion* office, given into the hands of two or three expert writers, and put into proper story form. As a matter of courtesy the manuscript was later to be sent to the person who had contributed the tale for revision or further suggestion.

The project was under consideration for two months or more, and at length Mr. Ford took the opinion of several authors, and perhaps publishers. Mr. W. D. Howells, then editor of *The Atlantic*, believed it would succeed and become an element of great strength to *The Companion*—a tremendous advertisement in fact. Mr. J. T. Trowbridge held a similar opinion, and I believe that Thomas Bailey Aldrich concurred. Certain other writers of fiction objected to it, however, as might have been expected.

Mr. Ford's failing health held the plan in abeyance for a year or more. Finally he said to me one day at his home, "I still have faith in that plan of ours. I can see great possibilities in it for *The Companion*'s subscription list. Working it skillfully, we could make the paper a repository and a chronicle of the domestic and family history of the nation!"

"But I confess," he continued sorrowfully, "that I do not quite dare start on it without further demonstration. I am far from well. (He looked very ill that day.) Probably I shall not be with you to see this plan in operation.

"But let's test it a little further," he added after a pause. "You must have many recollections of your boyhood at your old home in Maine. Write out some of these reminiscences as stories. We will print them and see how they are received. If our readers like them we can go ahead with the general plan."

Acting on his suggestion I began to write the tales of our old farm neighborhood—memories of my boyhood at the old Squire's place or recollections of stories told to me by the old gentleman or others of his generation—more than two hundred of which have since appeared in *The Companion*. At first I supposed I would be able to remember no more than twelve or fifteen incidents that could be told as true stories. But as time passed, I found that more and more of these boyish remembrances came to my mind, and that whole volumes of stories could be made from recollections of our family and those of our neighbors. The favor these tales have won seems to have proved that the true story idea might be adopted with success.

Following this brief sketch of my earlier days in *The Companion's* service, therefore, I have ventured to append a little sheaf of those stories, written at Mr. Ford's suggestion those many years ago—several of which now appear in print for the first time. They may not be the best, but they were among the earliest efforts in the true-story line.

A longer version of the preceding introduction was written by C. A. Stephens for *Stories of My Home Folks*, a collection of stories that was originally published as a subscription premium by *The Youth's Companion* magazine in its centennial year, 1926. By that time, Stephens had been writing almost exclusively for the *Companion* for fifty-five years, during which time he had contributed more than fifteen hundred separate stories or serial episodes to the publication.

Indeed, at the turn of the century—just before movies and radio were to become the nation's preferred form of popular entertainment—*The Youth's Companion* was the most widely read family magazine in America, and C. A. Stephens was indisputably its most popular writer. His stories were so commercially successful, in fact, that in order to maintain the "diversity" of its contributors list while, at the same time, filling its magazine with articles that were sure to be read, *The Companion* published almost half of Stephens's stories either anonymously or under several dozen pseudonyms—including those of "Zu Behfel," the German engineer, "Stinson Jarvis," the sea captain, and "Marcus Vanderpool," the Amazon adventurer.

Stephens also wrote under a number of female pseudonyms, including "Henrietta Crosby," who wrote of life on her New Hampshire farm, and "Charlotte H. Smith," the author of "Wintering in a Dugout," which was serialized in *The Companion* through December 1891. Originally written from the point of view of the spunky and independent frontierswoman, the story prompted several marriage proposals received at *The Companion*'s office from lonely, although obviously literate, settlers.

The stories that gained the most fervent readership, however, were those written under his own name, the majority of which involved his relatives—both real and fictional—and their hundreds of adventures in the woods and on the farms in and around "the Corners" at North Norway, Maine. These stories became so popular that just before the turn of the century, Stephens invented a "competing" author, Charles Adams, who wrote dozens of stories about the folks from the anagrammatic village of "Waynor," Maine. One of these stories, "When the Bank Was Robbed," is included in this collection. It was not uncommon for stories by both C. A. Stephens and Charles Adams to appear in the same issue of *The Companion*.

The reason for Stephens's remarkable popularity is easy to accept. It resulted almost entirely from the fact that his stories were so easy for the public to accept.

His stories were acceptable because they were innocent of religiosity, pedantry, saber rattling, muckraking, and most of the other habits of popular journalism of the day. In this respect, Stephens was fortunate that he had joined the staff of *The Companion* only a few years after Daniel Sharp Ford became its sole owner and editor. Prior to Ford's arrival, *The Companion* had been quite sternly moral in its tone, and Ford, although quite sternly moral himself, realized that if the magazine were to become a truly popular journal, that is to say, if it were to become the growing financial enterprise that he envisioned, it would have to become less dogmatic and more spirited. If it were to induce increasing numbers of "average" families into its readership, it would have to include more middle-of-the-road subjects within its pages.

Stephens was perfectly suited to producing this type of material. He had grown up on a farm, had chopped cordwood, mown hay, gone to the fair each fall, coasted downhill in the winter, and swam from a rowboat in the middle of Lake Pennessewassee in the summer. He had put himself through college, gone eagerly out west, and returned somewhat meekly back east. He had also gotten himself published in several of the leading family magazines of the day. Maturin Ballou, editor of two of these publications, had said at the time that Stephens was "the most promising young man in America."

In addition to experiencing the physical rigors and realities of farm life, Stephens also came of age in a time and place of enormous political, social, and religious upheaval. When Stephens was born, George Washington's war was less than seventy years past, and Abraham Lincoln's just seventeen years ahead. He was born into a community that was only one generation removed from its settlement by hardheaded and hardworking frontier evangelists. In fact, he received his middle name from Bishop Francis Asbury, the renowned itinerant Wesleyan evangelist of revolutionary America. Two other even stronger influences on his youth, however, were his cousins, Byron and Addison Verrill, who were just a few years older than Stephens and who lived in neighboring Greenwood, Maine, less than an hour's walk from the Stephens farm. The former was an extremely influential, and for his time, a remarkably open-minded, local educator. The latter, an early student of Louis Agassiz at Harvard, became one of the most respected natural scientists of his day.

Addison is a central character in dozens of Stephens's stories in which he is always portrayed as a young man of unquestioned intelligence and integrity, whose character and forthrightness prevail both against the challenges of nature—as in "Cutting Cordwood" and "At the Hay Meadow"—as well as against various narrow-minded or unscrupulous denizens of the frontier—as in "The Black Squirrel," "At Anticosti," and "The Queer Amethyst Quarrel." In a number of stories,

Addison matches wits with, and eventually makes a goat of, a visiting fundamentalist preacher, a rabidly partisan legislator, a particularly dull-witted schoolmaster, and a number of other figures of self-declared authority who are eventually revealed to have no moral authority at all. Through these tales, Stephens finds in Addison a marvelous combination of intellectual independence, commercial practicality, skepticism of the powerful, and respect for the common person.

These abilities and attitudes that Stephens so greatly admires in young Addison are the same qualities that give the Old Squire such a presence in these stories. Politically, the "old gentleman" sits squarely on the fence. Since all newspapers of the day were rousingly partisan, the Old Squire always reads two of them—one Democrat and one Republican—in order to keep a balanced view of events, and when, for example, the town erupts into political turmoil over the continuing nonresults of the Hays-Tilden election, the Old Squire ends the fray by inviting everyone to a party at his maple sugar camp.

Morally, he is a nonpareil. In "The Old Squire's Rozzum," he sells at his prewar cost to the military a stash of rosin that wartime demand has made almost priceless. In "The Queer Amethyst Quarrel," he refuses to quibble over newly discovered and valuable property rights because he had settled the property line years ago—not by a survey, but on his word. In an almost unbelievably admirable gesture, he refuses to dispute a patent on a line of potatoes scurrilously stolen from "The Old Squire's Eden." When reminded by Addison that the strain is rightfully his own and he is therefore entitled to the profits it generates, the Old Squire is simply pleased that the product is available to the public, regardless of the source:

> "Of course, of course," replied the Old Squire, still smiling.
> "But after all, the main thing for us to accomplish in life is to
> keep this old world of ours going ahead for the better."

Moral, however, does not mean moralistic. Indeed, in the Old Squire's world, there is room—warm and affable room—for all manner of people—immigrants, itinerants, waifs, even the perpetrator of "The

Unpardonable Sin." He is curious about everyone and everything around him. And when this curiosity lands him in the middle of the inevitable controversy, he prevails through self-deprecation, acceptance, and humor. He is not so much a teacher, a moralizer, an organizer, or a leader, in the traditional senses of these words, as he is a charmer.

Indeed, Stephens's particular skill as a writer—which met so well the needs of *The Youth's Companion* of 1870—was his own ability to charm the reader. From the point of view of a curious observer, often only casually involved in the action, he describes charming outcomes to believable circumstances. He doesn't seek out challenges as Addison does, nor does he stumble into them as does the Old Squire, but rather he convinces the reader that he coincidentally saw, or heard about, or perhaps was brought along to help in some event that was enlightening, amusing, or of some minor interest to the reader.

Even in the introduction above, which is as autobiographical and personal as Stephens ever becomes, it is Mr. Ford who is presented as the important character. The young writer is "bashful" and "modest" in his first meeting with the editor, and even after many years of work on *The Companion,* he credits Ford with suggesting—and finally insisting upon—an initial scheme for finding and writing stories based upon true-life events, and a final directive for Stephens to write about his own life on the farm in Maine. Stephens's descriptions of these incidents are utterly unpretentious. He colors them with such homely details—the two long flights of stairs, the tall coal stove, the two five-dollar bills and four ones from the hand of Miss Gorham—that we are convinced the entire, charming story about the derivation of his many other charming stories must be as he says: as a youth just out of his teens, he began writing for *The Companion;* the stories were based on true-life events from the author's "boyhood at the Old Squire's place"; they were developed in a fairly orderly fashion beginning at a specific time about thirty years into Stephens's writing career, and the stories included in the collection are among the earliest the author wrote on those subjects. We are convinced that Stephens didn't make up these tales; they are true. And Stephens is not so forward to imagine that the readers should have stories of *his* life thrust upon them; Mr. Ford made him do it.

The real charm of this introduction, however, is that it is really just another story. Stephens was hardly "a youth just emerging from his teens" in January 1870. In fact, he was in his twenty-seventh year. Nor is it likely that he received his "first earnings as an author" from *The Youth's Companion* since no fewer than ten of his stories, including a twenty-two-part serial, appeared in three other nationally known journals before "A Scrimmage with a Bear" was published in the *Companion* in March 1871.

Moreover, Stephens wrote a number of stories about his youth on the farm before arriving at the office of *The Youth's Companion*, and the stories in the book for which he wrote the introduction in question were almost all works from the end of his career, not the beginning. He and his cousins grew up before the Civil War. None were orphans. And Stephens, prior to his leaving home for boarding school, never lived with anyone other than his own mother and father. Finally, the Old Squire and Grandma Ruth themselves appear not to have been single historical figures but amalgams of Stephens's grandparents both on his mother's and his father's sides of the family.

But because of Stephens's narrative simplicity, which is continuously grounded by his almost offhand inclusion of minor physical details, and because of his narrative objectivity—his posture as merely a curious observer, even in declaredly autobiographical tales, such as "My First and Last Duel"—the stories, just like the introduction above, *feel* entirely authentic.

When Stephens wrote for *The Youth's Companion* of growing up on a small farm in New England, he attracted an audience of three broad categories of people: Many had actually grown up on small New England farms, themselves, had gone to war or gone out west and found in Stephens's stories fondly remembered details from their own youths. Many more were children and grandchildren of America's small farmers, whose lives were spent in burgeoning mill towns and cities and who yearned for the simplicity of the life that Stephens described. The Lynch sisters in "The Old Cider Mill" perfectly represent this type of reader, and certainly, if Cad or Lorette (They must have been actual neighbors of Stephens's, don't you think?) had happened upon the story, they would have wept bitterly for the world they had lost. Finally,

Stephens's largest audience, and the one that he would have most completely entranced, were the vast population of "average" Americans who wanted—and probably needed—to feel that sincerity, simplicity, and honesty were possible, that these virtues had, in fact, actually existed not too long ago, and that they were therefore a "real" part of their inalienable national heritage.

The power that these simple tales had for America's readers is demonstrated by the fact that even today—almost seventy years after Stephens's last story appeared in *The Companion*—loyal and ever more elderly readers write to our local librarian here in Norway, Maine, or stop by on their summer trips, and want to know the whereabouts of the Old Squire's farm, and whatever happened to Addison and Theodora, and whether or not there are any of Stephens's stories still in print. Indeed, many of our visitors were born after *The Companion*'s demise, but they tell us that their parents or grandparents had read to them stories of C. A. Stephens from treasured and well-thumbed issues kept in an old trunk in the attic.

In conclusion, C. A. Stephens composed the above introduction to charm you into his book. He wanted you to know that it was his kindly old editor who nursed the Old Squire tales from him, but that, more importantly, they are really true stories about real life in Maine. And of course, they are.

1

When the Old Squire Broke the Punch Bowl

AN OLD WEDGWOOD PUNCH BOWL AND A SILVER flagon with a tall, slim neck were among the heirlooms that Grandmother Ruth brought to Maine from her girlhood home in Connecticut when she and the Old Squire first began housekeeping, long ago.

Flagon and bowl were part of the "setting-out" that Great-grandmother Pepperill had given her daughter, Ruth; for the Old Squire had married in the days when it was customary to brew punch for visitors, and to take a stimulant on almost all occasions. The evils of intemperance had not then developed into the abuses that afterwards disgraced the state of Maine.

Addison, my four other cousins, and I,* who came to the Old Squire's during the Civil War, never really saw that punch bowl. The flagon, however, was still in existence, and we young people were always keenly but quite silently interested in it. But it had had its long neck wrung and was lying back out of sight on the top shelf of Grandmother's

---

*While Stephens refers to the protagonist by the name of Nicholas in one story, elsewhere, particularly in the stories written before the series was formalized in 1899, he is called Kit and sometimes Christopher. For the sake of consistency, the editors have identified him as Nicholas throughout this volume.

little cupboard in the front hall—disabled, so to speak, gone quite out of business, and out of good repute. It was never taken down in our day, but we sometimes inspected it curiously when we went to the cupboard; we wondered—after school expenses began to trouble us—how much it would bring if sold for old silver.

The fate of the punch bowl and the wrung neck of the flagon were part of a tragedy so painful that neither Grandmother nor the Old Squire liked to refer to it. It was one of those occurrences that are best buried in the unhallowed grounds of memory.

The tragedy happened on the day—a great day in the history of the old hometown—when they raised the frame of the Congregationalist meetinghouse. An inscription over one of the two inside doors gives the date as May 18, 1836. The Old Squire was still a young man then, and Parson Elihu Hessey was the minister at that time.

There had been previously a small, low-posted meetinghouse, but the new church was to be a pretentious edifice, with posts twenty-two feet high, so that there could be an elevated gallery around three sides. It was to be seventy-two feet long by fifty feet wide, with a belfry having four corner spires—a large church for a rural town. The frame, hewn from old-growth pine and oak, was made very heavy; there were sills of timber ten inches square; massive cock-tenant posts; seven-inch plates; rafters thirty feet long; thick ribs, and girts of tough, white ash to support the heavy galleries.

Old man Jason Cummings was master carpenter and had been at work on the frame for three weeks. The townspeople calculated that it would take a hundred men to lift up the broadsides. The raising was planned to come off on the fiftieth anniversary of the settlement of the town, and, to make it a great occasion, Parson Hessey, who had preached there for eighteen years, was to name the frame, according to custom, when the ridge pole was pinned. He was to break a bottle on the pole— then called the rum pole—and to deliver a befitting "sentiment."

Word had gone forth that all the able-bodied men in town should assemble on the eighteenth at one o'clock in the afternoon, and it was expected that the raising would begin at two.

The master carpenter had everything ready in advance. Both broadsides were ready to hoist, and long, strong poles, or shores, were attached to the plates with ox chains, to hold and to steady them when they were raised. Plenty of white ash pins had been made and laid handy for instant use; pike poles, too, lay on the ground in a long row, ready to catch the uprising plate when it was breast high. In the sill, at the foot of each post, stuck a broadax for guiding the tenon into its mortise.

Conveniently near lay the long ladder by means of which Parson Hessey was to mount to the rum pole to name the frame when it was raised.

Everything was ready, including a barrel of West India rum, a barrel of hard cider, and three gallons of molasses, and, lest that might not be enough, an additional half barrel of cider had been bespoken. This supply of stimulants may seem large, but it was quite in accord with the ideas that then prevailed. A supply that large was considered necessary for a raising, a muster of the militia, a town meeting, or any other public gathering. For it has to be confessed that at that time Maine was the banner state for drunkenness. Matters had come to such a pass that every other man in the state was a hard and habitual drinker.

Drunkenness, indeed, was so common, so universal, that everybody appeared to take it for granted. It is a fact that at the muster of the militia the previous year the men were so intoxicated that they could neither wheel nor march. More than half the battalion, including the colonel and two of the lieutenants, were lying about the muster field, unable to keep their feet, and they remained there until late the following night. Fine defenders of home and country!

A good many of Maine's hard drinkers had no homes or were in grave danger of losing what they had. Two out of every five farms in town were advertised to be sold for unpaid taxes. And the highways were so neglected that it was highly dangerous to be out after nightfall.

As a matter of course, on that long ago afternoon in May, the assembled raisers paid their respects to the two barrels that had been set on tap in the shade of a nearby apple tree. Some took cider; some, West India rum and molasses, and some took both. This was the usual thing. Even Parson Hessey took a swig—three swigs, certain watchful boys said.

The day was exceptionally warm for the time of the year. Everyone was perspiring. In the words of one old-timer, it was "one of them kind o' days when rum bites well." It bit so well that by the time they were ready to lift the broadsides many of the men were considerably exhilarated and the shouting was prodigious.

"Are you all ready?"

"All ready!" came the tumultuous response.

"Then take her up!"

And up she went, right valiantly. Strength was not wanting, but some lifted harder and faster than others; the men were beyond attempting teamwork.

"Steady! Steady there! Steady, you! Foller with your shores there! All together now! Heave ho! Up! Up! Hold now! Hold all! Steady, and pin your stays!"

The lofty broadside was upended, and old Jason cried: "Well done, men! Ten minutes to take breath in!" This interval many improved by paying further respects to the barrels in the shade. Added hilarity prevailed when the master carpenter summoned them to raise the other broadside. They got it up and stayed after a manner. The crossbeams at the end of the frame were then filled in, timber by timber, and the end plates were raised and pinned—at least it was supposed so, for pins were tossed to those aloft, and the sharp crack of mallets was heard. Braces and studs were then filled in, and these, too, were pinned, or it was supposed that they were.

The body of the frame was now up. Then rafters, ribs, and ridge pole were added. There followed another interval of rest and refreshment. After this, forty of the younger men mounted the frame and laid hold of the rafters as these were handed up to them by the men below. And then, working in groups of six, they yoked these long timbers in pairs at the peak of the roof; next, the ribs were laid on, connecting rafter to rafter, and then, amidst great enthusiasm, the ridge pole was passed up and the frame crowned.

Thus far all had gone fairly well. One man had his foot cut with a broadax, and another had his toes jammed when the foot of a post went into its mortise, but these were minor accidents. Now, all was ready for the naming of the frame. The crew aloft ranged themselves along the plates, to cheer at the proper moment, and, according to old custom, the master carpenter mounted a pile of lumber and shouted: "Hear all! Hear all! Behold a fine frame! It deserves a good name. Who will name it?"

Three active young men sprang forward to raise the long ladder for Parson Hessey to ascend to the rum pole. But it was then discovered by those nearest the minister that he was in no fit condition to go far from the ground. Sad to say, he could barely walk to the foot of the ladder. Charitable deacons gathered around him; they persuaded him away from the ladder and at last seated him on the head of one of the barrels, under the apple tree. There he delivered the sentiment of dedication, in a manner not wholly edifying, but when he had finished, the crews aloft and on the ground cheered heartily. Some of the young, spry fellows on the frame even crowed and danced, and chased each other round the plate, twenty-two feet from the ground. The frame was secure, or should have been.

Suddenly, however, a loud crack was heard, followed by warning shouts from below. The whole structure began to wobble. At one end the crossbeams fell out and then the entire frame, with forty men on it, lurched over and went down with a frightful crash.

Evidently someone had failed to drive the pins home, or had driven them in the wrong place, for the tenons of the supporting crossbeams had pulled out of the mortises. The supposition was that this duty of pinning had been trusted to one or two who, for the time, did not quite know what they were doing. Those who were on the ground ran for their lives to get out of the way of the falling timbers; those aloft had to go with the wreck.

Outcries and groans of distress followed the crash. One young farmer was killed outright, crushed beneath one of the heavy rafters. Another was so injured that he died a few weeks later. Still another had a broken leg; another, a dislocated shoulder, and more than a dozen received serious bruises, cuts, and bumps, from which they were many days recovering.

The then young Old Squire had been one of those standing on the frame at the far end, but when he had felt it going, he had jumped clear of it and landed on a heap of fresh earth a few yards back from the sills. Beyond being badly shaken up, he escaped un-injured.

A sorrowful week in town followed the disaster, and the meeting-house frame lay there until the next spring before anything further was done. Parson Hessey preached the funeral sermons and spoke feelingly of the deaths as "that sad dispensation of Providence with which the Lord has of late chastened us."

There was more immediate chastening. Despite the gravity of the accident, numbers of the raisers continued drinking after the frame fell—to help them to bear up under the calamity, perhaps; at least, that was one excuse offered.

Not far from the Old Squire's there was then living a young neighbor who always became dangerous after he had imbibed freely. He came home from the raising in a homicidal temper. Shortly after dark his little boy, five years old, appeared at the Old Squire's door, crying dolefully and saying that his father was chasing his mother with an ax.

Hastening to the house, the Old Squire and Grandmother Ruth—then a vigorous young woman—found this neighbor, ax in hand, yelling like a wild Indian at the foot of the chamber stairs. His wife had escaped to the loft above. Only the fact that he was too much intoxicated to ascend had prevented the alcohol-crazed maniac from following to strike her down with his vicious weapon.

They had to overpower him by main strength and to tie him, hand and foot, to prevent another tragedy. It was three o'clock in the morning before the man was sufficiently calmed to make it safe for them to untie him and to go home. More than once in after years the Old Squire related these circumstances to me, and I have no doubt as to their entire truth, even to the smallest details.

Day was just breaking, he told me, when Grandmother Ruth and he got home, and they sat down to rest awhile in the sitting room of the old farmhouse before going about the duties of another day. They were more than weary; they were depressed and filled with a sense of indignation. For some time they sat silent.

"Joseph," Grandmother finally said solemnly, "things in this town have come to a dreadfully bad pass."

"Yes, they have," her young husband agreed, with equal earnestness.

"It's rum, rum, everywhere!" Grandmother Ruth exclaimed. "I'm sick of it—sick of it—sick of it!"

"No sicker than I am, Ruth."

"Something ought to be done!" Grandmother Ruth cried. "Let's see if we can't do something to put a stop to this drunkenness."

"Let's begin right here at home, then, and never have another drop of liquor in this house!" her young husband exclaimed, jumping up from his chair. His eye fell on the flagon and the punch bowl, then always kept on a little sideboard near the fireplace. Snatching up the bowl he dashed it on the hearth, breaking it in a hundred pieces.

Not resenting the destruction of her heirloom, and equally bent on showing her own deep feeling, Grandmother Ruth seized the flagon and tried twice, with all her strength, to wring its long neck. But the thick silver was too stiff for her; she was unable even to bend it.

"Well, if you can't, I will!" the Old Squire exclaimed, and catching it from her hands, he wrung the neck halfway around at a single twist, for he was a strong man in those days.

That was the beginning of their lifelong fight against the rum evil in our hometown. For ten years, aided by others equally earnest for the public weal, they labored without ceasing, until the Maine Law was on the statute books.* And, with the enforcement of that law, came wonderful improvement throughout the state: new schoolhouses; more savings banks; better highways; improved farms, and greater prosperity everywhere.

---

*Maine passed a statewide prohibition law, championed by Neil Dow, in 1851. It remained in place until the Eighteenth Amendment (national prohibition) was repealed in 1934.

2

When the Savings Bank Was Robbed

FROM 1846 TO 1856 WAS A TIME OF PROSPERITY IN Norway. Abundant crops were raised, for most of the farms were new, and as yet the soil was rich enough without fertilizers. The storekeepers at the "Center" shared in the general prosperity. Savings were accumulating in farmhouse chests and bureau drawers, and in the fall of 1851 Newell Chapman, who had been one of the selectmen for six years, proposed to start a savings bank.

That was then a new idea, but it found favor at once. Chapman became president, and Henry Barron was named as cashier. The necessary legal steps for incorporation were taken that winter, and in March the Norway Savings Bank opened for business in a room at the rear of Henry Barron's shoe store, rent free.

Very little expense was incurred. The president and even the cashier served without salary. The office furniture consisted merely of a desk and two chairs, a table, two blank books, and a small iron safe of most primitive construction. The cashier carried the key of the safe in his pocket along with his jackknife.

There was little fear of professional bank robbers in those days. I do not think that these inopportune gentry had even been heard of in

Norway. The sole use anticipated for the safe was that it might afford security in case of fire.

President Chapman was a long-headed Yankee, who knew how to invest funds safely, and almost every prosperous farmer in town was a trustee. Bank examiners were not needed.

Chapman and Barron were shrewd and close but strictly honest. It had not occurred to bank presidents then to use deposits for stock speculations. People brought in their savings, and Chapman and Barron invested them as fast as they could in mortgages bearing the legal 6 percent interest, with sometimes a "bonus" in advance, which was also legal where both parties agreed on it at the outset.

In 1856 the bank had in investments $192,000, not a dollar of it drawing less than 6 percent, and much of it more, owing to Chapman's shrewdness.

The entire bank expenses that year—largely costs of foreclosures of mortgages, registration fees, and so forth, with some necessary traveling expenses on the part of the president and cashier—were $78.20.

This was before the great financial panic of 1857. That crisis, however, was little felt by the Norway bank. The deposits were in farm mortgages, upon which the panic had no effect.

But during the season of 1856 they heard of a savings bank robbery for the first time in Maine. The bank at Bethel had been entered by night and the door of the safe broken open. Everyone felt that it was a crime too audacious, too outrageous to have been committed by any ordinary person or resident of the town, and the idea prevailed at once that it was the work of some new and desperate kind of reprobate.

President Chapman called a meeting of the savings bank trustees to talk over this new danger. He was a wary man. What had happened in Bethel might happen in Norway, he said. If such daring rascals were roving about the country it behooved them to be on their guard; for the bank often had considerable sums of money in the safe.

From accounts of the robbery at Bethel, it was conceded that no safe door or brickwork could withstand such resolute rogues. Chapman came to the conclusion at once that a watchman was the safest precaution.

But to hire a watchman at a dollar a night was a piece of extravagance that shocked the minds of the trustees. Chapman himself recoiled from it. Three hundred sixty-five dollars a year was not to be thought of.

Chapman held to his idea, however. He and Barron fixed up a little sleeping room directly over the bank, and by judicious persuasion prevailed upon a young fellow, named Pinckney Danbridge, to sleep there. Then Chapman—who never took a cent in payment for his own services—worked privately for two days on a contrivance for waking young Danbridge in case the safe in the room below was approached in the night.

In some way a wire was conducted from beneath the floorboards in front of the safe, up the wall, and through the floor of the chamber to a clock alarm. If anyone trod on that board in front of the safe door the alarm would go off close by Danbridge's head.

What he had to do then was to throw up his chamber window and fire a double-barreled gun, which would wake not only Barron, who lived in a house directly across the street, but everyone else in the vicinity.

Chapman arranged it all himself, even to the loading of the gun, and he or the cashier looked to the wire every evening at six o'clock, when they locked up, for the Norway Savings Bank of those days was open from seven o'clock in the morning till six in the evening.

For sleeping there Danbridge was to receive ten dollars a year and his room rent, and Chapman did not fail to impress on his mind, at frequent intervals, a profound sense of his responsibility to the bank and to the public. There is no doubt that Danbridge felt it.

One might have doubted it, however, for he was a great, smiling youth, loose jointed, and very lathy to look at. He and his mother had come to Norway from Norfolk, Virginia, four years before, and Danbridge, now eighteen or nineteen years old, worked in Long's woolcarding mill at the lower end of the village.

He slept over the bank for a year or more, and it was one of Chapman's rules that he should be in his room every night at half past nine. Chapman took no chances at a boy's carelessness. He or Barron wound that clock and set the alarm every night.

The apparatus was all right, and would have worked according to schedule every night of the month and year. But Danbridge had become enamored of a maiden living at the other end of the hamlet, and it has to be said of him that he fell into a habit of making long calls at her house in the evening. Bashfulness in part may have led him to conceal these visits. But it has also to be related that he was accustomed to go to his room over the bank at eight o'clock, and leave it privately later in the evening, after Barron and Chapman had gone home, supposing that he was snug in his bed upstairs.

This was all very wrong, of course, as the events proved. For the bank robbers really came one night in August, while Danbridge was making a protracted call at the other end of the village.

There were two of these robbers, and one of them, as afterward transpired, knew the place very well. The night was wet and foggy, on the dark of the moon, but the robbers pried up a side window of the bank room and entered without difficulty.

Beyond doubt they trod on the board by the safe and set off the alarm upstairs. But no Danbridge was there to fire the gun. The robbers appear to have heard the alarm, and beat a retreat for the time being, but as no one stirred they went back and wedged open the safe door at their leisure.

There were, as it happened, about eleven thousand dollars in the safe, besides promissory notes, mortgages, and other papers of value to the bank. The men took all these, put their booty in an old leather valise, and decamped by the window, as they had entered. One can but smile to think how easily a bank could be robbed in 1857. There were no time locks or chilled-steel vaults to contend with then.

But it chanced that Danbridge was now tiptoeing his way back to his bedchamber, and in the fog and darkness he nearly ran into the robbers as they emerged from the narrow alleyway between the shoe store and the building next to it. He was stealing home so quietly that the robbers did not hear him, but he heard them: in fact, he had heard them getting out at the window, and surmised instantly that mischief was on foot. He stood quite still as the two men hurried past him, and he heard them go down the middle of the road, so as to make no noise on the plank sidewalk.

Danbridge's suspicion was fully confirmed when, on going in between the buildings, he found the bank window open. Owing perhaps to these nocturnal trips, he carried matches in his pocket. Striking one, he held it in at the window. Then by the fitful light, the open safe door caught his eye, and he knew what had happened.

He was conscience stricken. What would Chapman say to him? What would Barron say? What would everybody say? It would all come out that he had been calling on Elsie Dunn. And now the bank's money was gone and he was to blame for it! Even while he stood there, striking matches, the robbers were escaping with all that money. He ought to follow them and see where they went.

That seems to have been what passed through Danbridge's mind, and it accounts for what he did. For instead of giving an alarm, he ran like a fox down the road after the robbers.

The miscreants had a wagon and horse, which they had left at the lower end of the village, hitched in a church horse shed. Danbridge heard them back out and heard the chafe iron squeak as they turned and drove away along the country road to the southward.

It was too dark to see them, but he ran on, and for a mile or more kept within hearing distance of the wagon. He was a long-legged youth and a good runner. They drove fast, however, and gradually drew out of hearing.

The pace, too, had begun to tell on Danbridge, and he now realized that he would be unable to follow them far. He was near the old Chase farm, a mile below the village, and pulled up to get his breath and think what to do.

As he stood there he heard the step of some animal, and made out the head and neck of a horse, looking at him over a gate by the roadside. The horse was standing in a stable yard.

Danbridge knew the Chase boys and, indeed, knew the horse. He considered the necessity so urgent that, without stopping to wake the family, he entered the stable, and by striking another match, found the headstall of a harness, and having bridled the horse, he mounted, bareback, and went on in pursuit of the wagon. In the course of an hour he heard the wagon ahead, and then followed on more cautiously for several miles. He was not cautious enough, however, for at the foot of a long hill in the town of Poland the robbers either heard the horse's hoofs behind, or from some other circumstance suspected that they were pursued. They stopped in the shadow of some pines a little off the road and lay in wait there.

It had now begun to grow light a very little for it was past three o'clock in the morning. Danbridge came on and did not see the team till he was within a few yards of it. He pulled up then, very suddenly and with good reason, for there stood the two men with derringer pistols pointed at his head.

"Halt, you!" one of them called out, in a tone so savage that it made the poor fellow quake.

"Where are you riding to?" the other demanded.

Danbridge was scared, but his wits stood him in good stead. Otherwise he would probably never have gone much farther.

"I'm going after the doctor!" he replied.

"Oh, you are," said the one who had halted him. "Who's sick? What's the matter?"

"There's a new baby at our house," said Danbridge. "They got me up and sent me in an awful hurry for Doctor Davis."

The two men looked at one another a moment. Then they laughed. "Go on, you yoho!" one of them said.

Danbridge put the horse to a gallop, and rode on ahead of them for as much as a mile; then coming to a crossroad he turned off on it, and leading his horse into some bushes, waited for the robbers to pass.

They came along in the course of a few minutes and drove by, keeping the main road.

Danbridge waited until they were well out of sight, for he knew that it would not do for him to let them catch sight of him again. Besides, it was getting lighter, and he could follow their track in the sandy road, all the better that there had been rain earlier in the night.

When they had been gone for fifteen or twenty minutes he followed them on the main road again, till between six and seven in the morning. He met one team, but was still able to follow the track of the wagon ahead.

They were now in the town of Yarmouth, approaching the sea, and soon after this, as he cantered on, he came to a little collection of houses, stores, and a tavern, known as Lombard's Corners. The wagon track turned in at the tavern.

As soon as Danbridge saw where the track ended, he turned back, and hitching his horse at a barn out of sight, went round in the rear of the tavern and entered the stable by a side door, behind the horse stalls. A very sweaty horse, with the harness still on, stood in a stall, eating oats, and there was a muddy wagon that had evidently just come in.

Danbridge noted this at a glance, also a fresh-faced, redheaded boy, apparently twelve or thirteen years of age, who was shelling ears of corn and feeding a flock of hens and turkeys outside the door.

He said "Hallo!" to the boy, and coming through the stable, asked him if he had a dozen eggs of his own that he would sell.

"Guess so," replied the boy, grinning, with a glance toward the tavern door. "What'll you give me?"

"Ten cents," said Danbridge. With another glance at the tavern entrance, the boy came into the stable and softly closed the great door.

"I'll get you a dozen," said he, "if you'll promise not to tell."

"I won't say a word," replied Danbridge. And while the lad was making a collection of eggs from several hiding places of his own, Danbridge asked him whose wagon and horse it was that had just come in.

"Don't know," replied the boy. "My, but they've been drivin'! Heard 'em tell the old man that they was sheriffs, chasin' a hoss thief. Said they wanted to feed their hoss and get breakfast just as quick as they could."

"Where are they now?" asked Danbridge.

"Eatin'."

"They didn't know there was anybody in the stable here when they drove in," continued the boy, counting his eggs. "But I was here, milking the cow. I was sitting down low on the stool, snug up to the cow, behind the stanchel boards. They looked round, and one of them said something kind of queer."

"What did he say?" Danbridge asked.

"Said, 'We'd better not carry it into the house. The folks might notice it and think it strange. Better put it out of sight here somewhere, till we start.'"

"Did you see what it was they had?" Danbridge inquired, with growing interest.

"Yes, I peeked through the stanchel boards. It was some kind of a leather bag," said the boy. "And I'll bet it's got pistols in it. Sheriffs always has pistols, you know."

"Did you see where they put it?" Danbridge asked, quickly.

"They put it in the old winnowing mill, there by the cow," said the boy. "One of them hoisted up the fan end and set it in under the fliers. But you'd better not touch it," the boy added. "It's got pistols in it."

Danbridge thought rapidly. "You must get me something to put these eggs in," he said to the boy. "I cannot carry them in my hands. Get me a basket, or a small box or a bag."

"Perhaps I can find a little bag somewhere," said the boy, doubt-fully.

"Quick, then, before anyone comes out!" exclaimed Danbridge. The boy disappeared through a passage into the ell, extending from the stable to the tavern, and the instant he was gone, Danbridge looked under the "fliers" of the red fanning mill. Hidden away there was an old leather valise, tied up with a bit of rope. It was quite heavy, and when Danbridge shook it, gave forth an unmistakable chink of silver money.

He slipped the rope enough to peep in, and could distinguish bun-dles of papers and packages of what seemed to be bank bills. He felt sure that it was the contents of the bank safe, and without waiting to conclude the transaction in eggs, snatched up the valise, ran out at the side door of the stable and back to his horse.

Fortune had strangely favored him, as she sometimes does favor people at hard spots in their lives. If he could but get back to Norway with that valise, he hoped that the recovery of the money would in some degree palliate his sins of omission as watchman, and he rode as fast as the tired horse would go.

Meanwhile the robbery of the bank and the mysterious absence of Danbridge had been discovered at Norway promptly at six o'clock that morning. The village was thunderstruck, and knew not what to think. Barron was amazed; Chapman was furious. He examined Danbridge's bedroom with suspicion, which soon grew to a conviction that the boy was himself the robber. The hamlet seethed with indignant excite-ment.

Then came tidings that a horse had been stolen during the night, at the Chase farm. This gave Chapman a clue as to the direction the thief had taken.

"We'll have him!" he exclaimed. "We'll run the rascal down!"

They summoned Swett, the sheriff, and hitched up two of the fastest horses the place could furnish. By half past seven the president, cashier, sheriff, and Hubbard, the schoolmaster, then a powerful young man, were off on the main road in hot pursuit. They met Danbridge eight miles below the village. He was sternly halted and bidden to give an account of himself. True, he was going the right way, not the wrong, but suspicion had been making havoc with his reputation.

Danbridge made no mistake this time, however. Chapman's grim eye was on him, and he told the whole story, with no attempt to excuse himself. Chapman and Barron meanwhile were examining the valise. They smiled again. The money and notes were all there.

"But we must catch the rascals!" cried Chapman. "We must chuck them into the state prison before they do any more damage."

Barron went back with Danbridge and the money, to restore the horse and make explanations. But Chapman, the sheriff, and the schoolmaster continued in pursuit of the robbers. By dint of hard driving they reached Lombard's between ten and eleven.

At the tavern a singular state of affairs prevailed. The two bank robbers, who declared themselves to be officers of justice in pursuit of a horse thief, had immediately missed their valise and raised a commotion, pretending that their handcuffs and warrant had been stolen from the wagon. They had so threatened the landlord that the poor man was much terrified, and they had searched first the stable, and then the house, from cellar to attic. The redheaded boy, for reasons of his own, appears to have remained closemouthed.

The rogues were ransacking a closet in the ell when the Norway party drove up, but catching sight of the newcomers, both of them escaped by a back window and ran across a field toward a tract of woodland.

Chapman and the schoolmaster are said to have overtaken and captured one of the robbers, but the sheriff lost his man in the woods, and he was never caught. Nor did they bring the one whom they captured to Norway. For, in point of fact, a most disagreeable surprise awaited Chapman when he took a look at his prisoner's face.

It was none other than his wife's younger brother, Wallace Codman, the "black sheep" of the family, who had run away fifteen years before. His first visit home to Norway had been for the purpose of robbing his brother-in-law's bank.

Neither the sheriff nor Master Hubbard could ever be brought to say anything of the matter, but a story came roundabout by the way of persons at Lombard's tavern, that Chapman gave the ne'er-do-well a terrific "licking" with two horsewhips, using them both up on him, and then let him go with a promise to put him in the state prison if he ever showed his head at Norway afterward.

Chapman did this out of regard for his wife, and never told her. She died eight years afterward without ever having heard of it.

When the particulars of the robbery were known and talked over, Barron, the schoolmaster, and the Old Squire, who was a trustee, were of the opinion that some reward or token of appreciation should be given Danbridge for the energy with which he had followed the robbers and recovered the bank's property.

But Chapman said, "No. If he had attended to his business as he ought to have done, the bank would not have been robbed at all!"

Though Danbridge's mother was a New England woman, for some reason she took her son back to Norfolk in the winter of 1860. He was drafted into the Rebel army, and two years afterward it was reported that he had fallen, fighting for the "Lost Cause," at the Battle of Cedar Mountain.

3

The Old Squire's "Rozzum"

WAR CAUSES STRANGE FLUCTUATIONS IN PRICES. DUR-
ing the Civil War in the United States, when the supply of raw cotton
from the South was wholly cut off from the North, cotton cloth rose
from seven cents a yard to sixty cents. But the greatest rise of price was
in rosin.

Before the war, in the fall of 1860, rosin sold in New York for $1 a
barrel, and in Portland, Maine, one lot of a hundred barrels went for
$110, which was less than a cent a pound. Dealers failed to foresee the
scarcity in rosin that the secession of the southern states would cause in
the North, although virtually the entire supply came from the pine
forests of the Carolinas and Georgia.

After the inauguration of President Lincoln, in March 1861, the
price of rosin rose by leaps and bounds to ten, fifteen, twenty-five,
thirty-five, and in some instances to fifty and even sixty dollars a barrel.
There was virtually no rosin in the market; you could not buy enough
even to roughen fiddle bows; fiddlers had to use spruce gum—a very
poor substitute.

In Maine they got a kind of rosin, or "rozzum," as the country
people called it, from old stumps of the white pine, the roots of which
were fat with red pitch. This touchwood, or lightwood, had previously
been used only for kindling fires, but now dealers were ready to pay
seven dollars a cord for it. Miles of stump fences were cut up and drawn

to a large retort; the pitch, when tried out, proved a fair substitute for rosin.

At the Old Squire's farm there was much interest in rosin and the soaring price of it, largely on account of an odd speculation that the old gentleman had made in the winter of 1861.

He had gone to Portland in January to deliver a thousand tamarack knees, which were then generally used in shipbuilding for the bends of vessels. Business was dull that winter, and several Portland wholesale dealers who were in financial difficulties were offering goods at low prices. At the Preble House, where businessmen from out of town usually stayed, the Old Squire learned that a certain firm had a hundred barrels of rosin in stock, which they offered at $1.10 a barrel. He thought little about it for the moment or during that evening, because rumors of secession and the possibility of war were the chief subjects of talk.

A little before three o'clock in the morning the Old Squire waked suddenly and sat up in bed. The subject of his thoughts was rosin.

"Rosin comes from the southern states," he muttered, "and if the South goes out of the Union and there's war, how shall we get it? The price is sure to advance."

The conviction took such firm hold on him that he was unable to fall asleep again; he lay thinking the matter over until daylight. After breakfast at seven o'clock, he went down to Commercial Street and bought that hundred barrels of rosin for a $110, with the privilege of keeping it in the warehouse there.

The more he thought about rosin the stronger grew his conviction that it would increase in price. During that day and the next he bought ninety-two barrels more, at less than $2.00 a barrel. And when, a few days later, a schooner came in from Newbern, North Carolina, with rosin, he bought fifty barrels more, at $1.50 a barrel. If that had not taken almost all the money that he had received for the tamarack knees, I think he would have bought a hundred barrels more.

On the way home, however, he began to fear that he had been oversanguine; indeed he now felt so uncertain about his venture that he did not say a word to Grandmother Ruth about it. He thought that it would trouble her and that she would reproach him for his rashness.

The dreary wartime drew on, with all its poignant griefs in North and South alike. The Old Squire's sons entered the Northern army, and one by one they fell in battle. Yet through it all the Old Squire's patriotism burned steadily.

Solicitude for the national welfare and grief over the loss of his five sons drove all thought of his investment in rosin out of his mind. Indeed, I doubt whether he remembered much about his rosin from the outbreak of the war until we had our war scare in Maine. A daring party of young Confederates entered Portland Harbor and seized the revenue cutter of the port, with some bold intention of bombarding the town. The vessel was immediately recaptured, but everyone feared that another and more successful attack might follow. That raid on Portland recalled to the Old Squire's mind his 242 barrels of rosin, stored near the waterfront. Deciding to haul it out of danger's way, he mustered nine double teams and drove to Portland for his rosin. When he had got it home he stored it, tier on tier, in the hay bay of the big west barn.

It was then that Grandmother Ruth first learned of his investment in rosin, and although she would have frowned on the venture if she had heard of it at first, she now hoped to get a fortune from it. For by this time rosin was selling at Portland for $18.50 a barrel.

Still the price rose, and with it soared Grandmother's hopes for the future. She did a deal of arduous multiplying with pencil and paper; 18 x 242, then 19 x 242, 22 x 242, and so on as the price of rosin mounted. In spite of all the sorrow that the war had brought her, the dear old lady began to plan for new carpets, new furniture for the parlor, fresh coats of paint on all the farm buildings, new cupolas and gilt vanes on both barns and the carriage house.

When the price of a barrel of rosin rose to $27, Grandmother Ruth tried to persuade the Old Squire to sell. She was growing impatient for those improvements, which now included a new buggy to drive to church in, a new black gown of silk that would stand alone, and a befitting bonnet.

But the Old Squire said, "No, not yet!"

Something, too, that Grandmother did not at all understand seemed to be troubling him. He did not appear to enter with full relish into her plans for beautifying the old farm. Whenever she talked of them he said little. As a matter of fact, he would have liked to tell her what was weighing on his mind, but knowing her more practical views of life, he hesitated to do so.

Businessmen in Portland knew that the Old Squire was holding a quantity of rosin, presumably for a greater rise in price. He received several offers for it, but refused them all. At last, in 1864, there came a letter from the navy department, which said that the government needed rosin for some purpose at its navy yards, and that it would pay him $34 a barrel for it, delivered at the nearest railway station.

The Old Squire hastened to put his rosin at the disposal of the government, and a few days later the great pile of dusty barrels that for three years had lain in the barn was on its way out into the world again. Even in those dark days of 1863 and 1864 the United States government was regarded as a good customer, and Grandmother Ruth's hopes ran high: 242 barrels at $34 a barrel made $8,228—the greatest windfall that had ever come to the old farm thus far.

Alas for those rosy anticipations!

Months passed. The Old Squire appeared reticent. When Grandmother Ruth questioned him, he admitted that he had been paid for the rosin, and he bought her the black silk and the bonnet. But the farm buildings went unpainted, no cupolas shone from the roofs, and Grandmother continued to drive to church in the old wagon. There was a certain mystery about it that disturbed Grandmother Ruth. Time and again she tried to pin the Old Squire down to an explanation.

"Joseph, what did you do with that money?" she asked more than once.

But he always replied, "Ruth, I do not feel that I can tell you yet."

As time went on she decided that he had speculated with the money and lost it. That indeed was the belief concerning the Old Squire's "rozzum" that prevailed in the family and among our neighbors at the time when we of the younger generation talked about it shortly after the war's end. The Old Squire never explained. Perhaps he thought that the truth of the matter would be more annoying to Grandmother Ruth than her own suspicion concerning the mystery.

Years later I had occasion to overhaul a trunkful of old papers—the receipts, contracts, and agreements of the Old Squire's business life.

Among them was a little bundle of letters from Vice President Hannibal Hamlin, who had been a schoolmate of the Old Squire when they were boys; one or two letters from our Maine senator, William P. Fessenden, regarding the impeachment of President Andrew Johnson, and another, dated June 15, 1864, that contained a government money order for $418.66.

The letter, which was in a clerkly hand, included memoranda setting forth that the money order was in payment for 242 barrels of rosin at $1.73 a barrel.

For a moment I wondered why that small sum had been sent in payment for rosin that at the time the sale was worth $34 a barrel. Then, knowing the Old Squire as I did, I saw that the question answered itself. His patriotism had led him to ask from the government only what the rosin had actually cost him in the winter of 1861. And then, to make his offering to his country complete, he had never presented the order for payment.

At the bottom of the letter were a few lines in another and peculiar handwriting, signed Gideon Welles. Welles, as I now remembered, was secretary of the navy from 1861 to 1869, first when Abraham Lincoln was president, and then under President Johnson. How like an echo from that time of great trouble and doubt were the words of his cramped marginal note:

"On behalf of the Government, and personally, I desire to thank you, sir. Public spirit like yours gives us hope and courage to go on."

4

Single Combat

THE LAST DUEL IN THIS COUNTRY—THE LAST, AT LEAST, that attracted public attention—was between the Hon. David C. Broderick and Judge Terry of California. It shocked the entire nation, and strong repulsion to the practice found expression everywhere. Several years later, however, another duel took place, but it failed to catch the public eye, although it was fought with the most remarkable weapons on record!

The duel of which I speak occurred soon after I went to live at the Old Squire's in Maine. At that time I was scarcely twelve years old, and I had known Tom Edwards only six weeks. He was a resolute boy of about my own age; I had liked him from the first, and we had soon begun to get acquainted.

One day the Old Squire gave me permission to go across the fields and visit Tom for the afternoon. As it was my first call at the Edwards farm, I put on my Sunday suit of dark gray cloth, and a white turnover collar and black bow tie. When I got there, I found that Tom was just setting out on an errand to a shingle mill, two and a half miles away.

I went along with him. But before we started we dug some angleworms and stowed hooks and lines into our pockets, for Tom declared that there were trout in the mill brook that would weigh two pounds. But for reasons that will soon appear we did not fish that day.

The fact is that we had a slight difference of opinion on our walk to the mill. That neither of us knew much about the subject of our argument did not prevent us from being very positive in our views.

It was about the transatlantic telegraph cable, which in 1858, after two failures, had been successfully laid across the Atlantic Ocean.

"Did you know," said Tom as we went along, "that Cyrus Field has strung a wire across the Atlantic Ocean, that people can talk through?"

"Well, they can't talk, exactly," said I.

"Oh, yes, they can," Tom insisted. "For I have read what they first said to each other. It was in the *Maine Farmer* last night."

"It's only little raps they give through the wire," I maintained. "They spell out words by that."

We walked on a little way in silence, and then Tom remarked that he did not believe I knew much about it.

I realized that there was a good deal of truth in that, but I replied hotly that I guessed I knew as much about it as he did.

"It isn't raps at all," Tom retorted. "It's electricity, and that is lightning, or just the same thing."

After that we went on to the mill without speaking. Round the mill were heaps of shingle bolts and long piles of logs, mostly fir, which farmers had drawn there to be sawed into shingles. As I sat on one of the logs, waiting for Tom to do his errand in the mill, I noticed the large, fat blisters of liquid pitch on the fir logs. When I punctured one of them with my pocketknife, almost a teaspoonful of the fir "balsam" gushed out. An ax was sticking in a log near by, and when Tom came back he showed me that by striking on the blister with the poll of the ax, he could make the liquid pitch fly fifteen or twenty feet in almost any direction he wished.

"I could take you right in the face with it, if I tried," he said. Then he looked at me defiantly and again opened the subject of dispute.

"They don't telegraph by raps," he declared. "They do it with electricity."

"Electricity makes the raps," I admitted, "but it isn't lightning electricity. It's a kind they make with chemical stuff in a battery."

Tom retorted that everyone who knew anything knew that Ben Franklin drew electricity down from the sky with lightning rods.

"They don't telegraph with that kind of electricity," I declared. "They use a tamer kind, and they have to tame it first in a battery."

"Tame your grandfather!" shouted Tom. "You don't know putty! I most think you're a fool. I'm ashamed to be seen out with you!"

I had read in a newspaper, not long before, that during a debate in Congress a senator had called his opponent an ass. I called Tom that, instantly and impressively. "You are an ass," I said, "and that is the worst that anyone can say of anyone else. A fool is nothing to that!"

My retort staggered Tom for a moment; then he flew at me and knocked off my cap and slapped me. According to the high precedents that I had gathered from my reading, I knew I could not honorably endure his assault without demanding satisfaction.

"Tom," I exclaimed, "I challenge you to fight a duel—right here!"

Tom was impressed by my manner and gazed at me almost admiringly. "What shall we fight with?" he said.

"That is for you to decide," I replied. "You are the challenged party."

Tom glanced round. "We haven't got any pistols," said he, "or any swords."

I folded my arms and assumed an air of indifference.

Tom was perplexed, and looked round again, but as his eyes rested on the fir logs beside which we stood, he cried with sudden animation, "We'll fire fir balsam at each other! We'll stand four feet off, and first I'll strike a blister, and then you will. We'll stick our faces out to it, and no dodgin'—take it right in the eyes, or anywhere!"

"Very good, sir. How many shots?"

"Till one of us says he's had enough."

"Very good," I repeated loftily. "It is well. Your choice of weapons is acceptable."

Tom seized the ax. "We'll stand here at the end of these logs. I'm the challenged one, so it's my first lick."

"That's as much as you know about dueling! But take your first shot, if you want it. I don't care."

"Face that blister, then!" cried Tom exultantly. "Nearer than that. Stick your old face up nearer. Now don't you dodge."

Splat came the poll of the ax down on a big blister, and splat flew the balsam; some of it splattered my face, some went into my hair, but

most of it hit my clothes. It smelled rank and felt very sticky, but I was glad that I had faced Tom's shot without flinching. Drawing myself up, I bade him hand over the ax for my turn.

As Tom thrust his head forward, about four feet away, he showed no sign of fear. He even grinned and made faces at me. For a time, indeed, there was not much for him to be afraid of. He was much more skillful at striking the pitch blisters than I was. My first shot flew astray, whereas, at his second, the pitch struck me square in the mouth and stuck my lips together. Although I was mad clear through, I kept myself in control, and managed after one or two more fruitless shots to hit him full in the face; the pitch spattered into his eyes and set him to prancing wildly. I felt a thrill of joy to think that at last I was acquitting myself well in this duel.

From blister to blister we moved along the pile of fir logs. Most of the pitch went on our clothes, but our faces were plastered with it, and before long our hands were so thickly covered with the sticky stuff that after striking a blister we could hardly let go of the ax. Our lips were stuck together, so that we could only mumble our defiances. I felt horribly uncomfortable. Tom was looking rather glum, and his abundant hair stood up in a pitchy mop.

For fifty shots or more we faced each other. Then a master stroke from Tom sent a full dose of pitch square into my left eye. That finished me. Prancing to and fro over the shingle bolts, I tried instinctively to reach the brook, where I could bathe my smarting eye. But water, when I did apply it to my eye, did little to ease the pain. Through blinding tears I caught a glimpse of Tom standing on the bank, with a wild grin on his pitch-smeared face. But I was too thoroughly frightened to care about him. I felt sure that I should lose my eye, for it seemed to be burning up.

Stumbling over shingle bolts and wallowing through a great heap of sawdust, I regained the highway and blindly fled the field of honor.

When I reached home, cousins Ellen and Theodora were in the kitchen, helping Grandmother to get supper. As I came in, they turned and looked at me, aghast at my appearance.

"What has happened to you?" Grandmother cried.

"I got some fir balsam on my face," I faltered.

"You poor child!" the old lady exclaimed, and put her arm about me to examine my eyes. Her arm stuck to me.

"Why—why—look at your clothes!" she cried.

"What have you been doing?"

I had sunk down in one of the kitchen chairs, and now, when I got up, I took the chair with me. At that, Ellen burst out laughing. Grandmother sat me down again, chair and all.

"Now how did you ever get all this pitch on yourself?" she demanded.

"It splattered," I said reluctantly. "Splattered from what?" she cried.

"From the ax."

"Whose ax?"

"Tom's ax," I confessed.

"The little villain!" she cried, surveying me with increasing dismay.

But my conscience assailed me. "I got some on his clothes, too," I confessed.

"As bad as this?" she asked in wonder.

"Yes," I said. "Almost as bad."

Grandmother regarded me soberly. "Now tell me, what were you doing?" she demanded again, and shook me, although not very hard, for I was very sticky!

"We were fighting a duel," I said at last.

"Fighting—with fir pitch!" the old lady cried in astonishment. "Your grandfather shall hear of this!"

At that moment, as it chanced, the Old Squire came into the house. Grandmother met him at the door, and informed him of my encounter with Tom and of the condition I was in.

The old gentleman looked me over critically. "Your eyes smart, do they?" he asked.

"Awfully," I admitted.

"Is Thomas as bad off as you are?" he inquired.

"Almost. Not quite, I guess," I said.

The Old Squire's lips twitched, but he did not smile. "You had better change your clothes, my son," was all he said.

Grandmother now smeared lard on my face and hands, and then with a dish towel scrubbed off the worst of the pitch. It hurt me almost as much to get the stuff off as it had to get it on.

The next day she immersed my Sunday suit in a kettle of melted lard, then soaked it for twenty-four hours in a strong solution of soap and water, but it was never much of a suit after that.

Later, Grandmother called on Tom's mother, to compare notes. She learned that Mrs. Edwards had put Tom through the same ordeal that I had undergone.

A few days later Tom and I met accidentally on the highway. When he saw me coming he drew to his side of the road. As we passed, we each looked the other way. After we were well by, however, I heard him say in a low voice, "Sorry that hit you in the eye," to which I replied in an equally low tone, "Huh, that's nothing!" We went on, without looking back, but within a fortnight we were as good friends as before.

5

At the Taking of Louisbourg

Part 1: "Run as you never ran before!"

AT THE OLD FARM, IN THE WINTER OF 1864, WE HAD twenty-three bushels of rusted beans to pick over, and we did it evenings, after school, a bushel at a picking; little white beans they were, scarcely as large as peas, and to keep our spirits up and prevent us from getting sleepy, our grandfather, the Old Squire, told us all the colonial stories he could think of.

There were six of us young folks—cousins whose fathers had been killed in the Civil War—who gathered about a scarred, old kitchen table where our fathers had formerly sat. Sometimes Grandmother would put on her "specs" and draw up; she was an expert at bean picking, and the bushel went out much faster when she gave a hand. But more frequently she had laundry and mending to do; then there were more than five quarts apiece for us, and it is a great task to pick over even one quart of badly rusted beans.

But with the prospect of a good long story and lots of talk about early times in Maine, when Maine was a part of the Massachusetts Bay Province, we could see the bean bag and dippers brought out with better courage.

It must have been something of a tax on the Old Squire to recall and relate so many stories. Sometimes he would attempt to beg off for a night, but we would hear nothing of that, claiming that if there was no story there should be no bean picking and exhorting him to put on his thinking cap. Frequently he would say that he couldn't think of anymore. Thereupon we would all sit back in our chairs, and the picking would wait.

Then from over at her light stand where she was mending, Grandmother would say, "Tell them about the time Lyman Glain shot the panthers in his sugar lot, at Gray;" or "there's the story of Ann Miriam Eastman and the Indian squaws, at Scarborough; you haven't told them that."

And one night—it must have been as far along as the seventeenth bushel—she suddenly exclaimed, "Why Father, you never have told them about Grandsir Pliny Eastman who went down to Louisbourg with Sir William. There's a lot about him: how he ran six miles through the woods when they won the Royal Battery; how he was paid for collecting cannonballs; how the captive girl hid him in the fanning mill; how he had to fight Indians after the siege was over; and what was in the silver box he found in the bombproof."

"Why so I haven't," said Grandfather, much encouraged, "I wonder I hadn't thought of that before."

"But I never heard of Grandfather Pliny Eastman before," said Theodora, who was most interested in our family history. "What grandfather was he?"

"Oh, it was your grandfather's grandfather, not yours," said Grandmother. "That was a long, long time ago. Before the Revolution. During the French and Indian Wars."

"In what year was it, Grandfather?"

"1745," said Grandfather; "and you can reckon up, boys, and see how long ago that was; four generations ago. Grandsir Eastman was only a boy of eighteen or nineteen then. He lived at Falmouth and enlisted there to go in General Pepperell's regiment; for he was a relation of the Bray and Pepperell families that lived at Kittery and Portsmouth."

"But what was it all about?" said Halse, my cousin from New Orleans. "What were they fighting for?"

"That is a pretty long story," Grandfather replied. "You must read about it in your *History of the United States*. The French people were very strong in America then. They had colonies in Canada, Nova Scotia, and Cape Breton Island, and Louisbourg, on Cape Breton, was the strongest of all their fortified towns, stronger even than Quebec; it was called the Gibraltar of America, which means it was one of the strongest fortresses in the world.

"Massachusetts, Maine, and all the rest of New England were then English Colonies, for that was thirty years before the Revolution, and so our folks took sides with England in all her wars with France, which were then quite frequent. These wars made a great deal of trouble between the French and English Colonies. The French were very active then and, generally, the Indians sided with them, for the French tended to treat Indians better than did the English, and the Jesuits and other Catholic missionaries had been among nearly all the tribes. Also, the French in Canada offered bounties on English scalps and bought English captives off the Indians, to be kept as slaves, at Montreal and Quebec.

"But what set our folks so resolutely to take Louisbourg, that spring, was the fear that all the coasting and foreign trade of New England would be destroyed by French privateers who made Louisbourg their port of refuge. Governor Shirley—who was the war governor of Massachusetts of those days—was very urgent and active in fitting out an expedition to capture Louisbourg. At first there was much hesitation; for some of our folks who had been captives at Louisbourg, described it as a tremendously strong place with walls thirty or forty feet high, defended by 150 of the heaviest cannon which were then cast. The great French engineer, Vauban, had planned the fortress, and France had spent thirty million livres in constructing it."

"Livers! Why not real, human livers?" said Wealthy under her breath. (Wealthy was cousin Ellen's little sister.)

"No! Not that. It was a coin—l-i-v-r-e—worth eighteen or twenty cents. Folks said that we never could take such a strong place and that it was of no use to go near it. But Governor Shirley kept agitating the matter, and finally out of fear for their trade, and hatred of the French and their Indian allies, our folks plucked up their courage and determined to go down and take it. The ministers preached sermons to encourage their congregations. Everybody was talking about it, and there was a great excitement throughout New England. But the French never learned a word of it, for no vessel going northward was allowed to sail from Boston, Salem, Portland—then called Falmouth—or Portsmouth. Volunteers were called for—just as in the great Civil War 120 years later. Four thousand men were called for, and they soon got them. Scores were carried away during the last two weeks before the expedition sailed. Had they known what was before them, it is not likely they would have been altogether so anxious to go; for more than a thousand of them were fated to lose their lives at Louisbourg.

"About forty-two hundred finally went, and of these, Maine, then only a small colony, furnished fully one-third; the expedition was commanded, too, by a Maine man, General William Pepperell, who lived at Kittery and traded at Portsmouth, New Hampshire. Afterwards, in the time of the Revolution, the Pepperells were Tories, or Loyalists. But Royalist or not, there is no doubt that General Pepperell was a very fine man, as well as a wise and prudent commander. For he took Louisbourg, although in the fogs and bogs of Cape Breton he contracted rheumatic disease of which he finally died.

"This was New England's first great military expedition. The army was divided into ten battalions and despite a lack of discipline it was an energetic force, brimful of resolution and daring. Young Colonel Gridley who afterwards built the redoubts at Bunker Hill, was the engineer. The governor of New York loaned Massachusetts ten cannon, but refused to cooperate otherwise. Most of the other cannon and one large mortar were taken from Fort William in Boston Harbor. The soldiers had flintlock muskets, powder horns and wooden cartridge boxes, and a part of them had bayonets; there had been so much haste, however, that they were but poorly supplied with tents and provisions. Fourteen small armed vessels were equipped to act as a convoy for the transports which carried the soldiers around by sea, and Commodore Warren with four English men-of-war from the West India Squadron, followed the New Englanders to Louisbourg where he contributed somewhat—not greatly—to the siege of the fortress. Many of our soldiers indeed heartily wished that Commodore Warren had never come; for he embarrassed General Pepperell not a little, in one way and another, and in the end prevented the New Englanders from receiving any of the prize money which should rightfully have fallen to them. Every sailor in Warren's fleet received 850 pounds prize money ($4,050) and the officers obtained immense sums. But the New England volunteers received nothing, and this was one of those rankling grievances which, remembered for years, rendered the colonials the more willing to renounce allegiance to England.

"There were over a hundred small transport vessels that sailed from Boston and other ports along the coast, during the last week of March; the weather proved fine and the ships all reached Canso Harbor in safety, sixty miles from Louisbourg. But the ice along the Cape Breton coast held them back for nearly a month, and it was not till the 29th of April, 1745, that they were finally able to sail for Louisbourg.

"Get your atlas and look at the map. Find the gut of Canso and Louisbourg, and then find, if you can, Gabarus Bay which is a small bay five miles this side of Louisbourg. That is the place where Governor Shirley had ordered Pepperell to land his men and make a night attack on the great fortress. But it was found utterly impossible to land there by night, and the landing was not made till next day.

"And now," said the Old Squire, "I'm going to tell you Grandsir Pliny's story—as nearly as I can remember it—as he used to tell it to me when I was a boy."

"I don't like to hear you call him grandsir, when he was so young," said Theodora. "Just think, he was my great-great-grandfather—and only eighteen then! Do you know how he looked?"

"No," replied the Old Squire, "but when I knew him, he was a straight old man whose cheeks were still red. I should imagine that he must have been a large, strong, well-favored boy. He had been out scouting against the Indians once or twice already, and was probably a good shot and a good woodsman. Like as not, he was a little rough of speech, for young men did not pick their words much in those days, but I think that he was a generous-hearted, rather jolly boy whom the girls liked."

"Well, I shall call him Pliny Great-great," observed Theodora.

"Very well," said Grandfather, laughing, as he dipped us out another quart of beans all around.

"As soon as we turned to"—'that was the way he used to tell it,' said the Old Squire—"we heard the French bells ringing at Louisbourg.

The wind was fresh from there: the bells jangled and clashed, as if there were a fire. The French had seen us and were giving the alarm. There had been a grand ball in the town the night before, and it was said that General Duchambon, the commandant, and all his officers were sleeping late that morning. They had not heard a word of our coming to attack the place. Alarm guns began to boom. Bugles blew, and we saw a column of the enemy marching across the flats toward the shore of the bay.

"As soon as our anchors were down, the boats were lowered and loaded with our guns and equipment and we embarked in them to go ashore. More than a hundred boats were putting off from the ships at once. There were not oars enough and the boats were loaded down with men. A surf four feet high was breaking on the beach. As soon as our boat came into shallow water, the lieutenant shouted. 'Over with you, every second man, and take the other on his back!'

"I jumped out—up to my waist, and I tell you that water felt cold! Nate Haskell and True Pennell were my mates, and Will Tufts who afterwards climbed the flagstaff of the island battery and put his red coat on it, was in the boat with us. Nate got on my back and I waded ashore with him. The surf wet us both throughout; he held our guns up and kept them dry.

"As soon as we were ashore we stopped to load our guns; for we saw the French about half a mile further along the beach toward Louisbourg; they began to fire at our men who were farthest that way, and we ran towards them. There did not look to be more than 150 of them, but we did not know how many there might be in the woods, back of the beach. We were not much afraid, for our men were now coming ashore fast. The French advanced through a swamp full of bogberry bushes; they cheered and fired by volleys, but our men were all running in that direction and outnumbered them in a few minutes. A great burst of firing ensued before Nate and I came near, and much powder smoke drifted back over us. The wind blew it out to sea, and then we saw the French running. Some of them ran to the woods. Our men chased them but did not follow them into the woods. We thought that there might be Indians lying in wait there. I heard the man in advance say that six of the French had been killed. A squad of the New Hampshire men had caught the French captain and led him past us, holding fast to his collar.

"Just then Captain William Vaughan came up, shouting, 'Come on boys! Run 'em into Louisbourg!'

"A part of the French were retreating across the flats in the direction of the fortress, and about forty of us started after them, Vaughan leading. It was a very weird, boggy place, little stony knolls and then hollows where one would go knee-deep in moss and water. One could not even run, if he tried. The French were about a quarter of a mile ahead of us, plodding through the bogs. Now and then one of them would turn around and fire back at us.

"After about two miles they reached some small houses, built of squared timber. We thought that they would make a stand there.

"'String out—and surround 'em!' Vaughan called to us. He was very canny, but not a trained officer—just a former mill owner from Damariscotta.

"Nate, Will Tufts, and I with fifteen or twenty others started to run around to the left of the houses, but had not gone far when the French left the buildings and made toward Louisbourg again. Smoke rose behind them; they had set the houses afire.

"We did not dare go much nearer the town, for we could now hear the drums and bugles very plainly, and as we stood there looking at the ramparts, a cannon was fired and the ball struck in a bog fifty or sixty paces in front of us, throwing up mud and water. On that side, the fortifications looked like a great green mound, three-quarters of a mile long, with roofs, turrets, and gables of many gray-colored houses, showing over them. Far around to the left we could see a great gate with mason work. It looked as if we could easily climb the ramparts, but in reality, there was a ditch thirty-feet deep and eighty feet wide just inside the glacis, or outer mound of green turf, and on the inside of the ditch was a wall thirty-five feet high which the glacis and counterscarp hid from our view. After looking at the town awhile we went back and found our men encamping along shore, near a little brook, and there we passed our first night on Cape Breton.

"Next day our battalion received orders to go around back of the little range of wooded hills, beyond the flats, and come to the harbor, above

the town. Vaughan went with us. We entered the woods and throwing
out flankers and sending scouts ahead, tramped for two or three hours
through thick fir and spruce forest. Small black flies nearly devoured us
here. At length, we came out in sight of the harbor, with Louisbourg
down to our right, and then the fresh sea wind blew away the flies. On
the shore of the bay, nearer than Louisbourg, was another fort which
they called the Royal Battery. From where we stood on the hill, Nate
counted thirty embrasures with heavy cannon in them. But nearer still,
no more than a quarter of a mile below us, stood six or eight long warehouses at the water's edge. We could see only three or four men about
them and Colonel Waldo at once gave the order to take and burn them.
Our whole detachment rushed down the hillside and surrounded the
buildings. Then there followed a great racket, smashing down the doors
with stones and large poles, taken from a pile of spars that lay on the
shore. We then searched the storehouses. Inside them were great quantities of cordage, tar, lumber, oil, paint, and other naval stores, brought
from France. In one of the buildings some of the men found several cases
of brandy and wine. Many bottles were handed around, but Nate and I
could not get one. Those who had tinderboxes began to set the storehouses on fire and soon they blazed up terrifyingly. I had never seen such
a fire before. The tar, oil, and cordage threw up thick black volumes of
smoke which the wind drove directly down toward the Royal Battery and
the town. I suppose that some of the men had taken draughts of the
brandy; for they now began shouting and cheering. Some hollered and
yelled like Indians. They made a tremendous noise, and this and the
dense black smoke produced a curious effect—very favorable to us. Our
men had no orders to attack the Royal Battery and had no notion of doing
so, but the French there, hearing the shouting, believed our whole force
was rushing to storm the works, under cover of the dense smoke. The
commandant, like a coward, ordered his men to spike the guns and escape
along the beach into Louisbourg, and this they did, without being seen
by us, the smoke was so dense in that direction.

"After the warehouses were on fire, our men started to return to
camp, but Vaughan passed word to fifteen or sixteen of us who had been
with him the day before, to fall out and stay with him. We went to a
deserted French house at the edge of the forest, where we secured some

dried venison, tea, and a copper kettle, and that night we camped at a dry place among the firs, a little way back of the hills.

"At daybreak Vaughan awakened us.

"'We will have a look at the Royal Battery,' said he. 'Follow after me and keep still.'

"We went along the crest of the hills, among the low spruces there, till we came down opposite the battery which had walls and was laid out like any fort. We could look down on it from the hill and the first thing Nate said to me as we peeped out was, 'Plin, there's nobody there.'

"There was no smoke, no sentries, not a soul in sight anywhere. We did not know what to think. 'They may be lyin' low,' Vaughan said. 'Watch awhile.' But not a soul could we see.

"Vaughan then drew a tiny bottle from his pocket and showing it to a Cape Cod fisherman in our party, said, 'Pete, I'll give you this bottle of nice French brandy if you will creep down and see who's there.'

"'Done, Cap'n!' replied Pete. 'But I want that bottle first.' "Vaughan gave it to him. He took a drink and then went directly down the hill. We watched him cross the dry ditch and climb in at an embrasure. He was out of sight a few moments, then appeared on the parapet and swung his hat. 'Come on!' he shouted. 'I've took the battery alone!'

"With that we all started to run down the hillside, but Vaughan caught me by the collar.

"'Plin!' he exclaimed, in great excitement. 'You've got good legs. Drop your gun and run round through the woods to camp. Tell old sleepyhead to send five hundred men here, double quick!'

"Vaughan who was a headstrong fellow did not like General Pepperell very well, and was inclined to speak contemptuously of him.

"He continued, shaking me. 'Run as you never ran before! Tell 'em we've taken the Royal Battery, with thirty cannon, and have only fourteen men to hold it!'

Part 2: *"You will not shoot me."*

"THEN, INDEED, I ran.

"If there had been a road, or a path through the woods, a trip of six miles would have been no great feat for me. But my route was through thick fir and spruce woods, over broken ground, first up a craggy ridge then down in a wet hollow where I went to my knees in soft moss and water. So rough was the country and so thick the growth, that I had great trouble in keeping to my course. The sun had not risen but the east was now very bright and I headed in that direction.

"On and on I ran, panting hard, for the morning was quite warm, or soon seemed so to me. At length the sun rose, and keeping it in view among the trees, I pressed on with less trouble about my bearings. But for the sun I could hardly have found my way.

"At length I heard a cannon fired. It was probably at Louisbourg, but I fancied that it was from one of our ships in Gabarus Bay, off our camp, and ran in that direction. It seemed to me that I had come at least ten miles already. A dozen times I thought that I must be lost, but at last I came out suddenly on the brink of a hill, fronting the open flats—with Louisbourg close down to my left. I was much too near the town, and to my no little alarm saw a party of French at a house, scarcely a gunshot distant. One was an officer, and he stood looking at our camp which I now saw a mile and a half away to the right.

"I had incautiously run out in sight on a bare ledge, and as I stood staring, trying to get my bearings, one of the enemy chanced to espy my red coat against the green boughs.

"'*Voila!*' he shouted, just as I turned and ran. I heard the Frenchy chasing me, and made a wide detour at full speed again through the woods to the right. Then after listening and making pretty sure that the enemy had not followed me so far, I ran down across the flats to our camp. One of Walcott's sentinels stopped me.

"'Take me to General Pepperell' said I, panting so hard that I could hardly speak the words. "The soldier who knew me by sight, pointed to Pepperell's tent near the beach, on the south side of the little brook. The general, who was a tall, pleasant-faced man, had but just risen when his orderly led me into the tent. He had not put on his coat, and his long hair which looks so nicely combed and powdered in the portraits of him, was in a fine tangle, I promise you, in spite of his pink bed cap.

"'What is it, my boy?' he said. 'You look very hot.' "'The Royal Battery's *took*, sir!' I panted. 'Cap'n Vaughan's took it, and he's only fourteen men to hold it with!'

"General Pepperell looked incredulous.

"'Can this be true?' he exclaimed, regarding me rather sternly.

"'True as the sun shines, General!' I exclaimed. 'I've run all the way here. 'Cap'n Vaughan wants five hundred men, double quick!'

"'Most important!' he exclaimed to Colonel Bradstreet who had followed me into the tent. 'We must get Waldo and his men up there at once.'

"They said no more to me, and I went out and threw myself down on the ground. My clothes were drenched from perspiration and my face burned. Moreover, I felt very faint, for I had had no breakfast. The ground was damp and the wind blew freshly from the sea. It felt very cool and comfortable at first. I lay there for as much as an hour, and was nigh falling asleep when Colonel Bradstreet came and spoke to me, and I found myself shivering from cold. When I rose my legs were so stiffened that I could barely walk. The cooks had prepared breakfast and when I had eaten, I felt better, but was still very stiff in the legs.

"Colonel Bradstreet to whom I related the particulars of our adventures at the battery and of my run to camp, bade me rather sternly never to leave my gun behind me again. 'When you have rested,' said he, 'go back and get it. A soldier should never leave his gun.'

"'Cap'n Vaughan told me to drop it, sir,' I replied.

"'Bill Vaughn is no soldier,' said Colonel Bradstreet gruffly.

"But I could not help thinking to myself that, soldier or no soldier, William Vaughan had gotten possession of the Royal Battery which was the greatest exploit performed by anyone thus far.

"The crews of the ships in the bay were landing cannon and ammunition. A detachment of Colonel Hale's men had advanced and were swamping a road across the flats, for hauling the cannon toward the town. Colonel Dwight's regiment advanced to the green hill where I had come out of the woods upon the French party, and it was there, I heard Colonel Gridley say, that the first of the siege batteries must be placed. Colonel Dwight, Captain Bernard, and Captain Gibson came to headquarters, while I was nearby, saying that it would be impossible for the men to draw cannon across the boggy flats on wheels. They agreed that wooden sleds would have to be made and the cannon lashed to them like logs, for the men to draw.

"Toward noon Jotham Farbell, another of Vaughan's soldiers, came through the woods, to inform General Pepperell, that our men had held the Royal Battery against an attack by the French in boats. The enemy had been beaten off, after a sharp fight at the beach. Waldo's men had arrived and they were now drilling out the vents of the heavy guns at the captured battery, which had been spiked with rat-tail files.

"In the course of an hour Farbell went back with a message to Waldo, and I accompanied him. We lost our way and did not reach the battery till sunset. I recovered my gun and box, and remained in the battery which was a strong fort with walls, moat, and a comfortable barracks inside. The cots were well bedded, and the French had left their blankets; there were also large stores of salt meat and ship bread, and those who had been in the magazine, said that it was full of powder, forty-two pounder shot, shell, and langrage. The smiths had drilled out two cannon, and at sunset, by Waldo's order, these pieces were trained on the town and opened fire. I had never heard such loud reports in all my life before. The shells fell into Louisbourg, and our men were in great glee watching the stir that they made in the city. People could be seen running along the streets, to take shelter in the bombproofs.

"I reported myself to Colonel Waldo who knew me well and asked him what I should do next.

"'Did Colonel Bradstreet bid you come back after you got your gun?' he asked me.

"'No sir,' I replied. 'He told me to come here and find my gun.'

"'Then you stay right here with us,' said Waldo, laughing. 'I want all the men I can get.'

"That order suited me very well; for Nate Haskell and True Pennell were there and a drummer I knew, from Berwick, whom they called Gust Larrabee. I went into the mess with them. We had a fine time that night in the battery. Our officers looked for a night attack from Louisbourg which was about three-quarters of a mile distant, but the French did not make another attack on the battery.

"Toward morning the men on guard duty saw three Indians crawling in the brush on the hill which commanded the battery on the land side, and as soon as it was light, Colonel Waldo ordered out a scouting party of fifteen men under Lieutenant Davies. True Pennell and I were in this party. Waldo had a sketch map of the whole island, and he ordered Davies to beat through the woods till he came to a long bay called the Meerah, or Mira. He wished to find out whether the French had a land force outside of Louisbourg.

"We went along the beach as far as the warehouses which Vaughan had burned, and then followed a cart road inland to the southwest, throwing out flankers into the woods on each side. It was a road that seemed to have been recently traveled by oxen, but we came to no clearings and met no one.

"The Mira is a long, narrow, winding bay with green hills on both sides of it. We reached it before noon, and then followed the road southerly along the shore for three or four miles. The cart road then turned to the west and crossed a little river on a log bridge. This river makes into the head of Mira Bay. Several of us ran down the bank to get a drink, and we then saw that the river was swarming with large, black-backed fish which the Lieutenant said were salmon. True and I waded into a pool below some ledges and threw out more than twenty with our bayonets—fish that weighed from six to ten pounds apiece. String sticks were cut and every man took one along.

"We went on, following the road, but had proceeded for no more than a mile beyond the log bridge, when we came to clearings and saw three groups of farm buildings close together. As many as sixty cows were feeding in pastures around them, and we heard roosters crowing, but saw no people.

"After watching awhile, Davies ordered his men to keep in the bushes on each side of the cart track, and sent True and me, with Pete, the Cape Cod fisherman, to see if any of the enemy were lying there.

"'If you are fired on, fall back here,' he said. 'We will cover you.' He gave True his flint and steel, bidding him set the stacks and barns afire.

"I felt frightened, for I expected we would be fired on from the farmhouse nearest us, which was a low stone building with a thatch roof and small narrow windows. But a soldier must go as he is ordered. We ran along the road with our guns cocked and came to the house, but the door was fast and we could see no one at the windows, nor about the barns. True turned in there, to go to the barns, but I ran to the next farmhouse which was situated on the other side of the cart road. The door of this house was partly open, and I saw a girl peeping out.

"'She's a Frenchy,' thought I, 'and I will scare her;' so I shouted, 'Surrender!'

"With that I heard wailing as of old people, somewhere in the house: *'Merci! Merci! Mon dieu! Mon dieu!'* But the girl opened the door as I ran forward, and did not seem much frightened. Not even at Falmouth had I ever seen so pretty a lass: about sixteen, with rosy cheeks and dark blue eyes. 'But,' thought I, 'you are nothing but a Frenchy, I don't care for you.'

"I was greatly astonished therefore to hear her speak. 'You will not shoot me,' she said. 'I'm English, too. I'm a slave here. Oh! I'm glad the English have come, for they will take me home!'

"'Where is your home?' I exclaimed.

"'At Annapolis, but our folks came to Canso to live last year, and the French took us all prisoners.'

"All the time she was speaking, the screaming and wailing in the house continued, and a trembling old voice cried 'Meeriam! Meeriam!" over and over.

"'Who's in the house?' I demanded.

"'Only old Monsieur De la Rue and his wife and their sister.'

"'No men?'

"'Only old Monsieur in his bed,' replied the captive girl, laughing at me.

"'It doesn't seem right to set the place afire,' said True who had now come across the road to join me.

"We went back and reported to our Lieutenant.

"'Zounds, no!' he exclaimed. 'We won't burn folks alive—even if they are French. Leave that to Ingins and Papists.'

"But he sent me back. "'Go ask the girl if there are any French soldiers or Ingins about, or have been lately,' said he.

"I ran back, and again the captive lass came out. She could scarcely conceal her great joy at seeing her own countrymen after being in captivity so long. She told me that there had been no troops or Indians about of late, for the latter had all gone south, into Nova Scotia, to besiege Annapolis; also that her young master, Paul De la Rue and his wife had gone into Louisbourg four days previously, and had not returned.

"'Nor will they,' said I. 'Louisbourg is close invested, and soon we shall take it and all who are there.'

"'And then—when you go away—you will not forget to take me!' the girl exclaimed, eagerly. 'You will not leave me a slave!'

"'That we will not,' said I.

"The peevish, feeble old voices indoors were calling 'Meeriam!' again, over and over.

"'Is that your name?' I asked.

"'Yes, Miriam Meserve, and my father's name is Obed Meserve; he came to Annapolis from Salem in the Bay.'

"I told her my own name and where I lived.

"'If you want good things,' said the girl, 'these farms abound. My master is a relation of Duchambon who commands at Louisbourg. He sells his produce to the garrison there. There are eggs in the barns, nests full of them, and there is milk for the milking and veal for the killing. You would do well to come and take what you want.'

"I dared not tarry longer; for our party waited, and Lieutenant Davies was a peremptory man.

"On our return to the battery that night, I gave the salmon, which I had brought home, to Colonel Waldo, for True Pennell and Pete had brought plenty for our mess. Waldo's grave face relaxed in a smile when he saw the quality of the fish. Davies had reported to him, but the colonel also questioned me as to what I had seen and heard. I gave him the intelligence which the captive girl had confided to me.

"'Ah, you youngsters,' said he with a laugh; 'beyond doubt if there are lasses you will find them.'

"There was twilight there until as late as ten o'clock at night, and four guns of the battery fired on the town throughout the evening. The French were replying, at intervals, and our men were obliged to keep close to the wall in the east angle of the works, for several solid shot and one shell fell into the battery. During the day our men had dragged two of the heavy forty-two pounder guns to the new battery which Colonel Gridley had constructed on the hill to the southwest of the town, fronting the King's Bastion. This battery had now begun to fire, both with cannon and with the large mortar brought from the fort in Boston Harbor.

"In the evening a scout came to us through the woods from this battery. He said that Dwight's whole battalion was out in the borders of the forest, binding fascines for a new, advanced battery which General Pepperell intended to erect in the course of two days. Pepperell's men, he said, were drawing cannon and ammunition across the boggy flats on sleds.

"Next morning the shot and shell fell so frequently into the Royal Battery, that all of Waldo's men save about thirty who served the four guns, were sent out of the works into the woods back of them. About a hundred were detailed to drag cannon around to the new battery, but the most of us did what we liked. Our discipline was far from strict. Unless detailed for duty, we did about as we pleased. Nate Haskell and I scouted in the woods, hoping to fall in with an Indian.

"Next day was Sunday and Parson Moody preached in the small Papist chapel inside the Royal Battery, but the town began firing, before he finished his sermon; the battery replied with shell.

"On either the next day, or the day after, as we were not on duty, Nate and I set off unbeknown, to catch more salmon. It was a long distance to go, but we ran for much of the way, along the cart road, keeping a sharp eye ahead for French or Indians.

"After reaching the stream at the log bridge, we soon caught all the salmon we could carry. I then bantered Nate to go on to the French farm with me, to see Miriam Meserve and get some eggs. He was a dreadfully bashful fellow—one of the kind of boys who never dare say a word to a girl—and would not go. He declared that we ought to hurry back to camp. I coaxed him and chaffed him. At length he agreed to go with me to the edge of the clearing and wait there, while I went for the eggs. He would not go any farther than that, and after a good look at the place to see if any of the enemy were about, I ran to it from the woods.

"Nobody was stirring outside the farmhouse, and I walked around the yard for some moments before the captive girl espied my red coat from indoors. She then ran out and, as before, seemed much pleased to see me.

"'Have you taken the town?' she exclaimed. 'I have looked for some of you everyday. It is dreadfully lonesome here. Master Paul and his wife have not returned, and old Madame and Monsieur do nothing save lament all day long. Oh, I am so homesick! When shall you take the town and go home?'

"'When we can,' I replied. 'Not at once. It is a very strong place. I have only come to get eggs—and see you for a moment.'

"'Eggs you shall have,' said she, and fetching out a large osier basket, led the way to a barn, despite piteous cries of 'Meeriam!' from indoors.

"'They call to me all day long!' exclaimed the girl impatiently. 'If I listened to all their outcries I should neither sleep nor eat. One would think I was their own flesh and blood and not a slave lass whom they have torn from her home!'

"The yard and barn swarmed with cackling poultry, geese, and ducks, and never in my life had I seen so many nests of eggs; nests everywhere, rolling over full. We filled the osier basket, packing them in barley chaff. Miriam carried one side of it with me out to the cart road.

"'Ah, it is good to hear one speak English again and speak it myself,' she exclaimed, and seemed loath to release her hold on the basket. 'Come and get more eggs tomorrow, and you will not take the town and go home without me?'

"I assured her we would not.

"All the while we could hear those pettish old voices, croaking, 'Meeriam! Meeriam!' in the house.

"Nate upbraided me for my long absence. We slung the basket on my musket and each taking one end of it, ran fast along the cart road, having two ten-pound salmon apiece over our shoulders, but night fell before we reached the battery.

"Again I gave the colonel a fine fish and also carried two dozen of the eggs to his mess cook. We feared lest we should be punished for our long absence, but no notice was taken of it.

Part 3: "She is no baby now, sir."

"NATE HASKELL would not go with me to the French farm the next day; he was, as I have said, a very bashful fellow, and moreover, he feared to be reprimanded for leaving our lines without orders. But I risked it; I thought that I would get two more salmon at the river and another basketful of eggs. I did not like to ask True Pennell or Will Tufts to go, for I was afraid that they might not behave quite right toward Miriam Meserve.

"I saw a large bear in the cart road near the log bridge and might have shot it, but was afraid that the report of my gun would be heard by some of the enemy scouts.

"I had taken the osier basket, and after watching the farm awhile from the edge of the woods, I ran along the cart road toward it. But I had not taken twenty steps when I saw the captive girl, at the end of the stone farmhouse, waving her hands toward me in what I thought a rather odd way; yet I recollected how very glad she had seemed to see us, and set it down to that.

"As I came nearer, she ran suddenly from the house toward the barn from which we had taken the eggs, and seeing her go there, I veered across the fields and went to the barn instead of the house. But as I approached the door and was about to speak, she said, 'Come in out of sight, quick!'—in a whisper. 'What made you come when I motioned you back? Didn't you see me motion to you not to come? I was watching all the morning and saw you when you first came out of the woods; I ran out to keep you from coming nearer.'

"'Why, who's here?' said I.

"'Songo, the Mic-Mac chief, and four of his men; they are in the house, talking with old Monsieur,' replied Miriam. 'I'm afraid they saw you. If they looked out they must have seen you. Hide here in the barn while I run in and see what they are doing.'

"I kept out of sight, and Miriam ran into the house. She was gone for a considerable time, but at length returned. 'I had to wait,' she said. 'They didn't happen to look out and see you, but I wonder; for they are in the front room, drinking brandy with old Monsieur. If you step out of the barn, they may see your red coat.'

"'Have they got guns?' I asked her.

"'Yes, and their faces were painted not long ago. They are talking about Annapolis and the English, and old Monsieur will be giving them a calf, for he called me and asked how many calves were in the pen beside the barn. You must hide in the barn here till they go.'

"There was a noise outside as she whispered this, and we heard one Indian speak to another.

"'They are coming for the calf now,' exclaimed Miriam, 'Oh, hide somewhere, quick! Where can you hide?'

"At the far end of the barn there was a rudely contrived machine for threshing barley, wheat, and oats, set in motion by large wind vanes attached to a shaft outside—such as one may see even now at French Canadian farms. Nearer the door stood a fanning mill, or winnowing machine, for separating grain from chaff. It consisted of a rack for sieves, connected with an axle fan, turned by a hand crank, and the fan was enclosed within a large rounded box, resting on the floor.

"'Get under that,' whispered the girl. 'I've been under it'—and she lifted up one end of it. In an instant more I was beneath the mill, with my head between two vanes of the fan.

"It was not a brave thing for a soldier to do, but I was in no haste to lose my scalp, and I thought that five to one was heavy odds. There was a round hole in the fan box, on each side, but in the dark barn, not even an Indian's eye would have discerned me.

"The girl who was as quick as a hare in her movements, pushed some straw against the fanning mill and threw my gun upon a mow of old hay. Then beginning to sing, she snatched a handful of eggs from a nest and went out at the door; for old Madame had been crying 'Mee-riam,' from the house,

"I lay quiet, listening in great anxiety. The Indians were dragging a calf from the pen. It bleated loudly as they cut its throat. They opened the large doors of the barn on the front side. From the hole in the fan box, I saw them truss up the dead calf to a beam over the open doorway, and dress it, removing the skin with their scalping knives. The manner in which they bolted great chunks of the raw, warm liver, as they butchered the calf, was quite horrible. Between fear and hatred of them, I earnestly wished for two muskets. I think that I would have fired on them as they stood there. Cold sweat broke out on me at the thought that they might possibly be led to examine the fanning mill and attempt to turn the crank. They looked about the barn for some minutes, as they waited for the carcass to drain. One of them stood with his moc-casined ankles within two feet of my face, laughing at his mate who ate an egg raw and smeared himself with the yolk. They chuckled, exchang-ing now and then a low word of comment on the contents of the barn. The liquor which they had been given indoors, had put them in a merry mood, for one of them threw his tomahawk at a post in the barn, four or five times, his mate grunting approval when it stuck in the wood. I could easily imagine what would befall me, if they chanced to find me there; I was much cramped but scarcely dared breathe lest they might hear me.

"After a time, another of the Indians, the chief probably, called to them from the house door, and immediately they cut the carcass of the calf in halves and slinging the meat on their backs, went away.

"Still I dared not stir. Before very long, however, the captive girl came softly in. "'They've gone,' she said aloud and lifted the sieve end of the fanning mill, for me to crawl forth. I made all haste to get my gun, asking her what direction the Indians had taken. She had watched them go along a path on the hither side of the Mira. From what she had overheard, she thought a party had come up from the south, the previ-ous night.

"I deemed these tidings of importance and resolved to report to Colonel Waldo at once, without tarrying to load myself, either with eggs or salmon. I was very hungry, however, and in this matter the cap-tive girl was able to give me good cheer; for immediately she brought from the house a shoulder of cold baked veal and a large wheat cake with butter, all on a great pestor platter; also a glass of wine with which, she assured me, the farmhouse was abundantly provided. She sat by me, inside a stall, while I hastily partook of this refreshment. Our parting, indeed, might have been thought an affectionate one, for Miriam held me by the hand while I again and again promised, that we would not sail for home without her. Then, after she had looked forth along the cart road, I set off at a great pace and reached the Battery before sunset.

"In consequence of the information I gave, Captain Gibson was dis-patched at daylight next day, May 10th, with a party of twenty-five men, to reconnoiter. Fortunately for me I was not detailed for this service, having made so long a trip the previous afternoon. Gibson and his men fell in with a large body of Indians and were all killed or taken, except the captain and two privates, and the prisoners—were first tortured, then put to death.

"A force of two hundred men was sent out immediately and there was some desultory fighting. Fully six hundred of the French and Indians were now said to be on the Mira, watching opportunity to attack Pepperell's army in the rear. I heard from Lieutenant Davies that some of the buildings at the French farm had been sacked and burned, but I could get no tidings of Miriam Meserve and felt much disturbed on account of her. I dared not now venture so far as the farm, however, for the woods were full of the enemy's scouts, and Colonel Waldo who had been aware of my peregrinations, 'out of the corner of his eye,' had called me to him one day, and bade me very sternly not to leave camp again without orders, 'neither for salmon, eggs, nor lasses': those were his very words.

"At this time, too, Nate and I were in a party of fifty, sent from Waldo's regiment to aid Pepperell and Bradstreet's men in drawing ammunition and fascines by night, from the camp, for the new batteries in front of the West Gate of the town. On two nights also we worked in the trenches, extending them out to the left of the advanced battery. This was very hard work. A great many of the men were sick, from standing in the mud and water so much. Our batteries and those of the enemy fired almost steadily now, from four o'clock in the morning to ten at night.

"Ammunition was so scanty on our side, that General Pepperell offered two pence apiece for every one of the enemy's cannon shot which we would find, when they fell, and bring to the batteries. When off duty the men were frequently running and searching for them with shovels. Nate and I, when not at work, would sit watching for them. The earth work in front of the batteries became packed with them. After dark the men dug them out. Often, too, they struck the top of the earthwork and went skipping across the flats, or bounded hundreds of feet in the air and fell in the woods behind.

"One night the French made a sudden and very determined sortie, and a hand-to-hand fight occurred; they carried a part of our trenches, but were bloodily repulsed before they got into the battery.

Next morning the ground in front of the works was dotted with bodies.

"During the forenoon the French sent out a flag of truce and were allowed to come and bury their dead. While the white flag was out, we saw men and women and even little children walking on the parapet of the town wall. From the trenches and the advanced battery, our men shouted 'Good morning!' to them, for the distance was only 750 feet. They replied, '*Bon matin*, Yankese!' and said something about *dejeuner*, which a few among us who knew French, said was an invitation to come into town, to breakfast. Our soldiers replied that they would come in to dinner by tomorrow or next day.

"Some of the French on the rampart had bottles which probably contained wine. They poured out glassfuls and holding them up, in the sunlight, drank to us. As many as a thousand of our men came forward to the long trench while the flag was out. Some of us even went a little closer. Seeing several women near the King's Bastion, I called and asked whether Madame De la Rue were there. I shouted twice. Presently a soldier replied in English:

"'Monsieur and Madame De la Rue are here.'

"'Tell them,' said I, 'that I have seen old Monsieur and Madame De la Rue, at the farm beyond the Mira, and that Miriam Meserve is with them.'

"The soldier went away, but returned soon, having with him a lady and a gentleman. The latter spoke to me in French, the lady also, but I could not understand them. Then the soldier shouted in English again, saying, 'Monsieur and Madame thank you for these tidings;' and after a moment, he added, 'They pray that God may have you and them in his holy keeping.'

"I thought that very strange—that they should send such a word to an enemy; for I supposed the French to be very wicked people.

"After about an hour and a half, a bugle blew; our drums rolled; the French on the ramparts disappeared from sight. The flag was going in, and we who were out at the trenches ran back as fast as we could.

"Cannon fire began again, hotter than ever. Our advance battery had knocked down the drawbridges at the great gate, and now and then, after a good shot, we could see parts of the wall there tumble down into the moat.

"At the end of the week we went back to the Royal Battery and were under Colonel Meserve's orders for four days, drawing cannon from the Royal Battery to a new battery which was built by night on the shore, nearer the town. This was called Titcomb's battery, from Major Moses Titcomb of Colonel Hale's regiment, who planned it. One day after Colonel Meserve had been giving me some directions for lashing a gun, I asked him whether he knew Obed Meserve of Salem and Annapolis, since his name was the same.

"'Obed Meserve is my kinsman,' he replied. 'What of him?'

"'He was a prisoner to the French at Canso,' I replied, 'and his daughter Miriam is a captive at a French farm hard by here, on Mira Bay.'

"He was much disturbed and declared that he would attempt to recover her. Miriam was a baby when Obed went to Annapolis,' said he.

"'She is no baby now, sir,' said I. 'She is the prettiest girl I ever saw, and the quickest witted.'

"Colonel Meserve regarded me for some moments in silence. 'Yes, that was fifteen or sixteen years ago,' he said at length.

"On the day following, a party of twenty, under Captain Lovering, was sent around the harbor to Lighthouse Point, so called, on the north side, opposite the town and opposite the enemy's strong battery at the center island, called the island battery, which prevented Commodore Warren and the men-of-war from entering the harbor and helping us take the town.

"Lighthouse Point is high and rocky. Our officers, especially Dwight and Gridley, had urged planting cannon here, for a plunging fire on the island battery, and at last despite the distance which the guns would have to be drawn, General Pepperell had given an order to attempt it"

"We crossed over the north arm of the harbor from the Royal Battery, in boats, and landed in a cove, called Careening Bay. While we were reconnoitering, one of our men who had gone into the water for a bath, discovered thirty heavy cannon which the French had sunk below the low-water mark. A boat went back with the tidings, and immediately Colonel Gridley and Captain Bernard's company crossed over. They rigged tackle to haul out the cannon, and our party labored all day throwing up an earthwork and binding fascines, from trees and bushes back of the point.

"The weather was foggy, and early next morning a tremendous cannonade was heard out to sea, for an hour or more. We feared that a French fleet had come to attack Commodore Warren and raise the siege, but before ten o'clock the fog rose and we saw that our frigates were still in the offing, and that another large ship was with them. Word came to us before noon, that the new ship was the French man-of-war, *Vigilant*, which Warren had captured: a sixty-gun ship on its way from France to bring supplies to Louisbourg. Our men at the batteries could be heard cheering clean across the harbor.

"Late that night we saw a great fire in the direction of the town. There was much shouting and screaming. Soon an explosion ensued which threw burning timbers to a great height. In the morning we learned that Captain Gibson and eight others had towed a schooner, which had been captured in the harbor, close under the town walls. The vessel had been converted into a 'fire ship' and filled with combustibles, including a quantity of powder and many loaded shells. When set on fire it burned fiercely, then exploded, destroying a part of the sea wall and several buildings, and clearly terrifying the townspeople.

"Colonel Gorham's battalion came around to Lighthouse Point next day, and it was most fortunate, for on the day after, Duchambon sent a strong boat force across the harbor to drive us away. The French made three different attempts to land, but were repulsed by our men. We lay behind rocks up the steep side of the point and fired at the boats with good aim. The boats carried fifteen men each, but so destructive was our fire, that some of them had hardly enough men left in them to row back, and one was abandoned altogether.

"We who were under Captain Lovering, were ordered back to the Royal Battery next morning; for there was now sufficient force to hold Lighthouse Point and build the new battery. The distance across the ship channel, from the point to the island battery, was only eight hundred yards, and all agreed that as soon as heavy guns were mounted there, the island battery could be silenced. There was therefore much surprise among our soldiers when we heard, that night, that a boat party was to be detailed to storm the island battery. We did not believe the report at first, for—as the men said—if the island battery was to be carried at once by a night attack, why had they begun to raise a battery on the point, to silence it? Besides, the island battery had walls and a ditch, and there was a strong force of the enemy's best artillery men there.

"The report proved to be true, however. Volunteers to form a storming party of four hundred men, were called for at sunset, from the different battalions. It was by General Pepperell's order and about fifty of Waldo's men responded.

"I remember that Nate Haskell, True Pennell, and I stood on the hill back of our works and looked across at the island battery for a long time, as the setting sun shone on it.

"'The walls look pretty high,' Nate said. 'There isn't a breach anywheres. How are we going to get in?'

"'Scalin' ladders,' said True.

"'The French will knock 'em down faster than we can put 'em up!' exclaimed Nate.

"'I don't like the looks over there,' said True. 'I will go, if I am ordered, but I won't volunteer. Let them knock it down with the Lighthouse Point battery, I say.'

"'So I say,' said Nate, and I was of the same mind.

"But Will Tufts volunteered. He was braver than we. The four hundred were raised easily enough. More offered than were wanted; yet nearly everyone wondered why the attack was to be made.

"The fact was—as was learned afterwards—that General Pepperell had been nettled and urged on by Commodore Warren to make the attempt, against his own better judgment. It was almost the only mistake that our general made during the entire siege. The British commodore who was doing little himself, had continually complained of Pepperell and as constantly urged him to do this, that, or the other, impossible thing.

"The storming party did not get off that night, however. They waited for fog. Nate and I who had been astir all that night were very tired next evening, having been hauling cannon again. We were both asleep in our shelter, when the storming party finally embarked, at about one o'clock the next night, May 27th. A tremendous outburst of cannon fire waked us a little later, and everybody in camp except the sentries and pickets, ran down to the waterside.

"*Bang—bang!* boomed the heavy guns at the island battery, the red flashes lighting up thin fog. Musketry flashed and cracked all around the island. We could hear the shouts of the officers plainly, and the hurrahs with which our men pulled in and rushed to the walls with their ladders. It was not a surprise. The French had seen them and opened fire with grape and lagrange on the boats, many of which were riddled and sank under the men. More than half of the force landed, however, and rushed bravely to the assault. The uproar then was something awful to hear. Yells, shouts, and a continuous cracking of muskets mingled with the sound of breaking ladders and the noise of heavy stones, or guns, tumbling down.

"We could gain little notion which side was having the best of it, and when, by and by, some of the boats began to come back, with half the men hurt, they did not themselves know much more about it than we did.

"About 180 of our men had climbed into the battery, and Will Tufts who had fought like a tiger among the first, hauled down the French flag and put his redcoat on the flagpole, shouting, 'The battery's ours!'

"But the veteran French soldiers, standing in the dark, inside their casemates all around the fort, and in the bombproof, opened a deadly musket fire on our men who were in the open space about the flagstaff, shooting them down like deer. About sixty were killed here in a few minutes, and the others finding that they stood no chance, surrendered.

"But on shore we could not find out what had happened, till daylight, when we saw the French flag flying over the island battery. At sunrise the enemy manned the parapet of the battery and cheered for a long while, dipping their flag to the town. Everybody knew then that the attack had failed. We had lost 186 men outright, besides many wounded.

"It was reported that General Pepperell sent word to Commodore Warren, in the morning, that thenceforward he should conduct the siege as prudence dictated, and that if Warren wished the island battery stormed, he might land his own marines there and storm it.

"Truth to say, our men were much dissatisfied and not a little disheartened that morning, for the scouts had brought in word that a numerous force of Indians and French was mustering on the farms on the Mira. Shortly after sunrise our drums beat to parade, when a hundred of Waldo's men, including True Pennell and myself, were detailed to form part of a column to go against them.

"Hitherto we had done service, arduous service, it is true, but now for the first time we expected hard fighting, since our orders were to bring the enemy to an engagement, if possible, otherwise to chase them into the Bras d'Or, or drive them southward across Canso Strait.

Part 4: "But did he not see Miriam Meserve again?"

"THE CANNON SMOKE lay low over the woods around the harbor and over Louisbourg, when we reached the hill in the rear of the Royal Battery where Waldo's men were encamped. The setting sun shone through it, red as blood. Our men were cheering. First one battalion took up the shout, then another, from all the camps and batteries around this town, and over at Lighthouse Point. 'Twas King George's day, and a tremendous bombardment had been going on ever since four o'clock in the morning. Twenty of our guns were still firing, the town replying, but wearily, as one would have said.

"I saw Nate Haskell standing by a gun sled, looking out on the harbor, and running down to him, asked what the cheers were for.

"'Look at the island battery!' he exclaimed. 'They haven't fired from it for two hours. Our guns on Lighthouse Point have knocked half their cannon off the platforms. The French are hiding in the bombproof. Some of them took to the water to escape the shells and swam across to Louisbourg!'

"It was at the island battery that our men had been so disastrously repulsed some days previously, and it was this same strong work which, all along, had prevented our men-of-war from entering the harbor. The French had excellent gunners there, and to see them taking to the water, caused tremendous cheering on our side.

"'The fleet will come in tomorrow!' the men shouted.

"During the night, however, Duchambon, the French commandant, who was a brave, resolute officer, sent boats across from the town to the island and made such repairs, that at daylight the battery began firing again. Our guns mounted on the high bluff at Lighthouse Point, sent shell and solid shot into it all day long. Neither on that day nor the next did the landside batteries cease firing for so much as five minutes, till darkness fell at night, and there was also sharp firing from the trenches.

"Two Swiss soldiers in the enemy's garrison deserted to us on one of these nights. On being taken to General Pepperell's tent and questioned, they declared that there was no longer food for the men in the town, and also that the supply of powder was nearly exhausted. The townspeople, they said, particularly the women, were entreating Duchambon to capitulate to Warren and the fleet. For word had been carried to them by a letter, that some of our men had been tortured and murdered by their Indian allies, at the farm on the Mira, and they were now in mortal terror lest the town should be stormed and taken by assault.

"The island battery was now so nearly silenced that Commodore Warren summoned courage to bring his men-of-war into the harbor. During the next forenoon eleven ships and frigates, carrying in all 540 guns, drew in and anchored close off the entrance to the port, and in plain sight of all our camps. That day a plan of attack, both by land and sea, was arranged between the doughty commodore and the New England general. The former was now maneuvering, underhandedly, to gain all the honor for himself and the fleet; although not a gun had been fired at Louisbourg from any vessel of his squadron. There was a great deal of hard talk against the fleet among the soldiers, that day.

"It was expected that the town would surrender by evening. The night passed, however, and the batteries opened fire next morning, as usual. Duchambon was too brave a man to yield until the last moment.

"At daybreak the preparations for a general assault began. Scaling ladders were carried forward and great bundles of fascines and poles for rafting the moat; also timber from a number of dismantled houses. On the harbor side a great number of boats were prepared. The plan was to attack on both sides at once; while the marines from the fleet stormed the gates in the sea wall, we of the land force were to advance at four different points, cross the moat and scale the ramparts. The battalion commanders called their men together and exhorted them most solemnly to do their full duty. There was little need for the exhortation. We all knew that we must take the town, and we had no doubt that we should do it.

"It was now nearing noon, June 15th; the men were in their assigned positions, and I think that the order to attack could have come soon, when a French officer appeared on the parapet near the King's Bastion and waved a white flag. As soon as he made sure that the flag was seen, he swung down by an embrasure, crossed the moat on some timbers and came forward to our trenches. As he approached, he called out in English that he bore a message for General Pepperell. Captain Wilmot conducted him to Pepperell and word soon went about, that Duchambon had asked for a cessation of hostilities until terms for capitulation could be agreed on.

"Some of our men cheered. Some found fault, saying that they would rather take the town by storm. But the most of us were glad, and felt little spite. The French had but fought as brave men should to defend the town.

"A favorable answer was sent back, and there was no further firing that day. Messages passed to and fro between Duchambon and General Pepperell. The terms of surrender which the former sought to obtain for the garrison were twice rejected. Early next morning, however, it was agreed that the French should surrender Louisbourg on the following day, but should be allowed to march out with the honors of war.

"Very early the following morning, however, it was discovered that Commodore Warren had sent a boat force to occupy the island battery, and had himself entered the town, from the harbor side, to take possession of it and receive the keys of the citadel, in advance of us. It seemed that he wished to deprive the New England army of the honor of its victory, and again there was much angry talk among the soldiers. But General Pepperell, unaware of Warren's stratagem, sent a message to Duchambon at noon, informing him that our army would enter the town at five o'clock in the afternoon. On learning this, Commodore Warren sent out a pettish message complaining of General Pepperell's haste and irregularity. But Duchambon who now began to perceive that the English commodore had assumed more authority than he possessed, made haste to clear an entrance at the much battered West Gate.

"There were about three thousand of us who marched in by this gateway. Pepperell's regiment led the column; Walcott's came next and Waldo's was fourth. As we passed through the shattered gate our men cheered, the drums beat, and those who had horns and trumpets blew loud blasts. Two of Pepperell's men had procured violins and one had a hautboy. These musicians walked beside the column, playing merry tunes; while here and there a lively young soldier would leap out and execute a double shuffle!

"The French folks stood in groups at the street corners and in doorways and when they saw how well disposed and jolly we were, they called out 'Bravo!' to our music, and some handed bottles of wine to the soldiers. In truth, they were as glad the siege had ended as were the besiegers themselves. Men, women, and children had been obliged to live in narrow, damp bombproofs and casemates in the walls. We could but pity them when we saw what their condition had been for forty-seven days. Not a house in the town but showed great gaping holes in roof and walls, where our shot and shells had struck them. Many buildings had been knocked wholly down. The streets were piled with splintered timbers, broken brick, stone, and mortar. Little wonder—for our siege batteries had used almost a hundred tons of powder and had fired more than four hundred tons of shell and shot.

"But when we began to walk about and viewed the strength of the defenses, the height of the parapet, the depth and width of the moat, the great guns, caserns, casemates, and bombproofs, our feeling was one of astonishment, and ever the wonder grew in us, that we had been able to capture so strong, so apparently impregnable a fortress.

"A little way within the gate there was a large stone building, much shattered by our shot. Here the French commandant, Duchambon, met General Pepperell and making low obeisance, tended the hilt of his sword in its scabbard which, however, our general requested him to keep. A French officer then gave to Colonel Bradstreet several large iron keys, bound together with a thong. Duchambon, who was a handsome old man and bore himself proudly, wore a blue coat having large gilt epaulets, and held in his hand a gold-laced hat. His hair was white with powder and his face cleanshaven, but brown.

"A thousand of our soldiers under Walcott and Bradstreet remained in Louisbourg that night, to occupy the fortifications, but the most of us went back to our camps. For Warren's men, who were on shore, strutted about arrogantly proclaiming that they alone had been responsible for Louisbourg's rapid capture. And there was scarcely a house fit to enter; the whole town smelled shockingly from neglect of filth.

"At sunrise next morning True Pennell, Nate Haskell and I started to go into town again, but as we came around the '*barasoi*,' or cove, between Titcomb's Battery and the West Gate, we met a French gentleman and lady coming outward on foot, accompanied by an old French soldier and a boy. I thought that the lady was she with whom I had spoken from the city wall during the siege, and as they approached, I asked whether it was not Monsieur and Madame De la Rue? The French soldier made answer in English, saying that it was so, and that they had set off in quest of their old parents at a farm on the Mira.

"I then said that I was the soldier who had accosted them from the trenches, and that old Monsieur and Madame De la Rue had gone to a fishery beyond the Bras d'or.

"The lady seemed much distressed that they were so far away; for they had no conveyance. "'Why did they go there?' the soldier asked me, for her.

"I was obliged to tell them of the massacre at Mira bridge, and that the farm buildings had been burned. Madame De la Rue, who was worn and ill from the privations of the siege, wept bitterly. I sought to give them comfort saying that the old people were, beyond doubt, well and safe, for Miriam Meserve was still with them.

"As our men were not doing duty that day, I determined to go with them, and asked True and Nate to accompany me. Nate, indeed, consented, but True preferred to go to Louisbourg again. I then attempted to find Colonel Meserve, but learned that he had gone aboard one of the ships that morning, on a business matter.

"I must needs confess that our trip to the Mira that morning was a most tedious one, for Madame walked but slowly, sitting to rest very frequently beside the way. Nate and I at length went on in advance. We had now little fear of the enemy; for word had gone forth already, that Louisbourg was taken. Nothing was left then to fight for. When therefore we reached the farm and found no one there, I resolved to go on to the fishery on the Arm, where I supposed Miriam Meserve to be, and if possible fetch back the old French folk to join their son and daughter. For although they were of our enemies, their case moved me. Nate consented to go on and after a hasty meal of eggs which we boiled in a kettle at the farm, he and I went on, leaving the kettle over the fire with a fowl boiling in it, for Madame when she should arrive.

"Nothing now delayed us, and we proceeded at a good pace for twelve or fifteen miles, when as we were passing one of the deserted farmhouses, previously described, we came upon an Indian, in full paint, at the very threshold of the door. Beyond doubt he thought us skirmishers from a force close behind, for he uttered a shout of surprise and ran to the woods. We could have shot him as he ran, yet would not now do so, but Nate exclaimed that we would do better to go back. 'That Mic-Mac has fresh paint on,' said he. 'He does not know of the surrender.'

"I did not like to go back and stood pondering the thing, when we were fired at from the woods at a little distance. My knee was grazed by a ball and another struck the stock of my gun. We sprang to shelter through the house door and made it fast with the beam of a loom indoors. As we did so we heard war whoops, and on looking out at a small window, saw six or seven Indians running toward the house. Nate knocked out the glass pane and I fired at them. Nate also fired. We both sprang aside to reload. The Indians ran up, thinking to break down the door before we could charge our pieces. They jumped against it, then struck their tomahawks into it; the blades came through, but we were not long ramming down each a cartridge. Hearing our ramrods play and finding that they could not get in quickly enough, the Indians suddenly ran around the corner of the house, where there was no window. There was what answered quite as well, however; for it was a log house and the moss stuffing was out at the chinks betwixt the logs. We saw the body of a Indian in front of a chink, and raising his musket, Nate fired through it. The piece recoiled, but the native was shot dead. We heard the others run off, and after that they kept out of sight in the bushes. We knew that they were lying in wait, however, and dared not show ourselves. It was an evil plight.

"'As soon as it is dark, they will burn us out,' said Nate.

"He was vexed with me for setting off on such an errand and with himself for coming. We looked about the house; there was a box containing a few quarts of dry barley, but no water, nor yet a well near it.

"We agreed to wait till dark, then try to steal out and get away. An hour or two passed very uncomfortably, for we were already thirsty, when we heard an odd voice, shouting as if to cattle along the cart road, and a little after a curious creaking and rattling.

"Standing back in the shadow, we could look out at the small front windows, and presently saw a yoke of little brindled cattle—cows they were—come out into the clearing, by the cart road, drawing a rack, set on two wheels. The team was driven by a French peasant wearing a fur cap, hot as was the weather, and brandishing a long goad stick over the cows' backs, while he continually shouted, *'Marche donc! Marche donc!'* The rack appeared to be half filled with straw, and partially hidden by the straw, sat several persons.

"Before the cart had quite emerged from the woods, however, the Indians stopped it, crying out, 'Yankese!' and pointing excitedly toward the farmhouse. The driver seemed alarmed and started to turn his yoke of cows back, but a woman sprang down from the cart behind and came forward, waving her straw hat. The moment she came out in sight from among the beech trees, I saw that it was Miriam Meserve.

"In my sudden joy at seeing her, I shouted her name from the broken window, and should have run out, I think, had not Nate, more prudent, pulled me back. Miriam came hastening to the door which I at once opened, and I fear that our greeting must have proved embarrassing to a young fellow so very bashful as Nate. He was watching the Indians, however, holding his gun ready to shoot.

"'Were you coming for me?' was Miriam's first question.

"I replied that we were, and asked who were in the rack cart.

"'Old Monsieur and Madame De la Rue and their sister and Catherine Edgecomb,' said she. Word came last night that you had taken the town, and that the French would all be sent home to France. I brought the old folks across the Arm at noon today in canoes. I said to them that they must come and find their children, and start at once, or I should run away; for I could not remain there another moment!'

"I then told her how we had been attacked by the Indians there, and that they seemed not to have heard of the surrender.

"'I will go tell them,' said Miriam, 'and make old Monsieur tell them also.'

"She ran back and we heard them setting forth the matter to the Indians who appeared to receive the news very sullenly.

"At length the cart came forward, leaving the Mic-Macs standing there among the trees. When the droll conveyance reached the house, Nate and I joined it and took our way back in company with Miriam and her charges. For several miles we were apprehensive lest the Indians might follow and attack us. But the tidings of the surrender probably overawed them. We were not molested on our road, and finally reached the farm by Mira bridge late in the evening.

"Young Monsieur and Madame De la Rue were there. The ardent joy and affection expressed by these afflicted French people at meeting, after so many dangers, touched the hearts of us who were from New England not a little. Nor were their kindly expressions hardly less warm to us who had assisted them, even though we were aliens and of the blood of their enemies.

"Next morning Nate and I went back to Louisbourg, where we found our soldiers doing heavy duty, clearing the streets, remounting cannon on the ramparts, cleaning the barracks, and guarding spoils which we had been promised, but, as it turned out, were not to share in. The French garrison had already been sent aboard vessels in the harbor. Louisbourg was ours, but now it must needs be garrisoned, and a great disappointment was in store for many of us who had hoped to return home when the city was taken. For now we were told that we would have to remain until regiments of artillery could be sent out from England to occupy it. A portion of our army, including such as had received wounds and were invalided from disease, and also those who had been captives to the French, were to be sent home at once, but we who were well were told that we must remain.

"During that day I obtained speech with Colonel Meserve and gave him word of his kinswoman at the farm. He himself went that afternoon to fetch her, and placed her on board a brig that was erelong to sail and put into Annapolis.

"A curious memento of the siege fell into my possession the next day as we worked. With a hoe I was laboring hard to scrape the earthen floor of one of the bombproofs in which the French had been pent up during the bombardment, and was digging deeply to remove the filth, when the corner of the hoe, entering at what seemed a soft spot in the hard-trodden earth, pulled out a small square object which proved to be a silver box. Apparently the box had been hastily buried there, as if for concealment. With some difficulty the lid was raised, and I found that the box contained thirty-one livre pieces, four gold louis d'ors of the value of twenty English shillings apiece, a necklace of red coral with a gold catch, a very large turquoise ring, a small ruby ring, and three plain rings of Spanish gold. There was also a silver toothpick, and the lid of a silver snuffbox.

"True Pennell who was at work with me, at once clamored for a division of the coins, and in truth I should have shared them with him and Nate Haskell, but then I had other views; for that evening it was my intention to go off to the brig on which Miriam Meserve was to have passage home.

"This indeed I did, and though on account of the number of people aboard, we could speak but little of what was in our minds, I gave the box which I had rubbed bright, and all that it contained into her keeping, as a pledge.

"Next day the brig sailed. But we of the army were left to guard Louisbourg for eleven long months, and that is when Nate Haskell and more than a thousand others died of a wasting disease which broke out among us, from the uncleanliness of the place. Their graves are on Rochefort Point beyond the old lime kiln, toward the sea."

"But did he not see Miriam Meserve again?" exclaimed Ellen, as Grandfather seemed to make an end of his story. The Old Squire glanced across at Grandmother.

"Well, I should think so," said she, laughing. "Why, children, Miriam Meserve was your great-great grandmother."

As she spoke she drew back from the bean table and going into the sitting room, unlocked a drawer of her old bureau. We heard her opening her necklace box, and then she came back, bringing a very thin, worn old gold ring.

"And this," said she, "was one of the rings in the box. Grandma Miriam wore it all her life long. She had another, too, with a King Louis XIV head on it, which young Madame De la Rue gave her. That one she lost for fourteen years, but found it again when Grandpa Eastman took down the old house and built their new large one at Portland. That ring she gave to my sister Eunice."

6

At the Maple Tree Camp

IN ALL MY BOYHOOD I NEVER HAD A BETTER TIME THAN
when three other boys and I made a trip in March 1865 to Bub Barlett's
Sugar Camp to procure "red-eyed maple" for violin timber.

At that time red-eyed maple had acquired a certain popularity as
violin timber; that is to say, for the "back," "ribs," six blocks, and "neck"
of the instrument. Expert authorities are agreed that these parts of a
violin should be of some kind of maple, and the front of pine, but I do
not know that it has ever been proved that red-eyed or gray maple is
really superior to white maple or sugar maple.

Probably the kind of wood is less important than the "depth" of the
violin, compared with its size and weight, the situation of the "f holes,"
the accurate position of the treble foot of the bridge on the sound post,
and even the matter of varnish; for it is easy to make a bad violin from
the best of timber, as the novice often finds out.

But sometimes a novice has been known to make a very good
"fiddle." Old Hughy Glinds made but one in his life, but that chanced
to be such a good one that it came near founding a violin industry in
Oxford County.

Glinds was an odd old genius, who lived in a little cabin on the borders of what was known in the region as the Great Woods. He made
baskets and oars for a living, and sometimes ox bows, goad sticks, and
ax handles.

The timber for these articles he selected in the Great Woods, often going long distances to obtain the kind of wood he wanted. He was hard to please in the matter of his "stuff," as he called it. He was also very secretive, and would never tell others where these particular kinds of timber grew.

His cabin was a place of resort for all the boys in the neighborhood, for the old woodsman was a remarkable storyteller. He must have been more than sixty years old when he made his famous fiddle. Being a "genius," he fearlessly departed from the traditions of violin making, and fashioned the curved front from seasoned hackmatack instead of pine. The back, neck and other parts were from red-eyed maple, procured at a natural open, or meadow, which he had discovered at the head of a pond near an abandoned sugaring camp ten or twelve miles distant in the Great Woods.

So closely were the little red eyes scattered through the wood that the back and neck of Mr. Glinds's violin, when seen a few feet away, were of a peculiar bright cinnamon color. The front of the violin, too, was almost red. It was a very clear-toned instrument, and although three or four tunes, like "Fisher's Hornpipe" and "The White Cockade," were all that the old man could play, his music was a source of great pleasure to all the boys. I believe the instrument was really a superior one.

Glinds did not keep his great fiddle more than three years. A young musician named Sonfeldt, from Philadelphia, who came to Maine to hunt one autumn, bought it, paying what was thought to be the large sum of fifteen dollars. Sonfeldt sold it for a good price.

He appears to have told curious stories of Old Hughy, whom he described as a hermit violin maker, possessing an "art" derived from remote ancestors in other lands. This yarn he repeated for gain, for he refused to disclose Old Hughy's place of abode, but entered into an agreement with him to furnish the fronts, maple backs and necks for violins.

These parts were afterward glued together and sold as "Glinds violins."

Old Hughy, giving up basket making, now sent off a large box of "fiddle stuff" every month.

One winter Hughy had been afflicted with rheumatism so badly that toward spring he was unable to go off into the Great Woods for violin timber. Now the red-eyed maple which gave "selling" qualities to the "Glinds fiddle" grew at a remote spot in the heart of the forest, so completely surrounded by craggy hills and mountains that there was but one time of year when access could be had to it with a hand sled.

This was in the month of March, or early in April, when the snow was crusted so that a long bog could be crossed, and one could thus avoid the high, steep hills, covered with thick scrub brush, which hemmed in the red-eyed maples.

Of the score of boys who habitually visited Old Hughy, Willis Murch was most after the old man's heart. He had taught Willis mink trapping and many of the mysteries of basket making. Now he came hobbling down to see this same boy.

"I wanter see ye particular 'bout somethin' up to my house," he whispered, taking Willis aside.

Willis went back with him, but not till they were inside the cabin did the old man tell what the mysterious "somethin'" was.

"I've allus known ye, Willis, as a boy I can trust. And now I've got rheumatiz, and I'm a-goin' to take ye in pardership with me."

He concluded by revealing to Willis the spot where the red-eyed maple grew, and offering him one-half the profits if he would go there and "sled" home a quantity of it.

Willis deemed this a grand opening, but the trip would occupy at least three days, and he did not like to go so far into the Great Woods alone. At first Old Hughy was unwilling to have any other boy know the locality, but Willis argued that he could pledge them to secrecy and would select boys whom he knew to be trustworthy.

Somewhat reluctantly Old Hughy at last consented, and that afternoon Willis, with a vast show of secrecy and caution, made application to Thomas Edwards, little Edson Wilbur, and myself. Willis took us in as partners, and pledged us to fidelity and secrecy.

He wished to set off for Bartlett's the next morning, but we could not all immediately get parental consent. This, combined with light snow and the preparation of food for the trip, so hindered us that nearly a week elapsed before we were ready to start.

We set off merrily on a fine, sunshiny, crisp March morning. It was an expedition after a boy's own heart. We had a secret mission; we expected to make some money; we were going to have a "sheepskin party" ("Sheepskin" was our name for that delicious maple candy, made by pouring a spoonful of warm syrup on hard-packed snow.); we hoped we might find some bolls of spruce gum for homeward chewing; and, above all, we hoped to "do something big."

We had two hand sleds and two axes. Willis took his gun and ammunition. In the Great Woods there were deer, lynx cats, and perhaps panthers and wolves. These possibilities of game and danger added to the zest of the trip.

Lashed to one sled was a box of provisions, two chisels to tie to the end of "gummer" poles, a coffeepot, kettle and "spider," with several dippers and platters. ("Gummer" poles allowed us to knock down spruce bolls out of reach.) To keep us warm by night we had four stuffed coverlets or "comforters," rolled up snugly and tied shut.

The other sled held a tapping auger, wooden "piggins," one great iron kettle, all the basins and pans our mothers could spare to catch the sap as it ran from the "spiles" set into the trees, and a shovel.

Entering the woods by a lumber road a little beyond the Murch farm, we proceeded northerly, and traversed the entire length of Loon Pond on the ice. Snow still lay at a depth of two feet, but it was crusted so that we could walk on it without snowshoes.

This is the best time, indeed, for traveling in the woods, for no deciduous foliage then obstructs the view, the footing is like that of a pavement, and the only risk the possibility that a sudden change of weather may soften the snow crust.

Willis led the way and commanded the expedition, following Old Hughy's directions as to the route. We entered the bog at the foot of Willy-wick-wock Pond, which is between three and four miles long, and has a pretty island near the southern end, and still another about midway of its length.

Willis had once been as far as the foot of this pond, but to the rest of us it was an unknown region. We contemplated the unbroken forests on its shores with a certain awe, as we reflected what a long way we had come into the woods.

Thus far we had seen no game larger than red squirrels and a partridge. But while traversing the bog, we had heard the crackling and rushing noise made by some animal, probably by a deer startled by the grating of our sleds on the snow crust. We did not go to its tracks, but went on up the pond, passing the islands, and by noon reached the little open meadow at the head of it.

"This is the place—just as Old Hughy told me!" Willis said. "There's the stump where he cut down a red-eyed maple last spring, and there's its top partly in the brook. Those four big trees just beyond, by the brook, are all red-eyed maple. See how red the tops are! That's one mark of it. And see how gray the trunks are; that's another."

It was a pretty place. There might have been four or five acres of this open meadow around the pond, with a fine growth of red-eye and rock, or sugar, maples extending along the upper borders. In conjunction with the ubiquitous spruce, rock maples as thick as four feet in diameter had mounted halfway up one of the mountainsides which enclosed the valley to the northwest.

Just at the foot of the mountain, in the shelter of a high, overhanging crag, the little abandoned "sap house" stood among the giant maples. It was a sturdy ten-by-ten log cabin, tall enough to stand up in, with thick log beams, and a nine- or ten-foot sharply pitched shingle roof. Above the crag rose the steep mountainside, on which the snow lay deep and white, its surface broken only here and there by growths of gnarled and stunted shrubs.

By this time we were hungry from our long tramp, but Willis said, "Just one doughnut apiece out of our box, before we make camp. When we've gathered firewood and cleaned up the cabin, we'll have a fire beside the stump of the maple that Old Hughy cut. Then we'll have dinner." He doled out the four doughnuts.

"Come on with those axes," he said. "I'm going to have the neatest little camp you ever saw."

When complete, with our comforters spread out inside, and a fire blazing in front, the cabin was picturesque and cozy.

"Isn't it a little beauty of a camp?" Willis exclaimed, as he stood off to admire it. "But I say, boys, how warm it's getting! The weather's moderating. See how I am perspiring."

"I guess it's because we are heated by working so hard," said Tom, throwing himself down on the comforters inside the camp.

"No, it isn't that at all," said Willis. "The weather's turned warm. You can tell by the sky. See how hazy and mellow the sun looks, and the crust is getting soft!"

Edson took the kettle and went to the brook to get water for coffee and to boil potatoes, while Willis fixed a spring pole across the stump over the fire.

"I saw a fish in that deep hole below the maple top," Edson remarked as he came back.

"It will be a good time to fish through the ice on the pond," said Willis. "We can take pork for bait. What if we try it? Old Hughy says there are pickerel and trout, too, in Willy-wick-wock."

"And not cut the maple today?" asked Edson.

"No, we will put that off till tomorrow morning. We've done wonders with the camp this afternoon," said Willis. "The sap has started. We can tap some of the sugar maples today, boil down the sap tonight, and have ourselves a "sheepskin" party breakfast.

"We can cut and hew out all the maples we can draw easily enough tomorrow. Then the day after we can chisel some of the spruce bolls I have seen and start for home."

Willis cut and trimmed two slender twenty-foot willow trees for "gummers." He carried them into the hut and propped them up against the ceiling. Meanwhile the rest of us whittled spiles from bits of dry maple wood Old Hughy had left behind. Tom then bored upward angled holes in twelve sugar maples, so that the spiles would slant down, permitting the sap to run. He set dippers under the spiles at first, and afterward most of the basins and pots. The sap flowed freely.

As soon as coffee was made and our dinner eaten, we took the axes and went fishing on the ice of the pond. Willis selected a place about a hundred yards from the mouth of the brook. We had to clear away the snow and then chop two holes through two feet and a half of ice.

After the holes were cut and cleared, we dropped in the hooks and were lucky enough by and by to catch two pickerel.

The camp, with the little wreath of blue smoke rising, looked very pretty from the pond where we stood fishing. Tom and I, after taking these fish, went to prepare firewood and look to the sap, leaving Willis and Edson to fish.

"Oh, but isn't it hot!" Tom exclaimed, repeatedly, as we worked; we both threw off our jackets and vests, and even then were much too warm. The sun, now nearly setting, had the mild, yellow appearance of late spring days, and the snow crust had softened much.

"There's a thaw coming on," Tom said, as we wallowed back to camp with the kettleful of sap. Even after the sun set there was not the least trace of chilliness in the air, but rather it seemed to grow warmer.

Willis and Edson came to camp with their pickerel as dusk fell, and we fried some of the fish. So we made a good supper of pickerel with our cooked food and cold sap to drink. But for the change of weather we should have been quite happy.

"I never knew it to change so warm, all at once," said Willis. "I don't like it, either."

We set the remaining sap to boil, arranged the order of our watches, and were sitting in the front of our camp when two owls began to hoot in the woods.

"That's a sign of rain," Willis said. "Old Hughy calls those 'rain owls.'"

The evening was not very dark. We could see clumps of loosened snow fall from trees, and hear the crust "give" here and there about the meadow. Soon the change of temperature affected the ice of the large pond. Pockets of it began to move, causing strange, long-drawn, gurgling and groaning sounds which appeared to traverse the entire length of the still water.

As we sat listening to these noises, a black animal about as large as a dog of average size went bounding across the meadow a short distance below the camp. It appeared to be a black cat or "fisher" marten. Willis took his gun and wallowed to the edge of the woods, hoping to catch sight of it again, knowing that the fur of this large American sable is valuable.

He did not like to go far into the woods, however, and the noise of his steps in the snow evidently frightened the animal away. Giving up the chase, he returned to camp.

As the evening advanced, the long walk and other toils of the day began to tell on us. We grew sleepy despite the strange roaring and groaning from the pond, and lay down in the cabin. Instead of needing the comforters over us, we found ourselves warm enough in our jackets, and in that condition we fell asleep.

An extraordinary meteorological change had taken place, one that many persons may still recall, even after twenty years, since it was attended in northern New England by a succession of slight earthquake shocks during three entire days, which caused much fear.

At about two in the morning, while Tom was watching the kettle, and we other three lads soundly sleeping, we were suddenly awakened by a frightful rumbling, jarring noise.

Edson, who fell apart in crises, was the first to be awakened by this rumbling, roaring sound. He sprang up, crying out, "Boys! Oh, boys! What's coming?"

Rubbing our eyes, we heard what was indeed a terrible sound—a deep, prolonged rumble that seemed to issue, with oscillations of the ground, from the hills and meadow.

Tom rushed in. "It's an earthquake!" he exclaimed in an awed voice. That was indeed what it was, but the convulsion was over before we had time to think much about it.

"The earth never opens and swallows up houses in the country!" said Willis, to reassure himself.

"But what made the hills roar so?" queried Edson.

"I s'pose 'twas the sound coming up out of the earth," suggested Willis. "But did you feel that bump that came after the noise? I wonder what could have made it?"

Not one of us could tell.

"I'll bet it scared the folks at home dreadfully," said Tom. "Do you suppose it shook the houses down?"

"I guess it wouldn't shake down a frame house," remarked Willis. "But it must have made the dishes rattle."

We went outside to look about. The sap had boiled half away in the kettle and most of the firewood was gone. The sky was cloudy, and there seemed to be a mist on the meadow, but it was not unusually dark.

"Let's gather some more wood and boil the rest of the sap down," said Tom.

Then again the same deep rumble resounded from the wooded hills and rose from the ground.

"There's another coming!" Willis cried, and we felt another earth jolt, followed by oscillations of the ground, for several seconds.

It frightened us almost as much as at first. We stared at each other in awe; then Edson, who tended to lose his head easily, ran into the camp and threw himself on the comforters. There he lay for several hours. The rest of us gathered more wood, then sat down in the front of the camp, talking about earthquakes and speculating with the gravity of perfect ignorance on their cause.

There was a third, lighter shock, barely audible, in the course of half an hour.

"I guess it's kind of petering out," Willis said. "Earthquakes never do much damage in this country."

"Oh, but there may come a big one yet!" said Tom. "What's to hinder?"

"I guess it's too far north," said Willis.

"It isn't so very much farther north than Lisbon, where the geography says that nearly sixty thousand people were swallowed up in six minutes," replied Tom.

"That's so. We had it in our lesson last winter," said I.

This discussion was cut short by the syrup foaming up to the top of the kettle. We threw a handful of snow into it to keep it from boiling over, and in less than half an hour we had boiled it down to a pint. After coaxing forth Edson, we began an early breakfast of sheepskins. For some reason spoonfuls of hot maple syrup, when cooled by being poured over hard-packed snow, has a delightful flavor. New snow works better than coarse snow on which the sun has shone for weeks and, fortunately, for several days previously light snow had fallen. We had but to scoop it up from drifts that still lay deep over some parts of the sugar lot, pack it into snowballs, place them on our plates, and pour on the syrup. It is truly astonishing how many such sheepskins a party of four hungry young people will consume at a setting. We must have finished off at least twenty apiece—and seemed none the worse for it.

While we were eating rain began to fall softly, and by six o'clock it was pouring like a summer shower. I have never seen snow turn to slush and water so rapidly as it did that morning. Within an hour the meadow was a yellow pond. The brook was full of water, and clogged on all sides by masses of broken ice. Before we had gained any idea that we were in a situation of peril our camp had been fronted with water, so that to descend the meadow to the red-eyes we would have waded knee deep.

"Boys," I exclaimed, looking out, "everything's under water! How are we going to get away from here?"

"I don't know but we shall be drowned out! The freshet has come awful quick, hasn't it?" said Edson.

The water from the brook covered our fireplace by the stump, and flowed back among the logs of our camp floor.

"We shall have to wade for it," said Willis. "But I don't believe the water will rise very high, for this place is higher than the pond. Let's stay here and chance it."

We could do nothing save sit and watch the rising water. Soon the logs of our floor were half awash, and the boughs on them became wet, but we improved matters a little by placing the two hand sleds side by side on top of the logs. On top of all we placed our comforters and provision box, and managed to find room to perch there ourselves.

Throughout the forenoon the rain poured steadily, without wind. The water from the brook did not rise much higher, and by ten o'clock began to drain off. The snow on the meadow had nearly all melted, so that we could see last season's dead grass and reeds.

"How we are ever to get down the pond with a load of fiddle stuff is more than I can tell!" exclaimed Tom, gloomily. "The pond's all afloat and the ice'll soon break up."

"We shall have to go over the hills and through the woods, and get home by some other route," said Willis.

"But we couldn't take any wood over the steep hills!" cried Tom. "And I intend to take out a load of red-eye, even if I have to swim with it!"

"But we haven't victuals for a great while," remarked Edson.

"Then we will eat less," retorted Tom, doggedly. "There's no need of stuffing ourselves if we are only to sit here and watch it rain."

A little before midday there was another earthquake shock—a prolonged rumbling, followed by a slight jar.

Soon afterward the rain ceased, although the sky remained cloudy till four o'clock in the afternoon, when there was lightning and low thunder, another unusual phenomenon for Maine in March. The wind began to blow from the west. The sky partly cleared in that quarter. The sun shone as it set; there was a manifest change in the air. The warm wave had spent itself over a country covered with snow and ice.

By sunset the water had so far drained away that we were able to kindle a fire in front of our camp and make coffee. A partridge flew across the meadow from the woods and alighted in the top of a yellow birch beside the brook, where it began eating the buds. Willis shot it, and we broiled it over the new fire we had started.

Dusk fell, but the west continued bright over the woods. Now and then a gust indicated colder weather coming.

"By tomorrow we can cut a maple and fix up a load of short, clear stuff," Willis said. "How much old, clear heartwood do you suppose we can haul on the two sleds?"

"Two hundredweight on each if the pond freezes up again," said Tom.

"How many fiddlebacks would that make?" said Edson.

"Well, I think a hundred fiddles," said Willis. "If it does, we shall get twenty-five dollars."

While we were making these hopeful estimates our attention was suddenly attracted to a loud snapping noise in the woods west of the meadow. It was as if a herd of cattle were rushing down the hillside.

"What do you suppose is coming now?" exclaimed Willis, turning to get his gun.

Tom and I snatched up the axes, and Edson laid hold of our long-handled frying pan as a weapon, for the crashing noise was alarming.

It was coming directly toward us, and soon we dimly saw five animals dash out of the spruce woods. They splashed noisily through slush and water, and came out within ten rods of our camp, when they stopped and faced about with a peculiar, short, whistling note.

"Deer!" whispered Willis. "Don't speak! If only I can get this shot out of my gun and a ball in, I'll have one of 'em!"

Pulling the ramrod slowly, he thrust it down the barrel and attempted to screw the worm into the wad over the shot.

The attention of the deer seemed occupied by some object back in the woods. As they stamped in the slush we heard in the brush a half-whimper, half-growl. Even in his eagerness to reload, Willis stopped to listen. Then another creature shambled out of the ever-greens.

"A bear!" exclaimed Edson.

At sight of the bear, the deer went spattering through the puddles toward the pond. Half-growling, half-whimpering, the bear pursued them, but turned aside to avoid the pools of water. The deer easily outran him, and stopped on reaching the pond.

As the bear approached, the deer leaped the brook and came up the meadow on the other side. The bear ran along the bank of the brook, looking for a crossing place as a dog often does in like circumstances, especially in early spring, but finally the big animal plunged through the water, and followed the deer up the meadow.

They passed our camp, but gave us no attention. They would run a few hundred feet, then stop and face the bear till he came near, when they would spring far away from him quickly. Circling around the meadow near the woods, they crossed the brook there, and again ran down the other side. The bear kept after them steadily, whimpering and growling petulantly. Meantime Willis was making frantic efforts to get the charge of shot out of his gun.

"Plague take it!" he muttered. "I cannot get that wad out. I've a notion to drop a ball in, and fire all together."

"But there isn't powder enough in to throw it much," whispered Edson. "If you only hurt that bear a little, he may attack us!"

"That's so, Willis," whispered Tom. "He is just out of his winter den and is awful hungry—or he wouldn't take after those deer so."

The deer would turn and "blow," as if ridiculing the bear's slow efforts to overhaul them. At length he stopped beside a puddle, and drank of the water as a dog would. In the deepening gloom we could now but indistinctly make out the group of deer. They had stopped near the willow copse by the pond, and appeared to be browsing, while the bear now sat beside the puddle and watched them.

"I'm going to put the muzzle of the gun inside the camp among the brush, and fire that small shot out, and then load with ball, quick!" Willis declared.

Just then we heard a noise on the other side of the meadow, and dimly discerned the black form of another creature moving toward the deer!

"Jiminy, it's another bear!" whispered Edson. "The thaw has started 'em all out of their dens."

"Or else the earthquake has waked 'em up," said Tom.

These conjectures may have been true, and numerous bears may have been abroad that night, ranging in the woods, hungry after their long winter nap. If so, they may have smelled the deer, and in the madness of hunger, pursued them.

Scarcely had the second bear passed out of sight, when we heard a slight noise behind the cabin, and looking around, perceived a third bear shuffling around the corner, also heading for the deer. The beast was not thirty yards away from us, and blocking our path to the cabin. In the gloom he appeared to be of enormous proportions.

The bear stopped and looked at our camp. We heard him snuff uncertainly several times, and then he growled, turning his head suspiciously.

Then the other bears began to growl and snarl loudly. The first one, still resting by the puddle where he had drunk, appeared to resent the appearance of another bear.

The third bear at once added his notes to the uproar. One who has never heard such an outcry in the woods at night can but faintly imagine our sensations.

It was too dark now to see the bears, but with their din and our growing alarm, we imagined that their roars sounded nearer. So when Edson uttered a howl of terror, we all stampeded. Abandoning our camp, we jumped the brook and climbed the yellow birch tree where Willis had shot the partridge. Such was our panic that we did not pause to reflect that bears can climb trees.

The birch was a large tree with low limbs, and I felt much safer when perched ten or twelve feet from the ground.

Still the bears snarled and roared—indeed, they kept it up for two hours. Failing to catch the deer they appeared to be attempting to devour each other. Savage chases and rushes to and fro through the slush and water took place with horrible growls.

It had not grown very cold as yet. Save for the discomfort of roosting in a tree, we were not uncomfortable, and the bears made sufficient music to keep us awake till near eleven o'clock, when their din ceased, and we supposed they had gone.

The waning half of the old moon rose over the wooded hilltops, the clouds cleared away. Soon we could see the entire meadow, and our courage revived.

"I'm not going to stay up here any longer," said Willis. "The bears have left, and I don't imagine they would have touched us anyhow. But Edson, here, was awful scared."

"I noticed that you clum' up here about as quick as I did," replied Edson.

"When I'm doing a thing I try to do it quick," said Willis. "But don't go and tell anybody about it."

"Oh, I guess none of us will feel like *tellin'*," said Tom. "Say, what's the matter with us? We never thought about how easy bears can climb trees."

With that we burst into laughter and dropped down. Willis took up his gun and fired it. The report started an owl to hoot on the hillside, but we heard nothing of the bears, and on going to our camp found things undisturbed.

Willis completed his "loading for bear," and by this time our courage had so returned that we lay down under our comforters and soon fell asleep.

The sun was shining when we waked, and the wind blowing through the boughs of our hut. The air was much cooler, the slush had frozen over, and the now empty pools were covered with frail shells of white ice. Willis rose, and going to the old red-eye trunk, plied the ax, prepared firewood, and kindled a cheery campfire.

"Turn out, boys!" he shouted. "Today we will get our fiddle stuff ready. It's a jolly morning. Sap will run. Up with you, Tom, and set dishes under those trees we tapped. Tonight we will have more syrup."

Tom rose, yawning, and went off with the basins and pans to set up for sap. We saw him by and by far down toward the pond, and shouted to him to come to breakfast.

"I've been looking at those bear tracks," said he, when he came back. "I tell you those old brutes did prance round there in the slush. There's blood on the ice, too. I guess they had a fight." A pair of speckled jays came, attracted by the odor of our frying pork, perched on the roof of our camp, and even fluttered about within three feet of the fire.

"Oh you rogues!" Willis exclaimed to them. "You like the smell of fried pork, don't you? Squall away, you can't have any!"

But when the spider was set aside, one of the jays carried off a scrap from it. They seemed crazy for a taste of the meat.

After breakfast we selected a red-eyed maple about thirty inches in diameter, which Tom and Willis proceeded to chop down. It fell with a crash which re-echoed from the hillsides about the meadow.

Taking turns with the axes, we cut the trunk into logs, four feet in length. Most of the forenoon was thus occupied. During the afternoon we selected the best of the straight-grained logs, split them in halves, and hewed off the bark and sapwood, so as to haul home nothing save the best of the heartwood. Six of these logs were finally selected for our loads. They weighed as much as seventy pounds each. Three of them on a sled made a heavy load for two boys to draw up steep banks and over uneven footing in the woods.

"Never mind," said Tom, "we can take our time and double up our team at bad places."

Indeed, when it began lightly snowing again, Tom proposed to put another log on each sled, and succeeded in persuading us to agree to this.

By this time the stock of cooked provisions which we had brought was running very low, and toward sunset Tom, Edson, and I began boiling down a new supply of syrup, while Willis went out in the woods to look for partridges. We heard the report of his gun.

"I guess he's got one," Tom said.

He could scarcely have had time to do more than load in haste, when we heard a second report.

"He's got among a flock of them," I remarked. "I wish he would get four, so that we could have one apiece. Swinging an ax all day makes me fearfully hungry."

But Willis did not fire again. We watched for his coming back, holding a couple of partridges by the legs, and we kindled a bright fire of chips to cook the birds. But we watched in vain.

Dusk fell, and still Willis did not appear.

It grew darker and darker, the snow became thicker, and we were beginning to be very much frightened about Willis, but not one of us dared to speak. At last Tom exclaimed, and we all started at his voice: "What do you suppose has happened to him?"

"I don't know. I sh'd think he'd come!" I gasped.

By about nine o'clock the syrup reduced to the required thickness, and as we took the kettle off the fire to cool, Edson cried out. "Hark! What's that? Did I hear someone call?"

Tom and I listened intently. "I guess not," said Tom. "Hold on! Yes, you did, too! I heard it then myself."

"That's Willis calling!" said Edson. "Oh my, I wonder if anything's got afoul of him!"

Tom stepped out a little distance and shouted as loudly as he could. We two followed his example. In reply we heard a far-off "halloo," seemingly from behind the hills to the northwest of the meadow.

"Oh, he's a dreadful way off!" cried Edson. "No knowing what's got him."

"But we must go and help him!" exclaimed Tom.

He seized one of the axes, and Edson took the other; I had no better weapon than a club-shaped stick. In much excitement, we made our way with difficulty uphill through the dark, thick woods, among rocks and ledges crowned with spruces. What was left of the original snow had frozen to ice and, thinly painted with fresh snow, it proved particularly treacherous footing.

By and by we gained the top of the ridge. We halted and shouted. A response came from the hollow behind the hills.

"What's the matter?" Tom shouted.

"I'm treed!" cried Willis.

"What's treed you?" I shouted.

"The only response was a loud growling.

"What a horrible noise!" muttered Edson. "Must be a bear's after him. Why don't he answer? Willis! Willis!"

"Maybe the creature's got him!" exclaimed Tom, as no reply came. "Come on, boys! We've got to go and help him."

We started down the hillside, over the slippery ice, among rocks and trees, but I am free to say we would rather have run the other way.

It seemed to me that we went half a mile downhill, though probably the distance was not two hundred yards. At last we came to an overflowing brook, crossed it on a log, and then beat our way through an alder thicket.

"We must be getting near where he is," Tom said, presently. "Call to him again."

Just then Willis spoke from not more than fifty yards away.

"Is that you, Tom?" he called.

"Yes. What's the matter with you?" shouted Tom.

"It's one of them cross bears!" And as if in confirmation, we again heard the bear growl.

"Say boys!" Willis exclaimed "Climb! Quick! He's snuffing toward you!"

With that we rushed for a large rock, the outline of which we could distinguish. An old hemlock tree had fallen across the rock. In much haste we clambered on this slanting tree, and got up seven or eight feet from the ground.

"If he comes after us, I'll let him have it in the nose," said I, flourishing my big stick and trying to keep the quake out of my voice.

"I guess he isn't really going your way," said Willis. "He's lame, but he's awful ugly. He acts as if he was going back into his den."

"Is there a den?" asked Tom.

"Yes, down under rocks and the root of an old tree. I followed his track up to his den. He came out at me as soon's I got near. I guess he had his foot bit in the fight last night, for he can't step on it, and he's awful cross."

"You fired twice at him?" shouted Tom.

"Yes, and I hit him once, too," replied Willis. "He took after me, and I climbed this little hemlock and pulled my gun up after me. He couldn't follow because he's so lame."

"Thank goodness, we're safe!" said Edson.

"I loaded again after I got into the tree and fired at him, but I didn't seem to hurt him much," said Willis.

"Well, why didn't you keep shooting him till you killed him?" cried Tom.

"I spilled all the caps among the brush, and I don't dare get down to look for 'em," replied Willis.

"Well, that's a pretty fix!" exclaimed Edson. "What are we going to do?"

"Would you dare to tackle him with your axes, you three?" said Willis. "I'll get down and pitch in if you will."

"No!" Tom said. "I don't want to tackle him."

"I guess he'll attend to that himself!" said Edson, and those were also my sentiments.

"Well, then, holler like all possessed!" said Willis. "I can see that it disturbs him to hear your voices. He thinks he's being surrounded."

So we yelled, first one, then another, then all together.

"Has he gone in?" Tom asked at length.

"No," replied Willis, "but he don't like it."

"Neither do we," said Edson.

We yelled till we were hoarse, but the bear only growled as if he longed to have it out with us all.

There we stayed for at least half an hour, I think, but failing to hit on any safe plan of action. I imagine that the wounded and suffering bear tired at last of standing on three legs, for Willis called, after a long silence: "He's crawled down into his den. I'm going to get down and see if I can find a cap."

He fumbled about, but, in the new snow, failed to find a cap, and finally came cautiously to us on the old hemlock trunk.

"Get down easy, boys," he whispered, "and let's run for our camp! It's of no use to go fooling with a bear. We can't shoot, and he's down in a deep, dark hole under rocks."

"Fooling with him! Who fooled with him?" exclaimed Edson. "You needn't think I want to! I'm 'most starved. We were waiting for you to fetch some partridges for supper, and off you went chasing on a bear track."

"I wanted to see where it led to," replied Willis.

"Well, now you know, don't you?" retorted Edson.

We were all cross and very tired before we got back to camp. It must have been after midnight, and by then a full-scale storm had enfolded. So thick and fast did the snow whirl down, that we could barely see ten feet ahead. To find the camp had not been easy. Several times we had fallen in the drifts. And once or twice we thought that we would be obliged to take shelter in the lee of some big tree trunk—to freeze, it might be.

The fire had gone out entirely. We rekindled it, reheated our new syrup, and solemnly ate more sheepskins. It was certainly near two o'clock in the morning before we had finished and turned in.

The storm continued unabated as we fell asleep. The wind howled over the crag and down against our little cabin. The snow whirled drearily against the shutters, and whisked through wide cracks in the door and chinks among the logs.

A strange and fearful sound awoke us, in great alarm—a swift, oncoming roar and rumble like the deep, heavy jarring of another earthquake shock! Then followed a sudden, terrible crash!

As we were to discover later, the crag's great mass of snow, at least twenty feet in thickness, had collapsed on the cabin. In an instant, our refuge had become a trap.

We all sprang up in the dark to listen. The roof and walls groaned continuously. And Edson cried out, "Boys! Oh, boys! What's happening?"

Tom exclaimed. "I think it's another earthquake!"

"But why is the cabin groaning?"

Willis struck a match and pulled at the door. In poured a mound of snow. He stuck his head and arm outside as far as possible.

"It's an avalanche, boys. The snow from the crag has fallen. We must be under a ton of the stuff."

"Can we get out?" said Tom.

"I don't see how," said Willis. "We're probably fifteen or twenty feet down. We don't have shovels. And even if we did, the snow would shift and bury us anyway."

"What shall we do? Oh, what can we do?" Edson kept saying. He had got a hard grip on my arm.

"Yes, indeed, what can we do?" said I. "A pretty scrape we've gotten ourselves us into. Now what should we do about it?"

It seemed we could only sit and listen and wait. We were already overdue. When we didn't arrive tomorrow, Old Hughy would be questioned, and a rescue party dispatched.

If the cabin didn't collapse, we could survive. In two days we wouldn't freeze. We had our comforters. We were deep in the snow. We wouldn't need food and we could eat snow for water. But what about our air? Would it last?

We sat there anxiously talking it over, speculating on possibilities. But the truth was we didn't know.

Suddenly in the midst of our wild excitement and frantic mental efforts, little Edson Wilbur piped out, "Get the 'gummers'! Get the 'gummers'! We can use the 'gummers' to poke 'blow holes.'"

We turned to stare—though we couldn't see.

It was a ridiculous little voice, but the practicability of his idea carried instant conviction to the bewildered wits of all who heard him.

That fourth day, Old Hughy sat in his cabin weaving baskets close before the dancing flames of his fireplace. He glanced out now and then to note the continuing storm, with a troubled eye.

With the approach of night, the old woodsman began to watch for us. Darkness set in wild and stormy, and still we did not come. A feeling of anxiety took possession of him.

An hour passed—two hours. The years weighed upon him, but there was no sleep for Old Hughy. His heart was with us up at Bartlett's camp. He was thinking how scared and hungry we must be.

Perhaps—he shuddered at the thought that would possess him—we might be caught in the drifts, somewhere on the way home, struggling and fighting and perishing in the storm. Often he thought he heard our cries for help, and hurried to the door to listen in intense agony of mind.

Thus, waiting, listening, watching he passed the long, bitter night. The storm continued in all its fury. But with the coming of light, Old Hughy took a calmer view of the situation. He believed now that we had been sensible enough not to venture out into the storm, but had remained at the sap house. He expected us every moment, now, and kept a lookout for us, while preparing a warm breakfast; for he knew that we would be very hungry. The morning passed and no boys appeared. Old Hughy then began to feel that surely some calamity had befallen us, and started out to look for us. A brief effort to struggle through the drifts convinced him that he could not reach the mountain. Turning about, he slowly hobbled toward the Murch's house, about half a mile distant, trampling a path for himself along the drifted road.

At the Murch's, a worried party of eight men and boys—the Old Squire, Addison, Halstead, Jim and Asa Doane, Mr. Edwards, Mr. Wilbur, Mr. Murch, and Ben Murch, Willis's older brother—were preparing to leave in quest of us, for our long absence had caused alarm at home. And they knew Old Hughy could tell them where we had gone. They were putting on their snowshoes when the front door banged open. Old Hughy staggered in.

"The boys hain't come back yet, Mr. Murch," he cried, as soon as he could speak. "They're up to the mountains at Bub Bartlett's sugar camp. With the quakes 'n' storm, I'm a'feared somethin' bad may have happened to 'em."

Hours later the rescue party stopped abruptly near Bub Bartlett's camp.

"Why, what is the matter, here?" exclaimed the Old Squire, with a bewildered expression. The grove, the crag, everything about it, had taken on an unfamiliar aspect! There, indeed, was the tall birch stub, standing stark and bleached above the white drifts. The spruce clumps with heavy-laden branches, still showed at a little distance through the maples.

"But where's the sap house?" cried first one then another of the party. "It warn't far off from the old stump!"

"Yes, and the crag! What's become of that?" several exclaimed.

They rubbed their eyes, looked again, and then looked at each other. No one said a word, and the only sound heard was the bleached leaves of the beeches that rattled dismally in the wind.

"There's been a snowslide down the mountain!" said the Old Squire, at last. "That is the top of the crag," pointing to a few jagged rocks, sticking out through the snow above us. "The sap house is below it, *buried!*"

"And the boys!" the others exclaimed, under their breaths.

"Are under there, I fear!" said the Old Squire. "But there's still a chance they may be alive and, God willing, we'll have them out."

They shouted, but there was no response. They all shouted, till the grove and mountain echoed. Following the echo, muffled voices—faint and far off it seemed—answered them.

"Dig us out! Oh, dig us out!" they could hear us calling to them, our voices sounding ominously thick and far off.

"Are you all right, boys?" called the Old Squire.

Our cries of "Yes! Yes!" came drifting down the bank. Addison later said our voices from the camp could now be heard distinctly, and all took courage.

"Where are you?"

"In the cabin!" we shouted. "Look out for the 'blow holes,'" followed Willis, and we took it up in chorus.

This must have been a surprise because "blow holes" or "bear pipes" are signs of hibernating bear dens. Such narrow, ice-lined air holes form as a result of the bears' naturally warm exhalations melting the snow above them.

(But acting on Edson's suggestion, we had retrieved our "gummer" poles, and whittled one pointed end on each. Aiming them upward through the open door, we thrust through the thick wall of snow, toward the surface. At first we didn't know if they were long enough to penetrate all the way. Light didn't enter because it was night. Then Edson suggested trying to breathe through the holes. We tasted fresh air, and knowing we had succeeded, we punched out one hole after another. And later daylight filtered through them, bringing us great comfort and a sense of time during our burial.)

In response to our cries, the rescuers fanned out, climbing slowly toward the cliff. Suddenly Mr. Edwards said, "There!" Everyone looked. He was pointing to a four-foot section of slide peppered with two-inch-round holes and resembling the embedded top of a gigantic shaker.

"Where are some shovels?" shouted the Old Squire. "Get some shovels!"

There were but two shovels there, that day: the one our rescuers brought along and the other, down by the sleds, that we had packed. But those were seized by first one and then another rescuer, who dug like madmen, driven nearly wild by our imploring outcries from within the drift. The others worked with pots and pans and sticks of wood brought in frantic haste from the cooking place.

For three or four hours the implements were plied furiously over and over again in short bursts. Occasional pauses lasted only long enough to allow us to punch open our "blow holes" again and again for more air. Yet progress in removing the fallen mass was slow. It was not until the sun had sunk behind the mountain, that our rescuers got down to the eaves of the sap house and uncovered a part of the opened door. Then one after one we four boys crawled out, shaken, but unharmed. The great maples, with their huge branches, had shielded the little cabin from the full force of the immense body of snow, and along with its sturdy construction, had prevented it from being crushed.

"Now you're going to catch it!" muttered Halstead, with a dubious shake of his head, when we all had been inspected.

But instead of taking us to task all appeared as glad to see us as we to see them and their packs of provisions. Thanks to the food and the extra hands at the loads, when we left the next morning, we were able to reach home by early afternoon, in much better plight than might have been expected.

Our profits from the violin timber were smaller than our estimates. Old Hughy pronounced it "good stuff," and sent off one box of backs and necks from it. But the public demand for the Glinds fiddle appeared to have fallen off, and the old man could give us but $7.25 as our share of the sales.

Still, our hopes had not been disappointed. We had all had an unforgettable adventure and Edson, especially, had "done something big." It is said that great crises in human affairs always bring forth leaders hitherto obscure. And in the midst of our crisis, little Edson had found his courage. From then on, he became renown in Oxford County for his wise and levelheaded actions in times of stress and danger.

7

Uncle Dresser's Money

Part 1

IT WAS PLANTING TIME, AND JOYOUSLY SANG THE robins in the great balm-of-Gileads in front of the old farmhouse that morning—the morning of May 2, 1865. Spring, so frequently tardy in Maine, had come with a rush that year. In a single week the last hard snowdrifts of winter vanished, the birds returned to us, the ice broke up on the lake, and cherry and pear plum burst forth in white blossom.

On these spring mornings we had breakfast at six, and work for the day was then talked over, the Old Squire giving us boys a word of advice as to seed potatoes and the proper distance for planting corn rows when pumpkin seeds were put in the hills.

The old farm was a little kingdom by itself, and the breakfast table a kind of open court for free discussion of our manifold labors. Sometimes there were grumblings and complaints which had to be adjusted. But quite as often breakfast ended in a gale of laughter, for we were lighthearted children.

That morning opened gaily enough. The day before we had observed that certain vegetables in the cellar had been gnawed, and at supper Grandmother remarked that the rats were bothering her again.

"Addison," said she to my older cousin, "you must set the trap down there."

That morning Addison found that he had captured remarkable game. No one else was yet astir indoors, and he carried his catch out behind the wagon house.

At breakfast he spoke of it. "I caught that rat last night, Grandmother," he said.

"You did!" she cried. "I'm glad of that."

"I thought I heard a noise down in the cellar in the night," said the Old Squire.

"Was it a large one?" asked Ellen.

"Yes," said Addison, "it was; no mistake. When I went to rap him on the head he bit my stick savagely. He had teeth more than half an inch long."

The Old Squire looked at Addison curiously—for he was not a boy who often exaggerated facts—but merely remarked that those were long teeth for a rat.

"Well, it was a big rat, sir," replied Addison. "He was so large that I had the curiosity to take the steelyards and weigh him."

"How much did he weigh?"

"Five pounds and two ounces," said Addison, slowly and impressively.

There was a general exclamation of astonishment, and the Old Squire cried, "Sir!" in tones at once incredulous and reproving.

"Now, Addison, what are you talking about?" said Grandmother.

"Why, about a rat," replied Addison, stoutly. "Ah, but you must have weighed him wrong," observed the Old Squire. "No rat on these premises ever weighed five pounds, or a quarter of that!"

"On the contrary, sir," replied Addison, with an air of pride, "I weighed him twice, and I am sure that I weighed him correctly. I would make oath, if necessary, that he weighs just what I state."

The Old Squire pushed back his chair with a loud squeak on the kitchen floor and rose from the table.

"You come out and show me that rat, sir!" he exclaimed, and he marched out through the wood house with an air of determination to know the full truth, now and at once. Addison followed him; much interested, the rest of us crowded after them.

In the wagon house Addison opened the back door, and reaching down beside the high step there, lifted up by its long, black, smooth tail an animal with coarse reddish hair, as large as a large cat.

It was a great muskrat!

A rat, indeed!

At that time I did not know myself what sort of creature it was, but a shout of laughter from Halstead let me into the joke. The girls, too, were laughing, and Grandmother made a sudden dash at Addison, but he leaped nimbly out of the back door. Grandmother stood and laughed until she was quite weak. As for the Squire, he had given vent to a single snort of discomfiture, and started to walk away—to "save his face," as we used to say.

We were in the midst of this merriment when we heard wheels in the yard, and saw a stranger driving in. He held up a yellow envelope.

"A dollar fifty to collect," said he.

"It is a telegraph message," said Grandmother, faintly, and sat down in sudden agitation.

The terrible memories of the Civil War, when the telegraph so constantly brought the news of fatalities on the battlefield, were fresh in her mind.

The Old Squire went out for the message. "It is for you, Ruth," he said to Grandmother, and Theodora brought it to her.

"Open it, child, and read it." And Theodora opened and slowly read: "Africa Dresser died yesterday. Funeral Thursday at two o'clock," and the signature was "Relatives."

The Old Squire said nothing. Grandmother also sat pensively without speaking. The rest of us were wondering as to the name, which we had never heard before—"Africa."

"Was she one of our relatives, Grandmother?" Theodora asked.

"It was my half-sister Abigail's husband," Grandmother replied, absently. It seemed very strange that a man should have been named Africa!

During the forenoon other new vistas of the family history were opened. The question of attending the funeral had arisen, and at the dinner table it was apparent that the Old Squire did not wish to go.

"It is eighty miles," he said. "It would be a long, hard drive for you to take, Ruth. Besides," he continued, "the journey would use up five days and more, and our farm work is pressing us hard."

"I know it, Joseph. I know it," Grandmother admitted sadly. "Still, it is my sister Abigail's husband," she added. "I do feel that we ought to go—some of us."

The Old Squire winced visibly. There was silence for some moments, and then the truer reason for his reluctance came out.

"You know, Ruth, how those brothers of Africa have gone on about the property there, and what they have done, and the accusations they have made. Ruth, I dislike to go near them and I dislike to have you go, or get mixed up in it again. I don't blame you for wanting to go to Uncle Dresser's funeral, but Aunt Abigail's been dead a good many years. Hadn't we better send our regrets and keep away? Wouldn't it be better all round?

"And there's that Molly, too," the Old Squire added. "I never knew what to say or think about that! There's nothing we could do to better things. Like as not Calvin and 'Rastus would take it all wrong, if we went."

Grandmother sat back and wiped her eyes silently, seeing which the Old Squire soon rose and went out to the field again. He hardly spoke as we worked, and during the afternoon went to the house alone, to have, as we conjectured, another talk with Grandmother about going to the funeral.

Later, at the supper table, we found that they had agreed on a compromise. Grandmother had consented not to go herself, but not wholly to neglect common usages among relatives, they had decided to have Addison and Theodora go early the following morning.

As this would mean four or five days' respite from work on the farm, Halstead and I deemed it a great privilege, and were on the point of grumbling. To our surprise, Addison did not wish to go. "My scions have come," said he. "I must graft those summer sweets tomorrow."

"Why, you can put the scions in the cellar for a few days," the Old Squire said to him.

But for some reason Addison was averse to going. He made other excuses, until at last, unwillingly the old people consented that I should go in his place, although there were doubts as to my entire ability to drive or find the way. In fact, Grandmother begged Addison to go, but he remained strangely obdurate.

So they started my cousin and me at five the next morning, dressed in our best dark clothes, with old Sol hitched in the driving wagon and a bushel of oats under the seat.

It's a proud moment of a boy's life when a horse is first given under his hand. The Old Squire told me about how fast to drive, when to use the whip and when not, and how to feed and water morning, noon, and night. It was plain that both he and Grandmother lacked full confidence in me, but I had enough in myself to make up.

To Theodora, as being older and wiser, was entrusted a small map of Maine, clipped from an old geography book, with the route traced from town to town in pencil. I was driver, but she was sailing master, so to speak.

We were instructed to reach Lovewell's Tavern in Waterville that night, a hostelry which the Old Squire knew well. By telling Mr. Lovewell who we were and where we were going, we would be sure of good entertainment. For our luncheon we had a box of food.

The envious Halstead jeered me as I took the reins, and Addison had turned away, smiling, but Grandmother followed beside the wagon as I drove down the lane.

"When you get to Uncle Dresser's," said she, principally to Theodora, and in a low tone, "you must not mind if things there are not just as we have them at home here. Try not to notice anything that happens, and, Dora, dear, try to be nice to Molly Totherly—even if she does seem a little queer."

The idea of Grandmother asking Theodora to be nice to anyone seemed very odd to me, for she was always a sweet-tempered girl. In fact, Grandmother appeared much disturbed about many things that morning.

And now began a journey which then seemed to me of vast duration and filled with immense personal responsibility. We sought to remember every turn and fork of our road, so as to be able to find our way back. Theodora constantly consulted the map, and we inquired as to the way of nearly everyone whom we met.

I locked wheels with a wagon driven by a woman who was not inclined to turn out, but as both horses were walking, no harm was done. I took occasion to inform her that I required my half of the road. We also clicked hubs with a boy who had a basket of pigs, and was, perhaps, driving for the first time himself.

"If I had a girl with me, like you have, to hold my reins," said he, "I would stop and lick ye."

"Hitch your horse! I'll wait for you!" I shouted after him.

Theodora attempted gently to make me understand that such asperities were bad road manners, but I was all for insisting on my half of the road.

The May day was fine and warm, with all the tree buds bursting into leaf, and a faint odor of liverwort stealing from the woodlands beside the road, and how busy were all the sparrows, robins, and thrushes, looking for places to nest! Dora never tired of watching them.

At about eleven that forenoon we came to the bridge over the Androscoggin River at Livermore, and an hour later we had our lunch and fed old Sol by the shore of a great pond which the road skirted.

Throughout the afternoon we drove on, arriving at Lovewell's Tavern in Waterville, on the Kennebec River, at about seven o'clock.

Well do I recall how badly my arms ached from the unusual exercise of holding the reins all day. Theodora had offered to drive, but I would not hear of that, and she was not one of those who bother a young driver with constant advice.

Often that day we had speculated as to our stranger relatives to whom we were journeying, particularly as to Molly Totherly. Something in the Old Squire's tone and words when he spoke of her had filled us with a vague curiosity. During the two years we had been at the Maine homestead these relatives had never before been mentioned.

At the tavern the next morning we were unable to get breakfast until eight, but Theodora and I were out at six, and went along Main Street to see the college buildings, Waterville being the seat of what was then termed Colby University.

From Waterville we had eighteen miles to drive, up past the village of Skowhegan. I am a little reluctant to name the beautiful town adjoining, where our relatives lived, from a fear that my story may not prove a credit to the place. It is as well, perhaps, to let it go without further identification.

A few miles out of Waterville we were misdirected as to our road for the first time, and before we got back to our proper route and reached the "old Dresser place," the relatives and neighbors had collected for the funeral service.

The house was a large old two-story building, painted red, with an ell fully 150 feet in length, which connected it to a stable and barns. The place had formerly been a tavern. As many as twenty horses were hitched about, but the people were now all inside.

"We had better go in as soon as we can," Theodora said. So we hitched Sol to a fence post, and then going to the house door, entered, feeling very strange indeed among all those sitting, silent people, who regarded us curiously.

A man who seemed to be in charge of the funeral came to us, and when Theodora told him who we were, he said, "Then you belong with the mourners," and took us through two rooms to the parlor, where fourteen or fifteen persons, all strangers to us, were grouped about the coffin. Among them were three boys of about my own age and a girl rather older and much larger than Theodora, who sat apart from the others.

I wondered at once if she was Molly Totherly. She had the most abundant, beautiful red hair, and the largest mouth I ever saw.

That was as much as I noticed at first sight, for my attention was at once directed to one of the boys, who was staring evilly, and when I looked, made a small but venomous face at me. In all my life I never conceived so sudden a hatred of anyone as of that black-haired boy, relative though he were.

At the head of the coffin sat three lean, gray old men in ill-fitting black coats. They, too, looked very hard and forbiddingly at Theodora and me—so much so that I saw my cousin's sensitive face change and grow quite pale, for the funeral, and everything in the room, affected her profoundly.

The minister who preached the funeral sermon had begun to speak already, standing in the door of the room. But in what seemed to me a rather hardy manner, careless of propriety, the large girl moved her chair over to where Theodora and I sat. Motioning me to make room, she placed it between us, and sitting down there at once, took my cousin's hand in her own.

I remember noticing with a passing surprise what a strong-looking girl she was, what freckles she had, and also her great, odd, light hazel eyes, or else it was her eyebrows which looked so odd; they were very thick and pale yellow.

When she moved her chair to sit between us there was another stir on the floor beyond where the coffin stood, and a huge old black-and-white Newfoundland dog, getting up slowly, came round, and with a glance into the large girl's face, lay down in front of us. Somehow I felt less ill at ease after this, and I could see that Theodora did, although the black-haired boy made another face at me. Owing perhaps to this disagreeable boy, the big dog, or the large girl, I remember nothing of the sermon except the text: "Behold, I show you a mystery; we shall not all sleep." Once or twice a lugubrious wail of singing rose and fell in an adjoining room, and then the people filed in for a last look at the dead face of their old neighbor.

Theodora shrank from this, and held me by the hand beside her; for by this time the large girl and the dog had gone out.

As Sol was tired from our long journey, and had not yet been fed, we did not go in the procession to the graveyard, which was three or four miles distant, but when the others had departed, busied ourselves putting our horse up at the barn.

Then having had nothing to eat ourselves since morning, we took our box of food from the wagon, and going far out into an orchard back of the house, made a joyless supper there. My cousin confided to me that she could never partake of a mouthful of food in that house where the funeral had been, and I felt much the same myself.

We wandered about the orchard for an hour or more, until a woman, one of the neighbors who was assisting at the funeral, came out, invited us into the house, and showed us to rooms upstairs, where, she said, we could sleep that night.

The woman was talking all the while, and told us that "Grandsir Dresser," as she called him, was sixty-nine years old, and that his granddaughter, Molly, had taken almost the entire care of him for the last three years. "And I do just hope Molly'll get the property!" the woman added, with a sudden flash in her eyes which at the time seemed strange to us.

She went on to inform us that Molly's mother had been dead nine or ten years. "She was Grandsir Dresser's only daughter," said she. "But he's got three brothers, more's the pity!"

"Is Molly's father living?" Theodora asked.

The woman did not seem to hear the question at first, but replied at last that she believed he was killed in the war. "I do hope the old man's left a will, and a good strong will!" the woman ran on, as if from a pent-up desire to express her feelings to someone. "But he probably didn't."

The old red house, which seemed to us very large and cheerless, was now for the time quite deserted, but ere long—the relatives and others returned from the grave in a body, to the number of twenty-five or thirty, and appeared to be having a consultation.

Presently we heard first one, then another shout, "Molly!" "Molly Totherly!" "You, Molly Totherly!" But there was no response. We had not seen the red-haired girl since she left us in the parlor, or the old dog, either.

Not one of them had spoken a word to us or seemed to notice us, and by this time we were both about as homesick as we could be. I can never describe what gloom the place, the funeral, and all had cast upon us.

We drew off to the orchard again till dusk fell, then returned to the barn, where we looked after Sol's comfort, and then stole into the house.

The parlor and other rooms downstairs were now lighted. The three brothers, with their wives and children, were having supper and talking together. They seemed to have taken possession of the house; yet we saw nothing of Molly.

After lingering about the door and in the hall a little, in the hope of again seeing the woman who had talked with us, we crept up the dark staircase to the rooms which she had shown us.

"I wish we had never come!" I exclaimed fervently.

"Oh, so do I!" my cousin echoed faintly, then burst into tears. She was unaccustomed to such usage.

Ah, the gloom of those dark old rooms, and the sense of neglect and of enmity that oppressed us! It seemed to me that we never could endure the night. This, however, was but the beginning of what we were destined to experience before morning.

Part 2

WHAT WE SAW AND HEARD that night at the "old Dresser place" can only be described as a very bad side of human nature. It will be better to give the reader a hint in advance as to the cause—a hint of which my cousin and I did not have the benefit. The plain fact was, they were having no end of trouble there over Uncle Dresser's money.

The old lumberman possessed some little property, consisting of the homestead, timber lands, and, it was thought, considerable money. None of his immediate family was living at the time except this grand-daughter, Molly Totherly. Molly's mother had been his only child. But he had three younger brothers, Erastus, Ethan, and Calvin Dresser, who had families of their own, and who conceived themselves to be the heirs to their brother's estate.

None of them had ever aided him in any way. On the contrary, he had often felt obliged to help them. For several years they had rarely visited him, or evinced the slightest interest in his invalid condition, there being ill feeling on account of money which they had borrowed from him and did not like to repay.

On the other hand, Molly had lived at home and taken good care of him up to the time of his death. From the age of thirteen she had done this almost wholly alone and unassisted.

Uncle Dresser's neighbors were unanimously for Molly, and the things they said of those brothers would have made their ears burn if they had been ears of the sensitive kind. No one could learn whether Dresser had made a will, but Molly said that her grandfather had told her he was going to give her his property. On the day of the funeral, however, which Theodora and I had journeyed eighty miles to attend, the three brothers, Erastus, Ethan, and Calvin, with their families, appeared at the homestead. They brought a lawyer with them, and virtually took possession, their plan being to ignore Molly Totherly altogether. And I now imagine that the reason none of them recognized us, or welcomed us even to the extent of a single word, was from suspicion that we were there to set up some sort of claim on the estate, on Grandmother's side. Little wonder that the Old Squire wished to keep out of the trouble!

"Would it ever be morning, so that we could harness old Sol and get away from there?" was the thought uppermost in my mind as I stood at the window of that dark little chamber. There was a bed in the room, but I recollect resolving not to take off my clothes, but to be ready to start early, and I am confident that my cousin was even more homesick than myself.

Downstairs we heard people going hurriedly about from room to room, as if moving furniture, opening and shutting doors. Their voices came up to us, sometimes low and earnest, then high pitched, as if in anger. We also heard them calling, "Molly!"

Presently the old dog barked wrathfully.

Theodora now came to my door and spoke. She, too, appeared to have no thought of going to bed. "Oh, what do you suppose it is?" she asked. "What are they doing?"

That was more than I could answer. We stood in the doorway and listened. A singular noise had begun below, as if a door or a desk were being pried open with a bar. We could hear the wood cracking, then a loud snap, as of a breaking bolt or lock. Presently there rose exclamations as of dissent or dissatisfaction. Yet it was not easy to distinguish what they said. Louder than the rest, however, we soon heard one voice exclaim: "We'll find it if we have to tear the old house down!"

Then another lower voice said, "He didn't make a will."

"That's more than you know!" said the higher voice.

After this they seemed all to go to another room farther away, where we could for a time hear nothing, until suddenly heavy blows shook the whole house. Dora and I now had wild thoughts of stealing downstairs and going to the barn, to harness old Sol and escape. The moon was shining brightly outside the windows. But, to be frank, we were afraid to go down.

Immediately, then, a number of persons—eight or ten, from the sound of their steps—came upstairs, one gray, elderly man leading with a lamp. He looked first into Theodora's room, then into the one where we both stood near the window in the dark. Then he turned away, as if he had made a mistake.

We heard them go stumbling along the narrow hall into the ell chamber, and knock at a door out there.

"We know you are in here, Molly Totherly!" one of them at last said, angrily. "You had better open the door!"

A woman's voice replied from within, but we could not hear what she said.

"Oh, yes, we have a right to!" the man's voice in the hall exclaimed. "We've got the law on our side, and we are going to know what's in this room!"

The voice within appeared to refuse to open the door.

"Well, then, we will break it down!" cried the man. "Yes, we do dare to!" he went on. "You'll soon find out. No matter what your grandpa said. The law is on our side. Open this door! You won't? We'll see, then!

"Get an ax!" he said to some one of those with him in the hall, and one of them went tramping heavily downstairs.

This so excited Theodora that she trembled violently. "It is Molly!" she whispered. "What will they do to her?" I was equally excited, and had mad thoughts of rushing forth to Molly's assistance, or to raise help.

The man came back with an ax, and again they ordered Molly to open the door. Apparently she still refused, for the next instant a frightful blow resounded through the house. Theodora clutched my arm in terror. Outside, in the yard below, the dog barked, and continued barking savagely as the ax strokes were repeated.

The door, however, held. They struck it more than twenty times, and now it sounded as if they were chopping it down. We could hear the splinters and chips falling on the floor. By this time I was so beside myself with a frantic impulse to do something that I pushed up the window of the room where we stood, and got out on the piazza roof. I was about to shout for help. The sound of those blows inside a house at dead of night was maddening.

But at once on stepping forth I caught sight of something which arrested my attention and put a new idea in my head. Far along the side of the ell a window was open, and in the moonlight I saw what looked to be a rope dangling from it, and even as I looked, a woman began to get out at the window, and laying hold of the rope, swung herself down rapidly to the ground, where the dog was still barking. Theodora looked out in time to see the apparition descend.

The instant the woman's feet touched the ground she caught up what appeared to be a black bag, then glanced up, and spying me on the piazza roof, raised her other hand, and shook it slowly to me, as if enjoining secrecy and silence. In a moment more she and the old dog had disappeared from view.

"It's Molly!" Theodora whispered, in wide-eyed astonishment. "She's got away!"

I crept back hastily into the room, and we ran to look along the hall again, where by the lamplight we saw one of the elderly men still planting blows in the door, and despite our alarm, we both laughed in nervous glee over the idea that Molly had given them the slip.

Blow after blow resounded horribly through the house, but at last there was a crash, followed by a sound as of beams or boxes falling down. The door had been so barricaded that it was several minutes more before the men could effect an entrance. At last they got in, and then Theodora and I could but laugh excitedly again at the snarl which one of the brothers gave when they found the window open and the bed cord hanging from it.

Away they all went, pell-mell, downstairs and out into the yard and round the house and barn. They began to call, "Molly!" and "Beave! Beave! Come, Beave!"

"I don't believe they will find her!" whispered Dora, exultantly.

"I don't," said I. But for a long time we sat there, listening in the moonlit window.

After a while they all went back into the house, and there was further talk in the parlor. Then our inhospitable relatives went to bed. The moon had now set, but it must have been near daybreak. Not long afterward we noticed, with a vast sense of relief, that dawn was lighting the hills, and we waited only for it to grow light enough so that we could steal downstairs and out at the front door.

It had been the longest night I had ever known, and the most exciting one. The morning, moreover, was cheerless and chilly. We shivered from cold. There was frost on the dooryard chips as we went on tiptoe over them to reach the barn, where we had left old Sol.

The horse was in the stall where we had hitched him. He whinnied when he saw us, in expectation of his oats.

"Not now, old Sol," said I.

"We will stop and feed him after we have gone a little way," Theodora said.

But when we looked for our harness, all that we could find was the saddle; the bridle, collar, tugs and hames were missing, and so was our box of food!

We searched the barn. I even climbed on the grain scaffolds, and my cousin cautiously explored the stable nearer the house. She found our hames and tugs, hanging there with another harness. After this discovery we searched the stable high and low, and finally, in a large grain box, found a bridle and a collar which we thought were ours.

By this time the sun was peeping up, for we had spent at least an hour searching for our harness. As we drove slowly through the dooryard we heard a jeering young voice, and saw the frowsy head of the black-haired boy at one of the windows.

"There goes the little down easter, riding with his sister!" he sang at us.

"Where did ye find your bridle?" he bawled, after we had got past.

"Don't notice him," whispered my cousin. But if anything could have tempted me back to that house, it would have been the chance of getting hold of that little villain for about one minute! We had no doubt it was he who stole or hid our box of food, and we were both grievously faint and hungry, having eaten hardly anything for the last twenty-four hours.

But a good Samaritan hailed us from the door of the house next below the old Dresser place. The woman neighbor who had talked with us after the funeral came out to ask what had occurred during the night.

"Now did you ever!" she exclaimed, scandalized by the few facts which we disclosed to her. "Did you ever hear of such works?"

When she learned that we had had no breakfast, she was for taking us into her house. We did not deem it best to stop, but she insisted on bringing out to us each a cup of coffee and a doughnut. While we were drinking the coffee, she improved the opportunity to free her mind again as to those brothers.

She would have said much more, but we drove on as soon as we could get away; for we thought it best to go four or five miles before stopping to eat.

No one can imagine what a relief it was to feel the distance lengthening between us and the old Dresser place! Theodora drew a long breath of greater hopefulness. "We will have breakfast at Love-well's," she exclaimed, "and tomorrow we shall be home again—after all!"

My own spirits rose, and I touched up old Sol. Just then, however, as we passed a road corner, we heard a cry of "Whoa up, there!" although we saw no one.

Instead of stopping, I applied the whip again, being resolved not to be captured. But Theodora exclaimed, "Why, it's Molly!" And then we both saw her coming out from behind some bushes at the fork of the road. She had a black leather valise in one hand and was leading the huge old dog by a long chain.

"Going right by without stopping, were you?" she cried with a broad grin that showed her wide front teeth. "Whoa up, there!"

I pulled up, and Molly came straight to the wagon. "Got room for another passenger?" she asked.

"I think we can make room," said Theodora.

Thereupon Molly tossed her valise under the seat, jumped in, and swung the dog's chain round over my head for him to run on behind. "Go ahead!" said she. "I'm in. But start up easy, so as not to yank old Beave.

"Saw me getting out of the window by the light of the moon, didn't you?" she exclaimed to me, as I started the horse. "Those old skinflints were hard after me. They nearly tore the house down last night. I didn't think they'd break into my room, but they did. They were that crazy after Grandpa's money and deeds!"

"Did they find the money?" I exclaimed, with a boy's curiosity. "Have you got it?"

"Ask me no questions and I'll tell you no lies!" retorted Molly, laughing in my face.

Theodora and I felt rather queer over that, although we were keenly interested.

"Did you see 'em swarm out and hunt for me?" cried Molly, after a moment's silence. "Beave and I were away down the road, harking to see which way they'd come," and she burst out laughing again, but stopped short and glanced first at my cousin, then at me. "Don't you go to thinking things!" she exclaimed. "I haven't done anything or got anything that doesn't belong to me. I haven't a thing that Grandpa Dresser didn't give me himself."

Molly's assertion may not have constituted legal evidence, but Theodora and I were inclined to believe her. But we felt ill at ease, the more so because she kept looking back along the road, as if fearing pursuit, and urged me to drive faster.

"He can go on down to Waterville!" Molly exclaimed, when I spoke of stopping to feed old Sol. "Let me drive him." When I declined, she winked good naturedly at my cousin. "I suppose it does look better to have the man drive," she remarked.

I insisted on feeding the horse, and while we waited beside the road for him to eat his oats, Molly led old Beaver back a little way to drink at a rill. She was apprehensive, she told us, that homesickness might induce the dog to turn back if she let him go free. "He was Grandpa's dog," she said. "I promised I'd take good care of him as long as he lived."

While she was gone Theodora and I compared notes. "Isn't she a queer one?" said I.

"She hasn't had very many advantages," my cousin admitted. "But do you think she intends to go home with us?"

"Only to Waterville, I guess," said I.

Theodora was far from sure as to this. "What would Grandmother and the Old Squire say if we brought her home with us? And that awful dog, too?" she whispered. Our responsibility for Molly loomed up suddenly large. She came back before we could settle what we ought to do, and we were rather quiet in the wagon as we drove on for several miles.

Stirring events were at hand. Six or seven miles above Waterville, Molly, who kept a wary eye back along the road, jumped to her feet.

"There they come!" she cried.

"Who? Where?" said I.

"'Rastus and Ethan!" cried Molly. "And that's Calvin and one of those mean boys of his in the wagon behind!"

Two wagons were certainly coming on at speed, a quarter of a mile or less behind us. Immediately, too, a distant shout of "Stop! Stop, you!" was borne to our ears.

So far from heeding the request, however, Molly snatched the whip from the socket and gave our steady old Sol the greatest surprise of his life! I had all that I could do to manage him, and for some distance we tore along, towing old Beaver after us in a manner which I fear must have been very painful to his infirmities.

Part 3

FOR HALF A MILE or more we went on at a great rate, Molly glancing back and using the whip. I had all I could do to hold the reins. Theodora clung to the arm of the seat. At best, however, our old Sol was never a fast horse. "They're gaining on us!" Molly exclaimed, desperately. The rattle of the pursuing wagons sounded louder.

Suddenly Molly reached for her old black valise under the seat and then stood up, clutching my shoulder to steady herself. We were passing a place where the road crossed a small brook, and there were clumps of black alder and elder on both sides. As we coursed round a bend here, just after crossing the brook, Molly threw her valise off into the bushes.

I glanced at her in some astonishment. But she shook her head at me, and on we went past the bushy place and along the road beyond for a considerable distance.

The first wagon was steadily gaining on us, being now no more than two hundred yards behind. Molly laughed and put the whip in the socket.

"Let 'em catch us if they want to," she said. "But don't you so much as yip, or snicker, either!"

I had little thought of "snickering"—and as for Theodora, she was so alarmed and so fully occupied holding on that she had hardly noticed what Molly did.

Old Sol soon slackened his pace, and immediately we heard the two wagons closing upon us. In the first were two of the elderly men whom we had seen at the funeral. One was driving. Their horse was breathing hard.

"Stop, I tell ye!" the other called out, authoritatively.

"What for? What business have you to stop me?" I replied, valiantly, swelling with a sense of our invaded rights.

"Business enough, you sassy boy!" said the voice behind.

"That's Ethan," whispered Molly. "Pull up. We may as well have it out with 'em."

I stopped accordingly, old Sol nothing loath, and Molly turned round.

"Good morning, Ethan Dresser!" said she, with a ludicrous assumption of politeness. "Did you want to see me for anything?" And with that she jumped out of the wagon and drew the lolling old Beave by the chain till he sat down close to her beside the road.

Ethan Dresser had also got out, but on the other side. He came to our wagon, peeped under the seat, and then felt the oats in our bag with his fingers. My cousin had a small traveling bag. Ethan seized that, shook it, and then looked in it.

"You've no business to do that!" I exclaimed.

He gave me a malignant look. "You shut up," said he, "or I'll warm your jacket for ye!"

Meanwhile the other wagon had come up, and it added to my sense of outrage to see that the boy with Calvin Dresser was no other than that black-haired imp who had jeered our departure that morning. He sat holding the horse when his father got out to come to us, and presently chanted one of his sweet little couplets at Molly:

> Red-headed Molly Tother-lie,
> With a mouth as big as a pumpkin pie!

Molly merely shot a glance at him; for a third wagon had now overtaken us, which proved to contain the lawyer whom the brothers had brought to the funeral the day before.

"Good morning, Mr. Dolan!" Molly called out to him. "I was quite sure I saw you at Grandpa's funeral yesterday."

The young man laughed and said, "Good morning, Miss Totherly!" I thought he looked a little ashamed of himself or of the company he was in. But he came up to our wagon and cast an amused but sharp eye into it, then said something to 'Rastus, who came and undid the boot on our fender to look in it.

Ethan then ordered my cousin and me to get out. I refused, but Theodora, who was greatly terrified, obeyed, and stood beside Molly.

"What have you in your pocket?" 'Rastus said to her.

"Nothing that concerns you, sir," Dora replied.

"Humph!" he grunted. Calvin meanwhile had jerked the wagon cushion from under me. He and Ethan looked beneath it, and also felt it with their hands. Their lack of success put them in an even worse humor. And now all three of them went up to Molly.

"We're going to know what you've got in your pockets!" snarled Calvin.

"I haven't any pockets!" said Molly.

"You are a sly, thievish hussy!" said Ethan.

"I am not. Don't you dare call me that again, Ethan Dresser!" cried Molly, her gray eyes suddenly aflame. And the old dog growled. "Beave would shake the life out of you if I gave him the word!"

"If I had an ax here I'd kill that dog!" cried Ethan. "Cal, cut me a good thick alder club! We'll see who's comin' out on top here!" Theodora fled to the other side of our wagon. Beave was now growling frightfully. Molly had put one hand in his collar and stood firmly at bay.

But Mr. Dolan now approached Ethan and said something to him in low tones, evidently cautioning him, for in reality they had no warrant for stopping or searching us on the highway. Probably no one knew it better than the young lawyer. They presumed on the fact that we were little more than children and far from home. Beyond doubt, too, they had strong reasons for suspecting Molly.

"Better not," we overheard Dolan say to them several times. "May make it serious for you."

He turned to Molly.

"Now, Miss Totherly," he began, in winning accents, "I am sure you would not wish to do what is wrong. Had you not better put all this in the hands of the law and have it settled legally and right?"

"What's right is all I want," said Molly. At this moment old Beave thought Ethan and 'Rastus were approaching too near, and jumped toward them with a growl. Molly barely held him, and the brothers drew hastily back.

"I'll let go of him if you come near me again," said Molly.

There was no doubt as to the dog's intentions, and they backed off a little. Young Mr. Dolan resumed his persuasiveness.

"I really feel for you, Molly," said he. "I should not like to see you have to go into court or to prison."

"You won't see me go to prison," said Molly, laughing. "I've done nothing to go to prison for and don't mean to."

"You know, Molly," said Dolan, "that you can bring in a legal bill by the week for all the time you took care of your grandfather, and the court will allow it at a good rate of wages. The law will deal justly with you, and generously, too."

"No need of any bill," said Molly. "I didn't take care of Grandpa for money."

"But you would want something," rejoined the lawyer. "You might be in need of it."

"Grandpa looked out for that," said Molly, smiling broadly.

"How so?" said Dolan, keenly.

"If you were my lawyer, I'd tell you," retorted Molly, laughing outright. And Dolan himself could hardly refrain from smiling.

"Well, Molly, that may come later," he said, with a not unprofessional glance at her. "But you had much better give up what you have taken illegally," he continued. "Your grandfather's estate must be lawfully administered. Now if you have his money here, or his will—"

"Mr. Dolan," said Molly, "I haven't a cent of money on me here, nor so much as a piece of paper."

Dolan regarded her thoughtfully. He evidently believed that she had spoken the truth, for he at once went on another tack. A boy can sometimes be startled or frightened into revealing facts. Like a flash he turned on me.

"Where's that money?" he shouted, with a savage suddenness.

But in this case the boy had not seen any money. "I don't know," said I. "I know nothing about this."

"I am sure I don't," Theodora added, earnestly.

Dolan looked nonplused. The brothers were snarling together at Ethan's wagon. Two teams came along and passed us, the people regarding us with much curiosity.

"Molly," said Dolan, confidentially, "are you going far? Where are you going?"

"Why, Mr. Dolan!" exclaimed Molly with assumed archness. "Did you want to see me home?"

The young lawyer laughed, but looked sheepish.

"You are a very nice girl, Molly," was all he said, and he went to speak with his three unpromising clients at their wagon. But immediately he returned to us and addressed himself to me much less savagely. "Are you going home by way of Waterville?" he asked.

I said "yes" before stopping to reflect that I was not obliged to give him information.

"Wait till we drive past you, then," said Dolan. "We want to drive faster than you do," he added, by way of an explanation, which was probably not the true one.

We waited accordingly, and first 'Rastus and Ethan drove scowling by us, then Calvin and his black-haired son. The latter had been obliged to sit in the rear and hold the horse, but had doubtless been an interested spectator of our humiliation. His father had now taken the reins, and as they passed, Calvin Jr., thinking himself safe under the parental wing, threw in his small contribution of spite to Molly again, singing out:

Sorrel-top! Sorrel-top!
You'll soon be in jail!

But he had sung once too often that day. Dropping Beave's chain, Molly was in the back of the wagon at a bound.

"You little tike!" she exclaimed, and gave him two slaps on the ears that sounded like firecrackers. She was out before Calvin Sr. could turn round to interfere, but the boy's howls told of fair work done. The lawyer was driving up behind to pass us. I looked quickly to see what he would do. He seemed to be shaking with suppressed laughter. But Calvin was muttering threats, and, indeed, Molly had done an unwise thing—as the event showed. They drove on, with backward glances of ill favor, until a turn and bushes beside the road hid them from view.

"Now you stay right here a minute," said Molly, after watching the three wagons out of sight. "I left something back beside the road;" and she set off to go back, still leading old Beave.

Theodora wondered what she had gone back for.

"She threw out her valise," said I. "She's gone back to get it."

"Oh!" cried my cousin, in fresh alarm. "Do you suppose that money they talk about was in it?"

"I don't know," said I. "Maybe."

"Oh dear, this is dreadful!" Theodora exclaimed. "Why, it's like stealing, isn't it?"

"But Molly says her grandpa gave it to her," said I.

"Oh, I don't know what to think!" cried my cousin. "Why, we may all be arrested for having that money in our wagon!" Such sudden terror fell on us that we had wild thoughts of speeding up old Sol and leaving Molly and her valise behind. Dolan's talk of the law had filled us with alarm.

Molly returned suddenly without the valise. "I've been thinking," said she, "that we had better not go to Waterville."

"But we must go on home," said I.

"I know," replied Molly. "But I don't believe we had better go to Waterville. Why do you suppose that lawyer was so particular to find out that we were?" said Molly darkly. "I believe they are going there! They mean to nab us down there! That's why they drove on ahead."

This put new fear in Theodora and me. "But we don't want to go back to the old Dresser place," said I.

Molly thought a moment. "We can go up to Pishon's Ferry and cross the river. There's a road on the other side. We can go to Belgrade instead of Waterville; that will be on your way home."

"It will seem like running away, as if we were guilty of something," Theodora objected.

"We might as well do a little running," replied Molly. "That Ethan's bound to raise some kind of a row—and they've got a lawyer to help 'em!"

Uncertainty of the darkest shade beset our minds. But the instinct to escape led us to turn old Sol and take the back track.

"Whoa up!" said Molly, when we came to the little brook and the bushes where she had thrown out her valise. "I dropped something here." she added, with a grin, and gave me old Beave's chain to hold, while she jumped out and looked in the bushes. "Here 'tis!" she exclaimed, emerging from the sweet elders with the valise and an even broader grin.

She put her valise under the seat, jumped in, and took the chain. "Now drive," said she, "if there's any drive in you!"

I drove back up the road to the little place called Pishon's Ferry, where we first blew a horn, and then crossed on a ferryboat to the west bank of the Kennebec. The ferry fee was ten cents, which Molly insisted on paying.

"Oh, I'm rich, if I've got all they accuse me of taking!" said she, with a great laugh. But Theodora and I felt wondrously uneasy.

A guidepost not far from the ferry pointed the way to Norridgewock, and we drove on for two or three hours, coming at last to a small village, where the pangs of hunger led us to buy three dozen crackers and a pound of cheese at a grocery. Molly, I remember, went back and bought two dozen smoked herrings.

Not to make a spectacle of ourselves in the hamlet, we drove on with such patience as we could summon for some distance farther, to the shore of a large pond, where we unhitched and fed old Sol, and then laid out our eatable on a large, flat stone by the waterside.

It was a beautiful place, and now that we were on the other side of the river, a false sense of security beguiled us into remaining for an hour or more.

Molly made birch bark drinking cups to set on the stone, and after we had eaten and fed old Beaver on herrings and cheese, she made him hold a cup of water on his nose. At the word "Fire!" from her, he would throw it high in the air and catch it in his mouth.

We should have done much better if we had hastened on toward home.

Part 4

THOSE COVETOUS BROTHERS had determined not to let Molly go home with us. They thought that she had Uncle Dresser's money and papers with her, or had concealed them. There were no grounds, however, on which they could obtain a warrant for her arrest—or, rather, there had been none until, unfortunately, Molly herself furnished them by cuffing Calvin Jr.

Calvin Sr., Ethan, and Erastus were not slow to avail themselves of this pretext. By their lawyer's advice, probably, they trumped up a charge of assault and battery against Molly, and on making application for her arrest before the municipal judge at Waterville, Calvin Jr. was coached to cry and sob as if he had really sustained a serious injury. The object was to bring Molly back, and frighten her into revealing what she knew of her grandfather's property.

Had the authorities at Waterville been aware of this, they would no doubt have refused to issue a warrant, but in view of the testimony as to the assault, the warrant for her arrest was issued. The deputy waited for us to come into town, and remained on the lookout until nearly noon.

We did not come, having turned back and crossed the Kennebec at Pishon's Ferry, as has already been said.

Satisfied now that we were somehow giving them the slip, the brothers, the lawyer, and the deputy set off up the road, and followed our wheel marks to Pishon's Ferry. There they learned that we had crossed the river, and crossing over themselves, gave chase.

From eleven to twelve o'clock or past we had been losing time by the shore of the pond in Smithfield. Now that we were on the other side of the river, we felt quite safe. We waited for old Sol to rest and eat five quarts of oats; we ourselves lunched on our crackers, cheese, and herring. We had planned to proceed as far as Livermore that night, and reach home the next day.

While we were here Molly first divulged her purpose of going home with us. She could hardly have failed to notice that Theodora looked ill at ease.

"I know I have not been invited, Cousin Theodora," said Molly. "But I'm your grandmother's grandniece, and I don't know where else to go.

"I want to talk with your family," she continued, tears coming suddenly in her eyes. "I want to have them tell me what I ought to do. For I mean to do the right thing. But I won't give in to 'Rastus, Ethan, and Calvin. I know just what Grandpa thought of them. Grandpa didn't mean them to have a dollar of his property. He said they had had enough out of him already.

"Grandpa always liked your family," Molly went on. "He said if I was ever in trouble to go to them, and that they would do the right thing." This was an entirely new view of the case. Theodora grew sympathetic. We began to feel that perhaps we ought to take Molly with us, although I remembered that the Old Squire had expressed himself as very averse to becoming involved in this property dispute. Molly and her valise were likely to bring trouble, but we could see no way of getting clear of her. And there, too, was that enormous dog!

We felt a proper loyalty to Grandmother and the Old Squire. They had given six of us children a home with them, and we made their table a full one. For us to bring Molly and her big dog back with us seemed indiscreet, if not ungrateful.

Thoughts of our responsibility disturbed us as we drove on that afternoon through the towns of Rome, Mount Vernon, and Fayette, to Livermore on the Androscoggin River.

Such a region of ponds and lakes I had never been in before. There were ponds on all sides of us. We saw more than twenty that afternoon, some of them large sheets of water.

Probably the roundabout route which we took rendered it difficult for our pursuers to keep on our track. Old Sol, too, being now headed toward home, made good time, trotting on vigorously whenever the nature of the road permitted. We did not reach Dolloff's Tavern, at Livermore, however, until after sunset, and for the last hour or two all three of us had been so sleepy that we could hardly sit up in the wagon. Theodora and I had not closed our eyes the night before, nor, indeed, had Molly.

At the tavern we wrote our names in a much-blotted old register. The people seemed rather curious about us, but gave us a good supper. I then went to the stable to look after old Sol, and gave him his oats myself, the Old Squire having cautioned me never to trust that duty to hostlers, who might give the oats to some other horse if they were not watched.

Mrs. Dolloff and her daughters were afraid of old Beaver, and objected to having him indoors. So, after feeding him, Molly hitched him by his chain in a shed at the rear of the stable.

Mrs. Dolloff showed us to our rooms upstairs, Theodora's and Molly's adjoining, but mine being at the other end of the hall. I was soon asleep, my last waking thought being the pleasant one that we would get home by noon the next day.

Our slumbers, however, were destined to be of brief duration. Ethan Dresser and the deputy sheriff reached the tavern at about ten o'clock in the evening.

After following us to Norridgewock, 'Rastus, Calvin, Calvin Jr., and Mr. Dolan had turned back and gone home, but the sheriff and Ethan kept on in pursuit.

Old Beave must have scented Ethan Dresser. The instant they drove into the yard he set up a tremendous baying and growling. Then someone knocked at my door, and shouted, "Wake up! Open the door!"

When I opened it, the tavern keeper, with a lamp in his hand, and another man—the sheriff—stood there. The sheriff said, "Seems to me you are mighty sound asleep! Where's that redheaded girl that came here with you?"

"I guess she is in bed," said I. They turned impatiently and spoke to Theodora, whom they had already wakened.

On looking into the hall, I saw that Molly's door was open, but there appeared to be no Molly in the room.

Mrs. Dolloff and Ethan Dresser now came up the stairs with another lamp, and they looked in all the rooms and closets. Theodora had dressed, and I made haste to put on my clothes. We then looked in Molly's room.

"Do you know where she is?" I asked my cousin.

"No," said Theodora. "I was asleep, but I thought I heard her door open just as those men were coming upstairs."

After searching all the rooms, the sheriff and Ethan Dresser came back to us. "Don't you know where she is?" Ethan asked me. "If you know and don't tell us, it'll be worse for you! That girl's a thief."

"I don't believe she is a thief!" said I.

"I don't, either," said Theodora.

"You little upstarts!" exclaimed Ethan. Then he turned to the sheriff. "Look in their rooms," he demanded. "She may have hid something there."

"My warrant doesn't call for that," the sheriff objected. "I've no papers for these young folks."

Ethan had no such scruples. He and the Dolloffs, who seemed to be in sympathy with him, looked in our rooms. I suppose that the tavern keeper may have had a right to do so, if he pleased. They found merely our small belongings, and soon went downstairs to search our wagon and the outbuildings.

But soon Ethan and the Dolloffs came back into the house to question us again.

"What did Molly have with her?" Ethan asked me.

"Her dog."

"I know that. But what else!"

"I don't know."

He turned to my cousin. "What did Molly have in her hand or her pockets?"

I was afraid that Theodora might reveal something concerning the valise, and tried to give her a warning glance. It was quite unnecessary.

"Mr. Dresser," she replied, indignantly, "after the way you have treated us, if I knew what Molly had I would not tell you."

"Didn't she say anything to you?" Ethan asked me.

"Yes," I said, "she did."

"What was it? "

"She said, 'Ask me no questions and I'll tell you no lies.'"

Ethan gave vent to an angry snort, and Mrs. Dolloff laughed. "I'd like to have the handling of that boy a few minutes!" we heard Ethan mutter, as he went out to consult with the sheriff again. They stabled their horse, and coming in, registered, and went to bed.

It was now half past twelve. Mrs. Dolloff, who seemed more friendly, came in and advised us to go to our rooms again. But it was not until day had dawned that I caught another nap. Once asleep, I did not wake until the breakfast bell rang.

On our way downstairs Theodora and I agreed to answer no further questions. Ethan and the sheriff were at the table, but did not speak to us.

After breakfast I wished to pay my bill and go on home, but for nearly two hours the tavern keeper put us off. It appeared afterward that Ethan wished him to keep us there during the forenoon, while they watched for Molly, thinking that she might come back.

She did not come, and at ten o'clock the sheriff and Ethan hitched up to drive away. When ready to start, Ethan went to the shed where old Beave stood, and attempted to unchain him, to take him away, perhaps, but the dog jumped at him so savagely that he gave up the effort, and they drove off. Theodora and I then harnessed old Sol, and after paying our bill, started to drive away. But Mrs. Dolloff came rushing after us.

"You must take that dog!" she cried.

"He is not our dog," I said.

"I don't care whose dog he is! You brought him here. I won't have such an awful dog as that left on my hands!"

As nothing else would appease the woman, I gave her the reins to hold, and Theodora and I went to the shed, not without misgivings as to how old Beave would receive us. He wagged his tail, however, when we approached, clearly numbering us among his friends.

After procuring food for him from the kitchen, we gave him water, then brought him to the wagon—Dolloff promptly retreating to the house. Dora thought that she could lead him if I drove slowly, so we got in and made a start.

"What will Halse and Addison say?" I exclaimed.

"Oh dear!" sighed Dora. "And what will Grandmother say?"

The old dog followed beautifully, however, for several miles. He appeared desirous of getting on even faster than old Sol trotted, and the horse was now doing his best.

But this willingness to follow terminated suddenly at a point where a cart track led up from the highway over a steep, bushy hill. Old Beave wished to take the cart track, and pulled back and growled when we passed it. He was on the point of getting away from Theodora, but I seized the chain. And we then caught a link of it on the boot stop, and so held him.

The dog continued growling and pulling back, and was constrained to go on only by the strength of the chain. Finding it useless to resist, he followed sullenly all the rest of the way home.

We made no halt for lunch that day; we were in too great haste. And never did safe harbor, after storm, look sweeter to distressed mariners than did the old homestead to my cousin and me as we drove up the lane that afternoon.

Home, home again, after such an experience of a selfish, sordid world as we had never encountered before! Why, it seemed as if we had been gone for weeks instead of for four days!

At the farm in summer we had supper between five and six, and did the dairy chores afterward.

The family was at table when we drove into the yard. Ellen was the first to see us.

"They have come!" we heard her cry. And then she ran out on the piazza, followed by Addison, Halstead, and Wealthy, with Grandmother and the Old Squire not far behind.

I suppose that some trace of our disturbing experiences was impressed on our faces, for Grandmother cried, "Why, you dear children! Are you well? Has anything happened to you?" But Halse had seen old Beave behind us. "What a dog!" he shouted. "What a tremendous dog!"

Addison, too, was demanding, "Where did you get that dog?"

That was a sore subject. Theodora burst into tears. Grandmother gathered her in her arms forthwith.

"Come in, come in, both of you, and tell me all about it!" she exclaimed. And while Addison and Halstead led old Sol and Beave away to the stable, we, the returning ones, were escorted indoors to the table, to eat our supper and to relate our adventures.

My cousin and I took turns telling what had occurred. As our narrative proceeded, and the disagreeable features of it grew in volume, Grandmother wiped her eyes disconsolately.

"Oh, to think that they should behave so!" she lamented. "To think that they should go on like that—when the name of Dresser has always been an honorable one!"

The Old Squire sat up stiffly. He would not trust himself to say one word, for fear of injuring Grandmother's feelings. His deep aversion to such property quarrels was evident.

Halstead and Addison, who had now come in, also asked many questions as to the big dog. Such a dog had never been seen in that locality before. The boys were a little afraid of him, for he appeared sullen and out of sorts.

"I think that he misses Molly," said Theodora, and now that all the circumstances were better understood, both Grandmother and the Old Squire were much disturbed as to what had become of Molly Totherly.

The Old Squire asked particularly whether we had seen the warrant for Molly's arrest and whether we were sure it was a sheriff with Ethan Dresser. We were quite sure.

"This is a grave matter, Ruth," he said to Grandmother. "If there is a warrant out for this girl she needs friends. Addison, you hitch up Jerry in the light wagon. Then get your coat and the lantern. We will drive over to Livermore this evening and see what we can find out about this."

Just then, however, Ellen caught sight of someone in the yard outside who seemed to be peering in. "Who's that?" she said.

We all turned to look. And to Theodora and me, even in the twilight, it was no stranger whom we saw there with an old black valise.

"Molly!" we both shouted.

"Yes!" exclaimed a laughing voice outside. "It's Molly. I was peeking in to see if I'd come to the right place!"

Part 5

AT THE SOUND of Molly's voice old Beave, out in the stable, barked uproariously. Theodora and I hastened forth to usher her indoors. She tossed her valise down in one corner. "I hear old Beave," she said, "so I know he's here. I saw his tracks in the road, too," she added, laughing.

"But where did you go last night?" I exclaimed.

"Oh, I just stepped out when I heard Ethan coming upstairs," said Molly. "I was bound not to let them get my valise. I ran along the road, then climbed up a hill among some bushes, and waited there all night for you to come along in the morning. I waited there till nearly noon.

You didn't come, and I got so hungry I went off to a house I saw across the pastures to buy something to eat.

"When I came back I saw by Beave's big tracks in the road that you had gone by, so I came on after you."

"Grandmother," said Theodora, remembering that our guest had not been introduced, "this is Miss Mary Totherly, a relative of ours."

"Yes, yes, child, I know," and Grandmother kissed the visitor.

Theodora then introduced the Old Squire and afterward Addison, Ellen, and the others in their turn.

"You had better call me Molly," our guest said. "I don't know myself as 'Miss Mary Totherly.'"

That set Addison and Halstead laughing. Meanwhile Grandmother had made a place at the table for her.

"Oh, what a tidy place this is!" she cried, and looked round the room. "Aunt Ruth, I kept Grandpa's house three years all alone, but oh, what a house I kept! I didn't know how at first, and afterward I was always hurrying things off. If only I'd had you to tell me, I might have done better."

Grandmother sat down beside her. "Was your grandpa a great deal of care?" she asked.

"Oh, no, not so very much," said Molly. "What bothered me most was cooking to suit him. I'm a very poor cook, Aunt Ruth! I sometimes think poor Grandpa was glad to die, to get away from my cooking."

The Old Squire laughed and rose to go. Molly followed him to the door.

"I want to speak with you, sir, this evening," she said. "I came on purpose to talk with you. I'm in no end of trouble. It's about Grandpa's property. I didn't dare to stay there at home any longer.

"You see, Grandpa gave me his property. He said all along that he wanted me to have it. But his three brothers are determined to get it. There are not many things I'm afraid of, but I am afraid of that Ethan Dresser."

"Did your grandfather make a will in your favor?" asked the Old Squire.

"Well, yes, a kind of a will," said Molly. "I'll show you what he wrote. But they say that I must have a guardian, for I'm not quite seventeen yet. I want you for my guardian."

"But, my dear girl," exclaimed the Old Squire, with a disturbed look, "I think that someone else would do better!"

"I've nobody else," said Molly plaintively. "Grandpa told me to come to you."

The Old Squire and Grandmother exchanged looks of consternation. Much as they had desired to keep aloof from this property wrangle, they seemed about to be drawn into it.

Theodora and I went out with Molly to see old Beave, whom we had heard barking at intervals to attract attention. We told her how he had hung back when we came to the cart road which led up a hill. "That was where I was waiting for you!" exclaimed Molly. "Old Beave knew I turned off there."

Theodora also told her that Ethan Dresser had attempted to unchain the dog, and that old Beave had jumped at him and growled.

"That made the sheriff laugh," said I. "'That dog'll eat you up, Dresser,' said the sheriff."

"The sheriff?" said Molly. "What sheriff?"

"The one that was after you. Didn't you know that a sheriff came with Ethan to get you? He had a warrant to arrest you, but he said that he did not have any for Dora and me."

"No, I'm sure I didn't know!" cried Molly, looking much alarmed. "I thought it was only Ethan, and perhaps Calvin or Dolan with him. Oh dear, what do you suppose they will do with me?"

"The Old Squire knows about it," said I. "He will stand by you."

But Molly continued to look much distressed. "If I'd known it was the sheriff I wouldn't have run away," she said.

That evening we gathered in the sitting room. Molly had brought in her valise and set it on the center table.

"Now I want to tell you all about it," she said, "and see what you think I ought to do. But I don't want any Ethans looking in!" and she pulled down one of the window shades which had not yet been drawn. She then opened the valise and took out a large calfskin pocketbook. "That was Grandpa's," she said. "It's got his money in it, in greenbacks, and there's a little over two thousand dollars."

"Did he give it to you, child?" asked Grandmother, solemnly.

"Yes, Aunt Ruth, You will see that he did. And here are eight notes."

She took up a long envelope. "They are for money that Grandpa lent to different people. One, for $400, is against Ethan Dresser, and one for $350 is against Calvin Dresser. Neither of them has ever paid. Grandpa could never get them to pay anything—even the interest money; he did not like it at all. And Ethan and Calvin never came to see him all the time I took care of him."

The Old Squire looked at the notes. The six others were secured by mortgages on farms in Kennebec County, and the sum of them was about twenty-eight hundred dollars.

Molly then took out of the valise another folded paper.

"This is the deed of Grandpa's farm where he lived," she said. "You can read what he wrote on the back of it. He wrote it one day last October. There was a great rainstorm, and he was feeling very bad. He did not think that he should live till morning, and about eight o'clock he told me to fetch him his little tin trunk that had his papers in it, and the inkstand. 'I ought to have made a will long ago,' he said. 'But I've kept putting it off, thinking I'd feel better. I guess I never shall. But I'll fix it so you'll have what I've got left, for you've been a good girl to me, Molly.' Those were his very words."

"Then he did not send for a lawyer?" the Old Squire remarked.

"No," said Molly. "It was raining hard, and he wrote on the back of the deeds himself. I lifted him up and put pillows behind him, and laid an old atlas book in front of him. He spread the deed out on that, and I kept dipping the pen for him as he wrote. I looked up the day of the month for him, to date it. Now you can read what he wrote."

The Old Squire read it, and afterward Grandmother and all of us read it. On the back of the deed of the homestead Africa Dresser, in a not very bad hand, had recorded the date and written as follows:

This is my will, my last will, and my only will.

My mind is just as clear as it ever was.

I shall not live much longer, and the weather is so bad I can't get out to a lawyer's office. So I write my will on this deed. I cannot go into all the words a lawyer would use, but what I mean is that my granddaughter, Molly Totherly, shall have the farm which this deed covers and the timber lands, covered by two other deeds which I will write on in the same way as this.

What money I have got left, I give to Molly now before I die, and I also give her my eight notes, against Hiram Frost, Amos Sweetzer, Charles Holt, William Foster, William Goodnow, Henry Decoster, Ethan Dresser, and Calvin Dresser, and it is my will and wish that she shall collect them all, for they are rightly due me.

What I mean is, that I am determined to give and bequeath to Molly Totherly all my property, real and personal, and that nobody else is to have one dollar of it. I hope this will be plain enough to everybody.

I haven't got any seal, but Ezra Coffin and wife are my witnesses, and this is my signature.

Africa Dresser

Below were the signatures of the two witnesses, Ezra Coffin and Sarah H. Coffin.

"This is in Africa Dresser's handwriting," the Old Squire remarked. "I recollect it very well. I don't know what the lawyers will say of the will—probably they will try to pick flaws in it—but beyond doubt this is genuine, and he was evidently of sound mind."

Much the same in purport was written on the other two deeds, which conveyed extensive timber lands. Africa Dresser plainly desired to give the lands to Molly Totherly and to no one else.

"These lots are valuable and growing more so," said the Old Squire thoughtfully. "You will be a very well-to-do young woman, Molly, if you can hold them. But who are these witnesses named Coffin? Where are they now?"

"It was a man and his wife who were working there at our place for Grandpa," replied Molly. "They left us last November and went to Bangor. I don't know where they are."

"They must be found. Did Ethan Dresser and his brothers know them, or know that they witnessed these papers?"

"I don't think they knew anything about it. They searched for a will, but could not find it. They may have found out something, for they were all the time inquiring. Little Calvin would come to the house, pretend-

ing to visit us, and peep into every cupboard and desk, and ask me questions by the hour. He is a sly little toad! I knew that his father sent him there to see what he could find out, but I never told him anything.

"Perhaps I didn't do right," Molly went on, after a little hesitation. "But the night after Grandpa died, before Ethan or any of them came, I took these deeds and notes and the money, and put them all in this valise, and hid it in my room. It seemed to me that they were mine. Then when they broke into my room, I threw the valise out of the window and slid down the bed cord."

"Well, it was not exactly legal procedure," said the Old Squire, laughing. "But you had unscrupulous persons to deal with. If those men had found these deeds and notes that night there is no knowing what would have happened. Your grandfather's will and last wish would most likely have been disregarded. So I think you did quite right."

"I'm so glad to hear you say that!" exclaimed Molly. "I hardly knew what I had done, and they say that a sheriff is after me!"

"No one can harm you for keeping papers safe from persons who were behaving as Ethan Dresser and his brothers behaved that night," said the Old Squire. "You need not worry."

"Do you think Grandpa's property is rightly mine?" Molly asked.

"I do," replied the Old Squire. "It is plain to me that your grandfather has willed his property to you. He failed to do so in strict legal form, and probably the lawyers on the other side will try to pick flaws in this paper, it being a deed as well as a will. But the property is rightfully yours, or will be when the estate is administered. But I have no doubt there will be trouble about it."

"You'll be my guardian, won't you, sir?" Molly exclaimed eagerly.

The Old Squire heaved a sigh. "Well, Molly, if the judge sees fit to appoint me I will do the best I can for you."

Molly jumped to her feet. "I shall thank you for that as long as I live!" she exclaimed. "I suppose you never will need care from me, but if you ever do I'll take as good care of you as I did of Grandpa."

"Do you think you could cook for me?" said the Old Squire, with a twinkle in his eye.

"Yes, if Aunt Ruth will tell me how!" cried Molly, and they all had a laugh at that.

We heard old Beave bark again.

"Hark!" said Theodora, softly.

"Someone's come," said Addison. "I hear wheels," and he went out on the piazza, but it was now very dark.

"Who lives here?" a voice called out.

Addison gave the Old Squire's name.

"I thought so," rejoined another voice, one that, although indistinctly heard, seemed not wholly unfamiliar to my ear.

"That's Ethan!" Molly exclaimed. And with a sweep of her hand she gathered the pocketbook and papers into the old valise.

Part 6

WE HEARD ETHAN and the sheriff get out of the wagon and come up the piazza steps.

"What's wanted?" said Addison, as boldly as possible.

"Isn't Molly Totherly in this house?" asked the sheriff.

"And what if she is?"

"I've a warrant to arrest her. I'm a deputy sheriff of Kennebec County. My name's Longley."

"And my name's Dresser, Ethan Dresser," said the too familiar voice. "I've good reason to be here, too. I'm after a thief. And you'd better not set your face against the law, young man."

The Old Squire went hastily to the door.

"No one here opposes the law," he said. "If you are a sheriff in the way of your duty everyone in this house will help you. May I see your warrant?"

Longley followed the Old Squire into the lighted sitting room, and Ethan Dresser came after. They glanced round, but Molly and Theodora had slipped out.

Grandmother always remembered the ties of kindred.

"How do you do, Ethan Dresser?" she said, quite hospitably. "It is a long time since I have seen you, but I hope we are still friends."

"I don't know about that!" snarled Ethan, glancing at all of us, and evidently looking for Molly. "That remains to be seen. Where's that girl that stole my brother Africa's papers?"

"I do not think my niece has stolen anything," replied Grandmother. "You had better not accuse her."

"So you are going to cloak her, are you?" exclaimed Ethan, angrily. "I might ha' known it. Your sister was just like you, always putting Africa against his own flesh and blood."

"Don't speak to me in that way of my dead sister."

"I say what I know! And I'll say further, that if you cloak and hide this girl and put her against us, you will get into trouble for it. We'll have the law on ye. What are ye hiding her for? What be ye putting her out of sight for?"

This was too much. Grandmother rose up in sudden indignation, but before she could speak Molly reentered the room. "Who says anybody's hiding?" she exclaimed, with one of her laughs. "Hello, Uncle Ethan Dresser! Did you want me for anything? Here I am."

The sheriff, who had been displaying his warrant to the Old Squire by the lamp at the other end of the room, now approached Molly, and said he should have to put her under arrest.

"What for?" said Molly. "What have I done?"

The sheriff read his warrant to her. "It's for assault and battery," he added, but smiled broadly in spite of himself. The Old Squire looked puzzled; Ethan scowled.

"Just for cuffing that little Calvin?" exclaimed Molly.

"She never hurt him at all!" I protested. "He didn't get half what he deserved."

"This looks to me to be a pretty small piece of business," the Old Squire remarked. "It's a shame to drag a young girl into court for such a trifle. But I imagine there were other reasons."

"Maybe and maybe," said Ethan. "But she's got to go back and answer to this at Waterville."

"Oh, I'm all ready to go back," said Molly. "Going to start now?"

The sheriff looked doubtful, as if he were not wholly desirous of an all-night drive.

"Of course not tonight," said the Old Squire. "This is a trivial charge, and it is late. You are both welcome to lodging and food—that is, if Mr. Dresser cares to pass the night under my roof. Otherwise, there is a tavern at the Corners, a mile and a half from here."

In fact, we all hoped that Ethan would go, but, as appeared afterward, he had a motive for accepting our hospitality.

"I must keep an eye on this young lady," said Longley. "Last night she gave me the slip."

"I will be responsible for her," said the Old Squire. "She will not try to escape. I shall go to Waterville with her. We will start at six in the morning."

Their horse was put in the stable. Addison then showed them to a sleeping room upstairs.

Meanwhile, out in the kitchen, Grandmother was lamenting the family disgrace. For her it was a terrible thing to have a sheriff come to the house. Never since the old farmhouse was built had an officer of the law had occasion to enter it in the discharge of his duty. It threw a gloom on us all. Theodora and I felt that we were largely responsible for bringing this calamity home with us.

But I was so sleepy that I could with difficulty keep my eyes open, for I had hardly slept at all for two nights. Yet all the time I was wondering about Molly's valise, and whether Ethan and the sheriff would get it.

"What has she done with it?" I found an opportunity to whisper to Theodora, as we were dispersing to bed.

"Oh, don't ask me!" she replied. "I don't want anyone to ask me a word about it."

In point of fact, the two girls had run out together to hide the valise when we heard Ethan coming in. They went to the basement of the wagon house, which was connected with the farmhouse by an ell, and put the valise inside an old stove, which was used for drying apples in the fall of the year.

All the time old Beave continued barking so loudly and with such determination at the stable that finally Molly and Addison went out with a lantern, and to prevent him from keeping every one awake that night, they led him away to the farther barn and chained him in a stall. Old Beave held his own ideas concerning Ethan Dresser; even the smell of him put the old dog in an agitated state of mind.

Once in my own bed, I fell asleep almost instantly, and did not wake till Halstead called me the next morning.

"Get up, sleepyhead!" he said, impatiently. "Why didn't you turn out and help us milk the cows? You will have to milk four after this, for Ad is going off with the Old Squire and that Molly to Waterville. You and I will have it all to do." He went out discontentedly and slammed the chamber door. But a few moments later, as I was dressing in haste, I heard the door open softly behind me, and there stood Ethan Dresser, peering in. At sight of him a feeling of animosity took possession of me. But, for a wonder, Ethan was smiling, or trying hard to smile.

"Tired, wa'n't ye?" said he, with an evident effort to be pleasant. "Long ride, wa'n't it?"

I did not feel like replying, being little more than half-awake as yet.

"Have to work hard here, don't ye?" Ethan continued. "Lots of work to do, ain't there?"

I said yes.

"I'll bet ye have to work," Ethan went on, "but Fourth o' July is coming. Got any money for firecrackers and lemons and things?"

"Not a great deal," I admitted.

"Well, now," said Ethan, confidentially, and he came inside the room and closed the door, "d'ye see this!" He opened his hand and showed me a new five-dollar greenback. "That would buy a lot of nice things for the Fourth. And I'll give it to you if you'll tell me what Molly Totherly brought here with her."

Five dollars has attractions for a boy, but the covert manner in which Ethan proffered it only made me despise him the more. "What makes you think she brought anything here?" I asked, putting on my jacket.

Ethan regarded me with disfavor. "Then ye won't tell me!" said he, still displaying the bill. "Nobody'd know," he added, craftily.

"No, I will not tell you," I said.

"You know she brought some papers here," he declared. "You don't dare say she didn't."

I would not say a word more, and after a long, hard look at me, Ethan backed out and went to his own room. But he had been astir for an hour or more, and out at the stable he had already learned something. Halstead had been giving the horses their grain, when Ethan came into the stable and asked him casually how the Old Squire and Addison and Molly and her trunk were all going in one wagon.

"She hasn't got a trunk," replied Halstead, off his guard. "She's got nothing but a small valise that will go under the seat."

"Small black leather valise, is it?" queried Ethan, and Halstead nodded before he thought what he was revealing. That bit of information was not lost on Ethan. He knew the leather valise in which his brother Africa always carried his papers.

The Old Squire, Molly and Addison had already taken breakfast. Grandmother, Theodora and I were at the table with the sheriff and Ethan. Hardly a word was spoken. Grandmother, indeed, had been shedding tears over Molly, grieved beyond expression that she should be in the hands of the law.

The Old Squire deemed the charge against her a trifling one, and was chiefly concerned about the will and the property. He feared lest, plainly as Uncle Dresser's wishes had been expressed, Iris's three brothers and their lawyer might succeed in having the will set aside. The witnesses to the will, too, must needs be found and kept under observation. As they were poor people, he feared that Ethan Dresser might find means to tempt them into giving testimony in his favor.

It was for this reason that the Old Squire had determined to take my older cousin, Addison, to Waterville, and have him go from there privately to Bangor, to look up Mr. and Mrs. Coffin. Addison was a prudent boy, to whom a matter of this sort could be safely entrusted.

Legal advice would also be necessary, and after the charge against Molly should be disposed of at Waterville, the Old Squire had resolved to take her and the papers to Portland, and put the case in the hands of a young lawyer there who had already won renown at the bar, and whose name is now a familiar one in national politics.

The Old Squire could hardly have slept much that night. At four o'clock he waked Molly, and the valise was quietly rescued from its hiding place in the wagon-house cellar. The deeds containing Uncle Dresser's will were taken out. Molly concealed these papers inside her dress, but the more bulky package of money in bills, with the notes, insurance policies, and other papers were left in the valise, which they locked up, with Grandmother's knowledge, in a chest in the Old Squire's sleeping room, adjoining the sitting room, on the ground floor of the farmhouse.

Halstead had already harnessed Ethan's horse. The sheriff got into the wagon and sat waiting, but Ethan himself lingered. Probably he wished to make sure that the black leather valise was put in the wagon. I believe that he meant to capture that valise by fair means or foul, during the day or at Waterville.

No valise was brought out, however, and Ethan behaved oddly, as if reluctant to get into the wagon with the sheriff and drive away. But immediately Halstead brought our team to the door, and the Old Squire got in.

"Shall we go ahead of you?" the Old Squire said to the sheriff.

"Suit yourself, sir," Longley replied. Thereupon our team drove off at a good rate, leaving Ethan and the sheriff to follow on.

Grandmother was still wiping her eyes; Theodora and Ellen gazed wistfully after the disappearing wagons, then went to feed old Beave and condole with him.

Halstead and I had grave responsibilities devolving on us. Hard work was staring us in the face.

"Plant the potatoes as fast as you can," the Old Squire had said to us. "The ground is all ready. The girls must help you drop the seed and plaster."

Our spring work was, indeed, pressing hard, and there was no saying when the Old Squire and Addison would return. We hastily finished the morning chores and turned the cows to pasture, then furrowed an acre for potatoes and drew the seed and plaster to the field. The seed potatoes had then to be cut in halves.

Meanwhile Halse had summoned the girls. "Come, Dora and Nell!" he called to them. "You've got to help us. Grandfather said so." And they came, but with wry faces, for dropping seed potatoes with plaster is anything but clean work.

All that long May forenoon we toiled in the field and planted half an acre, but there were three acres more to plant and the pasture fences to mend.

Old Beave whined piteously when I went to carry him water at noon. While we were in the field that afternoon the old dog broke loose, and pushing open the slide door with his nose, coursed round the house and took to the road, dragging about half his long chain after him. Grandmother saw him, but deemed it useless to call us.

We had other troubles. That night the sheep, which had been driven up to the back pasture two days before, came down to the barns, apparently much frightened. After counting the flock the next morning, we found that a ewe and her lamb were missing, and on going to the pasture, we saw the sheep's pelt, where a bear had torn it off. Halstead now attempted to start a bear hunt, but found our neighbors lukewarm on the subject, as they were very busy with their work.

On the following day our cows and young cattle escaped from the pasture, and one of the steers became mired in a bog. It required all our efforts for several hours, with old Sol and a tackle and block, to extricate the animal.

These untoward incidents of farm life wasted our time. We planted hardly more than an acre in the three days. The next day was Sunday, but on Monday we set to work with goodwill. We furrowed another acre, and by three o'clock that afternoon had it planted. The girls, who had now grown interested in the work, urged us to furrow another acre.

"Nothing hinders today," said Ellen, "but there's no knowing what will happen tomorrow."

Halstead hitched old Sol to the plow, but we had made only two furrows for potato rows when we saw our little Cousin Wealthy coming to the field in great haste.

"We've got company!" she cried. "You must put up their horse."

"Who's come?" asked Ellen.

"I don't know; they're strangers," replied Wealthy. "It's an old man and a boy. And I don't believe Grandmother's very glad to see them, either."

"Why? What did she say!" asked Theodora.

"She said, when she saw them out of the window, 'For the land's sake!' But they sat there in their wagon right in front of the window, and at last Grandmother went to the door.

"'Howdy do, Ruth!' said the old man. 'Lookin' just as fair and rosy as when I used to visit forty year ago!'"

"My!" gasped Ellen. "What did Grandmother say to that?"

"She never smiled," said Wealthy. "But she looked straight at that old man and said, 'Calvin Dresser, what's brought you here?'"

At the name of Dresser Theodora cast a frightened look at me. "It's old Calvin and little Calvin!" she cried.

Part 7

AT THE AGE OF THIRTEEN I was so near forgetting the duties of hospitality as to think of drubbing Calvin Jr. at sight. Our harness which he had hidden, the ugly faces he had made, and the jeering songs he had sung at us clamored for satisfaction.

"I'll pay him up now," said I, as we went to the house to take care of their horse, and even Theodora's eyes gleamed at thoughts of squaring accounts.

"But we mustn't, not while he is here visiting," she said.

When we reached the house Calvin Dresser had hitched his horse to a post at the stable and gone indoors, but Calvin Jr. came out and drew near as we unharnessed.

"Hello!" said he, keeping off a bit.

Theodora said, "Hello!" rather coldly.

Calvin Jr. drew a little nearer and said, "Hello!" to me again with a grin.

Thereupon I turned and looked him in the face.

"What did you hide our harness for? Why did you make faces at us and sing mean songs at us?" I exclaimed.

"Oh, it was only in fun," said Calvin Jr.

"Don't!" whispered Theodora to me. "Don't do as Molly did."

The thought of Molly in jail, for aught we then knew to the contrary, for cuffing Calvin Jr. had a somewhat sobering effect on my temper.

"You had better not play any of your tricks here," I said. "What are you here for?"

"Pa and I came to make a visit."

We put up their horse, but none of us could understand why they had come; they had never visited us before.

At the supper table that evening, however, one would have supposed to hear Calvin Sr. talk that they were our dearest friends. The old man ran on at great length about former times, when he and Grandmother were young. Then he talked to Theodora and to me, and afterward to Ellen and Halstead, and even to little Wealthy, asking us all about ourselves, and what we liked and did not like. I think that he quite disarmed Grandmother's first suspicions, for he mentioned his brother's death and spoke of Molly Totherly, saying he hoped the law would do the right thing by her. Little Calvin sat by and grinned at us steadily.

Yet despite all the old man's effusiveness, there was a note of insincerity in his voice which Theodora and I both noticed, and even Ellen, who had never seen him before, said in the kitchen after supper that she believed he was an old snake in the grass!

Later in the evening Grandmother ushered father and son to one of the front chambers to sleep.

In those days of youthful toil nothing less than an earthquake would have waked us boys. The next morning, however, as I brought in the milk from the barn, Theodora asked me if I supposed Mr. Dresser was sick in the night.

"He was up," said she, "about in his stocking feet. I heard him striking matches ever so many times."

But at breakfast he appeared to be well. He talked more than ever, and little Calvin sat and grinned and watched all our faces.

Theodora and I had our suspicions, but there was little that we could do. We all went to the field to work. Our guests remained at the house, visiting Grandmother.

During the afternoon Wealthy came out where we were at work, bringing us water. "How do you like that boy?" Halse said to her.

"I guess he is a funny one," she answered.

"Why?" Ellen asked. "He's peeking into everything," replied Wealthy. "He asks mean questions."

Our suspicions, which had been growing all day, now took form. "I believe they are trying to find Molly's valise," Theodora whispered.

"Where did you and Molly hide the valise?" I asked, for I did not know.

"It is locked up in Grandmother's room in the Old Squire's chest," she replied. "But you know Grandmother keeps the key in her lightstand drawer, where anybody could find it."

"Let's go and see," I said, and we set off for the house, leaving Halse and Ellen looking curiously after us.

As it turned out, Calvin Sr. and his worthy son had been searching the house, on the sly, all day. While one of them talked with Grandmother out in the kitchen, the other had been looking high and low for Molly's valise. Ethan had told them that the valise was surely in our house. At last, one or the other of them had looked in Grandmother's room, found the key to the chest and opened it.

We ran all the way to the house, but approached from the rear of the buildings and entered by the back door of the stable. Here the first thing we saw was Calvin Dresser's horse, which had just been led from the stall and hitched to a post. The collar of the harness had been put on his neck, and the old wagon had been turned, ready for the horse. In fact, the old man had already begun to harness, but had gone back into the house for something he had left, or else to speak to Grandmother again.

"Why, they are going away!" whispered Theodora, and this seemed strange to us, for from what they had said we supposed that they intended to stay several days.

I looked out at the stable door to see if Calvin Jr. was about, but saw nothing of him. Theodora, meanwhile, ran up the back stairs of the ell and passed through into the farmhouse chambers, to see, as she explained afterward, if they had taken their belongings from their sleeping room and were really going away.

As she entered the upper hall of the house she glanced from the front window, which commanded a view of the lane and of the highway to the northeast. She caught sight of little Calvin, running from the foot of the lane along the road. And she saw that he had in his hand Molly's valise!

She turned instantly and ran back downstairs and out into the stable in great excitement. She had been gone hardly a minute. Calvin Sr. had not yet come back; we could still hear him talking to Grandmother.

"That boy's got Molly's valise!" were Theodora's first words. "He's running down the road. Chase him! Catch him!"

With that I dashed out at the rear door and ran across the back field to head him off. Theodora followed fast after me; she could run well in those days. Reaching the stone wall that bordered the road, I jumped over and looked both ways, but could see nothing of Calvin Jr. Theodora overtook me as I stood there.

"Here are his tracks!" said she, breathlessly, and we ran up the road in pursuit. There were bushes on each side of the highway, and we ran on for a quarter of a mile or more, for we could see his tracks in the sand and were resolved to catch him.

Even then we could see nothing of him, but, running on, we came upon him suddenly, sitting on a rock at a gap in the wayside bushes, where a cart road diverged from the highway. He had stopped and was sitting, with the valise on his knees, waiting for his father to come along. They had not dared to carry the valise out to the stable past Grandmother in the kitchen, but Calvin Jr. had slipped out at the front door with it and run down the lane, knowing that his father would soon overtake him.

When he saw us he jumped up and turned to run, but he had a high set of bars across the cart road to climb, and the valise bothered him. I was over the bars as soon as he was and shouted to him to stop.

"Father! Father! Father, help!" he screamed, and started to run across the field. I caught him and held him.

"Give up that valise!" said I.

"I won't!" said he, and struck me with it. I threw him, and Theodora, who had come up, snatched the valise from his hand. Then I let him get up, but he flew at me like a young tiger, and being about of an age, we had a pretty spirited set-to for some moments. I got him down, and then Theodora interposed.

"The sheriff will be after you," she whispered. "Let go! Let go!"

I "let go," and Calvin Jr. got up, crying, and called to his father again, then snatched up a stone and threw it. I dodged it, but it came near striking Theodora, who stood behind me. I went for him again, fully resolved now to give him his deserts.

Just then, however, we heard a wagon coming along the road at a great rate. The boy heard it, too, and screamed, "Father! Father!" Beyond doubt it was Calvin Sr., and fearful of contending with a raging parent, I let the son go, and ran with Theodora and the valise to a growth of young white birches on the lower side of the field. We gained cover before Calvin Sr. appeared, and then ran on through a pasture to the forest lots beyond. We were afraid that the old man would return to the house instead of going home, and perhaps take vengeance on me for drubbing his son.

At last, toward sunset, we made a circuit of a mile or more through the woods, and came round in sight of the farm buildings, and there we hid the valise carefully in a "double wall" bordering the fields. Theodora then went to the house to reconnoiter, promising to blow the dinner horn for me if it was safe to return.

I soon heard the horn. Calvin Dresser and his son had not come back, and Grandmother, Halstead, and Ellen were wondering what had become of Theodora and me. I was somewhat scratched and disheveled, but for the time being we kept quiet.

At the supper table, however, Theodora glanced at me, then said, "Grandmother, are you sure they didn't find Molly's valise!"

"Why, yes, child," said Grandmother. "They couldn't have found it, for it's locked up in my chest."

"Well, that boy was in your room, Grandmother," said little Wealthy. "I saw him come out."

"Hadn't you better look and make sure?" said Theodora. "They did start off kind of quick and queer," said Ellen.

Grandmother rose and went to her room. She was always very sure that no one would ever think of looking for her key in the light-stand drawer! From the dining room we heard her open the drawer and then unlock the chest. The next moment she came out in great distress.

"That valise is gone!" she gasped.

It was cruel of Theodora and me to sit quietly as we did. Theodora, indeed, was usually the most tenderhearted of girls, but such fights as we had been in that afternoon make children cruel.

Halse and Ellen, who knew nothing of our encounter, rushed to the chest to see for themselves, then came back in great excitement.

"They did get it!" cried Ellen.

"They've got it!" exclaimed Halse.

Grandmother sat down, quite weak and overcome. "Oh, what will Joseph say to me?" she moaned. "And Molly!"

"Yes, they took it," remarked Theodora, coolly. "But don't fret. We got it away from them."

"What!"

Thereupon we told the story of our pursuit and battle with Calvin Jr.

"The deceitful creatures!" exclaimed Grandmother. "To come into my house, pretending to visit us, and behave like that! Calvin Dresser is a wicked old sinner!"

"Molly said that boy was 'a sly little toad,'" remarked Ellen. "What I'm afraid of is that they will be back here in the night."

"Well, they won't find the valise," said I.

"But where is it?" Grandmother asked. And when we told her, she insisted that we should bring it to the house and replace it in the chest. "That's where your grandfather put it and that's where it is going to stay," said she, firmly.

None of us thought that this was wise, but after dark I brought the valise to the house, and restored it to the chest. Grandmother consented, however, that Theodora should take the key and hide it in her room.

Calvin and his son did not return, and the next day we resumed our much interrupted spring's work. Little Wealthy acted as sentinel. If any of the Dressers appeared she was instructed to run to the field and summon us.

Nothing occurred during that day, and at the supper table Grandmother declared that Calvin and Ethan would be ashamed to come to our house again after what had happened. And anyone would think so. About eight o'clock that evening, as we were talking in the sitting room, we heard wheels in the yard outside.

"I guess that's Grandfather and Addison!" cried Ellen. We had been looking for them for five days.

"And maybe Molly, too," said Theodora.

Halse and I went out on the piazza, the girls following us. It was a dark evening, but I could discern two teams in the yard. They had stopped, and were standing there.

"Is that you, Grandfather?" said Halse.

There was no reply, but two men got out and came to the steps, where the lamplight shone on their faces. One was a stranger; the other I knew instantly. It was the young lawyer, Mr. Dolan, who had been with the Dressers when they stopped us on the road below Skowhegan. He said, "Good evening!" very politely.

"I hope our business here will not alarm any of the womenfolk," he said. "But it is believed that the private papers of Africa Dresser are concealed in your house. We have a warrant to search for them, and shall do so, as by law authorized. I must warn you to make no resistance and put no obstacle in our way. The penalty for doing so is severe," he added impressively. "You will do much better to aid us. The best and safest thing for you will be to hand these papers over to the officer here without compelling us to search for them."

A week before so portentous a speech in the name of the law would have frightened us all into abject compliance. Grandmother, indeed, was alarmed. "My husband is not at home," she said. "I sha'n't resist the law. We are law-abiding people."

But there had been so much threatening in the name of the law during the last few days that the first terrors were wearing off for us young people. I bethought myself of what the Old Squire had said to the sheriff. "Show us your warrant," I said.

"Yes," said Halstead, "we want to see your warrant."

"You are not obliged to show the warrant to minors who do not own the house," Dolan said to the officer.

"No, we are not obliged to show them the warrant," snarled a well-known voice behind them. And then we saw that it was Ethan Dresser and his brother Erastus who had come with Dolan.

Halse and I backed into the doorway. At sight of Ethan our distrust and combativeness rose. "You can't come in till you show your warrant!" we cried, stoutly.

Dolan and the stranger hesitated, but Ethan came past them.

"Get out o' the way!" he shouted, and pushed both of us back into the room. His brother came close behind him, and Dolan and the alleged officer followed them into the sitting room.

"Give us that valise, or it will be worse for ye!" shouted Ethan, who seemed beside himself with fury. He shook his fist and looked ugly enough to do murder.

Poor Grandmother was cowed. "I sha'n't resist! I sha'n't resist the law!" she cried. "Joseph wouldn't if he was here. Theodora, bring me my key! Where are you, child?"

Part 8

BUT NEITHER Theodora nor Ellen was to be seen.

"Bring me my key! Where are you, child?" Grandmother cried again. But no answer came to her call.

At the first sound of Ethan's voice outside Theodora and Ellen had run upstairs to their room. The chest key had been entrusted to them for safekeeping. They got it, scudded down the front stairs to Grandmother's room, and unlocked the chest. They had barely done so when they had heard the scuffle as Ethan thrust us boys from the door.

Seizing the valise, they ran up the front stairs again, and then, after listening a moment, went on tiptoe through the long ell chamber, down the back stairs into the stable, and thence out to the dark garden and orchard, where they hid behind the stone wall and listened fearfully to the sounds in the house.

For Ethan was now in full voice, and Grandmother, badly frightened, was imploring Halstead and me to find Theodora and bring the key to the chest. The wily Dolan, too, was exhorting her to give up the valise at once and save trouble for us all. Halstead, who always lost his head under excitement, had run to the wood house to get an old gun, which we kept loaded for crows, to shoot Ethan. But roughly as he had pushed us, I knew better than to do such a thing as that, and withstood Halse in the kitchen, holding fast to the gun.

It appeared that Calvin Dresser, after his unsuccessful "visit" to us, had driven all the way home that night. He had told Ethan and Erastus about the valise and chest, and this raid on us under cover of the law was the result. They were bent on capturing that valise at any cost, and they would have done so but for the presence of mind and pluck of those two girls. So well had Ethan and Erastus been informed as to matters in our house that when Grandmother was unable to produce the key, they both forced their way into her room, determined to break open the chest.

They found the key in the lock and the chest open, and the cry of baffled cupidity and rage with which they rushed back into the sitting room was heard by Dora and Ellen way out in the orchard.

Ethan shook his fist at Grandmother, quite beside himself. Erastus was nearly as bad.

They went on in so outrageous a manner that Dolan and the officer—if he was one—became alarmed, and tried to stop them. Little Wealthy, who had gone to bed before the invasion, waked in great fear, and was crying upstairs. Grandmother went to quiet her and did not return.

Halstead and I stood at the sitting room door and watched the enemy. Erastus looked in Grandmother's room again. Ethan searched the parlor, then overhauled things in the dining room and kitchen. Evidently they had hoped to frighten us into giving up the valise and were now at a loss as to what to do.

Ethan took us in hand again. "Do you know what will happen to you if you don't tell where that valise is?" he exclaimed. "You'll go to jail! That's where you will go unless you tell us, and tell us right off, too!"

Halse retorted that Ethan was more likely to go to jail than we. "Where's your search warrant?" he cried. "I don't believe you've got any. The Old Squire will fix you for this."

Ethan seized Halstead by the collar and attempted to thrash him. I laid hold of Ethan's arm, and we were having a lively time when Dolan hastily separated us.

The young lawyer laughed but looked anxious; the affair was not turning out as they had planned it.

"Be careful, Dresser, be careful what you do," we heard him whisper to Ethan. "You will get us all into trouble."

"Yes," said Halse. "You had better be careful. You had Molly Totherly arrested for cuffing young Calvin. Now we will have you arrested for cuffing us." Ethan glared at him and would have cuffed him again, I think, but Dolan pulled him away. They then continued looking about the house. Halse and I sat and watched them. I felt sure that the girls had taken the valise from the chest, but we said nothing.

Dolan appeared to suspect something of the sort. He came presently and asked me where the girls were.

"Perhaps they have gone to bed," said I. "It's bedtime."

This reply appeared to disconcert him. They refrained from going upstairs, and soon after went out to look to their horses.

Halstead now went upstairs to find Grandmother, but I slipped out to watch our visitors put up their horses in the stable. They had a lantern. I stood by the garden gate and saw them feed the horses from our grain bins.

As I stood there someone came up behind me in the dark and touched my arm. I jumped in surprise. It was Theodora.

"Sh!" she whispered. "Come into the orchard. Nell and I have the valise, but what shall we do with it?"

She was all aflutter from fear and dread. I followed her out behind the orchard wall, where Nell was hiding. They were both dreadfully frightened at what they had done and at being out in the dark alone. Yet despite our fears as to the consequences, we felt exultant.

"They never shall have it!" whispered Nell, her teeth fairly chattering from cold and nervous excitement.

"But what shall we do with it!" Theodora whispered.

My first thought was to take the valise and go to our nearest neighbors, the Edwards family, and ask them to shelter us. "Perhaps they would think we ought to give it up," said Nell, and that we were now fully resolved not to do.

I had some thought of going to the house of a relative who lived six miles away. "But Grandmother would worry," Theodora objected. "Let's go over to the Aunt Hannah lot."

The Aunt Hannah lot was a farm once owned by the Old Squire's sister, and adjoined the home farm on the west side. A cart road led to it across the fields. The old house now stood empty. We set off hastily, and following the cart track, passed the sugar maple grove, and at last reached the dark old house. The door was fastened, but we knew of a window at the farther end which could be raised. I climbed in, then opened the door for the girls.

There was a stove in the kitchen and matches in a box on the mantel. We kindled a fire and warmed ourselves, and we were soon very sleepy, for by this time it must have been eleven o'clock. The old house was bare of all furniture, however, except a few broken chairs. We sat about the stove, falling asleep at intervals, till daybreak.

Cheerless enough the morning dawned. After an anxious debate, we decided to hide the valise, and then go back before anyone was astir.

Accordingly we put the valise under some shelves in the pantry, and ran for home. It was a sharp morning. There was a white frost on the dry grass of the fields. Our toes ached from the cold.

As we neared the farm buildings, Theodora and Ellen ran to the rear of the house, to enter by the back door of the kitchen. But I came round by the front side of the south barn. I peeped round the corner to see if anyone had come out. There stood Ethan Dresser in the stable door! They had remained overnight, to search the premises by daylight.

Ashamed to ask lodging of Grandmother, all four had spent the night in the stable on the hay. Ethan was out early; perhaps he had not slept well. He looked very sour as he stood there, but he saw me the instant I peeped round.

I drew back hastily, but had taken hardly three steps when Ethan dashed round the corner. "Young man," he cried, "where'd you come from so early? Where've you been?"

"That's my business," said I.

"You're not out so early for nothing!" he exclaimed. "You're up to some mischief!"

He made a sudden rush and cornered me between the barn and an oxcart which stood close to it. He got a hard grip on my arm. "Now you tell me where you and the girls have been," said he.

I would not say a word.

He shook me. "I'll have it out of ye!" he cried.

With that I shouted, "Help!" three or four times. I thought that Halse might be coming out. Ethan kept shaking me. "Stop your noise! Shut up, or I'll wring your neck!" But I shouted for help again, and immediately Dolan appeared, and after him Erastus Dresser.

"Don't hurt him, Dresser!" cried Dolan, but Ethan was in a rage.

"He's got to tell! I'll have it out of the tike! The papers were hid last night. This boy knows where, and he's got to tell!" And Ethan gave me such a grip that I yelled again at the top of my lungs. A moment later Theodora and Nell came running from the house, but stopped short at the corner of the barn, then turned and ran back to call Halstead.

"Tell us where that valise of papers is!" Ethan kept saying, gripping me harder and harder. "You know and you've got to tell."

"Is it in this barn?" said Erastus.

"No, it isn't!" I yelled; for Ethan hurt me so badly I must needs cry out.

"Is it under it?" queried Dolan.

"Look and see!" I exclaimed.

Thereupon they walked me with them round to the farther end of the barn, where a wide basement door opened into the barn cellar. But here Dolan's quick eyes caught sight of our tracks in the white frost, where we had come across the field.

"They've been away somewhere, and have just come home," said he. "They've been off to some of their neighbors."

"Where've you been?" snarled Ethan, savagely, shaking me. "Them your tracks?"

"That's for you to find out!" said I, but I got an awful grip for it.

"Where they've come from we can follow back," said Dolan. "And we must make haste before the sun gets up."

They set off across the field on our tracks in the frosty grass. Ethan marched me along with them; his hard old hand felt like a vise. When we came to the gate that led from the field to the cart road the tracks were less distinct, and I led them to the sap shed among the maples, where we made maple sugar in the spring. Here they searched for some time among the sap buckets and kettles.

But Dolan, who was very keen, soon suspected my ruse. Going hastily back to the road, he found our tracks again. A little farther on we came in sight of the house at the Aunt Hannah lot.

"That's where the tracks lead!" Erastus exclaimed, and they marched me along till we reached the house door.

Dolan glanced at my crestfallen face and laughed.

"It's here," said he. "An unoccupied house, too. Good! We can search it without a warrant."

They pushed and thumped at the door, which I had propped when we left it a few minutes before. At last they forced it open and drew me inside with them. I had now no doubt that they would get the valise. When they entered the old pantry I expected to hear Ethan's shout of triumph. In truth, I was astonished that they did not find it.

The fact was that nimbler feet than ours had reached the old house ahead of us. When Ellen and Theodora saw them following on our tracks across the field, they ran out through the orchard, and keeping in the hollow of the south field, came round through the wood lot to the Aunt Hannah house.

Ellen crept in at the window and brought out the valise, and when Dolan, Ethan, and Erastus arrived—leading me captive—those two girls were lying up in a little thicket of pines on the border of the wood lot, below the old house, watching what went on. They had the valise, and, at first sign of discovery or pursuit, were ready to flee into the depths of the forest.

While Dolan and Erastus were searching the rooms on the ground floor, Ethan stood holding me, but he grew impatient, and at last thrust me into a rear bedroom and shut the door. Once clear of his hard hands, I lost no time in prying up the window, then ran for home.

Grandmother and Halstead had been wholly at a loss to account for our absence, nor could I give them any certain tidings of Theodora and Ellen.

In the course of an hour Ethan and Erastus and Dolan came back from the Aunt Hannah lot, looking very glum. The stranger had remained with their horses at the stable. We did not offer them breakfast, nor did they ask it, but harnessed and drove to the tavern at the Corners. By nine o'clock they returned and began to search the premises again.

"You will have your labor for your pains," Halse said to them. "That valise is far enough away!"

They continued searching, however, till past noon, then drove to the houses of three of our neighbors, where they asked questions and told odious stories concerning us. Again they returned, but after questioning and threatening poor Grandmother awhile to no purpose, they finally left about two o'clock.

From a covert in the south pasture Ellen and Theodora had seen them drive away. But fearing lest they might come back, the girls did not venture to show themselves at the house, although they had eaten nothing but checkerberries all day. But our troubles were over. About four o'clock the Old Squire and Addison—so long expected—drove up the lane. Molly was with them, and old Beave behind. Theodora and Ellen had seen them, and came running to the house.

The Old Squire, Molly, and Addison were in high spirits. The charge against Molly had been dismissed by the municipal judge at Waterville as trivial.

On proceeding to Bangor, Addison had found the two witnesses to Uncle Dresser's irregular will, and had induced them to return with him to Augusta.

Meanwhile the Old Squire and Molly journeyed to Portland by railway to take legal advice, and so well did the young attorney manage the case that two days later the will was admitted to probate at Augusta and the Old Squire appointed Molly's guardian.

But when the Old Squire learned of the outrage to which we had been subjected he was tremendously indignant.

"They shall suffer for this!" he exclaimed. "I will know whether they had a warrant to search my house or not!"

Indeed, he was much inclined to set off in pursuit of Dolan and the Dressers that very night. Grandmother, however, begged him to let it pass.

"Don't stir it up anymore," she urged. "It's such a disgrace! And we are all so mixed up in it."

"But an outrage like this ought not to be passed over," the Old Squire remonstrated. "It's wrong to submit to it."

However, after pondering the affair overnight, he concluded to let the matter drop, and the next day we resumed our interrupted spring's work.

Neither Ethan nor his brothers made any further move against Molly's rights, and as her guardian, the Old Squire looked to it that they paid their notes in full, with interest.

Molly remained with us during the summer, then went to attend the fall term of the academy at Hebron, Maine. She was there for three years, and kept old Beave with her as long as he lived.

At the age of twenty-one she married, under somewhat romantic circumstances, the captain of a steam whaler, and for many years she accompanied her husband on his annual voyages from San Francisco to the Arctic.

8

The Doctor and the "Black Squirrel"

WHEN LITTLE COUSIN WEALTHY CAME DOWN WITH diphtheria in the summer of 1865, a young visiting physician was called but could not save her. He was the famous Dr. Horton, whose well-known "syrup" now invigorates all lands.

To be sure, the world had not then recognized him as a great genius. When I go out past that little heap of smoky stones, across the road in the pasture, I am amazed to think what a part they have borne in the sanitary welfare of the globe!

And memory goes back to a night in June, hoeing time with us then as now. The day's work was done; twilight and dusk were falling. A half dozen of us, boy neighbors, were lying under the great balm-of-Gilead tree, planning for the Fourth of July and talking over one thing and another, when from out of the shadow of the butternut trees, which skirted the road, there emerged a stranger; a tallish man in plaid trousers and double-breasted waistcoat, sauntering leisurely along, swinging his cane, and looking this way and that. On the grass in the shadow we were silently eying him, when suddenly spying us out, he stopped, looked a moment, then glancing around caught up half an old sled stake lying by the path, and, with a "Hullo there, you young cubs!" sent it whirling high in the air, with an aim which, in a second more, would have landed it in the midst of us. We jumped up and sprang away to avoid this salutatory missile.

"Come out here, every one of you." The act, though rather violent, was evidently sportive; we all edged out toward him. "Here, you boy with the sheepskin face!" seizing me by the collar. "How is your mother?"

I hastily explained that, because of our fathers' deaths, my cousins and I were at that time residing with my grandparents.

"Just so. How's your grandmother, then?" I gave him to understand that Gram was in a fully average state of health. "Glad to hear it. I've come to make you all a visit. Run in and ask her if I can stay a few days; then go to the village for my carpetbag."

But young Molly Totherly, whom we had recently rescued from evil relatives, had moved in with us, and taken possession of the spare room with all her bags and bundles, and Grandmother couldn't accommodate him.

"Guess we can keep you, over to our house," said Tom Edwards, when this was announced.

"Come on then—" taking Tom by the collar, and marching off with him.

"Isn't he a queer stick!" was the general exclamation. And the whole neighborhood was soon of the same opinion.

He was a young doctor from the city, Mrs. Edwards reported the next day, and he wanted to stay a week or two if she would keep him— he was "rusticating"; though just what sort of a process that might be wasn't so clear to the dear old ladies.

In the course of a week the doctor had made a general acquaintance with all the boys about; was a boy with us in his way. Wherever he went a troop followed. And he amused himself by playing off all sorts of rough tricks on us, from throwing our thumbs out of joint, and instantly setting them with a most excruciating snap, which he actually did, to "turning us wrong side out," which he didn't actually do, but made us implicitly believe he could on occasion.

Week after week went by. Why the doctor, such a great man as he evidently was, should be spending the whole "season" up there "doing nothing," was a mystery to all the old farmers—one they never solved. Since then, however, I've formed a theory relative to the object of that visit.

The doctor had avowed himself an amateur botanist. Every few days he would make an excursion down into Quog-hoggar, the cedar swamp and bring up great bundles of one and another kind of weeds growing there. But he didn't attempt to classify, arrange, or press them—not at all. On the contrary he used to borrow Mrs. Edwards's brass kettle, cram them into it, and then boil them down. We boys helped him build a stone arch (still to be seen out in the pasture) to set the kettle in; for after the first mess, Mrs. Edwards wouldn't have it in the house; for of all the nauseous stews—but never mind!

What mortal use he put, or meant to put, the liquor to, was for some time a problem with us. But one morning Tom and I caught him turning a dose of it down "Old Vete" (the dog) with a junk bottle. After that we were in the secret, and were privately instructed to lure in all "stray" dogs. The *modus operandi* was to entice them into the pig house, give them a dose (there was a good deal of growling about swallowing it) and detain them overnight to observe the effect. Patients soon began to get scarce. We seriously sickened several dogs, even killing one outright, for which we were much ashamed, burying him clandestinely among the pigweeds behind the sty. Generally, though, they would *scoot* out the moment a crack in the door was opened in the morning, and it's needless to say we never got the same dog into our infirmary twice. Whenever any of the doctored dogs had business past the place, they would put their tails between their legs and go by like a dart.

Well, not more than a year after, the doctor's name began to appear in all the newspapers, in connection with "The Greatest Discovery of the Age." "A common Weed growing wild in Our Pastures had been Discovered to possess Properties that would Cure," etc., etc. I have no need to expatiate. The world knows all about it. The doctor is now a man of immense wealth. Last week I saw his income stated at one hundred thousand dollars per annum. So Addison's theory is, that a vision of patent medicine was in the doctor's head during that summer he spent with us. And, seeing he's made so good a thing out of it, we all thought he ought to "pony over" something handsome for the use of the brass kettle and to compensate the owner of the dog he killed getting it up.

But botany didn't occupy all his time. Another specialty of his was squirrels; he delighted in their active motions and knowing ways. Out in the old butternut tree, hanging from the lower branches, he had no less than half a dozen cages—wooden ones hastily made—containing a noisy assortment of them. All day long they chickered and chirred, the doctor often lying at full stretch on the grass beneath watching them; now and then cracking a big "oilnut" to toss up through the gratings. One cage of "grays," large as cats almost, were his especial pride; he took them with him when he returned to the city. "And if I could only get a black one," he used to say, "my squirrel garden would be complete, and I should be perfectly happy."

When the township was first settled, there used to be black squirrels here. The old folks speak of them, and describe them as larger than the grays and black as jet. But there are none now; at least, there hasn't been one seen about here for twenty years. But nothing would convince the hardheaded doctor; he knew there must be black squirrels about. He had with him a great volume of natural history, and proceeded to show from it that black squirrels were still quite abundant in the Maine forests. And one day, coming in from one of his weed expeditions to the swamp, he declared he had seen one.

We all knew better; it might have been a black mink, or a skunk, like enough. He owned to having merely got a glimpse of it, but *knew* it was a black squirrel, and forthwith carried down all his traps to set for it—I need hardly add without success.

At the end of his first fortnight with us, a phenomenon on the doctor's countenance began to attract our attention. His mustache, which had been jet black when he came, was fading into a sickly yellow. The change seemed to be radical too; that is, it began at the roots and worked out to the very tips. At first we had feared for his health. Even a doctor might die! But he continued hearty and frolicsome. At length, just as conjecture grew weary, Tom whispered his suspicions to me, that the mustache had been colored with some kind of dye, and was now just outgrowing it.

The summer went by, and the since prosperous doctor went away forever. We missed him. In spite of all the outrageous tricks he used to play off on us we had rather liked him. He was one of those peculiar men who will nearly kill a fellow by way of sport, without raising any permanent resentment.

"Kind of sorry the doctor has gone," said Tom, a few days after his departure, as we strolled past the stone arch, where the old kettle had boiled out the problem of the future panacea. "How he used to knock us about, though! Pretended to be only holding my hand, and threw my thumb out of joint, on purpose—Moses! How that hurt! I meant to pay him for that, but he got off before I saw a chance. Suppose he really did see a black squirrel down in the swamp?"

"No indeed!" said I.

"Tell you what!" exclaimed Addison, suddenly. "We might have *sold* him on that!"

"How?" said Tom.

"Why, get up a big black squirrel for him."

"How could we make a black squirrel?"

"Oh! Take a big gray one and *black* him!" said Addison.

"What with, for pity's sake?" I interjected.

"Well—with *hair dye!*" cried Addison. This idea struck us so funnily that we had to roll on the grass and laugh over it.

"And we might do it now!" shouted Tom, jumping up; "and send it to him!"

"Agreed!" we cried.

That afternoon we set all our old box traps, and soon captured plenty of squirrels; though it was several days before we got one large enough to suit our notion. Meanwhile Addison had gone down to the village, some miles below, and procured from the barber a bottle of hair dye. The next thing was to *dye* the squirrel. A difficult job too! For he was an *old settler*, and resented all handling with savage bites. But we found a couple of pairs of old leather gloves, and then took him, trap and all, up into the garret, to prevent an escape in case he should break loose during the operation. Drawing on the gloves, Tom and I undertook to hold him, while Addison scrubbed in the dye with an old hairbrush, in spite of a most vigorous squirming. To prevent the fur from becoming matted and streaky we held him up in the sun and brushed till he was dry.

At the end of an hour we had a black(ed) squirrel; also some blackened hands which defied all soap and water. A cage-box, to send him on in, was now needful. We made one about two feet square, with strong ashen bars on one side, and putting in the squirrel, with a quantity of oilnuts, directed it to the doctor, from "his young friends in Maine." Down at the village, we put on a "Please give this young gentleman a safe passage," and placed it in the hands of the expressman.

"All we've got to do now," said Addison, as we rode homeward, "is to let the thing work itself out."

In a few days came a joyful letter from the doctor, starting off with, "My Dear Boys"—thanking us over and over again for the "B.S."; dilating on the joy he felt in showing him to all his friends who had never before seen one, and winding up with a reminder that he had told us there were black squirrels about there.

"All right, doctor!" cried Addison, rubbing his blackened hands together as I read the above. "We'll wait a bit."

Three weeks passed. "Should think his hair would begin to grow out by this time; doctor's mustache did," remarked Tom one evening. But another week passed, and another, when one night came a second letter, directed in a destructive-looking hand and launching out with—

YOU LITTLE SCAMPS: You don't know what a scrape you've got me into. More than a thousand people have called to see that squirrel, and now he's coming out a "pepper-and-salt" all over. My office boy says it's nothing but a gray squirrel colored, and I believe him. What the (unmentionable) did you daub on to him?

Next day we sent the following—

DEAR DOC.: Nothing in the world but hair dye; same thing you put on your mustache. Better put some more on him. Keep him black. Best and *only thing* you can do now. Perhaps some of that "fire-weed" juice would answer. We'll get you up another if you say so. Remember putting our thumbs out, Doc.?

Yours,
Tom, Addison, and Nicholas

The doctor didn't resume the correspondence, and we never knew how he came out with his "black squirrel."

9

At the Hay Meadows

DURING THE FIRST FEW YEARS AT THE OLD FARM WE had each laid by a little fund of our spare cash at the village savings bank. The Old Squire constantly encouraged us to do so. "Have something in your own names," he used to say. "It gives one self-respect. It will make you better citizens."

By July 1865, Addison had, I remember, forty-seven dollars in the bank, Theodora eighteen, and Ellen sixteen, but I had been able to accumulate only eleven.

Shortly thereafter, the Old Squire announced at the breakfast table—with some approach to solemnity—that if we five grandchildren really desired to get a liberal education, first at the village academy and afterward at college, we would have to start saving for it; he would oppose no objection, and would aid us as much as he could, and that as a beginning this fall we might keep, for educational expenses, all the monies we earned from haying at the Boundary Camp meadows.

His offer was exceedingly generous. The Boundary Camp meadows lay far up in the Great Woods. And during the winter, that hay would bring a good price at several logging camps only a few miles away.

"But to get a liberal education will prove a long, hard struggle for you," the old gentleman continued gravely. "It will take you seven or eight years. You will have to nerve yourselves for it. You must expect to encounter many privations and setbacks."

I suppose he deemed it best to throw us on our own resources at an early age to find out if we desired an education enough to really work for it. And listening to his words with equal seriousness, we had resolved to succeed in this first great adventure of our lives.

So on a morning in August 1865, we all set off in a boat up Lurvey's Stream, with a full haying outfit of scythes, rakes, forks, and a grindstone, to go to the Boundary Camp hay meadows.

Lurvey's Stream is a small and, in this portion of its course, not a rapid river. We had to pole our boat seventeen miles, and in consequence did not reach the scene of our coming labors till afternoon.

It was the first time I had ever seen the place, although Addison and Halstead had been there the year before.

In truth, these meadows were then a veritable wild paradise; yet there was that in the dark aspect of the pointed firs and the enclosing mountains which filled me with awe. It was all much as nature made it, a tract of natural grassland, extending for six or seven miles along the stream, sometimes in plats of several acres together in the broad crooks and bends of the river, or notched irregularly back into the fir woods on both sides. There were scores of these curiously linked little openings, half-isolated one from another by rings and belts of chokecherry, mountain ash, moose maple, willow, and alder.

Through it all wound the stream, its course marked by a few water maples and elms, where herons built their nests, and a profusion of high-bush cranberry.

On the north and west rose the dark-wooded boundary mountains. In some of the wetter places grew rank green clumps of Indian poke round sloughs where stood numerous muskrat houses, but most of the meadow was firm land which could be "hayed" over with scythe and rake. One season fifteen years before the Old Squire had obtained hay enough here to supply the ox teams at four logging camps on the stream below. At that time, too, efforts were made to seed these bottoms with "foul meadow," bluejoint, and even redtop, with some degree of success.

On the west bank of the stream, near the falls at the head of the meadows, where the spruce woods began, stood the Boundary lumber camp, consisting of two quaint structures, the "man camp" and the "ox camp," built of logs and roofed with riven splits. The man camp was our home during this haying venture. It was forty feet long by eighteen in width, and contained not only bunks, but a large old stove, very useful for cooking.

That afternoon Theodora and Ellen had us divide the camp midway its length into two rooms, by putting up a partition made of the splits from the roof of the ox camp. This done, they began their housekeeping labors (for which they shared in the profits). In fair weather we took our meals at a table, made also of splits, just outside the camp door, in the shadow of a large gnarly yellow birch which grew by a rock on the very bank of the stream a few rods below the falls.

We had brown doughnuts and cheese, pies, great pots of baked beans, and brown bread, and in the morning popovers, Jersey butter, crisp bacon, and delicious coffee, to say nothing of broad, thin "wheels" of "salt-rising" bread and great round yellow pones of johnnycake.

Close by the birch, a little nearer the water, we set up our grindstone and a few hundred yards lower down on the meadow, where bluejoint grew to the mower's waist, our first haymaking operations began and our first stacks were built.

It is almost needless to say that we soon became aware that haymaking at the meadows was hard work, far harder than on a well-equipped farm. For we not only had the thick, heavy grass to mow, spread, and rake, but we had to carry all the hay together on hay poles.

Building the stack, too, was no light task. A large pole, twenty feet in length, had first to be cut in the woods, brought to the spot, and set firmly in the ground. A circular "bed" had then to be constructed round the base of the pole to keep the hay up from the damp ground. These beds were formed by setting crotched stakes two feet high in the earth, and laying cross poles and fir boughs on them.

Much depends on the way the hay is "laid," however. Beginning at the bottom, it must be piled slanting outward, in order that the "weather" may not get into it. Our rule was to lay each stack twelve feet in diameter on the bed, and gradually increase this diameter to fourteen feet at a height of about eight feet from the ground, then gradually thaw it inwardly to the apex, where it was "bound in" to the pole with a withe, and a "weather cape" of rushes or fir boughs tied on to keep water from running in at the top. After it was laid and bound in, each stack was

"dressed," or raked down, so as to make the sides shed water. Such is a properly constructed "bottle" stack. Addison had learned the art of stacking—for it is an art—under the Old Squire's own eye the year before.

In truth, the work proved unexpectedly hard. Grandfather probably looked for us back at the farm in a couple of days, although we had taken food for a week.

During the first three forenoons Addison and Halstead mowed, while I spread out the swaths to dry with a fork. In the afternoon we raked up the hay and stacked it.

Two, and sometimes three, tons of hay were put in a stack, and we placed the stacks with a view to carrying the hay as short a distance as possible. For carrying the hay was very toilsome. First, two long hay poles were laid parallel on the ground, two feet apart, and about two hundred pounds of hay loaded on them. One boy then went in front of the load, another behind, standing each between the two ends of the poles.

"Now!" said the boy in front, and both ends of the pole were raised at once. Then began the march to the stack. One can get very tired carrying three tons of hay that way.

The weather favored us that week; it was fair and not uncomfortably hot. But Halstead complained bitterly of the hard work, and I have doubts as to the result if Addison had not hired three French boys whom we espied one afternoon fishing in the stream. They had come down through the woods from Megantic, just over the boundary.

These boys were wild-looking fellows, who wore fur caps. They could not speak English, and were very bashful with the girls at the camp, but they knew how to "hay," and by means of signs Addison struck a bargain with them to help us at a dollar a day and board. I must say of those French boys that they were the best boys to work whom I have ever seen—on either side of the boundary. We kept them mowing steadily, and we did the stacking.

On Friday afternoon Addison went home in the *bateau* to get more food and money to pay our new help. For those French youngsters ate as resolutely as they worked.

So strong was Addison's faith in this haying venture that he had determined to close out his savings to pay for help, and he also induced Theodora, Ellen, and myself to write and sign orders on bits of paper, that allowed him to do likewise for us.

After this we went on haying for twenty-three days, till September 4, and put up twenty-six stacks of hay, which we estimated at sixty tons. So far from exhausting the grass on the Boundary Camp meadows, I may say without exaggeration that we might have put up three times as much.

But our money for hiring help was exhausted, and the time for the county fair was approaching.

This was always an event of interest at the old farm, which usually contributed exhibits of cattle, fruit, and many other products. Four days, at least, had usually to be devoted to the fair.

We therefore finished our haying and returned home, leaving the stacks to stand in the meadows until winter, when the hay could be drawn to the lumber camps. There would be, Addison estimated, nearly eleven hundred dollars' worth—to gain which we had invested ninety-two dollars, in addition to our labor and food supplies from home, which, however, the Old Squire never charged up against us. It looked like a fine stroke of business, with profits sufficient to pay expenses for a term at the academy, with a surplus.

But danger impended—danger which we had not anticipated. Our stacks were soon in peril.

August had been unusually dry that year, and the first half of September proved drier still. During fair week the sky grew very smoky; there were forest fires up in the Great Woods, and we noticed that the Old Squire cast uneasy looks in that direction. He was thinking of his logging camps.

On the day following the fair the old gentleman was at the fairgrounds on prize committee business, and he had Ellen and myself go with him to help pack up our fruit and dairy exhibits. Thomas Edwards and Catherine were also there. But Addison and Halstead remained at home, working hard to finish digging a field of potatoes, that we had not gotten to because of our haying. Theodora was also at home, assisting Grandmother.

At about three o'clock that afternoon the boys, as they plied their hoes, saw a rheumatic old trapper and hunter named Hughy Glinds, who lived up in the borders of the Great Woods, hobbling across the fields toward them.

"What do you suppose Old Hughy wants of us?" said Halstead.

They were not left long in doubt.

"Thar's a big fire ragin' up in the woods!" he hailed. "It's workin' down onto them hay medders. You're goin' to lose them stacks o' yourn, sure's you're born!"

They dropped their hoes. "We must go right up there!" exclaimed Addison.

"Wal, ye can't go too quick!" cried Old Hughy. "And you'd better take a scythe and ax along," he added, "and a couple of buckets and a hoe and shovel. Ef I wa'n't so pesky lame. I'd go with ye."

The boys left everything, ran to the house, got tools, and hitched old Sol into the buckboard; for the water was now too low in the stream to go in the *bateau*, and they had to take the winter trail by way of the Old Slave's Farm. Addison ran into the house to get food to carry, and to tell Theodora where and why they were going. Somewhat to his annoyance, at first, Theodora wanted to go with them.

"Oh, no, Doad, you had better not," he said.

"I'm sure I can help!" she cried. "I can put on that glazed cap of yours and my old rubber waterproof." Indeed, she insisted on going, and came out all ready as the boys drove through the yard. So all three set off together and put Sol at his best pace.

The winter trail was far from being a smooth road, however, and Sol was by no means speedy. It was long past six when they reached the camp at the head of the meadows. The early September dusk was falling, but to their great relief, no fire was in sight, and there appeared to be no immediate danger. Yet the wind blew in fitful gusts from the west, and a vast amount of smoke that smelled strongly of burning spruce and pine was drifting low over the meadows. As it grew dark, too, the sky over the forest, all round to the westward, was lighted by an ominous red glare.

This and the great amount of smoke rendered them very uneasy. There was not much that could be done in the night, however. Theodora got supper at the camp, and they watched till as late as ten or eleven o'clock. Then, as no fire was very near, Addison urged Theodora to catch a nap. "I will call you if there is any need of it," he said to her.

She accordingly retired to the little apartment which Ellen and she had contrived for themselves while we were haying. The two boys appear also to have fallen asleep not long after in the bunk of the living room and slept soundly.

Addison was the first to wake and go out. It was already light. A sense of danger oppressed him, for he had become aware of a far-borne, roaring sound, with which blended low, distant crashes, as of falling trees. The smoke was much thicker than on the evening before. It made his eyes smart. Vast white columns of it were rolling skyward over the woods. Flakes of white ashes were fluttering down. Across the stream he saw two otters loping along the bank, and heard robins crying in a disturbed manner.

"Halse!" he cried, running back indoors. "The fire is close on us! Get up and help wet down the stacks!"

Halstead started up from sleep with an odd cry. He seemed dazed, and stared wildly about him; then dashing out, he crossed the stream and ran into the open meadow to look round. After a single glance he came rushing back. Addison noticed that he was pale.

"We never can fight it alone!" he cried. "The woods are all afire! I'm going for help!"

"No, no!" said Addison. "You must stay right here and help me wet down the stacks!"

But Halstead was quite wild, either from sudden fear for himself or some erratic notion of what he ought to do. Before Addison could remonstrate with him he ran to the ox camp, untied old Sol, and jumped on his back. Addison rushed after him, shouting, "Stop! Come back, Halse, and help me wet down the stacks!" Theodora, too, who had now emerged from the camp, called to him several times.

"We need a big crew!" was all the reply chasing him, for he had put Sol at a gallop down the trail and was soon out of sight.

With another wrathful glance after him, Addison, in turn, ran out into the open meadow to see for himself the progress of the fire. Theodora, equally astonished and bewildered by Halstead's unexpected behavior, came hastening after. At a distance of less than half a mile the entire forest, all round to the west and northwest of the meadows, was on fire. Magnificent in the still faint dawnlight, ruddy pillars of flame were climbing to the very tops of the firs. Immense writhing columns of yellowish and white vapor rolled upward into the sky.

For the moment awe fell on them both, awe and the instinct to escape.

With Addison, however, it was the instinct of an instant only. Thoughts of our haystacks and a determination to save them roused his courage. "If only Halse had taken the buckboard and you with him, Doad, I wouldn't have cared!" he exclaimed.

"But I wouldn't have gone!" cried Theodora, indignantly. "I will help you, Ad. I would stay and help if I burned up!"

"Come on, then!" shouted Addison.

Together they sped back to the camp, where the tools were still on the buckboard. First Addison hung the scythe in the snath, then got the buckets.

"Fetch the rake and hoe, Doad!" he exclaimed, and ran down the meadow on the west side of the stream, to where the nearest of the stacks stood. While he mowed swaths round them, Theodora hastily raked the dry grass away, clearing a little space round each one, so that the fire, when it came to run in the grass, might not so readily reach them.

Addison was strong and quick; he worked fast; within fifteen minutes they had cleared the grass from round the base of the eleven stacks to the west of the stream. Addison then caught up the hoe and dug a little ditch across the westward side of each in the soft black loam.

But already the firs all along the border of the meadow on that side were ablaze, with a tremendous crackling and roar. Fortunately, the wind blew but fitfully as yet. The chief danger was from blazing cinders and sparks whirled upward with the smoke.

The rush "cape" on top of one stack suddenly began to blaze, but seizing a bucket, Addison dashed water over it from the stream. Theodora brought another bucketful. They put the blaze out, then wet down all eleven of the stacks, running to and from the stream, bringing more than fifty bucketfuls within ten minutes—all this in a rain of ashes, amidst smoke so thick that they panted as they worked. The roar of the conflagration, too, nearly drowned their voices.

For a few minutes it looked as if they might succeed, but glancing across the stream, Addison saw, to his consternation, that one of the stacks on the east side was blazing; also that sparks had set the dry grass over there on fire in several places.

"Doad, it's getting the start of us!" he cried. "Come on, quick!"

He splashed through the stream, dipping up a bucketful, and then ran to the stack and put out the blaze. Theodora followed him, filling her own bucket, and they wet the stack down. But even as they did so another stack began to smoke—and there were fifteen stacks on that side!

Then began a desperate struggle against what seemed hopeless odds. There was now no time to mow round all these stacks or dig trenches. With a few hasty slashes of his knife, Addison cut bunches of green alder bushes by the stream.

"Take these, Doad, and whip out the little fires in the grass as fast as they catch!" he exclaimed. "Keep them from running to the stacks."

This for a time she succeeded in doing, darting this way and that, up and down the meadow. Addison, meanwhile, had snatched up the buckets again, and filling them, rushed to the burning stack, the whole top of which was now afire. He quenched it, however, partly with water, partly by whipping out the blaze.

But by this time still another at a distance was smoking. They had to run fast to save that one; there was no rest even to take breath. Fires in the grass were starting on all sides. Flying sparks scorched their faces and burned dozens of little holes in their clothes. Time and again they had to throw water on each other.

It was little wonder, indeed, that such frantic exertion proved too much for Theodora. While running with her bucket of water, she was suddenly overcome, either by the smoke or heat. Turning to take the bucket from her, Addison saw that she had sat down in the grass, very pale, panting for breath.

Self-reproach smote him. "Doad!" he exclaimed, helping her to her feet. "Go up on this side of the stream to the falls and sit down there beside that big rock by the water. The fire will not get to you there, for there's sand and gravel all round. Sit there till you are rested. Don't come down here again!"

"But, Ad, I want to help!" she still urged.

"Go!" he exclaimed. "Don't bother!" And very reluctantly Theodora left him there.

While this was happening two more stacks had taken fire, and one of them burned in spite of all Addison could do with bucket and bushes.

While rushing with his buckets to a bend of the stream, he saw the alders on the other side part, and a large bear that the fire had driven from the woods plumped into the water up to its neck, and stood there, wheezing for breath. Addison did not stop for bears, however; he got more than fifty bucketfuls from the same pool where the animal stood. Deer, too, were bounding across the meadow, and a cow moose and calf went galloping by.

His clothes repeatedly took fire as he whipped the blazing grass, and to keep from blazing himself he jumped into the water time and again, then, all dripping, sprang out and rushed to the fight again. He simply would not give up, but fought on with grim determination, regardless of the outlook or of the passage of time.

He had now wet down all the stacks on the east side of the stream, but by this time one of those already wet on the west side was afire! Then began the worst, most disheartening part of the struggle; for by this time the dry grass was afire all over the meadows, as well as the fir woods on both sides. The smoke and heat were well nigh unbearable. It was only by plunging into the stream repeatedly that he was able to endure it and go on.

Addison had succeeded in putting out the burning stack on the west side, and once more drenched the entire eleven over there. But the heat and smoke rapidly dried them; he found that he must keep wetting them, going from one to another as fast as he could run. Before he was aware—there were so many of them partly hidden from view by trees and bushes—another down the stream on the east side was ablaze past quenching. After this he ran from one to another of the stacks, dashing water on them, six or eight bucketfuls apiece, and kept them all dripping wet.

Toward noon the conflagration seemed to abate a little, and hopes of winning encouraged Addison. The sky had darkened. Through the smoke, clouds could be seen gathering, but immediately gusts of wind, from a shower passing a mile to the northward, sent sparks and flame eddying across the meadows again, and before he could run with water and his alder brush three stacks were afire, one of which burned despite his efforts.

Wind eddies now seemed to come first from one quarter, then from another, and for two hours Addison was constantly running up and down, quenching new outbursts of the fire. Then came a smart shower, which rendered the danger less imminent, and gave him a moment's respite.

All the time anxiety concerning Theodora disturbed him. When the shower began, he started to find her, but to his great relief he met her bringing a pot of coffee in one hand and a pie in the other. Nor had she been all this time making coffee. Theodora, indeed, had been fighting fire on her own account, and almost as successfully as Addison himself.

After resting by the great rock in the cool of the falls for a few minutes, she had felt much better, and had started to go back down the meadows, but the fire was now burning all round the little clearing in which the Boundary Camp stood.

Suddenly she perceived that the roof of the ox camp was smoking. In fact, it was ablaze before she could do anything to put it out, for at first she could find nothing with which to carry or throw water. At last she snatched a kettle off the camp stove, and used it as a bucket.

The ox camp burned in spite of Theodora's best efforts, however, and the blazing cinders from it and the burning woods would certainly have set the roof of the man camp on fire if she had not thrown water smartly for an hour or more, wetting both roof and walls repeatedly.

While Addison was saving the stacks, Theodora saved the camp, with all we had in it. And that old camp was yet to be the scene of several remarkable adventures.

Meanwhile, down at the farm that morning, we had been uncertain what to do, not knowing the extent of the fire, and deeming it possible that Addison and Halstead together might be able to look out for the hay. We had got home from the fair, with our stock and other exhibits, late the evening before, and were not astir very early. In fact, we were at the breakfast table, between eight and nine, when Halstead, the panic-stricken, came home, running old Sol and looking very wild indeed.

On the way down, his imagination appeared to have run away with him completely. His first words to us as we rushed out were, "The Boundary Camp meadows are all afire! The stacks are all burnt up!"

"But where are Addison and Theodora?" the Old Squire exclaimed. "Why did you leave them?"

"I came for help!" cried Halstead, in a strange, high-pitched voice. "It needs a big crew! We must raise a crew and go back!" He was nearly in tears.

"Did you leave Addison and Theodora in the camp?" the Old Squire questioned him.

"Yes!" cried Halstead, vaguely. "But it is all burnt up before this time! The fire was close by! 'Twas the awfullest sight I ever saw!"

This, of course, was very alarming—if true. The Old Squire called in our two hired men from the field, and sent me off in haste to summon Mr. Edwards and his son Thomas, and as soon as they came, two of the farm horses were hitched into a double-seated market wagon and we set off up the trail.

Halstead was so excited and upset that the Old Squire told him he need not go back.

The day proved very hot for September, and all the way up through the Great Woods the air was so full of smoke that our eyes smarted from it. Driving as fast as possible, however, we were unable to reach the meadows till after four o'clock—in the midst of that shower.

It was a strange sight. Stumps, logs, and fallen trees were still burning on all sides, and the entire stretch of meadowland, where the fire had consumed the dry grass, was now smoking and steaming in the rain.

The horses kept snorting, and they were very loath to go past the worst of the fires, but we urged them on. In truth, we were in great anxiety. It was plain that a mighty conflagration had been raging there. And what had become of Addison and Theodora?

At last we came in sight of the camp, and to our great relief perceived that it was still standing, unconsumed. What we saw there as we drove up was Addison, sitting on the "deacons' seat" near the door, eating a crust of pie, and Theodora just emerging from the door with a dishful of hot oatmeal porridge!

But at first glance we hardly knew either of them, they were so muddy, singed, and blackened, Addison in particular. His clothing was sodden, caked with dry mud and burned full of holes, as was his hat. His eyes were red ringed, his hands blistered, his boots burned and crumpled yellow. In truth, he was the worst looking boy I ever saw!

But he grinned through his grime when he saw us drive up. For the fight was won—a wonderful fight, too, for a boy, fifteen. He had saved five hundred dollars' worth of hay.

The Old Squire got out, and going down the meadows among the stacks, ran an experienced eye over the mute evidences of the struggle that had gone on there, then came back to camp.

"Addison," said he, "you're a man, every inch a man!" and gave him a hearty handshake.

We never said much about this to Halstead afterward. Not every boy inherits a good head for emergencies. But it must have bothered him. When Addison, Theodora, Ellen, and I left for the academy two years later, he stayed home and spent his money on a horse instead.

10

Bear Tone

ONE DAY ABOUT THE FIRST OF FEBRUARY, CATHERINE Edwards made the rounds of the neighborhood with a subscription paper to get singers for a singing school. A veteran "singing master"—Seth Clark, well known throughout the country—had offered to give the young people of the place a course of twelve evening lessons or sessions in vocal music, at four dollars per evening, and Catherine was endeavoring to raise the sum of forty-eight dollars for this purpose.

Master Clark was to meet us at the district schoolhouse for song sessions of two hours, twice a week, on Tuesday and Friday evenings at seven o'clock. Among us at the Old Squire's we signed eight dollars.

The singing school did not much interest me personally, for the reason that I did not expect to attend. As the Frenchman said when invited to join a fox hunt, I had been. Two winters previously there had been a singing school in an adjoining school district, known as "Baghdad," where along with others I had presented myself as a candidate for vocal culture, and had been rejected on the grounds that I lacked both "time" and "ear." What was even less to my credit, I had been censured as being concerned in a disturbance outside the schoolhouse. That was my first winter in Maine, and the teacher at that singing school was not Seth Clark, but an itinerant singing master widely known as "Bear Tone."

As opportunities for musical instruction thereabouts were limited, the Old Squire, who loved music and who was himself a fair singer, had advised us to go. Five of us, together with our two young neighbors, Kate and Thomas Edwards, drove over to Baghdad in a three-seated pung sleigh.

The old schoolhouse was crowded with young people when we arrived, and a babble of voices burst on us as we drew rein at the door. After helping the girls from the pung, Addison and I put up the horses at a farmer's barn near by. When we again reached the schoolhouse, a gigantic man in an immense, shaggy buffalo coat was just coming up. He entered the building a step behind us.

It was Bear Tone, and a great hush fell on the young people as he appeared in the doorway. Squeezing hurriedly into seats with the others, Addison and I faced round. Bear Tone stood in front of the teacher's desk, near the stovepipe, rubbing his huge hands together, for the night was cold. He was smiling, too—a friendly, genial smile that seemed actually to brighten the room.

If he had looked gigantic to us in the dim doorway, he now looked colossal. In fact, he was six feet five inches tall and three feet across the shoulders. He had legs like mill posts and arms to match; he wore big mittens, because he could not buy gloves large enough for his hands. He was lean and bony rather than fat, and weighed 320 pounds, it was said.

His face was big and broad, simple and yet strong; it was ringed round from ear to ear with a short but very thick sandy beard. His eyes were blue, his hair, like his beard, was sandy. He was almost forty years old and was still a bachelor.

"Wal, young ones," he said at last, "reckonin' trundle-bed trash, there's a lot of ye, ain't there?"

His voice surprised me. From such a massive man I had expected to hear a profound bass. Yet his voice was not distinctly bass; it was clear and flexible. He could sing bass, it is true, but he loved best to sing tenor, and in that part his voice was wonderfully sweet.

As his speech at once indicated, he was an ignorant man. He had never had musical instruction; he spoke of soprano as "tribble," of alto as "counter," and of baritone as "bear tone"—a mispronunciation that had given him his nickname.

But he could sing! Melody was born in him, so to speak, full-fledged, ready to sing. Musical training would have done him no good, and it might have done him harm. He could not have sung a false note if he had tried: discord really pained him.

"Wal, we may's well begin," he said when he had thoroughly warmed his hands. "What ye got for singin' books here? Dulcimers, or harps of Judah? All with harps raise yer right hands. So. Now all with dulcimers, left hands. So. Harps have it. Them with dulcimers better get harps, if ye can, 'cause we want to sing together. But tonight we'll try voices. I wouldn't wonder if there might be some of ye who might just as well go home and shell corn as try to sing." And he laughed. "So in the first place we'll see if you can sing, and then what part you can sing, whether it's tribble, or counter, or bass, or tenor. The best way for us to find out is to have you sing the scale—the notes of music. Now these are the notes of music." And without recourse to tuning fork he sang: "Do, re, mi, fa, sol, la, ti, do."

The old schoolhouse seemed to swell to the mellow harmony from his big throat. To me those eight notes, as Bear Tone sang them, were a sudden revelation of what music may be.

"I'll try you first, my boy," he then said, pointing to Newman Darnley, a young fellow about twenty years old who sat at the end of the front row of seats. "Step right out here."

Greatly embarrassed, Newman shambled forth and, turning, faced us.

"Now, sir," said the master, "catch the keynote from me. Do! Now re—mi," and so forth.

Bear Tone had great difficulty in getting Newman through the scale. "'Fraid you never'll make a great singer, my boy," he said, "but you may be able to grumble bass a little, if you prove to have an ear that can follow. Next on that seat."

The pupil so designated was a Baghdad boy named Freeman Knights. He hoarsely rattled off, "Do, re, mi, fa, sol," all on the same tone. When Bear Tone had spent some moments in trying to make him rise and fall on the notes, he exclaimed: "My dear boy, you may be able to drive oxen, but you'll never sing. It wouldn't do you any good to stay here, and as the room is crowded the best thing you can do is to run home."

Opening the door, he gave Freeman a friendly pat on the shoulder and a push into better air outside. Afterwards came Freeman's sister, Nellie Knights; she could discern no difference between do and la—at which Bear Tone heaved a sigh.

"Wal, sis, you'll be able to call chickens, I guess, because that's all on one note, but 'twouldn't be worthwhile for you to try to sing, or torment a planner. There are plenty of girls tormentin' planners now. I guess you'd better go home, too; it may come on to snow."

Nellie departed angrily and slammed the door. Bear Tone looked after her. "Yes," he said, "'tis kind of hard to say that to a girl. Don't wonder she's a little mad. And yet, that's the kindest thing I can do. Even in Scripter there was the sheep and the goats; the goats couldn't sing, and the sheep could; they had to be separated."

He went on testing voices and sending the goats home. Some of the goats, however, lingered round outside, made remarks, and peeped in at the windows. In an hour their number had grown to eighteen or twenty.

Dreading the ordeal, I slunk into a back seat. I saw my cousin, Addison, who had a fairly good voice, join the sheep, and then Theodora, Ellen, Kate, and Thomas, but I could not escape the ordeal forever, and at last my turn came. When Bear Tone bade me sing the scale, fear so constricted my vocal cords that I squealed rather than sang.

"Sonny, there's lots of things a boy can do besides sing," Bear Tone said as he laughingly consigned me to the outer darkness. "It's no great blessing, after all." He patted my shoulder, "I can sing a little, but I've never been good for much else. So don't you feel bad about it."

But I did feel bad, and, joining the goats outside, I helped to organize a hostile demonstration. We began to march round the schoolhouse, howling "Yankee Doodle." Our discordant noise drew a prompt response. The door opened and Bear Tone's huge form appeared.

"In about one harf of one minute more I'll be out there and give ye a lesson in Yankee Doodle!" he cried, laughing. His tone sounded good natured; yet for some reason none of us thought it best to renew the disturbance.

Most of the goats dispersed, but, not wishing to walk home alone, I hung round waiting for the others. One window of the schoolroom had been raised, and through that I watched the proceedings. Bear Tone had now tested all the voices except one, and his face showed that he had not been having a very pleasant time. Up in the back seat there still remained one girl, Helen Thomas, who had, according to common report, a rather good voice; yet she was so modest that few had ever heard her either sing or recite.

I saw her come forward, when the master beckoned, and sing her do, re, mi. Bear Tone, who had stood waiting—somewhat apathetically—came suddenly to attention. "Sing that again, little girl," he said.

Encouraged by his kind glance, Helen again sang the scale in her clear voice. A radiant look overspread Bear Tone's big face.

"Wal, Wal!" he cried. "But you've a voice, little one! Sing that with me."

Big voice and girl's voice blended and chorded. "Ah, but you will make a singer, little one!" Bear Tone exclaimed. "Now, sing 'Woodland' with me. Never mind notes, sing by ear."

A really beautiful volume of sound came through the window at which I listened. Bear Tone and his newfound treasure sang "The Star-Spangled Banner" and several of the songs of the Civil War, then just ended—ballads still popular with us and fraught with touching memories: "Tenting Tonight on the Old Camp Ground," "Dearest Love, Do You Remember?" and "Tramp, Tramp, Tramp, the Boys Are Marching." Bear Tone's rich voice chorded beautifully with Helen's sweet, high notes.

As we were getting into the pung to go home after the meeting, and Helen and her older sister, Elizabeth, were setting off, Bear Tone dashed out, bareheaded, with his big face beaming.

"Be sure you come again," he said to her, in a tone that was almost imploring. "You can sing! Oh you can sing! I'll teach you! I'll teach you!"

The singing school that winter served chiefly as a pretty background for Bear Tone's delight in Helen Thomas's voice, the interest he took in it, and the untiring efforts he made to teach her.

"One of the rarest of voices!" he said to the Old Squire one night when he had come to the farmhouse on one of his frequent visits. "Not once will you find one in fifty years. It's a deep tribble. Why, Squire, that girl's voice is a discovery! And it will grow in her, Squire! It is just starting now, but by the time she's twenty-five it will come out wonderful."

The soprano of the particular quality that Bear Tone called "deep tribble" is that sometimes called a "falcon" soprano, or dramatic soprano, in distinction from light soprano. It is better known and more enthusiastically appreciated by those proficient in music than by the general public. Bear Tone, however, recognized it in his new pupil, as if from instinct.

The other pupils were somewhat neglected that winter, but no one complained, for it was such a pleasure to hear Bear Tone and Helen sing. Many visitors came, and once the Old Squire attended a meeting, in order to hear Bear Tone's remarkable pupil. "In Days of Old, When Knights Were Bold," "Dear Old Juanita," and "Roll On, Silver Moon" were some of their favorite songs. Still a goat, and always a goat, I am not capable of describing music, but school and visitors sat enchanted when Helen and Bear Tone sang.

Helen's parents were opposed to having their daughter become a professional singer. They were willing that she should sing in church and at funerals, but not in opera. For a long time Bear Tone labored to convince them that a voice like Helen's has a divine mission in the world, to please, to touch, and to ennoble the hearts of the people.

At last he induced them to let him take Helen to Portland, in order that a well-known teacher there might hear her sing and give an opinion. Bear Tone was to pay the expenses of the trip himself.

The city teacher was enthusiastic over the girl and urged that she be given opportunity for further study, but in view of the opposition at home that was not easily managed. But Bear Tone would not be denied. He sacrificed the scanty earnings of a whole winter's round of singing schools in country school districts to send her to the city for a course of lessons.

The next year the question of her studying abroad came up. If Helen were to make the most of her voice, she must have it trained by masters in Italy and Paris. Her parents were unwilling to assist her to cross the ocean.

Bear Tone was a poor man; his singing schools never brought him more than a few hundred dollars a year. He owned a little house in a neighboring village, where he kept "bachelor's hall"; he had a piano, a cabinet organ, a bugle, a guitar, and several other musical instruments, including one fairly valuable old violin from which he was wont of an evening to produce wonderfully sweet, sad strains.

No one except the officials of the local savings bank knew how Bear Tone raised the money for Helen Thomas's first trip abroad, but he did it. Long afterwards people learned that he had mortgaged everything he possessed, even the old violin, in order to provide the necessary money.

Helen went to Europe and studied for two years. She made her debut at Milan, sang in several of the great cities on the Continent, and at last, with a reputation as a great singer fully established, returned home four years later to sing in New York.

Bear Tone meanwhile was teaching his singing schools, as usual, in the rural districts of Maine. Once or twice during those two years of study he had managed to send a little money to Helen, to help out with the expenses. Now he postponed his three biweekly schools for one week and made his first and only trip to New York—the journey of a lifetime. Perhaps he had at first hoped that he might meet her and be welcomed. If so, he changed his mind on reaching the metropolis. Aware of his uncouthness, he resolved not to shame her by claiming recognition. But he went three times to hear her sing, first in *Aida*, then in *Faust*, and afterward in *Les Huguenots;* he heard her magic notes, saw her in all her queenly beauty—but saw her from the shelter of a pillar in the rear of the great opera house. On the fifth day he returned home as quietly as he had gone.

Perhaps a month after he came back, while driving to one of his singing schools on a bitter night in February, he took a severe cold. For lack of any proper care at his little lonesome, chilly house, his cold a day or two later turned into pneumonia, and from that he died.

The savings bank took the house and the musical instruments. The piano, the organ, the old violin, and other things were sold at auction. And probably Helen Thomas, whose brilliant career he had made possible, never heard anything about the circumstances of his death.

11

The Queer Amethyst Quarrel

THE MURCH BOYS HAD TRAPPED A BEAR IN THEIR SHEEP pasture that night, and came round in haste early next morning, to raise a party to run the animal down.

The bear, evidently a good-sized one, had gone off with the trap, making for the Great Woods, dragging after him a heavy green beech clog, attached to the trap by a strong chain.

Nothing, except a fire, will bring out a party quicker than the prospect of hunting down a bear. Several men and ten or a dozen boys— among the latter my cousin Addison and myself—set off with guns and two hounds. But there was no need of dogs; the trail made by the beech clog was as plain to follow as a cow path. At every leap the bear had taken, the heavy log had torn up the turf, moss, and dead leaves.

We expected that the creature would soon get "hung up" from the clog catching under roots or between tree trunks. But that did not happen, and the bear hunters had a long chase—first over the pasture lands, then through woods and across swamps and brooks, for four or five miles, to the foot of Birchboard Mountain. Now and again the clog had caught fast, but judging from the tracks, the bear had cast it loose with paws or mouth. Apparently he was heading for a densely wooded valley on the other side of Birchboard Mountain which here sloped gradually upward for a mile or more and was wooded with a noble growth of yellow birch. A long gully, formed by a small brook, extended up the slope, and the bear had followed the bed of it; we could see where the trap and clog had torn a little furrow among the small stones and gravel of the now dry watercourse.

The Murch boys and two or three of the men were some distance ahead—we could hear them calling out to each other—but Addison and I had fallen behind. It was a warm May morning, and we had begun to reflect that it was not our bear, exactly, and would not be ours when caught. We had run for much of the way, and beside being hot we were nearly out of breath. The Old Squire, in fact, had laughingly advised us not to go, and now we were beginning to wish that we had stayed at home.

We were toiling on up that watercourse, when Addison caught sight of something that interested him far more than the chase; anything in the way of minerals, indeed, always enlisted his attention. Where the clog had dragged among the little stones, brought down by the water, lay a purple crystal as large as a hen's egg. Addison caught it up. "Amethyst!" he exclaimed and examined it curiously. It was a crystal having hexahedral facets, but had been much battered, and worn by contact with stones in the brook bed. Yet in some places one could still look into the clear heart of it where the rich deep purple tint shone forth.

"Amethyst, sure," Addison repeated. "The finest I ever saw!" He turned it over slowly, then handed it to me. "Wonder if there's more!" he said, and began pawing over the stones and gravel.

We got some strong sticks and for half an hour or so dug up the pebbles and gravel in the bed of the gully, first for a little way below, then above the place where the crystal was found, following the gully upward for several hundred yards.

"No doubt this was washed down from somewhere above here," Addison said. At last we found another fragment of amethyst of the same tint, but smaller, and feeling certain now that the amethyst came from higher up the mountain, we followed the gully to where it shallowed, toward the summit ledges, but found no fissure, vein, or matrix where the crystals had formed.

We seemed now to be off the track of it, and after some further search went home; for it was nearing noon, and the bear hunters had long ago passed out of hearing.

We learned later that they had got the bear and had gone back by another way. Tired out or grown desperate from the pain of the trap, the animal turned at bay in a swamp on the other side of the mountain, and was shot without difficulty or danger to its pursuers. They secured the bear's skin, but at that season of the year, it was of little value.

Addison had much the prettier trophy to show the folks at home. The Old Squire, I remember, held the crystal in his hand for a long time. "This is as beautiful as a flower—and far more enduring," he said.

As time passed, our thoughts often reverted to that watercourse at Birchboard Mountain, and late that fall, a party of we young people, including Halstead, Theodora, and Ellen, also Kate Edwards and Willis Murch, who had trapped the bear, went up there to search further. This time we took hoes and gave the bed of the rivulet another overhauling. But one little shim of amethyst was all that we found.

Still another trip was made there two years later, after we had begun attending the village academy, when the preceptor and nine or ten of our classmates accompanied us. Merely a few broken bits of amethyst were picked up. Nonetheless Addison remained confident that somewhere up the mountain, if we could only find it, there was a fissure or a crack in the quartzose ledges where these amethyst crystals had originally formed. And I think it was on Sunday morning following that last school excursion, that he suddenly put his head—not yet combed—in at my chamber door and exclaimed, "I dreamed we found that amethyst vein last night!"

"That so?" said I, not yet very fully awake.

"Yes!" he cried. "And I believe I can find it, now. Let's go up there this afternoon, after meeting."

I did not feel very enthusiastic, at first, but when our usual three o'clock Sunday dinner at the old farm was over he and I set off quietly, saying nothing to anyone else, and tramped up to Birchboard Mountain again.

Truth to say Addison had not dreamed out very explicit directions, but I suppose that his mind had been running on the subject in sleep, and this had wakened new interest in it, as dreams often do.

As we proceeded up the bed of the gully, a partridge flew across it and stirred the low hemlocks which at that point masked the left bank, and this led us to notice that, partly hidden by the evergreen boughs, a little side gully entered there—one we had not previously seen. It was, in fact, little more than a ditch only three or four feet deep and six or seven across, whereas the main gully we were in was thirty or forty feet in width and nine or ten in depth.

"That looks to be a little watercourse," Addison remarked. We climbed up to explore it, and found that it was, indeed, the bed of a rill where water rushed down, after heavy rains, from farther along the summit of the mountain. It was much overgrown, but we followed it upward and coming to a bed of loose stones and gravel, Addison poked this over with his boot toe, when almost the first thing he saw was another amethyst crystal of the same deep, lovely, violet hue.

"At last we are on the right track!" he exclaimed. "That vein is somewhere up this little watercourse!"

We followed on, and less than a hundred yards farther up, came where there were ledges on both sides, and presently, under the overhang of a crag of coarse yellowish rock, caught sight of a slantwise fissure only a few inches wide, from both sides of which the points of amethyst crystals stood forth like the teeth of some huge saw. As far as we could thrust in our fingers the crevice was jagged with crystals some of which were two or three inches in diameter.

To a lover of beautiful minerals it was, indeed, a glorious sight. "My dream!" Addison cried.

"I guess it was that partridge!" I said.

"I don't know but it was," he replied, laughing. "But never mind that. We've found it at last. And aren't they beautiful!"

The outermost crystals, however, had been sadly marred and broken, as if someone had pounded them with stones. A wandering hunter or Indian, perhaps, in earlier days, had found the place and attempted to break off the points of as many of the crystals as were easily accessible. Shims and fragments lay at the foot of the ledge, and afterwards, all along the bed of that little gully down to where it joined the larger watercourse, we found numerous clear bits and purple fragments, washed along by the rush of water in time of freshets.

We had brought no tools, as it was Sunday, and after feasting our eyes on what we could discern in the fissure, and picking up what we found lying loose below, we returned home, agreeing on the way to say nothing of our find outside of our own family, since if it were told, many persons might hasten there and do still further damage by rude efforts to secure specimens.

The Old Squire, who was almost as much interested as Addison, went up to the mountain with us on the following Tuesday, and after packing the fissure with cotton batting, we drilled holes in the abutting rock, and made three powder blasts, in order to reach the more perfect crystals that lay deep within the fissure. In spite of every precaution we could take, however, many of them were broken, but we secured eleven that were quite perfect, and gathered up fully half a bushel of the less perfect or broken crystals—all of the same deep, full, royal purple tint.

"I really think this amethyst is valuable," Addison declared. "I do believe it is fit for gems."

"Well, valuable or not, they are very beautiful," the Old Squire said. "We will make a cabinet and keep them to look at."

We returned there on three other days that fall, did considerable further blasting, and in fact worked the fissure as far as the amethyst appeared to extend. Deeper down the fissure appeared to close solidly in. Altogether we had secured enough to fill a good-sized cabinet having five shelves.

While there one afternoon the noise of the blasts attracted two hunters who came where we were at work and picked up specimens to carry away. They told us they were from Lurvey's Mills, five or six miles to the westward of the mountain. I suppose these men may have spread reports of our discovery. Till then no one had learned of it.

The lines of forest lots were not carefully marked. In a general way we supposed the place was on land, owned by the Old Squire, which included the birch growth on the side of the mountain. At first, however, we had not deemed the matter of ownership of the land of much consequence, for the locality was far back in the woods, and anything found on unimproved forest lands had always been held to be the property of the finder.

About a fortnight later Addison and I were therefore disagreeably surprised at receiving the following curt, badly spelled note from our former schoolmaster, the incredibly inept Sam Lurvey, of Lurvey's Mills.

It will be as well for you to give up them perple stones you took off our land, and not be too long about it either, if you don't want to be sued.

Samuel B. Lurvey

When this unneighborly missive was deciphered, Addison and I expressed indignation openly.

"Well," the Old Squire said, judicially, "the line between our lots and those of Zack Lurvey crosses the top of the mountain not far from where you got these crystals. But the lines were never run very carefully. Possibly the place is on their land. Maybe they think so. But to be certain, a new survey of that entire tier of lots would have to be made by compass."

"And there's iron ore in that mountain," the Old Squire added. "There might be compass deviation."

We guessed that after hearing we were blasting there, the Lurveys had made a hasty effort to trace the line, and had concluded that the place was on their forest lot.

"But isn't that like those Lurveys to claim something away off up there in the woods!" Grandmother Ruth exclaimed.

"They do not like us," the Old Squire remarked. "Old Zackary would enjoy making trouble for us if he could, but if these amethyst crystals were really on his land, he has a certain right to complain, although to claim them all is, of course, rather hoggish."

"Sam Lurvey would never have found the crystals, himself!" Ellen exclaimed.

"Nor known what they were, if he had!" Theodora added.

"Still, that doesn't alter the case much," Addison said. "What do you advise us to do, sir?" he asked the Old Squire.

"The lines must be resurveyed by a sworn surveyor and solar compass," the Old Squire replied. "Then, if we are at fault we will settle for it. We had better see Surveyor Matthews at once," he added.

But Surveyor Matthews lived eight miles away, and when Addison found him that afternoon, other engagements for his services, already made, rendered it impossible for him to undertake work for us that fall.

Matthews, moreover, was the only surveyor in the county who made use of the solar compass. For the present therefore we concluded to let young Lurvey's rough and threatening letter go unanswered.

Three mornings later, however, he drove into the yard, and when Addison and I went out, burst forth without even the courtesy of good morning, in an angry demand for those crystals.

"I'll thank ye to hand over them purple stones you took off'n our lot!" he exclaimed with vehemence.

"But how do you know they were on your land?" Addison asked.

"We follered the line and we know!" he cried.

"Have you had the line resurveyed?" Addison asked him.

"I tell ye we know where the line is!" shouted Sam. "And you may as well give them stones up!"

"All right, Sam, as soon as we find out where the line is we will talk about it," Addison said.

That made him angrier still. He evidently thought that we would surrender the crystals to him. "If you don't hand them over I'll get a writ and come here with the sheriff and search your house for them!" he threatened.

"Thanks, Sam, for warning us," Addison replied, laughing. "Come on with your sheriff!" We went indoors and left him.

But the Old Squire, who had heard the loud talk, sauntered down the lane and along the road, and when Sam had turned in the yard and went driving away, the old gentleman stopped by the roadside and spoke pleasantly. "I'm on my way to the post office," said he. "Could you give an old fellow a lift?"

Rather gruffly Sam pulled up. The Old Squire got in beside him, and as they drove along, talked of matters in general, until they were nearly at the office. He then broached the subject of the crystals and tried to smooth away Sam's ugly mood, assuring him, and also bidding him tell his father, that we wished to do the right thing.

"Wal, you've got to give up them stones!" Sam insisted. "If you don't we will sue ye."

"But instead of going to law, with costs of suit, both sides, wouldn't it be better, Sam, to leave the matter to three disinterested neighbors, to say what is right?" the Old Squire suggested.

"Oh, you want to pick somebody that'll favor ye!" Sam exclaimed.

"Not so," the Old Squire replied mildly. "You and your father are well acquainted with Selectman Harvey who lives near you at the Mills. Let him name three referees, to decide on the right thing for us."

But Sam would not agree to it. He was bent on making us give up the crystals.

"I thought it possible to appeal to that boy's sense of right and fair play," the Old Squire explained, after he came home. "But I made a mistake," he added dryly. "I found he didn't have any."

We remained quiet and waited for what would follow. We did not believe the Lurveys could obtain a writ to search our house, if they tried, but we thought it likely they might begin a lawsuit.

Old Zackary, however, was a much wiser man than his son. After he had heard from Sam what the Old Squire proposed, he sent over a short but civil letter, by one of his hired men, saying he thought that would be a very good way of settling it. "I agree to it," he added. "And so will Sam."

Three referees were therefore chosen, as suggested, and proceeded to give their verdict.

The only drawback to settling controversies by referees is that these good men often wish to please both parties and hence conclude to "split the difference" between them rather than make a really just decision.

That was what happened in our case. The verdict of the referees was to divide the crystals equally, and each side take half.

This was done—although truth to say it hurt our feelings sadly, Addison's especially, to give up those beautiful amethysts. The Old Squire asked the referees to divide what was in the cabinet and they did so. It seemed to us—looking on—that our half was much the smaller. I believe that Theodora went away and shed tears over it.

This, however, was not the end, nor yet the most mortifying part.

When, finally, Surveyor Matthews came round to retrace the lines of the lots, in May the following year, it was found that the fissure from which we had taken the amethyst crystals was fully thirty feet on our side of the line!

It was all rather laughable.

But Addison was now chiefly intent on recovering the crystals. He and I hitched up and drove over to Lurvey's Mills, in quest of Sam, and having found him we demanded that he surrender those crystals, forthwith.

He refused, in terms not necessary to record here. The referees had awarded them to him, he said, and no one could make him give them up. "Go to the law if you want to," he cried. "I don't care where the line is. You proposed referees, yourselves, and the referees gave me the stones." It transpired that he had sold the crystals already, for a trifle—and spent the money—and as he was now in his twenty-fifth year, his father declined to be responsible for his acts.

"Boys, the joke is on me!" the Old Squire confessed, as we talked the incident over at home. "I had better have kept quiet. My peace plan was premature."

We kept the amethysts that were left us, for a number of years. Several of the crystals were given to friends who were making collections of minerals. Eventually some of the best were sold to a metropolitan jewelry firm to be cut as gems, and for these we received a good price. No finer amethysts have thus far been found in New England.

What was left of the crystals, along with the cabinet that held them, were lost in the old farmhouse fire, many years later.

12

The Bees of Gehenna

THE REVEREND JASON WHITLOCK OF THE MAINE
Methodist Conference was presiding elder of the district during the
first three years we young folks were at the Old Squire's place. He came
regularly, once in three months, to preside at the quarterly meetings of
the local church, and although our family were Congregationalists, Mr.
Whitlock was wont to pass Saturday night and Sunday at our house,
Grandmother Ruth having a more commodious "spare room" than
most of her Methodist neighbors.

Judged by almost any standard, Elder Whitlock would have passed
for a cultivated man. By nature, too, he was an interesting preacher, one
who avoided solemn, doctrinal sermons and nearly always enlivened his
discourse with occasional anecdotes very interesting to us boys. He was
also wont to expound biblical history in an entertaining way, relating,
for example, where the Garden of Eden was supposed to be; and
describing the palm groves of the Shat-el-Arab; or picturing Babylon
and its mighty walls; or Nineveh, which a great inundation of the Tigris
overwhelmed; or the region of Mount Sinai and the nature of the
manna on which the children of Israel subsisted. My cousin Addison
especially was very much attracted to Elder Whitlock.

Within our family circle, Mr. Whitlock's visits were welcome occasions. He was of a naturally joyous disposition, often merry, told stories, joked, and often went out to the barn or the fields with us—in
complete contrast to Elder Ezra Colvin who succeeded him; for the

latter was an austere, silent man who rarely addressed a word to us young folks.

In my boyish mind there was only one drawback to Elder Whitlock's quarterly sojourns with us, namely, his penchant for baths. Those were the years before the Old Squire installed a hydraulic ram to force water up from the east brook to our farm buildings, and contrived a large bathroom in the old farmhouse. All the water used indoors had to be brought from a nearby well, and as Elder Whitlock liked a warm bath every night and a cold dip in the morning, quite arduous preparations were necessary to ensure his comfort. A bowl and pitcher of hot water had to suffice for the bath at night. But for the cold dip in the morning someone had to tote up a large tub to the spare room, the night before, and fill it with at least four bucketfuls of water from the well.

Cousin Theodora usually had charge of the bowl and pitcher, as also a smaller pitcher of hot water for shaving purposes at an early morning hour. As time passed, too, it came to be Addison's business to transport the big tub upstairs and set it in the far corner of the spare room on a plat of oilcloth (he fell downstairs with it one night!), while to me was allotted the duty of carrying up the four or five buckets of water from the well—and I found the task an onerous one. Once I shirked it, and said nothing. But the day of reckoning dawned in the morning, very early, too, and there came such sharp reproof that I never ventured on a second offense. The glum Elder Colvin who came later had this if nothing else in his favor, he wore a beard and, as far as we ever discovered was satisfied with a pitcher full of water a day.

On the memorable Sabbath morning in June 1866, to which I now refer, Elder Whitlock had been spending the night with us, and we boys had risen at five or earlier, so as to get the farm chores done before breakfast. The sun was just up, looking very red, for there was a good deal of smokes in the sky from forest fires. As we went out with the milk pails we heard a considerable buzzing at the bee shed, and noticed that bees were rising in the air over it and going to settle on a limb of one of the two large balm-of-Gilead trees that stood directly in front of the old farmhouse.

"They are swarming," Addison said, and went partly round to the front of the shed to see from which hive the swarm was issuing.

"It's those 'Holy Land' bees," he explained, coming back where I stood. "They're beginning to 'cluster' on that balm-of-Gilead. We ought to wake the Old Squire and get him out to help us hive them.

"But they will be sure to hang on there for an hour or so before dying away," Ad continued, after watching the bees awhile. "So I guess we had better milk the cows and get them off to pasture before we begin with bees."

Readers who are interested in apiculture may know something about Holy Land bees. They, or the original swarms, are alleged to have been brought from Palestine, though there has been doubt expressed as to this. I think ours came from an apiary in New York State. In early days we had only native black bees in Maine. Afterwards yellow Italian bees were largely substituted for the native black swarms. At one time the Old Squire had a queen from a swarm of Tauridian bees, said to have been imported from the Crimea in Southern Russia, and he also had quite an experience with Egyptian bees. The old gentleman possessed a knack of handling bees and rarely was stung by them.

As we went in with the milk, Cousin Ellen met us in much excitement. "Something's the matter with Elder Whitlock up in his room!" she exclaimed in low tones. "He is splashing water tremendously and calling out strange words! Doad heard him first. She is afraid he is taken crazy. She has called Grandmother Ruth."

We followed Ellen to the kitchen and through the sitting room to the front hall. Grandmother was ascending the stairs. She went to the spare room door, knocked and spoke. "Don't come in, sister! Don't come in!" the elder shouted excitedly. "Call your husband!"—and we heard water splash against the windows and the walls. Then a chair went end over end!

"Ah, Elder, what's the matter!" Grandmother implored. "Can't I help you?"

"Don't come in! Don't come in! I'm in my bath!" the elder repeated wildly. "Call your husband! Call your menfolks!"—and again the water flew over the room.

By this time the Old Squire was hastening up the stairs, and approaching the spare room door, cried, "What has happened, Elder? What has befallen you?" Splash, splash, and then sounds of the tub's upsetting and rolling across the room, was the sole response for the moment; then a distressed, muffled voice replied, "It's bees! A whole swarm of your bees came in at the window while I was in my tub. I'm stung all over! The room is full of them! I'm under the bed now, behind the valance. I'm not dressed and cannot reach my clothes. Send away the womenfolk, Squire, then open the door a crack and I will try to run out into the hall.

"But look out for yourself! The room is roaring full of bees!" he continued. "They've nearly stung me to death!"

Grandmother and the girls scattered promptly. The Old Squire then shouted, "Ready!" and half opened the door when out dashed the afflicted elder, smiting furiously with both hands. Quickly as he had clapped the door to, a gust of bees came out with him and there was a lively fracas in the hall, till the elder got into another room and shut himself in!

How to get his clothes to him was the next question—not an easy one. The spare room was literally full of bees, thousands of them. They had come in at the open window en masse. Apparently after "clustering" on the balm-of-Gilead limb a few yards away, the swarm decided to take up its abode in the spare room.

It is said that before a swarm leaves the parent hive, scout bees go forth in advance to find a new home, either in an empty hive, a hollow tree in the neighboring woods, a crevice in a crag, or some other nook or cranny that will afford the swarm shelter to begin their new housekeeping. The spare room window had been open a little way, overnight and for twenty-four hours previously, to air the room in anticipation of the elder's arrival. The scouts must have been in there exploring and concluded to take possession of the room as their future home; so after the queen came out, and they had clustered awhile in the tree, the whole swarm streamed in at the window and surprised the elder in his bath.

It was imperative that the elder should have his clothes immediately, and after a hasty canvass of expedients, the Old Squire sent Addison to the attic for a quilting pole. By driving a nail transversely through one end of it Addison contrived a makeshift hook. Then opening the door a chink and thrusting in the pole, the much-needed garments were hastily hauled forth one after another. Several bees came with them, and some minutes passed before the upper hall could be cleared of them. Addison was twice stung in the scrimmage.

By this time the elder had arrayed himself and came forth, but in bad case, with face and hands much swollen and reddened. Diluted ammonia and dabs of wet soda afforded some little relief. A box of honey was also opened for his benefit at breakfast, honey internally being supposed to be an antidote for bee stings.

But when all was done, it was a badly disfigured Elder whom Theodora and I drove to church two hours later in Grandmother Ruth's chaise, to preach the quarterly sermon. If he felt as badly as he looked, he was indeed a sufferer. Nose, chin, and one cheek were puffed out of all proper proportion. One eye, too, was nearly closed. On rising in the pulpit to face the congregation, the poor man felt it necessary to offer some explanation. As if it were yesterday, I recall what he said, and the grotesque aspect of his countenance as he tried to smile! "Dear Brethren and Sisters," he began. "The Lord has seen fit to chasten me grievously this morning. Perhaps it was for my spiritual good. Perhaps I had sinned consciously or unconsciously. I hardly believe it can have been on account of pride for my good looks, for I never had the looks. But it is probably best not to seek reasons for the dispensations of Providence, better to take them as they come and make the best of them. My present disreputable appearance is the result of nothing more reprehensible on my part however than a conflict with bees, honey bees. At the good friend's house where I was kindly entertained last night, a whole swarm of them came in at the open window and attacked me venomously. This good friend informs me that those bees came from Palestine, that they were Holy Land bees. But I doubt it! I am convinced those bees came from Gehenna!"

Neither the Old Squire nor Grandmother Ruth attended church that forenoon; the latter was too greatly concerned over the state her "spare room" was in. The bees were in full possession of it; they had to be got out somehow. Addison also stayed at home. They listened at the spare room door and took counsel together. The enraged bees within were now trying to settle their disturbed affairs. First the deep hum of the queen bee could be heard, then a roar of buzzing in response to her call from all the worker bees.

"Yes, she is in there," the Old Squire said. "Good. Now I guess we can manage them. We must get her out without hurting her, if we can, and place her nearby, outside, where the swarm can hear her call. I think they will follow her."

He brought out the "bee rig"—the veil for the head, gloves, wristlets, anklets, and thick frock—which he kept for use when angry bees had to be handled. With Addison's help he also contrived a little cage of wire gauze for imprisoning the queen when caught. As Addison's more youthful ears were better than the Old Squire's, he offered to don the rig, enter the room, and attempt the capture of her apian majesty.

"You will probably find her crawling on the wall, or on one of the bedposts," the Old Squire said. "You can readily distinguish her from the workers, she is so much larger."

That was the plan they followed. On slipping quietly in, Addison found that most of the bees were now gathered along one side of the room, and after listening for her hum, he located the queen, captured her in a loose wad of cotton batting and brought her out. They jockeyed her gently into the little gauze cage, and then fetching a ladder, Addison climbed into the balm-of-Gilead tree and attached the cage to a limb a few yards away from the spare room window. It is a fact that in the course of half an hour, the greater part of the bees in the room went out and clustered in the tree.

Once outside, they were smoked and hived in the usual way when swarms have clustered in a tree. Such bees as persisted in remaining in the room were then smothered with the bee smoker. Of these and others that had perished in battle with Elder Whitlock, nearly a quart was swept up later.

In fact, Grandmother Ruth's spare room was in sorry plight. Not only was the carpet water-soaked, but the bed as well. Much of the wallpaper, too, was streaked and ruined by water and crushed bees. If the dear old lady made a few irritated remarks that day, I feel sure the recording angel wrote "excessive provocation" after them.

13

The Old Squire's Eden

ON THE UPPER SIDE OF THE NORTH FIELD AT THE OLD Squire's farm was a great rock overshadowed by a huge sugar maple; just below the rock was as pretty a little field as you could wish to see. It was not much larger than a good-sized house lot, but its soil was of deep, clear, yellow loam, and it had a gentle southern slope that caught the sunshine. To the north and west the woods above the rock sheltered the field from cold winter winds and fierce summer thundershowers. It was such a pretty spot that we called it the Old Squire's "Eden," and sometimes the Old Squire's "garden," although he never raised flowers there, or even garden vegetables—except one kind. In point of fact, the best name for it would have been the "potato-ball garden," for there, season after season, during more than twenty years, the Old Squire had been experimenting with potato balls.

As farmers well know, the various varieties of potatoes tend to run out in time—or did so tend under former methods of cultivation—and have to be replaced by new ones. Several varieties had run out at the Old Squire's, and he was constantly trying to grow new varieties by planting the seeds in the potato "ball." Two or three seasons are needed to grow edible potatoes in that way. The first crop is usually immature. Nor can you ever be sure what kind of potatoes you will get from planting the balls of even the best varieties. It is usually a poor kind, but occasionally a very good variety appears.

A fine new variety of potato is likely to be very profitable to its grower; he can sell it at high price for field planting, until other farmers get enough potatoes for the seed.

The Old Squire hoped to grow an extra good variety in his potato-ball garden, and to make us all rich. The old gentleman was always optimistic—"schemy," Grandmother called him—and usually had high hopes for the success not only of his potatoes but of his hops, sweet corn, and other farm products.

Every spring, and sometimes also in the fall, he planted potato balls from different varieties up there by the great rock. In September he dug up what had grown during the summer and put them into several carefully labeled bins in the farmhouse cellar; the next spring he replanted them, each kind by itself. He repeated that process for two or three or four years, until he had produced well-matured potatoes, and could see whether they had real merit as a new variety.

In time the Old Squire came to be somewhat of a potato expert. Many of the varieties that he raised proved valueless, but now and then he grew a pretty good variety that he could recommend farmers to raise. There was one small kind that he called the Nest Egg, because it was white and smooth and shaped much like a hen's egg. Another kind he named the Round Reds, and another Ruth's Favorite, because Grandmother liked them for roasting. Then there were the Beauty of the Forest, the Irishman's Dinner, the Pearl Whites, Irish Dumplings, and Long-Live-in-the-Ground, so-named because the seed lived in the patch and for three successive winters survived the frosts.

But the best variety of all was the Bobolink. The name came from a pet bobolink that Theodora had tamed that summer. The bird was a vociferous singer, and whenever the Old Squire went up to his potato garden, the little bird flew after him, perched on some tall weed stalk, and then burst forth into his merry song. After these flights in the free air the bobolink would always return to its cage to be fed.

The Bobolink was a superior sort of potato, and bade fair to become very profitable to us. As I remember, it was yellowish white in color, of good size but not too large, in shape a little elongated and ovoid. It had a thin, smooth skin, from which the soil dropped off cleanly, and its "eyes" were not deep sunk but on the surface. When it was boiled the skin cleaved off: and when either boiled or baked it was very mealy and had a fine flavor. Moreover, it grew fast and ripened early; the tops showed no tendency to "rust," and it kept sound throughout the winter. Another good point was that the potatoes grew in a compact cluster in the hill and could be easily dug.

There were three rows of Bobolinks, each about twenty yards long; the Old Squire thought that there would be at least five bushels of them. His plan for getting the variety known was to give one or two of them to various farmers, far and near, that they might be examined and eaten. He felt sure that many would want the Bobolinks for seed, and that as their fame spread abroad there would be a steady demand for all we could raise, for ten years, perhaps.

It was then about the tenth of September, the beginning of the harvest season. One cloudy evening I had been at our nearest neighbors', the Edwardses, playing checkers with Tom. We got interested in a long, slow game, and it was almost eleven o'clock before I started for home by a path across the fields.

I hurried—for bears were sometimes roaming about at that time of year—and just as I was passing behind our west barn, to reach the back door of the farmhouse, I heard a queer little noise, like the clink of a hoe on a stone. I was thinking more of bears than of hoes, I guess, and as I knew no bear had made that noise, I went on indoors and stole up the chamber stairs. The house was dark, for everyone was in bed. As I undressed, it occurred to me that it was very odd to hear a hoe clink at that time of night. As I now remembered, the sound had seemed to come from up near the woods north of the west barn—the direction of the Old Squire's Eden. Even then I did not suspect anything in particular. Instead of getting into bed, however, I went to my cousin Addison's room and waked him.

"What do you want?" he muttered sleepily.

"Ad," I said, "what do you suppose anyone is doing with a hoe up in the Old Squire's Eden at this time of night?"

"Who is?" said he. "How do you know?"

"I heard a hoe clink up there as I came in," I explained.

Addison sat up, now thoroughly awake. "That's queer!" he muttered, and then asked me whether I was quite sure.

"Pretty sure," I replied.

He thought a moment, then jumped up and began to dress. "Let's go up and see," he said. We went quietly downstairs. It was very dark. We lighted one of the barn lanterns—which shows how little we really thought we should find thieves—and proceeded up to the Old Squire's Eden. All was as usual.

"Guess you imagined that noise," Addison remarked, and then, holding the lantern low, he glanced along the potato rows.

"By Jingo!" he suddenly exclaimed. "Someone has been digging potatoes here! Look at the fresh dirt. It's the Old Squire's Bobolinks, too, and"—following fast along the three rows—"they've dug every blessed hill of them!"

"Those thieves can't have gone far!" I cried.

"That's so. We'll catch them!"

We blew out the lantern, and then Addison went in one direction, out toward the highway, and I in the other, towards the Edwards farm. We ran softly, listening as we went, but heard no sound of anyone stealing away.

We now hurried back to the house and roused the Old Squire. He was at first incredulous and, taking a lantern, went up to the rock to satisfy himself. Such a thing had never happened before. Our first conjecture was that hunters or woodsmen had stolen the potatoes for food, but if that were so, it seemed very queer that they had not touched any of the other kinds growing there. At the head of each row of Bobolinks we had set a little stake with the name of the potato written on it. Every hill in those three rows had been cleanly dug, as though the thief had intended to get every potato.

The more we thought about it, the more certain we became that the motive of the thief, or thieves, had been to obtain complete possession of this valuable new variety of tuber. Of course all our neighbors, and in fact many farmers in the vicinity, knew of the Old Squire's potato garden. The neighbors, however, were above suspicion. Indeed they all helped us in the attempt to get on track of the rogues. But these had apparently planned the theft with care; at any rate, they left no trace behind them.

We had never seen the old gentleman so downcast by a loss. He had been experimenting so long in the potato-ball garden, and was so proud of the fine new variety, that the thought of the Bobolinks having been stolen merely to boil for food—perhaps—grieved him to the heart. He could hardly bring himself to speak of such a thing.

About a mile and a half from us lived a young farmer of not very good character, and we soon suspected that he had been concerned in the theft. Addison heard that this man had been seen on the morning after our potatoes were stolen, driving on the road with two barrels in his wagon; he told several people that the barrels contained pears that he was carrying to Portland to peddle from house to house.

There was little doubt that this fellow had known all about the Old Squire's experiments in the potato garden, and that he was aware of the value of this new variety, but we were unable to get any proof of our suspicions regarding him. What he could have done with the potatoes, we could not imagine. It would have been impossible for him to plant them himself, or to sell them for seed to any farmer in Maine, without our learning of it. Two years passed. The loss distressed the Old Squire so much that he let his potato garden lapse and seeded the patch down to clover.

Then at last in a western agricultural periodical some of us read about a new variety of potatoes, called Pacificas, that were being advertised for seed. According to the description, their fine qualities were so similar to those of the lost Bobolinks that the Old Squire wrote asking to have a little package of them sent him by mail.

No potatoes came, and he wrote again, but received no reply. He wrote a third time, and at last a letter came saying that the stock of seed was exhausted. Notwithstanding, the advertisement continued for months to appear in the agricultural paper; this seemed so singular to us that we finally addressed the postmaster of the town where the owner of the seed potatoes lived, and inquired about his character and his standing as a citizen.

The postmaster's reply was peculiar; it neither vouched for the man's character nor alleged anything against him. In the same letter the postmaster remarked that there was, apparently, a large sale for the Pacifica potatoes, and added that he himself had also raised them one season and would be glad to send us a few of them. A day or two later he mailed the Old Squire a small package of four potatoes.

From the moment the package was opened, neither the Old Squire nor any of the rest of us had the slightest doubt that the Pacificas were our lost Bobolinks. They were like them in every particular.

Meanwhile another peculiar circumstance came to light. Through one of our hired men, a relative of the young farmer whom we had suspected of the theft, we learned that the fellow had an uncle living in the West, a farmer of the same name as the owner of the Pacifica potatoes. Further inquiries proved that the uncle was indeed the man who had advertised the potato seed.

Evidently this young farmer had stolen the Old Squire's Bobolinks and sent them west, where his uncle had rechristened them Pacificas. That he had realized large profits from them was indicated by the fact that he had recently sold his small farm, purchased a larger one, and stocked it expensively.

We younger members of the family wished to take action at once against the two rogues, but the Old Squire pointed out that we could never bring them to justice, for our case against them had one fatal defect. We could not produce in court a single specimen potato of the original Bobolinks that had been stolen. And a court of law would be unable to take our unsupported word to the effect that this western seed potato was the same as the Old Squire's Bobolink that had been stolen two years previously.

Even if we could have proved it, the western uncle might have declared that he had been secretly growing seed potatoes from the ball, and that he had hit on a variety similar to our own.

So we had nothing to do except let the case drop.

Curiously enough, from the moment that the Old Squire became convinced that the Pacificas and his lost Bobolinks were the same, he cheered up. He began to laugh over the whole affair.

"I was afraid someone had eaten them," he explained. "That would have been a pity. But now they're spreading and doing good in the world—just as much, perhaps, as if I had sold them myself."

Addison, however, was inclined to see the matter in a different light.

"That money was yours, sir. You surely ought to have it!" he exclaimed.

"Of course, of course," replied the Old Squire, still smiling. "But after all the main thing for us to accomplish in life is to keep this old world of ours going ahead for the better."

14

Cutting Cordwood

IN NO OTHER WAY CAN THE NATURAL FEATURES OF A region be so indelibly fixed in the memory as the remembrance of hard work in the region will fix them there. I mean hard physical labor at which one perspires and puts forth his utmost bodily strength. Not alone the brain, but the muscles will seem to remember the place where the effort was put forth.

A few weeks ago, while tramping around the Old Squire's farm in Maine, I went through the "west field" and through the "further field," then up into the "horse pasture" and across the "hollow" and up into the "sheep pasture" on the mountainside, where the bears used to come in from the Great Woods.

Thence I went back into the "upper field" and across the woody valley on the east side over the trout brook, and up into the "Hannah lots," where Cousin Addison, Halstead, and I cut cordwood fifteen years ago.

A young growth of white birch, maple, poplar, and beech has sprung up there now, thickets of it with saplings as large as one's arm. But amidst it the old stained, blackened stumps, covered with "wood stools," still stud the hillside—stumps of the trees, the great rock maples and yellow birches which we then cut down.

I knew almost every one of these old stumps individually, recognized them as one does old acquaintances, and remembered the very day and time of day—when we cut the tree, and what the girls brought us over for luncheon after we had felled it.

Great hopes had centered in young breasts about that job, cutting cordwood. There we all were then, five of us cousins at Grandfather's, living on the old homestead farm—after the despair, tears, and havoc made by the Civil War.

As time passed and we got to be fourteen, fifteen, and sixteen years old we wanted to go to the village academy, and some of us to colleges and to scientific schools. And naturally the "Old Squire," as the neighbors called Grandfather, didn't feel quite able to undertake all this for us, his "second crop" of children, as he used to speak of us collectively to these neighbors.

But he did find ways to help us help ourselves!

"I'll tell ye what, boys," he said to us, one November morning—how like bright beams of sunshine his words dispersed the clouds of our discouragement and dissatisfaction!—"I'll tell ye what 'tis, boys, there's plenty of standing wood over in the 'Hannah lots,'" that I'll let you cut.

"The railroad folks pay four or five dollars a cord delivered at the depot. I'll guarantee ye a dollar a cord for all ye'll cut, and you shall have half the profit there is over and above the bare cost of hauling, on top on't. That ought to be about a dollar a cord more. And I'll let ye off from regular farmwork two days every week right through the year."

"But how much may we cut—how many cords?" Addison asked, wishing to make this good offer a sure thing. "Oh, all you want to, a thousand cords ef ye say so!" responded the Old Squire, with what seemed to us a joyous recklessness; "but let's say six hundred. I'll let ye a job of six hundred cords to cut, at a dollar a cord."

We were all at the breakfast table, just finishing.

"'Pa,' it'll be too hard work for them," Grandmother interposed, smiling, but looking a little concerned, nevertheless.

Dear, kind old lady, I can see her now, sitting behind the big coffeepot, her fair, full face still a little ruddy from her exertions in getting breakfast, and her abundant gray hair combed upward and backward in a fluffy roll above her forehead.

But we scoffed at the idea that any work would prove to be too hard for us, if there was good money in it.

"All right!" Halstead cried out. "We'll take it, Grandpa."

Addison asked if we could begin work at once that very morning, and Grandfather consented.

"This is Friday," he said, "and you may take the last two days of each week for your work."

Theodora and Nell sat looking, interested, yet a trifle dispirited.

"There doesn't seem to be any such nice job for us," said Dora, with the lonesome tone of one who sees herself left out of a good thing.

"But we have to work as hard as the boys do," Nell remarked, discontentedly.

"Indeed you do, girls," Grandmother interposed, "and I think that if you wash and mend the boys' clothes for them, and knit their socks, and cook their food, and take their dinners over to them in the wood lot, you ought to have a share in the wood money."

They made so strong an argument of our daily dependence upon them and their labor that, a little reluctantly, we at length agreed that one-third of the entire receipts should go to them.

But twelve hundred dollars! What a lump of money that looked to be to us then! Why, there seemed complete educations for five in it. What piles of books even half that sum would buy!

From breakfast we three boys started for the woodshed—the moment morning prayers were finished—to secure each a "chopping ax" and a "splitting ax" from the stock of tools laid away there. A kettle of hot water was brought out to the grindstone, and for half an hour we turned for each other to grind the axes.

Then each laid off a foot measure on the handle of his "chopping ax" and marked it with a brass brad, filed off smoothly so that it might not catch in the hand.

Small whetstones were looked up in the "scythe house" to carry in our pockets. The box of iron wedges, for splitting the logs, was overhauled, and three old "beetles"—huge mallets with long handles, and having the wooden heads strengthened with strong, iron rings—were brought out. These tools, with an eight-foot pole for laying out the cord piles, completed our outfit.

Thus equipped, we strode off through the fields and across the valley to the wood lots—Grandfather coming after us on this first morning, the more accurately to designate to us the particular tract on which we were to cut the wood. It was a broad slope of land, rising from the brook to the crest of a long, mountainous ridge, at that time densely wooded with maple, birch, beech, and hemlock, great rock maples and yellow birches two feet in diameter, by no means soft to cut or easy to split.

"Now understand, once and for all, boys," said the Old Squire, in the tone of voice which we knew meant that he was in earnest; "this wood is to be cut four feet long from peak to scarf, and well split.

"The brush is to be ricked up in piles so that we can get in here comfortably with teams after snow comes. The cleft wood is to be put up in cord piles, each eight feet long and *four feet and a half high*. Remember that *half-foot* is for shrinkage; four feet and a half high every time. If any pile falls short when measured, I shall scale it down by just so much off the dollar.

"The rest of the money, I'll pay you every time the railroad pays me for delivery to its depot in the village.

"You may have one, two, or three years to do the job in, but I will measure up at the end of every month if you want your pay, and mark the piles paid with red chalk on the end.

"If you yourselves are unable to complete the job alone, you may hire all the help you need, at your own expense, for whatever you choose to pay. But at the end of three years, you will have to have cut and delivered at least six hundred cords of wood."

Such were the terms.

We began work with all the enthusiasm of boyhood—to which the whole world seems in store—in the bright November weather. How the old woods echoed our ax strokes!

But trouble and wrath came very shortly. Halstead's first tree, instead of falling as he had chopped it to go, fell back against Ad's and mine carrying them the wrong way, and lodging all three in the top of a great shaggy hemlock. We had both warned him what would happen, but he would not listen to us.

We were obliged to cut the hemlock, a tree we did not wish to fell, and when at last the four trees were down, they lay on the ground in a bad place and in an ugly jam. So the most of the forenoon had been wasted.

"A fine beginning!" cried Ad, with scorn. "Hereafter, Halse, you and I will work a little farther apart." And Halstead retorted, "The further the better!"

It was a beechnut year. Under the thick coat of yellow leaves on the ground there were still a great many of the sweet little three-sided nuts. The woods were alive with chickering, chirring red squirrels, with here and there a sly, quiet gray with his beautiful tail, stealing through the treetops. When they came near, we would stop chopping and shy great flat chips after them, but never could hit one.

After a tree was down, we stood on the log and chopped a scarf into it on each side till they met at the center, and the four-foot section fell off. That was one "cut." The great maple trunks often had fifteen and eighteen "cuts." Such a tree would make a cord or more, and it was indeed a hard day's work for a youth of fourteen to cut, split, and pile a cord of rock maple wood.

Before noon of the first day, we had all three of us raised blisters on our hands, just where the fingers emerge from the palm—nor were our hands unused to farmwork.

About one o'clock Dora and Nell came up to us through the woods directed by our ax blows, bringing a tin bucket well stocked with newly fried doughnuts, bread and butter, and cold ham and, with the bucket, a two-quart bottle full of milk. They had eaten dinner before starting, but sat by to keep us company for half an hour, while we disposed of their welcome burden.

The already waning sun looked warmly down into the little opening which we had made. We sat on the freshly cut logs, and the girls said that Ad had cut the smoothest scarfs. It seems to me that today I smell those fresh maple and birch chips.

Then the girls went to pick up beechnuts in the tin bucket while we betook ourselves with beetle and wedges, to the harder task of splitting the four-foot logs.

First we would strike the splitting ax into the scarfed end of the log, thus making a slight crack or cut, which would offer "toehold" for the blunter iron wedge. Then, having started in the wedge by hand and a few light strokes, we would drive it in with the beetle.

But even the wedges—three or four of them—sometimes failed to open the tough, gnarled logs. We would have to turn them and begin afresh on the other side or the other end. Some of the logs, after half an hour's hard work, we were obliged to abandon altogether.

On the other hand, many of the trees split well. We could open the logs with the axes alone, first one striking in, then the other two working together on the same log. On an average, the splitting was as hard a job as the chopping, and with some trees much worse.

It was disheartening to get a large tree all cut up into four-foot logs, and find that not one of them could be split. We could commonly give a pretty good guess beforehand, however, whether a tree would split well or badly by the way it "chipped" when we felled it. But if we cut a tree down we were expected to work it up, and not leave it lying on the ground to decay.

We had next to "cord" the wood up in piles. First we laid off eight feet on a level plot of ground, and set up two end stakes. Or a standing tree might take the place of a stake at one or both ends of the pile. Trees were better, for they did not have to be braced, and were not liable to give way and spread.

"Stringers" were next laid three feet apart between the stakes, to keep the wood off the ground. We were then ready to tier in the wood, and it is twenty or thirty minutes' work to pile a cord of wood—very hard work, too, for one unused to it.

We did not put up a cord apiece on that first day, nor on any subsequent day that autumn. Of "second growth" white birch, poplar, or maple of good rift, we could probably have cut and piled a cord in a day even at that time, when our muscles had not been trained and hardened by work, but this was "old growth" wood, solid to cut and tough to split.

Later on we sometimes bored the toughest logs with an inch-and-a-half auger, and, having put in about three ounces of gunpowder and a safety fuse, tamped it down with cedar plugs and blasted the logs open. But this method never pays at a dollar a cord, for it requires fifty cents' worth of powder and five cents' worth of fuse to blast up a cord of tough logs.

It uses up a great deal of time, too. A man needs to work nimbly to blast twenty logs four feet long and two feet in diameter in half a day. Then after they are blasted, it will require another half-day to finish splitting them, ready for cording up, with ax and wedge.

In taking jobs to cut cordwood, the point where the boys get disappointed in the result, is in the splitting, whether the trees split well or badly. If the logs prove to be tough, no price which is likely to be offered, will enable them to earn very good wages.

Great stories are told of the number of cords, which this or that famous woodcutter has put up in a day. I know of one man who cut and split, but did not pile five cords in a day. The wood was white birch and white maple, second-growth trees, about a foot in diameter and "long-bodied," that is to say tall, straight trees. It was done in March, after the sap had started and the wood was soft. A single blow of the ax would split the four-foot logs.

Even after all these explanations, some woodcutters may look upon this as a large story. Two cords a day, in fair wood, is a good day's work for an experienced chopper.

Next day, in the afternoon, we built a camp in the wood lot, so as to have a shelter in case of sudden storms, and even to pass a night in if we were so disposed. The walls were of large poles, laid up log-house fashion, and the roof was completed piecemeal with bits of boards and slabs which we brought over from the farm.

It was a small structure, ten feet by twelve, with a door and one window which was closed by a shutter board—a very rude and primitive affair—but if it had been a palace, we could not have had more fun in it.

Later we set up an old cookstove in one corner, and the girls would concoct all sorts of dishes for us, which having keen appetites from the hard work, we used to relish exceedingly. They enjoyed it as much as we did, for they would pretend to keep house there, and were forever playing practical jokes with our victuals.

It was far from being all sport, however, and perhaps I am getting somewhat in advance of my story. On the Friday forenoon of the second week—our third day in the lot—Addison and I, who were working near together that day, were startled by a sharp cry from Halstead, who, since the first forenoon, when he had been so careless about the fall of his tree, had worked apart from us.

It was a cry of pain! and we both dropped our axes and ran to where Halse was working. He was sitting on the ground holding his right foot in both hands, writhing and crying out. He had on a nearly new pair of high-topped boots, and we saw the bright blood gushing out at a long cut through one of them, from the toe up to the instep.

"Oh, I've cut myself! I've cut my foot clean open!" he screamed out, as we came up.

I seized him firmly by the shoulders, and Ad pulled off the boot. His stocking was already soaked with blood, but we peeled that off also. The blood gushed in a stream, for it was a savage cut, extending across the great toe and half up the instep.

Ad first tried to bring the edges of the wound together and tie his handkerchief around the foot, but finding that he could not stop the flow of blood and that Halstead was getting very white in the face, he seized my handkerchief, knotted it loosely about his ankle and then, catching up a stick, thrust it inside the loop and twisted it around twice.

But before we had accomplished this, Halse fell over sideways in a fainting fit. That alarmed me, but Ad kept tightening the band around his ankle, and immediately the flow of blood ceased.

With a knife we then scraped some lint off a pair of cotton drawers, and putting this on the cut bound it up. I then ran for water, but before I could fetch it, Halstead had revived, and was sitting up. Addison kept the ligature round the ankle for about fifteen minutes, then gradually released it.

Not much more blood flowed, and we presently set off to help him to the house. It was difficult to do so, for Halse could step only on his left foot, and made use of our shoulders as a crutch. Then the doctor had to be sent for from the village seven miles away, so that day was as good as lost for all of us.

It was three weeks before Halstead set that foot to the ground again. Next year, poor fellow! he cut the other foot, and the third year he cut his right foot again.

Neither Ad nor I ever happened to cut himself, but it is an accident which may befall even the most careful wood chopper. If one is cutting wood alone in the woods, it may become a very serious matter. There are numerous instances where wood choppers have bled to death from ax wounds.

Grandfather was constantly cautioning us on this, that or the other point, and about once a month he would be sure to advise us something like this: "Always when you've cut a tree, boys, and you see it start to fall, step back behind the stump. Never stand sideways to the trunk of a tree when it goes down."

I did not for a long time see the force of this advice, and failed to pay much attention to it—till one day Ad and I had cut a tall beech, about a foot and a half in diameter. As it went down, I stood aside a little, but did not step back.

As the tree fell it struck some obstruction, and the butt hit me and knocked me about twice my length, with an ease and suddenness which abundantly impressed the subject of the Old Squire's caution upon my mind. I was a good deal shaken up, though not seriously injured. Yet such accidents are sometimes fatal.

Another of Grandfather's old saws to us was: "Always when you go to a tree to fell it, first glance up into the top and knock two or three times on the trunk of it with the poll of your ax—particularly in soft woods."

By soft woods the old gentleman meant spruce, pine, or hemlock in distinction from the hardwoods—maple and birch.

This also was one of the cautions which we heard, but failed to heed for a time. One day we began to chop down a large rock maple. Ad opened a scarf on one side while I worked on the other, but we had not got our first chips out, when down came a piece of dry branch out of the top, struck Ad exactly on his head, and felled him in his tracks!

He scrambled to his feet, somewhat dazed and not a little astonished! His hat had protected his head, in a measure, but the blow set his nose bleeding. The dry stick which had hit him was only about as large around as an ax handle, and not more than a foot and a half long, but it had fallen from a height of sixty or seventy feet, and came with great force.

After the winter school began we used to go over to work only on Saturdays, and by February the snow had become too deep to chop wood in the woods. Throughout the following spring and summer rainstorms often prevented us from working on our "liberty days."

We were hampered so much by these circumstances that I do not think we got up over sixty cords apiece during the first year. Halstead did not get so much as that, for he had much bad luck.

As time went on, we did not agree among ourselves on all points, and concluded to work each on his own hook. Practically, therefore, the job took the form of two hundred cords for each. Ad kept a little ahead of me, a few cords. He was two years older than I and had a good head, as well as good muscles for any kind of work.

We did not have the wood measured till September. At that time we drew on the Old Squire for what we had cut. Ad and I, with Dora and Nell, had arranged to go to the village academy for eight weeks, and we wanted the pay for our expenses.

To keep down costs, we carried food from home and often stayed in the village at an empty house the Old Squire owned. Some weeks we would go down to the village on Sunday evenings and return home only on Thursday evenings, so as to get in our two days of wood-cutting.

The girls, too, were obligated to assist Grandmother on those last two days of the week. They had also to cook our food which we carried with us to the village, and do a hundred other little things. In fact, they worked fully as hard as we boys did, and richly deserved their third of the wood money.

We studied during evenings, and in all odd hours, and kept well up with our classes at the academy, in spite of the lost Friday.

Dora and Nell were beginning algebra and Latin that fall. Ad had studied Latin a year or two, and was reading Caesar, I was trying to read it, too, but he was far the best student. And oh, we did have some of the cheeriest, most enjoyable evenings in October that autumn! For after the day's work cutting wood, we often spent the evening at our camp over in the wood lot.

We had a fire in our stove, and also a campfire outside. We used to carry over apples, and would pop corn there and make cornballs. Two young people, neighbors of ours, named Tom and Kate Edwards, who were also attending the academy with us, frequently came over to the camp to pass the evening.

We had a long bench and a rude table, rigged just outside the camp door, and there we would sit and get out our Latin lessons. Kate, Dora, Nell, and Tom were all reading Aesop's Fables, in Harkness's *Latin Reader*. Ah, they did have great times puzzling out those fables and eating cornballs! They named our camp the "Branch Academy."

At about ten o'clock we commonly started to go home, and lighted birch bark torches stuck on the ends of long sticks, to show the way out of the woods, across the brook, and up through the pastures to the house. It seems to me now, that I never enjoyed life half as well as while reading Latin over at the "Branch Academy" in the wood lot!

One evening three or four owls came about our campfire, and flapping their wings in the dark treetops, treated us to a fearful serenade. They stayed with us for more than an hour, and gave vent to some of the most singular sounds which I ever heard from owls.

On another evening a hare—chased by some wild animal, I presume—took refuge under the very bench on which we were all sitting.

On still another night which we boys spent at the camp, a bear came sniffing about a kettle set outside the camp door. Ad heard the noise, and getting up softly from our bunk suddenly pulled the door wide open. This surprised the bear so much, that he uttered a yelp more like a dog than a bear, and tumbled headlong over the big chopping block in his eagerness to escape.

There had come about an inch of snow earlier in the night, and the next morning we saw by the bear's tracks, that he had walked four or five times around the camp at a distance of twenty or thirty yards from it, before venturing up to the kettle.

Halstead had concluded not to attend the academy. He decided to use his money in buying a colt. During the second winter we cut about twenty more cords of wood than we had done the first year. But Addison did less, for he was that winter offered a chance to teach a small school three miles from home, and tried his "'prentice hand" as a pedagogue for the first time.

So the job continued on into the second summer, and in September we began a term at the academy again. This second autumn we had new books to buy, including an Andrew's *Latin Lexicon* which cost us four dollars and seventy cents, and accordingly had need of all our wood money.

Halse had now cut his other foot, and was laid up over a fortnight in October. Poor boy, he was always having bad luck, and we may sometimes have failed in proper charity toward him. He grew discouraged.

There were several other circumstances which tended to turn him the wrong way at about this time, and he was led to commit an act for which I am sure that he felt great shame afterwards.

Grandfather was now measuring the wood, and paying us every month. As fast as he measured and paid for the cord piles, he marked each with a letter P for *paid*, on the end of one or more of the sticks of wood in the pile. Halse so far yielded to a dishonest impulse as to cut the P off one of the measured piles—one pile every month for four months.

There were so many piles that the Old Squire did not notice the trick, and so Halstead drew his pay for four cords *twice!*

Something which he said later about the sum of money he had made caused Ad and myself to mistrust him. We could tell his piles by sight from ours, and kept an eye on them after that, with the result, that we were able to identify a pile the following month, from which he had hewn off the P.

We hardly knew what was the best course to take in so grave a matter. We disliked to expose him outright to the Old Squire, who trusted us all implicitly. For that very reason we were the more angry and the more determined that he should not be cheated.

We talked with Dora about it. She thought that we had better speak with Halstead, but Ad did not favor that plan, for Halse was somewhat hasty and peculiar. We looked over the piles, and made sure that this last was the fifth pile from which he had removed the mark. The thing we at length did, was to go the night before the Old Squire measured the wood that month, and privately put five P's on to as many of Halstead's new piles; he had seven that month, six beside the one which he had "doctored."

"Why, you haven't done much this month, Halse!" the Old Squire exclaimed, when he went to measure Halstead's wood, and found only two piles without P's on them!

Halstead did not know what to say or think! He felt guilty, of course, and probably was afraid that Grandfather had already found him out. He hung his head and offered never a word, nor so much as said that he had done more, but took his two dollars in silence.

But I think that he saw us looking a little amused at lunch that day, for he burst out in a passion, and said that he wished other people would mind their business, and let his affairs alone.

"Halse," said Ad, "if you know when you are well off, you will keep quiet."

That was all there was said. Halstead flushed as red as a beet, but concluded to follow Ad's advice.

He was always ashamed of what he had done. On several occasions subsequently, when we had caught him in a little crookedness, we would make a P on a piece of paper or a slate, and hold it up to him. That always had the desired effect. The Old Squire and Grandmother never knew of his trick. He did not cut much more wood, however.

The job dragged along into the third season. Three years is long addition to the lives of youths of fourteen and sixteen. We had somewhat outgrown the wants and conditions under which we took the job, and had done better otherwise. We had earned more money from Ad's bird's-eye maple scheme and the sale of Shasky-Legs. Ad could now get fifty dollars a month for two terms of school every winter, for he was quite successful as a schoolmaster. That winter, I also set up as a pedagogue in a small district school. We had, moreover, taken to canvassing for a horse rake and mowing machine, and had several other schemes for turning a penny.

However, we were determined not to let the Old Squire down and were able to hire help to cut the rest of our 600 cords. We paid the three diligent young French Canadians, who had previously worked with us in haying, the same dollar-a-cord price the Old Squire paid us. In all, they cut about 120 cords while we cut not far from 535 cords ourselves. And although it was an experience which we did not care to repeat, yet Addison, Dora, and Nell now often agree with me, that some of the most pleasant memories of our life at Grandfather's old farm, Down East, are associated with that three-year job of cutting cordwood.

15

~~~⟡━━━⟡~~~

A January Thaw

JUST BEFORE SCHOOL CLOSED IN 1867 A DISAGREEABLE
incident occurred.

It was one of the few times that the Old Squire really reproved us
sternly. Often, of course, he had to caution us a little, or speak to us
about our conduct, but he usually did it in an easy, tolerant way, ending
with a laugh or a joke. But that time he was in earnest.

He had come home that night just at dark from Three Rivers, in
Canada, where he was engaged in a lumbering enterprise. He had been
gone a fortnight, and during his absence Addison, Halstead, and I had
been doing the farm chores. The drive from the railway station on that
bleak January afternoon had chilled the old gentleman, and he went
directly into the sitting room to get warm. So it was not until he came
out to sit down to supper with us that he noticed a vacant chair at table.

"Where is Halstead?" he asked. "Isn't Halstead at home'"

No one answered at first; none of us liked to tell him what had happened. We had always found our cousin Halstead hard to get on with.
Lately he had been complaining to us that he ought to be paid wages for
his labor, when, as a matter of fact, what he did at the farm never half
repaid the Old Squire for his board, clothes, and the trouble he gave.
During the old gentleman's absence that winter Halstead had become
worse than ever and had also begun making trouble at the district school.

His special crony at school was Alfred Batchelder, who had an
extremely bad influence on him. Alfred was a genius at instigating

mischief, and he and Halstead played an odious prank at the school-house, as a result of which the school committee suspended them for three weeks.

That was unfortunate, for it turned the boys loose to run about in company. Usually they quarreled by the time they had been together half a day, but this time there seemed to be a special bond between them, and they hatched a secret project to go off trapping up in the Great Woods. They intended to stay until spring, when they would reappear with five hundred dollars' worth of fur!

Addison and I guessed that something of the sort was in the wind, for we noticed that Halstead was collecting old traps and that he was oiling a gun he called his. We also missed two thick horse blankets from the stable and a large hand sled. A frozen quarter of beef also disappeared from the wagon house chamber.

"Let him go, and good riddance," Addison said, and we decided not to tell Grandmother or the girls what we suspected. In fact, I fear that we hoped Halstead would go.

The following Friday afternoon while the rest of us were at school both boys disappeared. That evening Mrs. Batchelder sent daughter Amanda over to inquire whether Alfred was at our house. Halstead, to his credit, had shown that he did not wish Grandmother to worry about him. Shortly before two o'clock that afternoon, he had come hastily to the sitting room door, and said, "Good-bye, Gram. I'm going away for a spell. Don't worry." Then, shutting the door, he had run off before she could reply or ask a question.

When we got home from school that night, Addison and I found traces of the runaways. There had been rain the week before, followed by a hard freeze and snow squalls, which had left a film of light snow on the hard crust beneath. At the rear of the west barn we found the tracks of a hand sled leading off across the fields toward the woods.

"Gone hunting, I guess," said Addison. "They are probably heading for the Old Slave's Farm, or for Adger's lumber camp. Let them go. They'll be sick to death of it in a week."

I felt much the same about it, but Grandmother and Theodora were not a little disturbed. Ellen, however, sided with Addison. "Halse will be back by tomorrow night," she said. "He and Alfred will have a spat by that time."

Saturday and Sunday passed, however, and then all the following week, with no word from them.

On Tuesday evening, when they had been gone eleven days, Mrs. Batchelder hastened in with alarming news for us. She had had a letter from Alfred, she said, written from Berlin Falls in New Hampshire, where he had gone to work in a mill, but he had not said one word about Halstead!

"I don't think they could have gone off together," she said, and she read Alfred's letter aloud to us, or seemed to do so, but did not hand it to any of us to read.

We had never trusted Mrs. Batchelder implicitly, and a long time afterwards it came out that there was one sentence in that letter that she had not read to us. It was this: "Don't say anything to any of them about Halstead." Guessing that there had been trouble of some kind between the boys, she was frightened; to shield Alfred she had hurried over with the letter, and had tried to make us believe that the boys had not gone off together.

Addison and I still thought that the boys had set out in company, though we did not know what to make of Alfred's letter. We were waiting in that disturbed state of mind, hoping to hear something from Alfred that would clear up the mystery, when the Old Squire came home.

"He has gone away, sir," Addison said at last, when the old gentleman inquired for Halstead at supper.

"Gone away? Where? What for?" the old gentleman asked in much astonishment, and then the whole story had to be told him.

The Old Squire heard it through without saying much. When we had finished, he asked, "Did you know that Halstead meant to go away?"

"We did not know for certain, sir," Addison replied.

"Still, you both knew something about it?"

"Yes, sir."

"Did either one of you do anything to prevent it?"

We had to admit that we had done nothing.

The Old Squire regarded us a moment or two in silence.

"In one of the oldest narratives of life that have come down to us," he said at last, "we read that there were once two brothers living together, who did not agree and who often fell out. After a time one of them disappeared, and when the other—his name was Cain—was asked what had become of his brother, he replied, 'Am I my brother's keeper?'

"In this world we all have to be our brothers' keepers," the Old Squire continued. "We are all to a degree responsible for the good behavior and safety of our fellow beings. If we shirk that duty, troubles come and crimes are committed that might have been prevented. Especially in a family like ours, each ought to have the good of all at heart and do his best to make things go right."

That was a great deal for the Old Squire to say to us. Addison and I saw just where we had shirked and where we had let temper and resentment influence us. Scarcely another word was said at table. It was one of those times of self-searching and reflection that occasionally come unbidden in every family circle.

The Old Squire went into the sitting room to think it over and to learn what he could from Grandmother. He was very tired, and I am afraid he felt somewhat discouraged about us.

Addison and I went up to our room early that evening. We exchanged scarcely a word as we went gloomily to bed. We knew that we were to blame, but we also felt tremendously indignant with Halstead.

Very early the next morning, however, long before it was light, Addison roused me.

"Wake up," he said. "Let's go see if we can find that noodle of ours and get him back home."

It was cold and dark and dreary; one of those miserable, shivery mornings when you hate to stir out of bed. But I got up, for I agreed with Addison that we ought to look for Halstead.

After dabbling our faces in ice-cold water and dressing we tiptoed downstairs. Going to the kitchen, we kindled a fire in order to get a bit of breakfast before we started. Theodora had heard us and came hastily down to bear a hand. She guessed what we meant to do.

"I'm glad you're going," said she as she began to make coffee and to warm some food.

It was partly the bitter weather, I think, but Addison and I felt so cross that we could hardly trust ourselves to speak.

"I'll put you up a nice, big lunch," Theodora said, trying to cheer us. "And I do hope that you will find him at the Old Slave's Farm, or over at Adger's camp. If you do, you may all be back by night."

She stole up to her room to get a pair of new double mittens that she had just finished knitting for Addison, and for me she brought down a woolen neck muffler that Grandmother had knitted for her. Life brightens up, even in a Maine winter, with a girl like that round.

Addison took his shotgun, and I carried the basket of luncheon. No snow had come since Halstead and Alfred left, and we could still see along the old lumber road the faint marks of their hand-sled runners. In the hollows where the film of snow was a little deeper, two boot tracks were visible.

"Halse wouldn't go off far into the woods alone, after Alf left him," said I.

"No, he is too big a coward," said Addison. It was thirteen miles up to the Old Slave's Farm, where the Negro—who called himself Pinkney Doman—had lived for so many years before the Civil War.

"We can make it in three hours!" Addison exclaimed. "If we find him there, we shall be back before dark. And we had better hurry," he added, with a glance at the sky. "For I guess there's a storm coming; feels like it."

In a yellow birch top at a little opening near the old road we saw two partridges eating buds; Addison shot one of them and took it along, slung to his gun barrel.

The faint trail of the sled continued along the old winter road all the way up to the clearing where the Negro had lived, and by ten o'clock we came into view of the two log cabins. Very still and solitary they looked under that cold gray sky.

"No smoke," Addison said. "But we'll soon know." He called once. We then hurried forward and pushed open the door of the larger cabin. No one was there.

But clearly the two truants had stopped there, for the sled track led directly to the door of the cabin. There had been a fire in the stone fireplace. Beside a log at the door, too, Addison espied a hatchet that awhile before we had missed from the tool bench in the wagon house.

"Well, if that isn't like their carelessness!" he exclaimed, laughing. "I'll take this along."

But the runaways had not tarried long. We found the sled track again, leading into the woods at the northwest of the clearing.

"Well, that settles it," said Addison. "They haven't gone to Adger's, for that is east from here. I'll tell you! They went to Boundary Camp on Lurvey's Stream. And that's eighteen or nineteen miles from here." He glanced at the sky. "Now, what shall we do? It will snow tonight."

"Perhaps we could get up there by dark," said I.

For a moment Addison considered. "All right!" he exclaimed. "It's a long jaunt. But come on!"

On we tramped again, following that will-o'-the-wisp of a hand-sled track into the thick spruce forest. For the first nine or ten miles everything went well; then one of the dangers of the great Maine woods in winter suddenly presented itself.

About one o'clock it began to snow—little icy pellets that rattled down through the treetops like fine shot or sifted sand. The chill, damp wind sighing drearily across the forest presaged a northeaster.

"We've got to hurry!" Addison said, glancing round.

We both struck into a trot and, with our eyes fastened to the trail, ran on for about two miles until we came to a brook down in a gorge. By the time we had crossed that the storm was upon us and the forest had taken on the bewildering misty, gray look that even the most experienced woodsman has reason to dread.

The snow that had fallen had obscured the faint sled tracks, and Addison, who was ahead, pulled up. "We can't do it," he said. "We shan't get through."

My first impulse was to run on, to run faster; that is always your first instinct in such cases. Then I remembered the Old Squire's advice about what to do if we should ever happen to be caught by a snow-storm in the Great Woods: "Don't go on a moment after you feel bewildered. Don't start to run, and don't get excited. Stop right where you are and camp. If you run, you will begin to circle, get crazy, and perish before morning." Addison cast another uneasy glance into the dim forest ahead. "Better camp, I guess," he said. Turning, we hurried back into the hollow.

A few yards back from the brook were two rocks, about six feet apart and nearly as high as my head. Hard snow lay between them, but we broke it into pieces by stamping on it, and succeeded in clearing most of it away, so that we bared the leaves and twigs that covered the ground. Then, while I hacked off dry branches from a fallen fir tree, Addison gathered a few curled rolls of bark from several birches near by and kindled a fire between the rocks.

We kept the fire going for more than an hour, until all the remaining snow was thawed and the frost and wet thoroughly dried out, and until the rocks had become so hot that we could hardly touch them. Then, after hauling away the brands and embers, we brushed the place clean with green boughs, and thus made for ourselves a warm, dry spot between the rocks.

With poles and green boughs, we made for our shelter a roof that was tight enough to keep out the snow. Except that we made a little mat of bark and dry fir brush, to lie on, and that Addison brought an armful of curled bark from the birches and a quantity of dry sticks to burn now and then, that was the extent of our preparation for the night. We had as warm and comfortable a den as anyone could wish for.

We decided not to cook our partridge, but to eat the food in our basket. After our meal we got a drink of water at the brook, then crawled inside our den and—as Maine woodsmen say—"pulled the hole in after us," by stopping it with boughs.

"Now, let it storm!" Addison exclaimed.

Taking off our jackets and spreading them over us, we cuddled down there by the warm rocks, and there we passed the night safely and by no means uncomfortably.

It was still snowing fast in the morning, but the flakes were larger now, and the weather had perceptibly moderated during the latter part of the night. The forest, however, still looked too misty for us to find our way through it.

"We might as well take it easy," Addison said. "If Halse is at Boundary Camp, he will not leave in such weather as this."

All that forenoon it snowed steadily, and in fact for most of the afternoon. More than a foot of snow had come. We opened the front of our snow-coated den, kindled a fire there, and after dressing our partridge broiled it over the embers. Still it snowed, but the weather now was much warmer. By the following morning, we thought, we should have clear, cold weather and should be able to set out again.

But never were weather predictions more at fault.

The next morning it was raining furiously, and our den had begun to drip. In fact, a veritable January thaw had set in.

All that forenoon it poured steadily, and water began to show yellow through the snow in the brook beside our camp. Addison crept out and looked round, but soon came back dripping wet. "Look here!" said he in some excitement. "There's a freshet coming, and Lurvey's Stream is between us and Boundary Camp. If we don't start soon, we can't get there at all."

Just as he finished speaking a deep, portentous rumbling began and continued for several seconds. The distant mountainsides seemed to reverberate with it, and at the end the whole forest shook with heavy, jarring sounds. We both leaped out into the rain.

"What is it, Ad?" I cried.

"Earthquake," said Addison.

And it reminded us both of an earlier encounter, in which I, and three friends, were buried alive by a winter 'quake.

Accordingly, we abandoned our rocky den and set off in the rain. We went halfway to our knees at every step in the now soft, slushy snow. Addison went ahead with the hatchet, spotting a tree every hundred feet or so, and I followed in his tracks, carrying the basket and the gun. In fifteen minutes we were wet to our skins.

For three or four miles we were uncertain of our course. The forest then lightened ahead, and presently we came out on the shore of a small lake that looked yellow over its whole surface.

"Good!" Addison exclaimed. "This must be Lone Pond, and see, away over there is Birchboard Mountain. Boundary Camp is just this side of it. It can't be more than four or five miles."

Skirting the south shore of the pond, we pushed on through fir and cedar swamps. Worse traveling it would be impossible to imagine. Every hole and hollow was full of yellow slush. Finally, after another two hours or so of hard going, we came out on Lurvey's Stream about half a mile below the camp, which was on the other bank. A foot or more of water was running yellow over the ice, but the ice itself was still firm, and we were able to cross on it.

Even before we came in sight of the camp, we smelled wood smoke. "Halse is there!" I exclaimed.

"It may be trappers from over the line," Addison said. "Be cautious."

I ran forward, however, and peeped in at the little window. Someone was crawling on the floor, partly behind the old camp stove, and I had to look twice before I could make out that it was really Halstead. Then we burst in upon him, and Addison said rather shortly, "Well, hunter, what are you doing here?"

Halstead raised himself slowly off the floor beside the stove, stared at us for a moment without saying a word, and then suddenly burst into tears!

It was some moments before Halstead could speak, he was so shaken with sobs. We then discovered that his left leg was virtually useless, and that in general he was in a bad plight. He had been there for eight days in that condition, crawling round on one knee and his hands to keep a fire and to cook his food.

"But how did you get hurt?" Addison asked.

"That Alf did it!" Halstead cried, and then, with tears still flowing, he went on to tell the story—his side of it.

While getting their breakfast on the third morning after they had reached the camp, they had had a dispute about making their coffee; hard names had followed, and at last, in high temper, Alfred had sprung up declaring that he would not camp with Halstead another hour. Grabbing the gun, he had started off.

"That's my gun! Leave it here! Drop it!" Halstead had shouted angrily and had run after him.

Down near the bank of the stream, Halstead had overtaken him and had tried to wrest the gun from him. Alfred had turned, struck him, and then given him so hard a push that he had fallen over sidewise with his foot down between two logs. Alfred had run on without even looking back.

The story did not astonish us. For the time being, however, we were chiefly concerned to find out how badly Halstead was injured, with a view to getting him home. His ankle was swollen, sore and painful; he could not touch the foot to the floor, and he howled when we tried to move it.

Evidently he had suffered a good deal, and pity prevented us from freeing our minds to him as fully as we should otherwise have done. The main thing now was to get him home, where a doctor could attend him.

"We shall have to haul him on the hand sled," Addison said to me, and fortunately the sled that Alfred and he had taken was there at the camp.

But first we cooked a meal of some of the beef, cornmeal, and coffee they had taken from the Old Squire's.

It was still raining, and on going out an hour later we found that the stream had risen so high that we could not cross it. The afternoon, too, was waning, and, urgent as Halstead's case appeared, we had to give up the idea of starting that night. During the rest of the afternoon we busied ourselves rigging a rude seat on the sled.

There were good dry bunks at the camp, but little sleep was in store for us. Halstead was in a fevered, querulous mood and kept calling to us for something or other all night long. Whenever he fell asleep he tumbled about and hurt his ankle. That would partly wake him and set him crying, or shouting what he would do to Alfred.

Throughout the night the roar of the stream outside grew louder, and at daybreak it was running feather white. As for the snow, most of it had disappeared; stumps, logs, and stones showed through it everywhere; the swamps were flooded, and every hole, hollow and depression was full of water.

That was Wednesday. We made a soup of the beef bone, cooked johnnycake from the cornmeal and kept Halstead as quiet as possible. We had left home early Sunday morning and knew that our folks would be greatly worried about all three of us.

As the day passed, the stream rose steadily until the water was nearly up to the camp door.

"If only we had a boat, we could put Halse in it and go home," Addison said.

We discussed making a raft, for if we could navigate the stream we could descend it to within four miles of the old farm. But the roaring yellow torrent was clearly so tumultuous that no raft that we could build would hold together for a minute, and we resigned ourselves to pass another night in the camp.

The end of the thaw was at hand, however; at sunset the sky lightened, and during the evening the stars came out. At midnight, while replenishing the fire, I heard smart gusts of wind blowing from the northwest. It was clearing off cold. Noticing that it seemed very light outside, I went to the door and saw the bright arch of a splendid aurora spanning the whole sky. It was so beautiful that I waked Addison to see it.

By morning winter weather had come again; the snow slush was frozen. The stream, however, was still too high to be crossed, and the swamps and meadows were also impassable. We now bethought ourselves of another route home, by way of a lumber trail that led southward to Lurvey's Mills, where there was a bridge over the stream.

"It is five miles farther, but it is our only chance of getting home this week," Addison said. We were busy bundling Halstead up for the sled trip when the door opened and in stepped Asa Doane, one of our hired men at the farm, and a neighbor named Davis.

"Well, well, here you are, then!" Asa exclaimed in a tone of great relief. "Do you know that the Old Squire's got ten men out searching the woods for you? Why, the folks at home are scared half to death!"

We were not sorry to see Asa and Davis, and to have help for the long pull homeward. We made a start, and after a very hard tramp we finally reached the old farm, thoroughly tired out, at eight o'clock that evening.

Theodora and Grandmother were so affected at seeing us back that they actually shed tears. The Old Squire said little, but it was plain to see that he was greatly relieved.

If the day had been a fatiguing one for us, it had been doubly so for poor Halstead. We carried him up to his room, put him to bed, and sent for a doctor. He did not leave his room again for three weeks and required no end of care from Grandmother and the girls.

Little was ever said among us afterwards of this escapade of Halstead's. As for Alfred, he came sneaking home about a month later but had the decency, or perhaps it was the prudence, to keep away from us for nearly a year.

16

~~~※※※~~—~~◇※◇~~

The Old Cider Mill

YESTERDAY THEY TORE DOWN THE OLD CIDER MILL AT the Lynches'. Its place, or rather its office, is to be taken by a little cast-iron one set in the stable.

Odd enough it will seem to go past the Lynch farm now, and miss the old mill, for it was a very conspicuous object where it stood, three or four rods back from the house, with its great hopper and mash wheel encircled by the deep-trodden path where old Sib used to plod endlessly through the brisk October days, grinding all the cider apples of the neighborhood. And there were the great posts and crossbeam of the press, massive pine timbers, eighteen inches square, that had a certain Cyclopean look, fit to make a boy stare, and put large ideas into his head. There, too, were the big, steaming heaps of tan-colored pomace (or "pummy") and the great sour-smelling trough into which the ground apple fell and was thence conveyed to the hoops.

For several seasons, however, the huge wooden jackscrews have been out of the lofty crossbeam, and the mash wheel has grown toothless. Indeed, the old mill has never been quite itself since the Maine Liquor Law made a revolution in the neighborhood. But the great pine posts stood fast, and bade fair to do so for another half-century, to the wonder of strangers.

"Say, old fellow! Is that the gallows?" a passing "runner" demanded of Uncle Billy Clives, who, one day, sat nodding under the balm-of-Gilead, a little beyond.

"Gallows!" quoth the old fellow, a steady consumer of hard cider. "Wal, first an' last it's sarved me a sight worse than a gallows could 'a' done."

But at present my story relates to the last years of the old mill's active career, during which it was at certain seasons put to a special, but less legitimate use, the precise nature of which long remained a mystery. This was when the Lynch girls, then verging toward young womanhood, were all at home—Lucreesh, Cad, Jess, and Lorette, a merry lot, rosy, and "full of the old cat."

We had a custom in that neighborhood—a custom not confined to that neighborhood, I may add—of hanging May baskets; a sort of paper valentine, made basket-form to hold more substantial tokens than mere poetry. The hanging part was generally followed by a hot pursuit of the hanging parties, who, if caught, were subject to no end of laughable ignominy. The Lynch girls, swift of foot as Diana herself, sometimes captured the lads who ventured to append favors to their door, and then came the droll part, the part which has to do with the old cider mill. Whenever they had caught any of the boys, there would be plenty of exultant *powwows* while they took him back to where the old mill stood, then extravagant outcries, often yells of genuine distress, and no end of humble begging. The girls did something to him there at the old cider mill. What it was, whether they stuffed his mouth with "pummy," or pinched his toes in the mash wheel, was not very clear to the other lads. And of the three or four boys they had thus misused, not one could be got to tell what the girls had done to him—it was something he didn't like to talk about.

Now, I will wager that someone of my readers is saying that he should just like to see the four girls that could hustle him back there to that mill and stuff *his* mouth with ground apple! Well, sir, I should just like to see how you would go to work to help yourself, with four girls all laughing and pulling at you. What would you do? Double up your fist? Ah, but you know that it's morally impossible to hit one of the soft, calico-ey things—after you've doubled it! It's about the best way to let 'em work, and bear it all with your best grin.

This sort of thing had been going on for two springs, when, late in May 1867, a some degrees removed cousin of the writer's came on from

New York, where his father resides, to make us all a visit and stay through the summer. His name, as he wrote it, was Horace G. Melcher, the G. standing for the late great editor, but we knew him as "Hod" simply. I wonder whether Mr. Greeley's early playfellows used to call him Hod?

Well, Hod was a pretty good sort of fellow. Of course, he had on a few airs, but then we expect that in city boys—at first. They do have a good many advantages over country lads, and I don't know that it is anything more than fair that they should snub us a little. Hod, by the way, was then fifteen past. He ridiculed the "style" of the young ladies of the neighborhood, and, no doubt, they seemed to him different from the girls he had been used to seeing. But he took a very lively interest in May baskets, and, although May had soon given place to June, we still kept up the fun on odd evenings—only now they were no longer May baskets, but June boxes—every fruit in its season.

Thanks to the good counsels which our mutual playfellow, Tom Edwards, and I gave him, Hod had thus far kept out of the clutches of the fair Lynches. But, like many another, he soon got impatient of advice. He didn't see the good of skulking behind fences and into bush clumps. He was very certain they couldn't catch him; indeed, he would like to see the girl that could catch him in a fair race. He grew bolder, and one night (the third June box, I think), the door opening close upon our knock, he dashed out into the road, yelled, and ran off in full view of his eager pursuers. We heard him go down the road at full pound, with a spiteful pit-pat of girls' shoes hard behind.

Very possibly he might have escaped them, but, coming where the unfenced common skirted the road, he assayed to tack off across it. Here a treacherous stone hole, masked by high brakes and blueberry bushes, received him all in a heap. The next moment the pretty Philistines were upon him. A peal of triumphant laughter from the common told us the rest; for Tom and I, meanwhile, had hurried off back of the house, past the old cider mill, and plunged into the thicket of balm-of-Gilead sprouts which had sprung up about the trunk of the old tree. Throwing ourselves full length under this green coppice, we lay quiet. The twilight had not quite faded out in the northwest; in the east the rim of the late-rising moon was just peeping over; it brightened as Hod's captors came back with him. Every few steps there would be a tussle; the prisoner seemed a good deal inclined to resist. Then followed by an invariable "No you don't, sir!" "Now, don't hold a fellow so!" we could hear Hod remonstrating. Then the girls would laugh mockingly, and exhort him to come along, telling him how ungallant it was to run away from young ladies. "Now, don't tear yourself away! See us home, do! We've got something pretty to show you—something you'll like!" etc.

On they came past the house, and made straight for the cider mill; then we heard boards rattle and the old wooden screws squeak. Secretly tickled, and not a little curious, Tom and I got our heads up and peeped out from amongst the sprouts.

"Now, what's the use!" Hod was pleading. "I say, you girls, what are ye going to do to a feller!"

Then came a prolonged scrimmage. Round they went, all over the backyard. Hod was making a desperate effort to get away. No use; they held on to him and brought him up under the high posts of the press again, all panting.

"I'll be blamed," whispered Tom, "if they hain't got him up on the bench where the pummy hoop is!"

Then came another struggle and clatter. "Now—now—now, please don't!" cried Hod. But the wicked sprites only laughed the louder.

"There!" muttered Tom, "if they hain't got him into the hoop and got the follower down on to him! Good gracious, Nicholas! I believe they're going to squeeze him! They're turning the screws!"

We began to be a little alarmed for Hod. Not that we thought they would "squash him up" knowingly, but they had an enormous power in hand, and girls sometimes lack discretion.

Creak—creak—squeak! We could see Cad and Jess turning the levers to bring the screw heads down on to the follower. Lucreesh and Lorette were holding the follower over him.

"Oh, you'll make a splendid cheese!" they were saying.

I don't think Hod fairly divined their intentions until the follower began to press him. Then he squirmed in good earnest, but they had him hard and fast.

"Now, boy," says Cad, "what was you at our door for?"

"To hang a June box" said Hod, candidly.

"Oh, you was! Who was it with you?"

"I don't want to tell that," said Hod, honorably.

"Don't you?" *Creak—squeak.*

"Oh!" *Creak—squeak.* "Oh!—Tom Edwards—Oh-h! and Nicholas—Oh-h-h!"

They eased up, laughing as only such a mischievous pack can.

"Where did Tom and Nick run to?"

"I don't know," said Hod, and really he did not know.

"Try and think," says Jess. *Creak—squeak.*

"I honestly don't know!" vociferated Hod. *Squeak—creak.* "Oh!—up the road. Oh-h!—over into the wood. Oh! Oh!"

Torture has made many a martyr lie, no doubt, when the truth wasn't satisfactory to his inquisitors.

"You're the fellow from New York, ain't you?" demanded Jess, "the one they call Hod!"

"Yes—yes! From New York! I'm Hod!"

"Hod is a droll name; what does it stand for?"

"Stands for Horace."

"Horace, what else?"

"Horace Melcher."

"Any middle name?"

Hod hesitated. He was then very sensitive about his second name, New York folks were laughing so much at his great namesake.

"Come, what's your middle name?" questioned Cad.

"My middle initial's G," replied Hod, trying to compromise it.

"Well, but what does that G stand for?"

No answer. *Creak—squeak—creak.* "Oh, now!" *Creak—creak.* "Oh!—Greeley!—oh!—Horace Greeley—oh-h!"

Then they eased up to laugh over him, and says Lucreesh, "How much is your father worth, Horace Greeley?"

"Nothing!" exclaimed Hod, irritated at the sound of his full name.

"Reckon again!" cried Cad.

We heard the screws going, and Hod very quickly arrived at different figures: "Oh!—forty thousand dollars—oh!" he roared out.

"That's good!" said 'Creesh. "But you don't like our *style*, I hear!"

"No, I don't!" muttered Hod.

"Don't you—now?" *Squeak—creak—creak.*

"Oh yes! I do! I *do!* I Do!! O-h-h-h!"

"Wouldn't you like to kiss us, Hoddy?" said Cad, after a pause.

"I'd like to bite ye!" growled the oppressed Horace.

"Oh, no, no, no! There's a dear boy! Kiss us, won't you?" *Creak.*

"Yes! Yes! I will! Let me up!"

"I'm afraid you'll back out, if we let you clean out of the hoops," said Jess. "We'll let you part way up."

And the jades actually made him salute them all round, with his head just up over the edge of the hoop and the follower held ready to crowd him down again, if he bit, instead. Then they let him get out and go with a chime of "Good night, Hoddy," and "How do you like our 'style'?"

Hod made himself scarce forthwith. Tom and I waited till the "coast was clear," then crept out and went home. Hod had gone to bed.

Next morning I heard Tom asking him what the girls did to him.

"None of your business!" said he, shortly.

But afterwards, whenever we found it necessary to take him down a little, we would sing out, "Oh!—Greeley—Oh!" That would "fetch him."

Ah, well, those days are all past and gone now, like the old cider mill. Hod is of late junior partner in the mercantile house of which his father is the head, and if this little story should come to his eye—well, I guess he will stand it; he stood a worse pressure in the old "pummy hoop."

The pretty Lynches are gone, too; they went "off to the factory," and that was the last of them, so far as concerns our home neighborhood. Last spring, one of them (poor Jess), quite thin and faded, and with eyes preternaturally bright, came back to cough out the few remaining weeks of her life; the others are now part and parcel of that great, dreary factory town—an ever hungry monster that has already devoured all the bloom and beauty of each rural neighborhood far around it.

17

A Night on the "Great Rock"

IT HAD BEEN A SEASON OF DROUGHT. THE PASTURES were scarred, and all the plowed fields were like ashes. The long corn leaves had curled into crisp rolls, and the grasshoppers had stripped the potato fields till nothing but the pale green stalks were left.

But the great wilderness to the northward, which stretches off toward Canada, presented the most dreary spectacle. Much of it is composed of what lumbermen call "black growth," spruce and hemlock. Myriads of worms had eaten these till the green leaves had turned to dull yellow. Thousands of acres looked as if blasted by fire. In passing through the forest, it required both hands to brush away the worms which came swinging down on their webs from the treetops to the ground.

Hunting parties came back empty-handed. There was no game, they said; no moose, no deer, and no partridges. In the woods there was an almost painful stillness. Last fall the forest had echoed to the chicker and chirr of legions of squirrels, red, gray, and black. But now they were gone—somewhere—starved, perhaps.

Early in September the corn (what there was of it) was gathered. "Huskings" were almost a mockery that fall, but the boys would make them, according to custom. One night, about the middle of the month, we were all invited to Zack Davis's—"Uncle Zack," we called him. It was a couple of miles to his house. Uncle Zack lived at the end of the road, from our house, which, like a river toward its source, dwindled to a mere path through the woods and up the ridge.

Ellen and I, with our neighbors Willis Murch and Tom Edwards and his sister Kate, five of us, started about dusk, though the moon, just rising, was beginning to make it quite light.

There were forty or fifty boys and girls, old and young, at the gathering. It did not take long to husk the corn. About a bushel of ears apiece would finish it, they said. So, after husking, and a supper of puddings and pumpkin pies, those who wished to do so were invited to remain for a "good time" in the long, unfinished kitchen. Our party were among the number who *wished*, of course.

There were all sorts of plays and games, with plenty of song singing, and it was considerably past midnight when we started homeward. The moon was high in the heavens.

"It was the noon of night." The silvery light rested over all. Beneath it all the dreariness of the long drought was softened. We sang, as we went down the valley, repetitions of the songs sung in the evening, and listened as the tones were echoed back from the wild sides of the valley.

About a mile below Uncle Zack's, the path left the valley and crossed an open pasture. We were still singing when Willis suddenly cried— "Hark!"

"Nothing but a dog," said Tom, as a sound, which did sound something like the howl of a dog in the night, came to our ears from the ridge to the northward.

We stopped to listen.

"I don't believe it was a dog," said Willis.

"What was it, then?" demanded Tom, as if to argue it.

"I don't know," said Willis, "but it sounded too wild and fierce for a dog."

Just then it rang out again nearer—a long, wild howl, that seemed to come from the upper edge of the pasture.

"I tell you that's no dog!" cried Willis.

"You don't suppose it's wolves, do you?" exclaimed Kate.

"Wolves, no!" cried Tom. "There hasn't been a wolf seen about here for twenty years."

We stood looking up toward the upper side of the pasture. Every stump and bush was plainly to be seen in the bright light. Suddenly, a dark object, an animal of some sort, came out into the open land, and ran swiftly along the edge of the woods for twenty or thirty rods. Then it stopped, and again we heard the long howl. The woodland echoed to it. Just then the forms of four or five others came into sight in the pasture.

"They *are* wolves!" exclaimed Willis.

"Oh, let's run!" cried Ellen, catching Kate's arm.

"Go ahead, girls," shouted Tom, "as fast as you can for your homes!"

They did not need any further urging, but ran like foxes. A pile of "four-foot wood" was lying near the path. Some of it was small and round. We each took a stick, and ran after the girls.

A dozen howls seemed to burst upon the air all at once.

"They're after us!" cried Willis.

Glancing over my shoulder, I saw the animals, a dark pack of them, rushing down through the pasture in full chase. The moment they saw us run, they had started in pursuit. The still forest rang out afresh with their howls. In a moment more we had overtaken the girls.

"What shall we do with *them?*" panted Tom. "We can't make our homes with them."

Kate turned round suddenly. "The Great Rock!" said she, breathlessly. "We're 'most to it. Can't we get upon it?"

"Run for it, quick!" cried Willis. "Perhaps so."

The "Great Rock" was a huge boulder—some would call it a ledge—flat on the top, but with steep sides. It lay a few rods from the road, on the lower side. We were now nearly opposite it, and, turning out of the path, ran down towards it for dear life. The wolves were close upon us. We could hear them tearing down the hillside, and crashing through the brush.

"Up quick! Kate and Ellen!" cried Tom. "Put your toes into that crevice. I'll 'boost' you up!"

They went up like cats. The top of the rock was nine or ten feet above the ground. There were several cracks and seams in the side. We climbed after them in a hurry, but had barely time to turn round with our clubs, before the wolves were at the base of the rock. With wild howls and yells they sprang up its side, their nails scratching the stone, and their white teeth gleaming in the moonlight.

One of them obtained a foothold on the edge of one of the seams, and, with a second bound, came to the top of the rock, his fiery, green eyes showing over the edge. We all three struck at his head, and, with a doglike yell, he fell back to the ground among his enraged fellows, who howled and snapped at him.

We drew breath again.

"Guess we can keep them down," said Tom.

"Here are stones to pelt them with," cried Kate, picking up several the size of goose eggs.

On the top of the rock was a space, with an uneven surface, as large as a room eighteen by twenty feet in size. Low shrubs, poplar and white birch, grew on it, rooted partly into the rock, and partly into the mossy soil which had collected there. And sure enough, as Kate had discovered, there were plenty of fragments of the rock lying embedded in the shoal soil.

Tom and Willis caught up several of them, and threw them, with all their strength, among the wolves.

They dodged and yelled like curs, when hit, but we couldn't drive them away. They would slink back a little, and then charge upon the rock the moment we stopped throwing.

Suddenly, one of them ran round to the other side of the rock and howled. The rest instantly followed as if he had called them. There were no cracks on this side, but the ascent was less abrupt. We stepped hastily across. The moment the wolves saw us; they began to leap towards us, but slipped back on the bare rock, tumbling one over the other.

When one came within reach, we gave him such a whack with our four-foot sticks as to knock him back to the bottom. But the next instant, he would leap up again, as fierce and eager as ever. One, a gaunt old male, larger than the others, got his feet upon the top several times. The hardest blows we could deal seemed only to stun him for a moment.

Finding they could not reach us there, they ran round to the side next to the road again, but, after a few fruitless leaps, they drew back, and sat down just like dogs, and watched us steadily. Several of them were "lolling," with long tongues hanging out, and they all, from time to time, snapped at each other and at their own bodies as if covered with fleas.

Tom counted them aloud, as they sat glaring up at us. "Eleven," said he. "Aren't they a wicked looking set?"

There was no disputing that. Hungry and ferocious enough they looked. The girls could not find courage to look at them, Kate and Ellen were none of the fainting, squeamish sort, either.

"Well, what's to be done?" said Willis, as we stood there with our clubs, ready to meet them in case they made another rush.

"How are we to get home?"

"We might shout for help," suggested Tom.

"We should not be heard," said Willis. "Our folks are all asleep, probably. They wouldn't think of sitting up for us. And they won't miss us, either, till morning. Besides, as it's 'most a mile from our homes, they wouldn't hear if they were awake."

"And if they should hear, and come to see what was the matter, wouldn't the wolves get them?" asked Kate.

That had not occurred to us before. There was danger of it, certainly. "Let's tough it out, then, till morning!" exclaimed Tom. "It won't be a great while, now."

"They'll go off as soon as it gets light," said Kate. "I've read that they always slink away at daylight."

As Kate was speaking, another howl was heard off in the forest. It was answered by the whole pack, and, in a few minutes, three others came straggling in. Thereupon, they all sprang, snarling and snapping, at each other. Then they ran round the rock again, and the newcomers made several attempts to leap upon it. But we were ready to receive them, and gave one of them so severe a stroke that he measured his length upon the ground handsomely. As he fell, the others rushed upon him as if to tear him in pieces, but he jumped up and shook them off.

After a great deal of growling and grimacing, they returned to their old position in front of the rock, and sat down to watch as Kate told a story she had read of wolves in Russia; how they chased a sledge in which a family were traveling, and how the father had thrown out two of the children to the wolves, in order to save the rest. And Willis told us how they catch wolves in India by digging pits for them.

"But those are not this kind of wolf," said Tom. "These are gray wolves."

The night air was chilly and damp. Despite the peril, the girls were shivering. "Let's give them another pelting, and so warm ourselves," said Tom.

We dug out another lot of stones, and, stripping off our jackets, let the girls wrap themselves in them while we pelted the wolves.

"All ready now!" cried Willis, balancing a stone as large as his fist. "Let's aim at that old gaunt one that came so near, getting up here twice—all three of us. See if we cannot kill him."

We all threw, and Tom hit him plump in the breast.

The wolves all sprang up, howling.

"Keep your eye on him!" cried Willis, catching up another stone.

We all threw again, and Willis hit him hard on the head, fairly knocking him over, but he sprang to his feet as the rest of the wolves crowded upon him. I think Willis's stone must have drawn blood, for all the others rushed at him, snapping their jaws. At our next throw, the stones by accident all hit the nearest wolf, bringing him to the ground instantly. He sprang up on three legs; the other seemed to be broken and helpless. The rest of the pack rushed upon him, and he ran limping off with them at his heels. We heard them go cracking away into the woods on the other side of the road. A great howling and yelling arose, and, in a short time they all came panting back again. All save the one that went off on three legs. We saw no more of him.

We stoned them at intervals during the night, but made no more such lucky hits.

It seemed as if morning never would come, the hours crawled by so slowly. At last day broke, and the moonlight gradually gave place to daylight. The wolves grew uneasy. They howled and hung about awhile longer; then, one by one, like evil spirits of the night, they sneaked off into the woods. We waited till we were sure they had really departed, then came down from the rock, and Ellen and I reached home just as the folks were coming downstairs for the day. You can easily imagine their surprise when they learned how we had passed the night.

The wolves skulked about the pastures during the rest of the fall. They were starved out of the forest, people said. Several other persons had narrow escapes from them.

I never go past the Great Rock without a thankful feeling that it was placed just in that particular spot. Had it not been there, or if Kate had not remembered its location, we should never have reached home alive.

18

Bethesda

IF ANYTHING WAS MISSING AT THE OLD FARMHOUSE—
clothes brush, soap, comb, or other articles of daily use—someone
almost always would exclaim, "Look in Bethesda!" or "I left it in
Bethesda!" Bethesda was one of those household words that you use
without thought of its original significance or of the amused query that
it raises in the minds of strangers.

Like most New England houses built seventy-five years ago, the
farmhouse at the Old Squire's had been planned without thought of
bathing facilities. The family washtub, brought to the kitchen on a Saturday night, and filled with pail water tempered slightly by a few quarts
from the teakettle, served the purpose. We were not so badly off as our
ancestors had been, however, for during the Civil War, when we young
folks went home to live at the Old Squire's, stoves were fully in vogue
and farmhouses were comfortably warmed. Bathing on winter nights
was uncomfortable enough, we thought, but it was not the desperately
chilly business that it must have been when farmhouses were heated by
a single fireplace.

In the sitting room we had both a fireplace and an "airtight" for the
coldest weather. In Grandmother Ruth's room there was a "fireside
companion," and in the front room a "soapstone comfort," with sides
and top of a certain kind of variegated limestone that held heat through
the winter nights.

So much heat rose from the lower rooms that the bedrooms on the floor above, where we young folks slept, were by no means uncomfortably cold, even in zero weather. Grandmother Ruth would open the hall doors an hour before it was time for us to go to bed, to let the superfluous heat rise for our benefit.

In the matter of bathing, however, a great deal was left to be desired at the old house. There were six of us to take turns at that one tub. Grandmother Ruth took charge: she saw to it that we did not take too long and listened to the tearful complaints about the coldness of the water. On Saturday nights her lot was not a happy one. She used to sit just outside the kitchen door and call our names when our turns came, and as each of us went by she would hand us our change of under-clothing.

Although the brass kettle was kept heating on the stove all the while, we had trouble in getting enough warm water to "take the chill off." More than once—unbeknown to Grandmother Ruth—I followed Addison in the tub without changing the water. He had appreciably warmed it up. One night Halstead twitted me about it at the supper table, and I recollect that the lack of proper sensibility that I had shown scandalized the entire family.

"Oh, Joseph!" Grandmother often exclaimed to the Old Squire. "We must have some better way for these children to bathe. They are getting older and larger, and I certainly cannot manage it much longer."

Things went on in that way for the first three years of my sojourn at the old place—until after the Old Squire had installed a hydraulic ram down at the brook, which forced plenty of water up to the house and the barns. Then, in October of the fourth year, the old gentleman bestirred himself.

He had been as anxious as anyone to improve our bathing facilities, but it is not an easy job to add a bathroom to a farmhouse. He walked about at the back of the house for hours, and made several excursions to a hollow at a distance in the rear of the place, and also climbed to the attic, all the while whistling softly:

Roll on, Silver Moon,
Guide the traveler on his way.

That was always a sure sign that he was getting interested in some scheme.

Then things began to move in earnest. Two carpenters appeared and laid the sills for an addition to the house, twenty feet long by eighteen feet wide, just behind the kitchen, which was in the ell. The room that they built had a door opening directly into the kitchen. The floor, I remember, was of maple and the walls of matched spruce.

Meanwhile the Old Squire had had a sewer dug about three hundred feet long, and to hold the water supply he built a tank of about a thousand gallons' capacity, made of pine planks; the tank was in the attic directly over the kitchen stove, so that in winter heat would rise under it through a little scuttle in the floor and prevent the water from freezing.

From the tank the pipes that led to the new bathroom ran down close to the chimney and the stovepipe. Those bathroom pipes gave the Old Squire much anxiety; there was not a plumber in town; the old gentleman had to do the work himself, with the help of a hardware dealer from the village, six miles away. But if the pipe gave him anxiety, the bathtub gave him more. When he inquired at Portland about their cost, he was somewhat staggered to learn that the price of a regular tub was fifty-eight dollars.

But the Old Squire had an inventive brain. He drove up to the mill, selected a large, sound pine log about four feet in diameter and hired old Davy Glinds, a brother of Hughy Glinds, to excavate a tub from it with an adze. In his younger days Davy Glinds had been a ship carpenter, and was skilled in the use of the broadax and the adze. He fashioned a good-looking tub, five feet long by two and a half wide, smooth hewn within and without. When painted white the tub presented a very creditable appearance.

The Old Squire was so pleased with it that he had Glinds make another, and then, discovering how cheaply pine bathtubs could be made, he hit upon a new notion. The more he studied on a thing like that, the more the subject unfolded in his dear old head. Why, the Old Squire asked himself, need the Saturday night bath occupy a whole evening because the seven members of the family had to take turns in one tub, when we could just as well have more tubs?

Before Grandmother Ruth fairly realized what he was about, the old gentleman had five of these pine tubs ranged there in the new lean-to. He had the carpenters enclose each tub within a sealed partition of spruce boards. There was thus formed a little hall five feet wide in the center of the new bathroom, from which small doors opened to each tub.

"What do you mean, Joseph, by so many tubs?" Grandmother cried in astonishment, when she discovered what he was doing.

"Well, Ruth," he said, "I thought we'd have a tub for the boys, a tub for the girls, then tubs for you and me, mother, and one for our hired help."

"Sakes alive, Joe! All those tubs to keep clean!"

"But didn't you want a large bathroom?" the Old Squire rejoined, with twinkling eyes.

"Yes, yes," cried Grandmother, "but I had no idea you were going to make a regular Bethesda!"

Bethesda! Sure enough, like the pool in Jerusalem, it had five porches! And that name, born of Grandmother Ruth's indignant surprise, stuck to it ever afterwards.

When the Old Squire began work on that bathroom he expected to have it finished in a month. But one difficulty after another arose: the tank leaked; the sewer clogged; nothing would work. If the hardware dealer from the village came once to help, he came fifty times! His own experience in bathrooms was limited. Then, to have hot water in abundance, it was necessary to send to Portland for a seventy-five-gallon copper heater, and six weeks passed before that order was filled.

November, December, and January passed before Bethesda was ready to turn on the water, and then we found that the kitchen stove would not heat so large a heater, or at least would not do it and serve as a cookstove at the same time. Nor would it sufficiently warm the bathroom in very cold weather even with the kitchen door open. Then one night in February the pipes at the far end froze and burst, and the hardware man had to make us another hasty visit.

To ward off such accidents in the future the Old Squire now had recourse to what is known as the Granger furnace—a convenience that was then just coming into general favor among farmers. They are cozy,

heat-holding contrivances, made of brick and lined either with firebrick or iron; they have an iron top with pot holes in which you can set kettles. The Old Squire connected ours with the heater, and he placed it so that half of it projected into the new bathroom, through the partition wall of the kitchen. It served its purpose effectively and on winter nights diffused a genial glow both in the kitchen and in the bathroom.

But it was the middle of May before the bathroom was completed, and the cost was actually between eight and nine hundred dollars!

"My sakes, Joseph!" Grandmother exclaimed. "Another bathroom like that would put us in the poorhouse. And the neighbors all think we're crazy!"

The Old Squire, however, rubbed his hands with a smile of satisfaction. "I call it rather fine. I guess we are going to like it," he said.

Like it we did, certainly. Bathing was no longer an ordeal, but a delight. There was plenty of warm water; you had only to pick your tub, enter your cubicle, and shut the door. Bethesda, with its Granger furnace and big water heater, was a veritable household joy. "Ruth," the Old Squire said, "all I'm sorry for is that I didn't do this thirty years ago. When I reflect on the cold, miserable baths we have taken and the other privations you and I have endured all these years it makes me heartsick to think what I've neglected."

"But nine hundred dollars, Joseph!" Grandmother interposed with a scandalized expression. "That's an awful bill!"

"Yes," the Old Squire admitted, "but we shall survive it."

Grandmother was right about our neighbors. What they said among themselves would no doubt have been illuminating if we had heard it, though they maintained complete silence when we were present. But we noticed that when they called at the farmhouse they cast curious and perhaps envious glances at the new lean-to.

Then an amusing thing happened. We had been enjoying Bethesda for a few weeks, but had not yet got past our daily pride in it, when one hot evening in the latter part of June who should come driving into the yard but David Barker, "the Burns of Maine," a poet and humorist of statewide renown.

The Old Squire had met him several times, but his visit that night was accidental. He had come into our part of the state to visit a kinsman, but had got off his proper route and had called at our house to ask how far away this relative lived.

"It is nine or ten miles up there," the Old Squire said when they had shaken hands. "You are off your route. Better take out your horse and spend the night with us. You can find your way better by daylight."

After some further conversation Mr. Barker decided to accept the Old Squire's invitation. While Grandmother and Ellen got supper for our guest, the Old Squire escorted him to the hand bowl that he had put in at the end of the bathroom hall. I imagine that the Old Squire was just a little proud of our recent accommodations.

"And, David, if you would like a bath before retiring tonight, just step in here and make yourself at home," he said and opened several of the doors to the little cubicles.

David looked the tubs over, first one and then another.

"Wal, Squire," he said at last, in that peculiar voice of his, "I've sometimes wondered why our Maine folks had so few bathtubs, and sometimes been a little ashamed on't. But now I see how 'tis. You've got all the bathtubs there are cornered up here at your place!"

He continued joking about our bathrooms while he was eating supper, and later, before retiring, he said, "I know you are a neat woman, Aunt Ruth, and I guess before I go to bed I'll take a turn in your bathroom."

Ellen gave him a lamp, and he went in and shut the door. Fifteen minutes—half an hour—nearly an hour—passed, and still he was in there, and we heard him turning on and letting off water, apparently barrels of it! Occasionally, too, we heard a door open and shut.

At last, when nearly an hour and a half had elapsed, the Old Squire, wondering whether anything were wrong, went to the bathroom door. He knocked, and on getting a response inquired whether there was any trouble.

"Doesn't the water run, David?" he asked. "Is it too cold for you? How are you getting on in there?"

"Getting on beautifully," came the muffled voice of the humorist above the splashing within. "Doing a great job. Only one tub more!

Four off and one to come." He had been taking a bath in each of the five tubs in succession.

"But, David!" the Old Squire began in considerable astonishment.

"Yes. Sure. It takes time. But I know Aunt Ruth is an awful neat woman, and I determine to do a full job!"

19

The Old Squire's Clocks

THE GARRET OF THE OLD FARMHOUSE DOWN IN MAINE had been a repository of castoff articles for three generations, and proved an attractive field for exploration to the young people who went there to live throughout the Civil War.

Hung up there were old surtouts, faded blue army overcoats and caps, and still older poke bonnets and hats. There were two old "wheels" for wool "rolls" and a smaller one for flax, "swifts" for winding yarn, and two large wooden looms, one for homemade cloth and blankets, the other for rag carpets.

There were saddles and brass-mounted harness and andirons with big round brass heads; old cradles, bread troughs, and wooden trays; three tall German silver candlesticks and six old whale-oil lamps; a Springfield army rifle and haversack, and a much older "Queen's Arm," with a wooden cartridge box hanging from the trigger guard.

Then, too, there were dusty chests, a dozen or more of them, pushed back under the eaves, some containing leather-covered books, Bibles, hymn books, sermons, files of the *Pine State News*, and many copies of the once popular *Columbian Magazine*.

Indeed, I could hardly more than begin to enumerate all there was in that garret, but I must not forget "Old Uncle Ansel," as we called it, a curious combination of flywheels, balance wheels, tubes, and other nondescript gear, set in an oak frame as large as a large table. The odd contrivance stood for the effort of one of the Old Squire's uncles, back in 1830, to solve the then fascinating problem of perpetual motion. It was a disagreeable bit of family history, and there was some sort of queer occurrence connected with it, of which the old people were disinclined to speak.

On rainy days we used to steal away up there to pore over the stories in those old *Columbian Magazines;* and Theodora and Ellen were accustomed to time their stay—when they knew that Grandmother could not spare them long downstairs—by giving "Old Uncle Ansel" a whirl as they read.

A smart twirl of the flywheel would cause the machine to revolve silently for almost exactly seven minutes, and two twirls stood for about a quarter of an hour.

By the time we had been at the farm three months, there was not much in that garret which we had not investigated—with one exception.

At the farther end of it, the end next to the kitchen ell, there was a small, low room, partitioned off by itself, like a large closet, although otherwise the garret was all one large loft, extending back under the eaves of the house on both sides, but having two small windows at each end.

The door of this little room was secured by a padlock. There was no peeping in at a keyhole; nor could we boys come round on the ell roof to look in at the window, for the green paper curtain was drawn close down, and there were nails over the top of the window sashes. No one appeared to know where the key was, and whenever any of us had asked what was in there, Grandmother always replied, "Nothing of any consequence."

But one day, when our elders had gone away, my cousin Ellen chanced to be rummaging for something or other on the top shelf of the high dresser, and knocked down a rusty key. "Now what in the world do you suppose that's the key to?" said she.

Neither Theodora nor Wealthy could answer that question, and they laid the key on the table, where we boys saw it when we came in from the field to our noon dinner.

"That looks like a padlock key," said Addison, and he examined it for some moments. "I tell you that's the key to that closet up-garret!" he suddenly exclaimed.

"Let's try it and see!" cried Ellen, and with that we all jumped up from the table and raced to the garret. For a long time our curiosity had been gathering strength concerning what was in that closed room. Grandmother's noncommittal replies had but whetted it, and although neither she nor Grandfather had forbidden us to unlock the door, we yet had the idea that there was something inside which, at least, they did not care to talk about.

Addison arrived first, but we were all close behind when he tried the key in the padlock. The lock was rusted and started hard. The key, however, fit it. Addison unhooked the padlock from the staple, then shoved the door open, and we all peered in.

And it was a strange sight!

"Clocks!" exclaimed Addison. "Only look at the clocks!"

The little room was dim with dusty cobwebs, crossed and criss-crossed, but on two sides of it were tiers of shelves, one above another, three tiers high, and on all those shelves, and on yet another shelf partly under the eaves, stood small clocks, three deep on a shelf, clocks with wedge-shaped tops and little pointed spires at the front corners.

"My, did you ever see so many!" cried Ellen.

"All just alike, too!" exclaimed Wealthy, laughing wildly; for so many clocks standing there all mute in that dim, cobwebby room actually looked uncanny.

We went in, Ellen brushing down some of the cobwebs with her kitchen apron, and began counting those clocks.

There were eighty-four of them—all of the same size and just alike, down to the figure of Father Time, painted on the glass of the little front door.

"Now where do you suppose they all came from?" exclaimed Halstead.

"And what makes Grandmother keep them hidden away up here?" said Ellen.

"She has never told us a word about them," Wealthy chimed in. "She always said, 'Nothing of any consequence in there.' Why, we might have a clock in each of our rooms!"

"It is queer about them, and no mistake," remarked Theodora.

"I guess the Old Squire must have robbed a clock factory at some time," said Addison, laughing, but of course we all knew better than that.

But eighty-four clocks! All just alike, and put away in this little garret room years and years ago, apparently.

Halstead brought one of the clocks out, set it on a chest, and we looked it over. It was a pendulum clock, about two feet tall, with the key tied to the striking bell, inside the door.

Addison wound it up. "New clock," said he. "It never was run any."

"There's a little label here under the striker," said Halstead. "Says, 'Smith & Skillings, Worcester, Mass., 1836. Brass works. Percussion Hammer. Warranted for Four Years. Price $6.00.'"

"Yes, siree!" cried Addison, again surveying the interior of the closet. "All nice, new, sitting room clocks. Worth six dollars apiece. Jingo, this is a clock mine!"

"But we must never let Grandmother and Grandfather know we have been spying here," said Theodora. "We must lock the door again and put the key back where we got it."

"I suppose we had better," said Addison. "But where in the world did they ever get all these clocks?"

"And why never speak of them?" exclaimed Ellen.

"There's some reason that we don't know about," replied Dora. "We ought not to have pried. So let's lock the closet again and put the key back on the high dresser. I think, too, that we had better say nothing about it. It is something they don't want us to know about, or they would have told us."

So, after yet another wondering look inside that closet, we locked the door. Ellen put the key back where she had found it, and we said no more about it.

In a way, too, Theodora was right. Those clocks had a history, and that old closet held a kind of family skeleton.

Twenty-nine years before, while the Old Squire was still a comparatively young man, he had set off for Portland, the week before Thanksgiving, with a two-horse load of dressed poultry, turkeys, chickens, and geese, which Grandmother had been raising and fattening during that whole season. It was understood that if Grandmother took care of the poultry, she was to have half the proceeds.

Thomas Fogarty

There was over a ton of the poultry, and with a part of the profits the Squire was to purchase for Grandmother twenty yards of black silk, best quality, to make a gown, and a "fitch victorine"—something like a fur shoulder cape.

The Squire sold the poultry for more than three hundred dollars, but he had to remain two nights in Portland, at the old Preble House, and while there fell in with a man named Skillings, of the firm of Smith & Skillings, Worcester, clock makers. Skillings had recently come to Portland, and had three hundred clocks with him. The retail price was six dollars, but he offered the Old Squire 115 of them at three dollars apiece, and succeeded in convincing him that he could double his money on them by peddling them in the home county that winter.

So instead of coming home light, with the money for the poultry, and the black silk and fitch victorine for Grandmother, the Squire arrived loaded down with clocks.

It is a matter of family record that Grandmother was not pleased, and that she met him with anything save an ovation. But the Squire was young and hopeful then; he expected to double his money selling those clocks. He rigged up a covered pung with a rack inside, which would carry twenty of them at a time, and began to make trips round and about the town and the adjoining towns.

But times were hard. It was easier to plan to sell them than to get the money. In fact, the Squire was able to get rid of but twenty-three of the clocks, and some of these at five and four dollars each. Some, too, he "trusted out" for payment the following year.

By spring he was sick enough of the investment, and when the farm-work demanded his attention, he drew home a load of boards, constructed the closet in the attic, and stored the ninety-two clocks there till another winter, when he sold eight more.

By this time the clocks had become such a sore subject between Grandmother and himself, and he so dreaded to fetch them down again, that he embarked in lumbering the third winter.

And from that day onward, down to our time, neither he nor Grandmother mentioned the matter, nor so much as said "clocks" to each other. That closet had not been opened for twenty-seven years—till we unlocked it that day, and we remained quiet about it for yet another two years.

But eighty-four clocks! All just alike! It was impossible to forget them, and one day, two and a half years later, when we had begun to attend the academy at the village, and had bills to meet for tuition and books, we thought of those clocks. The idea of selling them occurred to us, and Addison and Ellen got the key again, and made another examination of the old closet.

"They are such old-style clocks, and so out of fashion, I don't believe anyone would buy them now," Ellen remarked.

But Addison thought that they could be sold.

"Brush them up, oil them, and varnish the cases, and those clocks would bring four dollars apiece," said he. "They are nice old clocks, with good works in them."

"They're doing nobody any good up there either," said Halstead. "Why those clocks might all be ticking and doing some good in the world! And do *us* some good, too."

"But I don't believe Grandmother and Grandfather would let us have them," Theodora remarked. "Those clocks have been put away up there for some reason we don't know of."

"Well, but they never go near them," urged Halstead. "Maybe they have forgotten all about them."

"Oh no, they have not!" exclaimed Ellen. "Grandmother knows all about those clocks and why they are there."

"But perhaps they would let us have them to sell," said Addison.

"I shouldn't like to ask them," said Theodora.

"I shouldn't, either," said Ellen

"Well, no more should I," Addison admitted. "I don't quite know why we shouldn't, but somehow it seems a little like digging up an old grave."

"Pooh! I'll ask them," said Halstead.

"No, don't!" exclaimed Theodora.

"No, Halse, not right out boldfaced," said Addison. "But perhaps we could bring it round easy, sometime when the Old Squire is feeling good natured, and he and Grandmother are laughing over old times."

"Maybe," assented Theodora, "if you were to do it just right."

"Well, wait a bit," said Addison.

He was the oldest and craftiest among us, and at last he and Ellen hit on a plan for broaching the subject.

Thanksgiving was approaching, and a day or so before that day Addison and Ellen went quietly up to the garret and wound up all those clocks, then with a goose feather and kerosene oil touched up the works, so that they would run. The clocks had been there so long that some of them could not be make to run at all, but they fixed up about sixty of them so that they could be started if the pendulum was given a swing.

What they did next was to set twenty of them at eleven o'clock, ten more at one minute past eleven, ten more at two minutes past eleven, and all the rest at three or four minutes past eleven.

At the old farm we always used to have our Thanksgiving dinner at three o'clock in the afternoon. Addison's plan was to go to the garret just before we sat down to dinner, and set all those clocks going, so that by the time we had got well along with our dinner, and everyone was feeling in a good and thankful mood, they would begin striking twelve, in platoons, so to speak, and keep it up.

None of us knew anything about this, however, except Addison and Ellen. They had thought best to keep it quiet; for we had three nieces of Grandmother's visiting us that week from Connecticut, and a girl named Mary Totherly, a distant relative, who was then attending school at Hebron Academy, about a day's drive from the old place. According to Grandmother's custom, the Thanksgiving dinner table was set in the sitting room, the largest room in the farmhouse. A door opened from it into the front hall, and after we had all been at table three-quarters of an hour, and the turkey was well disposed of and the plum pudding was brought on, Ellen suddenly exclaimed against the heat of the room.

"Do, please, Grandmother, let's have the door into the hall open," she said.

"Why, yes child, if you are too warm," replied the old lady. So up rose Ellen and set the door wide open. Addison had already left the door to the attic stairs ajar.

The plum pudding followed the turkey, as usual; the mince pie was being handed round, and Grandmother was beaming on her company, and the Old Squire was turning a joke of former dinners at the farm, when suddenly a horological commotion broke loose in the garret.

Twenty clocks, all starting in to strike at once, raised a tremendous tintinnabulation. Everybody at our Thanksgiving dinner table—save Addison and Ellen—sat up in astonishment.

Dong! Dong! Dong! Ding! Ding! Ding! Dang! Dang! Dang! on as many different keys, with new ones breaking in!

The Old Squire's hearing was not what it had once been. He looked first one way, then another, and then out of the window. "Seems to me I hear music," said he. "Where is it? Has anybody hired a brass band?"

But Grandmother exclaimed, "For mercy's sake, what ails the clock?"

There came a little lull, but immediately the next platoon opened on yet a different key, some striking fast, some slow!

"Appears to have lost the time!" the Squire remarked, with his hand up to his better ear.

"Joseph!" Grandmother exclaimed, severely. "That's clocks striking. Can't you hear? And it isn't the kitchen clock," she added, with a perplexed look.

By that time Molly Totherly and Halse were up from the table and out in the hall, investigating; the rest of us sat spellbound. For by this time platoon number three had got at it: *Cling! Cling! Cling! Clong! Clong! Clong! Clung! Clung! Clung!*

Our relatives from Connecticut were amazed, but Addison and Ellen now jumped up from the table, to keep from shouting with laughter. Halstead and Theodora ran upstairs, then came rushing down again.

"It is in the old closet, up-garret!" Halse cried. "Sounds as if more than fifty clocks were striking at once in there!" for all the rest had now started in, as if executing a grand *finale*, for which the previous efforts had been merely the overture! But no sooner had Grandmother heard the word garret than she turned quite pale. The Old Squire was out in the hall. Theodora came hastily round to the back of Grandmother's chair. "No, no!" she whispered in her ear. "It is just one of Ad's pranks," at which the old lady sat up.

"Oh, the rogue!" she cried, and then she began to laugh, and laughed till she was breathless.

"Come back here, father!" she finally called to Grandfather. "They have found your load of clocks at last."

The Old Squire returned to the table, looking a little queer.

"We found them almost by accident," Theodora explained, hurriedly. "We didn't really mean to pry into anything."

"But do tell us, Grandmother, how there came to be so many of them!" cried Ellen.

"Oh, that isn't for me to tell!" cried Grandmother, airily. "They are not *my* clocks. You will have to ask your grandfather about that."

"Oh, tell us, Grandfather!" Ellen exclaimed.

Never had we seen the Old Squire so embarrassed; he looked actually sheepish.

"You will have to tell them now, Joseph!" cried Grandmother, exultantly. "You will have to own up to those clocks now!" She fell to laughing again.

But he would not enter on the subject at much length. "Oh, I took a consignment of clocks off a man's hands once," said he, in an offhand tone. "They didn't sell quite as well as I thought they might. And those you saw upstairs were some I had left over."

"Yes," said Grandmother, with intense irony. "Just a few clocks left over! That's all!" and she relapsed into another fit of laughter. Clearly, she considered that the Old Squire's description of the transaction was wholly inadequate.

But here Addison, who had been watching his chance, put in a word. "Those are pretty good clocks," he remarked. "They're a little out of style, but I think I could sell them. What will you take for the lot, sir?"

"Before there's any trading done," said Grandmother, "I want to say that I've got a black silk dress and a set of furs sunk somewhere in those clocks."

"Yes, yes, Ruth, that's so, that's so," replied the Old Squire, hastily. "You shall have all that the clocks bring."

With that, Addison addressed himself more particularly to Grandmother. "What do you say, Grandmother, to about a dollar apiece for those clocks?"

But she had dealt with too many tin peddlers in her day to be caught napping. "That's not enough," she said. "But as it is all in the family, Addison, if you will give me a hundred dollars, you may have them and no more said."

Addison hastily consulted with Ellen and the rest of us. We all went upstairs and looked again at the clocks. It seemed a promising speculation; so we wound up that Thanksgiving dinner with a bargain for the Old Squire's clocks, all amidst much hilarity on the part of our guests.

The next day we bought two pounds of castanea nuts, pressed out the oil with a warm flat iron, and then, without taking the works apart, oiled all those clocks as well as we could. We also bought a quart of varnish, and Addison and Theodora varnished the cases.

By this time it was good sleighing, and on the following Monday morning Addison and I set off with fifteen of the clocks packed carefully in the back of the "grist mill pung," to peddle them out. After much discussion on all sides, we had fixed the retail price at $3.50 each.

"Now talk up to people," Grandmother exhorted us, from the piazza steps, as we drove away. "Those are good clocks, and you must tell people so."

The Old Squire was there, too. He said nothing, but smiled broadly. Very likely he was thinking of his own fruitless efforts to sell those same clocks thirty years before.

Apparently, too, times had not changed very much. We called at every house that we came to that day, and made a circuit of twenty miles through three adjoining towns. But every family appeared to have quite as many clocks as were needed, although we had numerous invitations to repair, oil, and regulate clocks. One woman bargained for a clock, but did not have the money to pay for it. In fact, the shortage of money that followed the Civil War had already made itself felt.

We did not sell a clock that day, and returned home discouraged. The Old Squire sat and smiled to hear us tell of it. But Grandmother cheered us up. We set off again the next morning, and that day we actually sold one clock!

The next day a man offered us ten bushels of oats for a clock. We took them and went home. The transaction gave us an idea. The Old Squire could use the oats at his two logging camps. We agreed on an exchange with him, and on Friday and Saturday we sold five more clocks for oats and corn.

The following week we "dickered" clocks for about everything in the way of farm products, and even exchanged clocks for cosset sheep, which we brought home to the Old Squire's barn, not wholly to his satisfaction, for they had to be fed there.

We also "swapped" four clocks, each for a cord of wood, delivered in the village seven miles from the farm, where we sold it.

But we grew so tired of such peddling that to this day I cannot endure the sight of a clock with a wedge-shaped top. We persevered, however, and canvassed nearly the whole home county. We swapped clocks for watches and revolvers, and exchanged watches and revolvers for poultry, and even for Newfoundland pups. We brought home almost every imaginable thing, alive or dead, the county produced. Grandmother and the girls usually hastened forth to meet us at night, when we arrived at home, and the old lady would stand and laugh until she was quite helpless, to see us unload.

Addison went on every trip; he was chief salesman. Halstead and I took turns going with him. The queerest trade of all was a clock for a bushel and a half of beans and a "coon cat." Once we swapped a clock for an old cookstove, and were cheated that time. On another day we traded a clock for a firkin of butter, which proved rancid.

Yet even by the middle of January we had disposed of but fortyseven clocks. The Old Squire, in 1837, could hardly have been more heartily sick of the clock business than we were.

On February 16 we still had twenty clocks on hand. Upon that morning Addison and I set off with them to drive to the town of Buckfield, twenty-five miles from home; for by the time we had canvassed all the nearer territory, some of it two or three times.

It was a bitter winter day. The wind blew, and the roads were so badly drifted that we were till sunset going twenty-five miles with our pung and span of farm horses. I never suffered more from cold than on that day.

That night we were furnished a lodging by a farmer named Hutchins, and he and his wife looked over our stock of clocks, but did not seem disposed to buy one. The next morning however, after breakfast, Hutchins said, "Come out to the barn and see my stock. I've got a two-year-old colt I'd like to show you."

We went out. "You see, I'm short of hay," Hutchins explained, confidentially. "I've got to sell something. I could spare this colt." And when he led him out of the stall, we thought that anybody who had him could spare him as well as not! Without exception it was the homeliest colt I ever saw. Apparently the animal had never been curried in his life. His hair was long and coarse, and just the color of faded yellow paint. He had a few hairs of mane on a long "spindly" neck that looked three sizes too small for his head. And he was rather light forward, but unusually heavy and high in the hindquarters.

We laughed, and Hutchins could not help laughing himself.

"You are sure it is a horse?" said Addison. "I've seen a good many, but I never saw one like that before."

"Oh, it is really a horse," said Hutchins. "I wouldn't tell you he was one if he wasn't. And I wouldn't part with him, either, if I wasn't short of hay. But I'll tell you what I'll do. I'll trade you this two-year-old colt for those twenty clocks of yours."

We didn't believe the colt was worth twenty dollars. But it was so bitterly cold that morning, the roads were so drifted, and we were so sick of facing the wind, that Ad cried: "Done, if you will throw in the halter!"

Hutchins agreed to that. We counted out the clocks to him and his wife, then harnessed and started for home, Addison driving and I leading the colt behind the pung.

"Oh, his name is Shasky-Legs!" Hutchins shouted after us, as we drove out of the yard.

It was another wintry day, but we got home with Shasky-Legs just at nightfall. The Old Squire and Halstead came out, followed by Grandmother and the girls, to see what we had captured this time. They all shouted when they saw that colt. But the Old Squire demurred on the spot. "We haven't hay for him. You will have to buy a ton of hay yourselves to winter him.

"That is the most foolish trade yet," he continued, a good deal out of patience. "I wouldn't give a dollar for such a colt."

We were obliged to use the oats which we had obtained in trade for clocks to feed to Shasky-Legs. It was impossible to sell him. We finally got him through the winter and turned him out to pasture. He grew well, and by September was a large colt for his age, but still so homely that it was painful to look at him.

We found a use for him. Addison, Theodora, Ellen, and I attended the fall term of the village academy, and by using Shasky-Legs, we were able to board at home, driving back and forth, seven miles, morning and night. We had a two-seated "beach wagon"—as it was called—and hitching in Shasky-Legs, the four of us used to go rattling along the road to the village. Everybody we met laughed, and at the academy door our fellow students generally cheered when we drove up.

All that autumn, for eleven weeks, we drove back and forth, and began to find that even if we made a late start in the morning, or were in a hurry to reach home at night, Shasky-Legs would get us there in half an hour, and that he did not appear to be blown or much fatigued by it. He was what horsemen call a pacer.

We fed him well, and that spin back and forth from the farm to the village seemed to be just about the amount of exercise which he needed. He kept in good condition, and was still growing. Every night and morning we let him go as fast as he would, and after the ground began to freeze at night, the way that old beach wagon rumbled and rattled along the road was really startling.

One of the selectmen at last spoke to the Old Squire about it, and he forbade our driving so fast. We were more careful when meeting teams after that, but when the way was clear, Shasky-Legs often made fine time. He liked it, and liked to pass other horses.

Now and then we had a brush with some young fellow who thought his own horse was speedy, but none of them could get away from Shasky-Legs. With those big hips and thick muscles, he could travel rapidly. Moreover, he was filling out into better proportions.

Nothing could change his coarse hair and yellow-paint color, of course, or make a handsome horse of him, but he was intelligent, and had a good twinkle in his eye that we liked. People began to look at him more critically, as well as laugh at him, and in November a man named Hawkes, who kept the village livery stable, offered to buy him.

We had several times seen Hawkes stop on the street and watch us as we drove past. "Mr. Hawkes likes the looks of Shasky-Legs," Ellen remarked one morning. And, in fact, he offered Addison seventy-five dollars for him. But Addison said, "No, we don't want to sell him."

On the ice of the lake that winter we had several brushes with other horses. Shasky-Legs was not a graceful pacer, but he did not let anything get past him. People began to realize that he was quite speedy. Moreover, he had what horsemen call fine "wind"; he seemed never to breathe hard. When other horses were panting, Shasky-Legs stood up as erect as ever, and twinkled his eye at us.

After January that winter, and while we were going back and forth to the academy during the spring term, some horse owner who we knew was certain to come round every day or two to "talk horse" with Addison or me, either to buy Shasky-Legs or swap for him. For the most part they wanted to swap, but Addison said "no" to them all, and refused to set a price on Shasky-Legs.

We were never late to school with Shasky-Legs, and in truth, we took a great deal of comfort with him—tempered slightly by the fear of being fined for fast driving, for the selectmen had warned us a second time. The Old Squire and Grandmother, too, were much disturbed lest we should have a smashup and break our bones. "Now don't drive fast this morning!" If we heard that once in those days, we heard it a hundred times. Shasky-Legs, however, was never skittish or refractory. He still showed a rather long, spindle neck, but he had a good knowing head on the end of it.

Toward the end of April Hawkes came round again, and this time he had a stranger with him, named Wilkins, who looked Shasky-Legs over, and persuaded Addison to take him out for a drive. When they came back Wilkins offered three hundred dollars for him.

Addison had considerable self-possession for a boy of eighteen. "Not for six hundred," said he; for by this time our ideas concerning Shasky-Legs were pitched higher. Besides, we liked him too well to want to sell him. He was growing better all the time.

But about a fortnight afterward this same horse dealer, Wilkins, with another stranger named Strong, followed us home from the village and had a talk with the Old Squire. They remained to supper, and

after some talk, told Addison that they had come to give him his six hundred dollars for Shasky-Legs.

"I said not for six hundred!" replied Addison, laughing.

With that, Wilkins affected to bluster, declaring that we had got them there under false pretenses, and he appealed to Grandfather to make Addison keep what they declared was his word to them.

The old gentleman declined to interfere. I, too, had heard what Addison said to Wilkins, and vouched for it.

Thereupon they came round on another tack, asked our pardon, and offered seven hundred dollars for Shasky-Legs. The Old Squire thought that we had better take it, but Addison stood out, and I agreed with him, for, boys though we were, it was easy to see that these dealers were bent on buying our three-year-old. They wanted to remain overnight, and the Old Squire found room for them. All that evening they argued and talked it over with us and got up to an offer of nine hundred.

Addison still said no and went to bed. We were both of us somewhat excited but determined to hold back. Each higher offer which they made only strengthened our resolution to keep possession of Shasky-Legs.

The next morning at breakfast the whole subject was argued over again. They sounded us for ten hundred, then eleven. At last they hitched up to go.

"Now hear our very last offer for that colt," said Wilkins, and jumped into their buggy. "We'll give you an even twelve hundred!" he said, impressively.

"Last offer or not, you cannot have him," replied Addison. "We mean to keep that colt."

But the Old Squire had become a good deal wrought up. He called us into the wagon house.

"Better take it," said he, hurriedly. "Don't let such an offer as that pass you."

Addison remained obstinate. Grandmother also came out and urged us to take it; yet Theodora and Ellen stood at the window, shaking their heads to us.

Thereupon the Old Squire rather took the matter out of our hands. "I shall ask for fifteen hundred. And they may have him if they agree!" he exclaimed, impatiently.

Wilkins and Strong had seemed in no great haste to drive away, and going out where they sat waiting in their buggy, the Old Squire offered to take fifteen hundred. Without another word Wilkins counted out fifteen hundred-dollar greenbacks, and five minutes later they were leading Shasky-Legs off behind their buggy. We never saw him again.

Of course it was a fine sum of money. Grandmother got her hundred dollars out of it—for those clocks—and the balance helped us on well with our school expenses for two years. Nonetheless, that was one of the few instances where the Old Squire's advice to us boys was not good. Within four months Shasky-Legs was sold in New York for six thousand dollars.

Some of our older readers who were familiar with turf events more than thirty years ago may recollect the pacer Mustapha, and his then very fast time of a mile in two minutes sixteen seconds. Well, that was our Shasky-Legs.

20

The Old Squire's Tonic

EVEN AFTER MORE THAN FIFTY YEARS I HAVE TO SMILE when I think of the Old Squire's tonic, or rather of the mortifying episode that grew out of it. The episode, by the way, arose from no fault of the tonic; that in itself was all right. The Old Squire took it every spring from March till the middle of April and thought it did him good. I rather think it did. At any rate, since he reached the advanced age of ninety-eight years and five months, there is fair reason to believe that the tonic did not shorten his days.

The tonic was made from an herb that we farm folks commonly call thoroughwort, the botanical name of which is *Eupatorium perfolatum*. It is called boneset and Indian sage. The earlier settlers of Maine made from it a lotion with which to saturate the bandages and the splints round a broken bone. The thoroughwort that the Old Squire used grew wild in a "beaver meadow" where one of our forest lots bordered Lurvey's Stream. There was a great deal of it there; the stalks were from three to four feet high, and in our latitude the pale, pinkish blossoms began to show during the first week in August. That was the time the Old Squire and Grandmother Ruth gathered it; they were wont to make a trip to the meadow annually and bring home two big bundles of the leaf stalks, which they hung up to dry in the attic of the farmhouse. The stuff cured well and hung there all winter.

On the first day of March Grandmother Ruth would put water to the amount of four or five quarts with a large wad of dry leaves, stalks, and blossoms to boil slowly in a bright brass kettle. Then she would add a pint of good sugarhouse molasses and let the whole simmer down to about a quart, which when cool she would cork up in a bottle.

From that bottle the Old Squire would take two swallows every morning before breakfast till the medicine was gone. That was the tonic, and that was the dose. He thought highly of it. But Grandmother Ruth did not like it; it was too bitter, she said. It certainly was bitter; we young folks liked it no better than she did. But as the years passed the Old Squire grew very fond of it.

"I look forward to taking it," he said to us one time. "As spring comes on I really long for it. I sometimes think it corrects many faults and failings of my physical and moral nature." At that Grandmother Ruth gave a peculiar and indescribable sniff of incredulity. To her such talk sounded hardly orthodox.

"But why not, Ruth?" the Old Squire rejoined, as if she had really said something. "A plant is a living thing and has life, good or bad, of its own. Now Indian poke has a rank, nauseous and, I believe, unmoral life. But thoroughwort, chamomile, and southernwood have clean, wholesome aromatic lives. Why should not a decoction from them produce a generally good effect on us when, as the year passes, we begin to get wrong internally?"

Grandmother Ruth's only reply was another sniff, a little more pronounced than the first, and accompanied with the slightest toss of her head.

The story of the tonic really begins in 1868 with the appearance of Dr. Orrington Califf, a man who styled himself a physician, and who perhaps was one. For several years he had edited a medical journal, but at that time he was traveling through Maine and New Hampshire, lecturing at district schoolhouses on medical topics. Dr. Califf came to our house and was with us three days. One morning he chanced to see the Old Squire taking his matinal two swallows from the bottle, and was curious to know what the liquid was. The old gentleman loved nothing better than to extol the virtues of that tonic.

Dr. Califf listened with quiet attention and seemed thoughtful.

"I have long held the medical qualities of *Eupatorium* in high esteem," he said at last. "It becomes almost a duty to make them known.

Others ought to share the benefits of your tonic. Thousands of people might be the better for taking it. You might become a great public benefactor!"

He talked in that strain for some time and found the Old Squire measurably ready to agree with him. He was in truth a very fluent speaker, and the upshot of the conversation was an agreement to make the tonic in considerable quantities and to put it on the market at a reasonable price.

There is no doubt at all of the Old Squire's good faith in the matter; he believed in the tonic, and felt certain that it would do good. The terms of the partnership, as I understood it, were that the Old Squire was to gather, cure, and furnish the dried thoroughwort in sufficient quantities, and that Dr. Califf should make and bottle the decoction. The doctor was also to undertake the advertising and the sale of it. In fact he was to carry on the business end of the enterprise and to have general control of it, paying the Old Squire a royalty of fifteen cents a bottle on all sales.

Articles of partnership were drawn up, but several hitches arose. Dr. Califf said that a certain percent of alcohol would have to be put into the tonic, as bottled, if it were to keep well. But to that proposal the Old Squire demurred at once; he would not be a party to the sale of anything spiritous. To do so he said was contrary to the law and to the sentiment in Maine. He declared that if the tonic were boiled down to the standard strength with molasses of good quality, and if proper precautions of sterilizing were taken, alcohol was not necessary. They debated the matter for one entire afternoon, but the Old Squire remained firm and refused to put his name to the agreement until an ironclad clause that fully prohibited the use of alcohol was inserted. At last Dr. Califf assented; at least, he signed.

Another disagreement arose in regard to the place of manufacture. The Old Squire wished to make the tonic in the "apple house" out at the rear of the farmhouse, and to have the doctor live with us or in the neighborhood, but the doctor urged family as well as various others reasons in favor of manufacturing at the city of Manchester, over the border in New Hampshire, and to that plan the Old Squire finally consented, although reluctantly. It may be said, in passing, that the state of New Hampshire had not enacted a law prohibiting the sale of intoxicants. At last the Old Squire and the doctor put the partnership on a working basis and Dr. Califf departed to make preparations.

There were numerous preliminaries. It was then March, and the start was not to be made until September, since the thoroughwort had yet to grow. All summer the Old Squire was making inquiries about new localities where thoroughwort was to be found. I remember that in July my cousin Addison and I made a trip up Lurvey's Stream as far as the Hay Meadows in quest of the herb. Later on, the Old Squire issued a standing offer of five cents a pound to the local herb gatherers for green thoroughwort. Our youthful neighbors, Kate and Tom Edwards, enriched themselves to the extent of sixteen dollars by bringing in as much as could be piled on a light driving wagon. They had discovered the herb growing abundantly in a meadow beside Bog Brook, where the stream wound its devious way through a great swamp locally known as "Quog-hoggar." Theodora and Ellen also gathered several bundles.

Throughout August and early September the Old Squire had the "apple house" hung full of the herb drying on poles; as fast as the thoroughwort dried he compressed it into sacks. In October Dr. Califf sent a team of horses across country to our place to get what the Old Squire had gathered and cured. There was a pile of sacks as large as a load of hay on the rack cart; the Old Squire said there was a half ton of the dried herb. Grandmother Ruth came out and viewed it with wonder.

"Joseph," she exclaimed, "I should think there was bitter enough in that load to cure or kill everybody in this state!"

The Old Squire did not go to New Hampshire, and never, I think, knew much about the details of the manufacture of the tonic. He and Dr. Califf wrote back and forth occasionally, but that was all. The medicine was called the *Old Squire's Tonic*, and the price was a dollar a bottle. The bottles were supposed to hold a quart, but I believe that Dr. Califf erelong reduced the capacity to about six gills. From time to time he sent us sample bottles, and the contents tasted much like that which Grandmother Ruth had made every spring. There was some correspondence concerning labels and circulars for advertising, but I think on the whole that the doctor went on with the work much as he pleased. We heard that he had a gaily painted cart and a span of horses, and that he drove about extensively, introducing the tonic. At times he reported sales to the Old Squire and sent him his royalty of fifteen cents a bottle. By June the old gentleman's royalties had amounted to more than one hundred dollars.

The Old Squire used to laugh about the business. I don't think he had ever taken it seriously; he was much occupied otherwise with his lumbering ventures. Yet he tried to do his share of work in the partnership by collecting all the thoroughwort he could find.

This went on for three seasons, and we came to regard it at the old farm quite as a matter of course, or rather as something to which we young folks scarcely gave second thought. Halstead indeed had already left home, and Addison was making preparations to leave us the coming autumn.

Then one day in August something disconcerting occurred. We were harvesting a field of oats at a distance from the house when Ellen came hastening into the field to inform the Old Squire that he had visitors. Four men had called and desired to see him.

"Do you know them?" the Old Squire inquired.

"Not certainly," Ellen replied, "but I think one of them is Sheriff Barrett."

A load of oats was ready to go to the barn; the hired men set off with it, and we followed after. Grandmother Ruth came out to the wagon house to meet us.

"They are in the sitting room," she explained, referring to the callers. "And, Joseph," she added, "it is something about that tonic."

The Old Squire laughed and entered the house. As the door of the sitting room remained open, much that the men said could be heard from the kitchen. The Old Squire knew Barrett well, and also two of the others; they introduced a fourth man, whose name was Farrington, as the county attorney. After the usual civilities had passed, Barrett remarked that their business was somewhat delicate; knowing that the Old Squire had been a prominent advocate of temperance, they had thought best to come and ask a few questions before instituting legal proceedings in the usual way against the unlawful sale of intoxicants. Then, noticing that the Old Squire looked puzzled, Barrett came more directly to the point.

"Are you engaged in manufacturing and selling a patent medicine called the *Old Squire's Tonic?*" he asked.

"Why, yes. I suppose I am. At least I am in partnership with a man named Califf, over in New Hampshire, who is making such a medicine; I furnish the herbs for it."

"Does the medicine contain an intoxicant?" Farrington queried.

"No, sir, not a drop," the Old Squire answered positively. "It is expressly stipulated in my agreement with Dr. Califf that no alcohol shall be put into it."

The county attorney glanced at the sheriff, who appeared to be a good deal amused, as were the others also. One of them went out to their carriage and brought in two bottles of the tonic.

"Is this the medicine you make?" the sheriff asked.

"It looks like it," the Old Squire said. "It has our label and the bottles resemble ours. Yes, there is the name blown in the glass."

"And you are not aware that these bottles contain an intoxicant?" Farrington asked.

"I am aware of nothing of the sort," the Old Squire replied with some heat.

One of the men then produced a corkscrew and, withdrawing the cork from a bottle, poured part of the contents into a glass. The sheriff then tasted the liquid and asked the Old Squire to do so. In fact they all tasted it.

"Strong stuff, isn't it?" observed Farrington.

"It certainly contains alcohol," the Old Squire admitted. "I can't account for it!" he exclaimed and, going to a cupboard, brought forth one of the bottles that Dr. Califf had sent us as samples.

When it was opened and everyone had tasted in turn, they all agreed that the stuff was quite a different thing and apparently had no alcohol whatsoever in it. Then the visitors looked at the Old Squire and laughed.

"There isn't much doubt that your partner Califf is a rogue," the sheriff remarked. "In fact we know he is one. For two years now he has been making trips over the line from New Hampshire into the border towns of our state, selling two kinds of this tonic. One, like the sample bottle he sent you, is for his temperance customers; the other is for those who like something stronger. The bottles seem to be the same, but the contents of the second kind is more than half whiskey. It is a rousing old tonic and no doubt has sold fast. We've been trying to catch him for some time," Barrett added, laughing. "For the last six months, however, he has been coming over mainly at night and has been leaving his medicine with certain confederates, who distribute on the quiet."

The Old Squire was astonished, painfully astonished. Out in the kitchen, too, Grandmother Ruth had heard enough to fill her with dismay and indignation. She sat down by a window and fanned herself vigorously without speaking.

Our disturbing visitors took leave presently, but cordially shook hands with the Old Squire as they went away.

"The law may have to take its course in this matter," the county attorney said, "but I assure you, Squire, that the proceedings, if there are any, will be merely formal so far as you are concerned. We are satisfied that you are guiltless of any intent to evade the law. But if you will allow me to advise you, I should say get rid of that partner of yours as soon as possible."

"You may be sure I will," the Old Squire replied earnestly. "I am greatly to blame; I ought to have kept better informed as to what he was doing."

We were all very quiet at table after they had gone. A sense of disgrace oppressed the entire family. Once Grandmother Ruth burst forth in wrath against Dr. Califf.

"I never liked his looks!" she exclaimed. "I knew he was a hypocrite when he lectured at the schoolhouse!"

"If you really knew that, Ruth, you should have told me at the time," the Old Squire remarked soberly. "He has deceived me completely."

The old gentleman set off for New Hampshire the next morning to find his crafty partner. Addison went with him, and they employed a lawyer to accompany them and give advice on such legal questions as might arise.

At Manchester they had some difficulty in finding Dr. Califf's "laboratory," as he called the obscure building where he manufactured the "tonic." When they did finally find Califf the Old Squire lost no time in serving notice on him that the partnership was dissolved, and, furthermore, he was not to use the label. Addison told us afterwards that the Old Squire gave the doctor a very plain talk.

No more tonic—of either kind—was made at Manchester, but we were subsequently informed that Dr. Califf manufactured and sold a thoroughwort "elixir," which he call the *Old Doctor's Tonic*, at Altoona, Pennsylvania. It was probably one of those patent medicines, once so common, that depended largely on alcohol for their popularity.

Altogether the Old Squire spent more than three hundred dollars to clear himself from his unwise partnership.

I may add that this awkward happening by no means impaired the old gentleman's faith in his tonic, as made in the home kitchen. He continued taking it every spring to the end of his long life.

21

The Unpardonable Sin

DURING THE FIRST WEEK IN MAY THE OLD SQUIRE AND Grandmother Ruth made a trip to Portland, and when they came back, they brought, among other presents to us young folks at home, a glass jar of goldfish for Ellen.

In Ellen's early home, before the Civil War and before she came to the Old Squire's to live, there had always been a jar of goldfish in the window, and afterwards at the old farm the girl had often remarked that she missed it. Well I remember the cry of joy she gave that day when Grandmother stepped down from the wagon at the farmhouse door and, turning, took a glass jar of goldfish from under the seat.

"Oh Grandmother!" she cried and fairly flew to take it from the old lady's hands.

Ellen had eyes for nothing else that evening, and as it grew dark she went time and again with a lamp to look at the fish and to drop in crumbs of cracker.

During the four days the old folks were away we had run free; games and jokes had been in full swing. There was still mischief in us, for the next morning when we came down to do the chores before anyone else was up, Addison said: "Let's have some fun with Nell; she'll be down here pretty quick. Get some fish poles and strings and bend up some pins for hooks and we'll pretend to be fishing in the jar!"

In a few minutes we each had rigged up a semblance of fishing tackle and were ready. When Ellen opened the sitting room door a little later the sight that met her astonished eyes took her breath away. Addison was calmly fishing in the jar!

"What are you doing?" she cried. "My goldfish!"

Addison fled out of the room with Ellen in hot pursuit; she finally caught him, seized the rod, and broke it. But when she turned back to see what damages her adored fish had suffered, she beheld Halstead, perched over the jar, also fishing in it.

"My senses! You here, too!" she cried. "Can't a boy see a fish without wanting to catch it?"

When she hurried back in a flurry of anxiety after chasing him to the carriage house, she found me there, too, pretending to yank one out. But by this time she saw that it was a joke, and the box on the ear that she gave me was not a very hard one.

"Seems to me, young folks, I heard quite too much noise down here for Sunday morning," Grandmother said severely when she appeared a little later. "Such racing and running! You really must have better regard for the day."

Preparations for breakfast went on in a subdued manner, and we were sitting at table rather quietly when a caller appeared at the door—Mrs. Rufus Sylvester, who lived about a mile from us. Her face wore a look of anxiety.

"Squire," she exclaimed, "I implore you to come over and say, something to Rufus! He's terrible downcast this morning. He went out to the barn, but he hasn't milked, nor done his chores. He's settin' out there with his face in his hands, groanin'. I'm afraid, Squire, he may try to take his own life!"

The Old Squire rose from the table and led Mrs. Sylvester into the sitting room. Grandmother followed them and carefully shut the door behind her. We heard them speaking in low tones for some moments; then they came out, and both the Old Squire and Grandmother Ruth set off with Mrs. Sylvester.

"Is he ill?" Theodora whispered to Grandmother as the old lady passed her.

"No, child; he is melancholy this spring," the old lady replied. "He is afraid he has committed the unpardonable sin."

The old folks and our caller left us finishing our breakfast, and I recollect that for some time none of us spoke. Our recent unseemly hilarity had vanished.

"What do you suppose Sylvester's done?" Halstead asked at last, with a glance at Theodora; then, as she did not seem inclined to hazard conjectures on that subject, he addressed himself to Addison, who was trying to extract a second cup of coffee from the big coffeepot.

"You know everything, Addison, or think you do. What is this unpardonable sin?"

"Cousin Halstead," Addison replied, not relishing the manner in which he had put the question, "you are likely enough to find that out for yourself if *you* don't mend some of your bad ways here."

Halstead flamed up and muttered something about the self-righteousness of a certain member of the family, but Theodora then remarked tactfully that, as nearly as she could understand it, the unpardonable sin is something we do that can never be forgiven.

Some months before Elder Witham had preached a sermon in which he had set forth the doctrine of predestination and the unpardonable sin, but I have to confess that none of us could remember what he had said.

"I think it's in the Bible," Theodora added, and, going into the sitting room, she fetched forth Grandmother Ruth's concordance Bible and asked Addison to help her find the references. Turning first to one text, then to another, for some minutes they read the passages aloud, but did not find anything conclusive.

The discussion had put me in a rather disturbed state of mind in regard to several things I had done at one time and another, and I suppose I looked sober, for I saw Addison regarding me curiously. He continued to glance at me, clearly with intention, and shook his head gloomily several times until Ellen noticed it and exclaimed in my behalf, "Well, I guess he stands as good a chance as you do!"

Two hours or so later the Old Squire and Grandmother returned, thoughtfully silent; they did not tell us what had occurred, and it was not until a good many years later, when Theodora, Halstead, and Addison had left the old farm, that I learned what had happened that morning at the Sylvester place. The Old Squire and I were driving home from the village when something brought the incident to his mind, and, since I was now old enough to understand, he related what had occurred.

When they reached the Sylvester farm that morning Grandmother went indoors with Mrs. Sylvester, and the Old Squire proceeded to the barn. All was very dark and still there, and it was some moments before he discovered Rufus; the man was sitting on a heckling block at the far dark end of the barn, huddled down, with his head bowed in his hands.

"Good morning, neighbor!" the Old Squire said cheerily. "A fine Sabbath morning. Spring never looked more promising for us."

Rufus neither stirred nor answered. The Old Squire drew near and laid his hand gently on his shoulder.

"Is it something you could tell me about?" he asked.

Rufus groaned and raised two dreary eyes from his hands. "Oh, I can't! I'm 'shamed. It's nothin' I can tell!" he cried out miserably and then burst into fearful sobs.

"Don't let me ask, then, unless you think it might do you good," the Old Squire said.

"Nothin'll ever do me any good again!" Rufus cried. "I'm beyond it, Squire. I'm a lost soul. The door of mercy is closed on me, Squire. I've committed the unpardonable sin!"

The Old Squire saw that no effort to cheer Rufus that did not go to the root of his misery would avail. Sitting down beside him, he said, "A great many of us sometimes fear that we have committed the unpardonable sin. But there is one sure way of knowing whether a person has committed it or not. I once knew a man who in a drunken brawl had killed another. He was convicted of manslaughter, served his term in prison, then went back to his farm and worked hard and well for ten years. One spring that former crime began to weigh on his mind. He brooded on it and finally became convinced that he had committed the sin for which there can be no forgiveness. He wanted desperately to atone for what he had done, and the idea got possession of his mind that since he had taken a human life the only way for him was to take his own life—a life for a life. The next morning they found that he had hanged himself in his barn.

"The young minister who was asked to officiate at the funeral declined to do so on doctrinal grounds, and the burial was about to take place without even a prayer at the grave when a stranger hurriedly approached. He was a celebrated divine who had heard the circumstances of the man's death and who had journeyed a hundred miles to offer his services at the burial.

"My good friends," the stranger began, "I have come to rectify a great mistake. This poor fellow mortal whose body you are committing to its last resting place mistook the full measure of God's compassion. He believed that he had committed that sin for which there is no forgiveness. In his extreme anxiety to atone for his former crime, he was led to commit another, for God requires no man to commit suicide, and his Word expressly forbids it. My friends, I am here today to tell you that *there is only one sin for which there is no forgiveness, and that is the sin for which we do not repent. That alone is the unpardonable sin.* This man was sincerely sorry for his sin, and I am as certain that God has forgiven him as I am that I am standing here by his grave."

As the Old Squire spoke, Rufus raised his head, and a ray of hope broke across his woebegone face.

"Now the question is," the Old Squire continued, "are you sorry for what you did?"

"Oh, yes, Squire, yes! I'm terribly sorry!" he cried eagerly. "I do repent of it! I never in the world would do such a thing again!"

"Then what you have done was not the unpardonable sin at all!" the Old Squire exclaimed confidently.

"Do you think so?" Rufus cried imploringly.

"I know so!" the Old Squire declared authoritatively. "Now let's feed those cows and your horse. Then we will go out and take a look at the fields where you are going to put in a crop this spring."

When the Old Squire and Grandmother Ruth came away the shadows at the Sylvester farm had visibly lifted, and life was resuming its normal course there.

They had proceeded only a short distance on their homeward way, however, when they heard footsteps behind, and saw Rufus hastening after them bareheaded.

"Tell me, Squire, what d'ye think I ought to do about that—what I done once?" he cried.

"Well, Rufus," the Old Squire replied, "that is a matter you must settle with your own conscience. Since you ask me, I should say that, if the wrong you did can be righted in any way, you had better try to right it."

"I will. I can. That's what I will do!" he exclaimed.

"I feel sure you will," the Old Squire said, and Rufus went back, looking much relieved.

"Did you ever find out just what it was that Sylvester had done?" I asked.

"Well, never exactly," the Old Squire replied, smiling. "But I made certain surmises. Less than a fortnight after my talk with Rufus our neighbors, the Wilburs, were astonished one morning to find that during the night a full barrel of salt pork had been set on their porch by the kitchen door. Every mark had been carefully scraped off the barrel, but on the top head were the words, printed with a lead pencil, "This is yourn and I am sorry."

"Fourteen years before, the Wilburs had lost a large hog very mysteriously. At that time domestic animals were allowed to run about much more freely than at present, and they often strayed along the highway. Sylvester was always in poor circumstances, and I believe that Wilbur's hog came along the road by night and that Rufus was tempted to make way with it privately and to conceal all traces of the theft.

"In spite of the words on the head of the barrel, Mr. Wilbur was in some doubt what to do with the pork and asked my advice. I told him that if I were in his place I should keep it and say nothing. But I didn't tell him of my talk with Sylvester about the unpardonable sin," the old gentleman added, smiling. "That was hardly a proper subject for gossip."

22

The Great Potato Picnic

THE GREAT POTATO PICNIC OF 1868 WILL NEVER BE forgotten by the people of Norway. While our district was nationally noted for its abundant variety of succulent apples, an unexpected resource had also been discovered. The rich soils of ridge and valley, when properly irrigated, produced potatoes in great quantity and of excellent quality.

But considering Aroostook County's potato boom, Norway potatoes never got the recognition they deserved. Though publicity schemes were undertaken on a large scale, nothing seemed to work until an enterprising selectman, Sol Upton, proposed holding a special "Great Potato Picnic" on the Norway fairgrounds, in September, a day before the annual fair.

Conceived of as a kind of grand potato "barbecue," it was advertised far and wide, attracted many thousands of people, and served to increase the fame and announce the resources of our district. It was indeed a spectacle! Exciting and perhaps thrilling, but not quite in the way we anticipated.

Committees were appointed to devise attractive features for the occasion, and, because the Old Squire was serving as selectman that year, I was put on the committee on sports, of which my friend, Tom Edwards, was chairman. We were told by the old gentleman that no ordinary program of sports would do, and that we must get up something picturesque, novel, and "startling."

"If it's to be picturesque," Addison said in one of the committee meetings, "it should be borrowed from some of this country's strangest and most colorful traditions."

We all remained silent and reflective a moment, and then Tom Edwards jumped up in some excitement.

"I have it!" he exclaimed. "We'll give them a bullfight!" We were struck almost dumb by the brilliancy of the suggestion, and adopted it by a unanimous vote.

But it was one thing to decide to have a bullfight, and another thing to get one up. The Old Squire told us that we must "put it through ourselves"; he had no time to superintend it. But we must guarantee that no one should be hurt in it, and that the animals should neither be killed nor cruelly treated.

We gave the guarantee, and set about organizing the "fight." Of course we knew absolutely nothing about bullfights. None of us were Westerners, and we knew nothing, except from books and hearsay, of the wild life of the mountains and the plains.

Nor could we find anyone who had had experience in bullfights. So much time passed while we were vainly corresponding with various people in the county, hoping to find someone who could direct a bullfight, that when we at last gave up searching and resolved to trust to our own resources, we had but three weeks left in which to prepare for the event.

I read all I could find in my family's new set of encyclopedias and then I went down to Norway and studied up the subject in the public library there.

My first proceeding on reaching home was to organize Addison, Halstead, Willis, Edson, and all the boys I knew into a corps of toreadors, picadores, chulos, banderillos, and matadors. Most of the boys wanted to be picadores, toreadors, or matadors, but Tom and I exercised our authority, seconded by that of the Old Squire, to such an extent that we finally filled up the ranks.

Then we appointed a subcommittee on costumes, and called in the assistance of Theodora and Ellen, Amanda Bachelder and Georgie Wilbur, and Kate Edwards and her mother, who had a gift for getting up all sorts of fancy dresses. I gave them my notes on the subject of bullfighters' costumes, and they set at work.

From a model which I obtained in Norway, I composed a beautiful announcement of the fight in Spanish. At the office of the *Lewiston Journal* this was converted into a magnificent and sufficiently startling poster, which proclaimed the fact that on the sixteenth of September a "Corrida de Toros" would be given at the Great Potato Picnic on the Norway fairgrounds. I threw in all the thrilling terms about splendid cavaliers and noble fighting beasts that I could find in the Spanish dictionary.

Everything seemed to be going on swimmingly now. One further important requirement in a bullfight had yet, however, to be met. We must have some bulls! This was the most difficult task of the whole enterprise. But at last we rented five handsome longhorn steers from a farmer near Lurvey Mills who had received a shipment of them as presents from his Texas rancher son.

For our arena, we proposed to have an enclosure of barbed wire at one side of the grounds where the Potato Picnic was to be held, in such a situation that the grandstand, put up for other spectacles, would command an excellent view of it. An entranceway from outside the grounds, through a gate at one side of the grandstand, and flanked on one side by that structure and on the other by an ordinary board fence, was to be constructed.

It seemed to us that a barbed-wire enclosure was much better than the ordinary arena of the Spanish and Mexican bullfights, because it would enable everyone to see plainly what was going on, at the same time it provided security for the audience. We brought the Texas steers to the town, and put them on short rations to make them ferocious. We did not intend to hurt them. Neither did we mean they should hurt us.

The costumes were to be the principal part of our Corrida de Toros; we were to have a sort of dress parade around the corral of handsome boys on handsome horses and on foot. The steers were to be driven about actively for some time, and a good deal of dust kicked up, and finally the attention of the people was to be diverted by a balloon ascension. We relied upon the novelty of the spectacle to please the people, and we knew that they would not be pleased by any exhibition of cruelty to animals.

We intended to have a full-dress rehearsal the day before the opening of the picnic, but the costumes were not quite done, and all the workmen in the town were so actively engaged in other branches of labor in preparation for the great event that our barbed-wire fence had not been put up. We were forced to wait for the corrida itself, to make the acquaintance of our *toros* in the ring.

The Potato Picnic was certainly an immense success. On one day, at least ten thousand people were present on the grounds. Eloquent and stirring speeches had been made; tons of roasted potatoes had been eaten; the bands were playing; and the enthusiasm ran high when the time appointed for the bullfight arrived.

We had been all excitement for hours. Our half-starved steers were in a barnyard near the grounds. Five minutes before the time, the gate of this enclosure was opened, and the live cattle were started by the toreadors and picadores for the picnic grounds.

By reason of my intimate study of the subject, I had been made chief toreador and master of ceremonies. I was mounted on old Nance, our family's gentle mare. We had one other toreador—Tom Edwards—and three picadores—Addison, Willis, and Edson—and our costumes, though made chiefly of cheap flannel and cambric, were, in gaudiness of color at least, a close imitation of those worn by Spanish bullfighters.

The cattle proved to be unexpectedly wild. One or two of them, touched up by one of the picadores, plunged about, fiery eyed and snorting.

After a good deal of trouble, they were driven into the arena, where they leaped and bellowed, and we five boys went careening madly in after them, amid intense excitement. The chulos, banderillos, and matadors, on foot of course, stood on a large dry-goods box just outside the barbed-wire fence, exactly opposite the entrance. From this point they could leap over the fence into the arena.

For their convenience in making their escape, three of four other dry-goods boxes were stacked inside the fence and against it.

As we rushed in, I saw the Old Squire in the grandstand, looking decidedly nervous. I doffed my sombrero in a grand manner to the people in the stand as we rode by, and then, coming to a halt, saluted

the crowd with a harangue in Spanish, not a word of which a Spaniard could have understood, announcing the beginning of the sport.

Then we began to chase the steers madly around the ring, with wild shouts, all in carefully selected Spanish. The steers, with eyes on fire and tails aloft, ran magnificently.

After some ten or a dozen of these circuits, I gave a signal to the chulos and banderillos, who, the moment we had passed them, leaped over into the ring and ran for the inside dry-goods boxes, where they began to wave in the air large sheets of red cambric.

Now came the thrilling moment. When the steers came around so that the red sheets confronted them, we expected them to be furious and to rush madly at them, whereupon the boys were to leap on the boxes and over the fence to a place of safety. This was to be continued until steers or the patience of the audience gave out, or the balloon went up.

But unfortunately the steers, instead of being filled with fury at the sight of the sheets, were scared almost to death. They turned about so swiftly that we who were on horseback almost rode upon them, but they dodged us, raced across the enclosure, huddled together with their tales to the fence, and confronted us with their long horns. Though I rode old Nance toward them as near as she would go—and she was disposed to give them a wide berth—they refused to budge. This was unexpected, and mortifying.

The crowd began to laugh and jeer. "Send the other boys around in back of 'em and let 'em punch 'em out!" someone shouted.

This was evidently the thing to do. I ordered—in plain English, this time—Halstead, one of the banderillos, to go around and punch the steers from behind, through the barbed wire. Willis, one of the picadores, handed him a lance.

Halstead, jealous over not being chosen matador, toreador, or picador, began prodding vigorously. And as soon as the steers were assaulted in the rear, they sprang forward with so wild a leap and such frightful bellowing that our five horses turned tail and ran frantically around the ring. They were simply uncontrollable. The steers were bellowing and running in every direction. The remaining boys in the ring, pale with fright, plunged almost headlong over the fence to a place of safety.

Our horses ran, and the cattle ran, each trying madly to get away from the other. The audience shouted with laughter. I screamed to my men, and they screamed back again, but the mad panic continued. There was really danger that a tragedy might follow.

In the midst of it, I saw Edson rushing on his horse out through the lane which led to the gate and thus out of the enclosure. Someone had prudently opened the gate, and that brave picador was taking to flight. Afterward I learned that the Old Squire had ordered the gate opened.

Another horse and rider lost no time in following the first. He happened to be just ahead of me, and in spite of all my efforts to control her, my mare went headlong the same way.

In less time than it takes to tell it, every toreador and picador had charged down that lane and out of the enclosure, and as we went out, the whole herd of steers came bellowing after us.

Out into the open space surrounding the grounds we rushed, with the now maddened *toros* at our heels. We could hear great shouts of laughter from within. Rows of faces appeared at the top of the grandstand, grinning at us.

I overhauled Tom Edwards.

"Tom!" said I, gasping, as my horse plunged—I was entirely out of breath, and so frightfully jolted by the riding that I could hardly speak— "Tom, where—are—you—going?"

"I'm—going—out—of town," said he, huskily, "and I ain't— coming—back till—this Great Potato Picnic is over!"

"So'm I!" I gasped.

We rode on, all five of us, toreadors and picadores, and did not slacken our speed until we were well out on the road toward the neighboring town of Oxford, where we put up for the night after notifying our families by telegraph. The last we saw of the steers, they were going up the road toward Lurvey Mills where they belonged at the clumsy trot that frightened cattle sometimes take.

The great Corrida de Toros was over. It ended very ingloriously for us. The Potato Picnic was an immense success. But for weeks we were the laughingstock of the town. And I have been told a thousand times since, but always with a grin, that the bullfight was the best thing on the program that day.

23

Sailing on the Ice

WHEN THE RAILROAD THAT RUNS THROUGH THE SEC-
tion of country in which the writer lived in his youth was finished, it
improved the market for lumber, and opened a new market for large
quantities of cordwood, which was then the only fuel burnt by the locomotives. Before the railroad came into use, firewood had been valueless
as an article of commerce.

In clearing the land, thousands of cords of the best of wood—rock
maple, yellow birch, and beech—had been burned where it grew. The
object of the settler was to get rid of the trees as easily as possible, and
the easiest way then, was to fell them and set them on fire.

Upon the large tract of land owned by my grandfather, there grew,
apparently, an exhaustless amount of wood. Until the advent of the railroad, only the pine and clear spruce had been thought worth cutting.
But the locomotives wanted the hardwood for fuel, and for a number of
years contracts were filled for hundreds of cords per winter, at four and
five dollars per cord.

The price seemed high, but it was only a fair remuneration; for it
was seven miles down the lake to the railroad station, and generally the
wood had to be hauled out of the forest, a mile or more, to the wood
yard on the ice at the head of Pennesseewassee. From this wood yard it
was about as much as a man and a team could do on a winter's day to
draw one cord down to the station; so that to cut and get out several
hundred cords was a "big" job, and required the services of many teams

with their drivers. Three or four choppers were also employed, for one cord a day was as much as the average woodcutter can chop and make ready for loading.

All winter long the woods and the lake's snow-clad shores echoed the strokes of the ax, the blows of the beetle, and the shouts of teamsters.

It was a busy scene. Each morning the loads went creaking out on the lake, and at evening the tired teams came plodding back to their log stalls.

To stimulate us boys to industry and economy, Grandfather had made us partners in a special three-year contract for six hundred cords of wood. He furnished the teams, their feed, and the wood on the stump; receiving as his share of payment half the contract price of the wood. We were to cut, haul, and deliver, or hire to cut, haul, and deliver.

Of course we were under a heavy expense, but Addison, Halstead, and I, usually had each spring—after paying off the girls—a net profit of about three hundred dollars to divide among us. We had, however, to work hard for our money, and attend sharply to business. The teamsters, if not watched, were apt to abuse the oxen, and stealing, lying, and drinking were vices which seemingly many of them took to naturally.

Not many words were used. If a man proved incorrigibly bad, he was abruptly discharged without a word of comment. That was an argument the men could understand.

At the close of the second winter to which I refer, we boys found that our share of the profits so far was about two hundred dollars apiece. As we made this sum by hard work and not by "grinding" the men, or by overworking the teams, I have always been a little proud of what we had accomplished.

But at the opening of the third winter, the indications were not favorable for a good season's work. We had about 80 cords still to deliver and about 220 to cut and deliver. Addison was now teaching at two winter schools and not able to provide much help. Halstead was laid up for a month after chopping his foot for a third time. (We had to hire the three young French Canadians who had helped us hay several years before as extra cutters.) And even the weather refused to cooperate. It was mild and no snow fell until December, which is not usual in that region. Finally, on December 4, the weather turned bitterly cold. The thermometer sank to 14 degrees below zero and ice formed on the lake ten inches thick. But there was no snow till December 8 or 9, when six or eight inches fell. Wind blew so hard that the glassy surface of the lake was swept bare, but in the woods there remained enough snow to enable us to draw the cordwood out upon the ice.

As is not uncommon in December, the wind blew almost constantly from the north and northwest, and sometimes very violently. The temperature remained below zero even at noon.

A day or two after the snowfall, we started with our loads of wood down the frozen lake. The oxen and the horses had been newly shod, and did not slip on the ice, though the steel-shod wood sleds almost slipped along without their aid. The horses trotted with the wind at their backs. We made the down trip of seven miles in an hour!

Several of the teamsters, taking off the oxen, went behind their sleds, and each shoved his cord of green wood with one hand. Noticing this, Halstead—who was interested in windpower—declared that if we rigged a sail we should have no need of the oxen, except to draw back the sleds.

Coming back we talked over his suggestion. At first our comments were half in sport, but the more we discussed the suggestion, the more feasible the idea seemed of execution.

At last we formed the grand plan of joining sleds together and raising a tall mast, so as to carry many cords of wood on one trip. I remember that the idea took such hold of us that neither Halse nor I slept that night.

The next day we framed a heavy platform, twenty-four feet in length by ten in width, and set it on four steel-shod sleds, two abreast. At one end of this platform, which was of timber, a "foot" was mortised for stepping a spar thirty feet in height.

How to steer our wood ship was a question we argued as we worked. It took all day to arrive at the plan we adopted. It was, I think, an original one.

At the apex of a triangle formed of two beams, resembling a harrow, and projecting in front of the platform, we set an old broadax. We had the poll or head of the ax drawn out by the blacksmith, so as to run up through a hole in the apex and turn easily in it. Upon the upper end of this elongated pole a strong level was fitted.

The triangle and level resembled somewhat a rudder and tiller, though it was placed at the bow instead of at the stern of our ice ship. Some of the wood was piled forward upon the triangle, so as to weigh down the ax blade, that it might take hold of the ice. When the ship was sailing, the lever was turned to the right or left, as we wished to direct our craft. Our "invention" never worked as well as a boat's rudder does in water, but by it the course of our rude vehicle could be changed sufficiently for our purpose.

For a sail we rigged a large tarpaulin, used to protect loads of hay from the rain. It was made of tarred canvas, and was about fifteen feet square. We cut it in the form of a leg-of-mutton sail, and attached it to yards. It was hoisted by a line running through a ring at the top of the mast. Our ship was not a handsome craft, for our idea extended only to the making of a serviceable wood sled, which should sail with its load down the lake rapidly and cheaply.

Early the next morning we loaded about four cords of wood upon our ship. Hitching horses to it, we drew it out on the lake from under the lee of the woods, and hauled up the sail. During that forenoon the wind was very light, and though when the sail would occasionally fill the load would glide along, yet we had to rely on the horses to reach our destination.

The following day and the day after there was but little wind, but the calm was followed by very cold weather and a three-days' gale. This was terribly severe. We had difficulty to keep from freezing even at our work.

That morning we piled seven cords of wood on the ship. A dull, cold haze was in the sky, and the sun seemed to have lost all its heat. The lake looked gray and bitterly cold, with the north wind sweeping the leaden-colored ice.

With our heads muffled up, we hauled the load from under the lee shore, and unhitching the team, without stopping, hoisted our sail. The wind filled it with a violent jerk, making our mast bend like a withe.

"Now for business!" shouted Halstead, jumping on the triangle, and seizing the steering lever in his mittened hands.

He had the warmest place, if there was any; for I had to stand on top and hold the sheet. The heavy load at first slid off slowly, but the wind grew stronger as we got farther from the woods, and we were soon going as fast as a horse could trot.

I kept lowering the sail lest we should lose all control of the craft, for it was a novel and alarming sensation to feel the heavy load moving so rapidly.

But soon we grew bolder. That afternoon we "sailed" down another load, carrying, at least ten cords. We let the ship run, and at times it went at railway speed.

A mile or more above the landing, at the foot of the lake, I dropped the sail, and the ship gradually slowed into port, and was greeted with admiration by the folks who had come out to see us.

It was thought to be a great feat. We sailed down the lake and unloaded our wood long before the span of horses, which started at the same time as we set out, would arrive to draw back the ship.

During the second day's gale we made three trips, carrying down nearly forty cords.

On the third day the wind blew so furiously that the sail drew all the wood we could pile on the ship. It was exciting work to steer the large load while going at swift speed. A cord of green wood will weigh about three tons, and on that day our loads weighed, at least, thirty-five tons each. As we plunged along, the ice would often crack with a report like that of a cannon, but ice at this season is tough, and we had but little fear of breaking through.

We got, however, too bold. About midway of the lake on the east shore, there is a rocky point called "Sabattus's Nose," from an Indian chief who used to live thereabouts. In sailing down, we had to bend round the "Nose," and, of course, we kept well off at first. But it was pretty trying work for Halstead's arms. The old ax blade had to be held very hard against the ice to keep the ship off far enough to clear the rocks.

In our first trip Halse did not run within a hundred yards of the nose; but, growing bolder, he kept reducing the distance and hugging the point a little closer each time.

"Fifty feet is leeway enough," he would say to my remonstrance.

But fifty feet was a small leeway with so uncertain a rudder. At least, we found it so.

For that day, as we dashed down with our third load, a violent gust caught us about half a mile above the point, and drove us in nearer up on the east shore. We were absolutely flying when Halstead shouted, "Drop the sail! Drop the sail, or we shall go on the Nose!"

I dropped it at once. Halse worked with might and main at his lever. We were under tremendous headway, and yet the wind swept us on. The nose seemed to be coming straight at us, and coming like a racehorse! A moment more and we were just upon it. Halstead let go the lever.

"Jump! Jump!" he shouted. "Jump clear, if you can!"

We both leaped for life, he from the triangle and I from the top of the load, and tumbling end over end, went sliding and sprawling on the ice.

The same instant I heard an awful crash. My eyes were full of water, and the air seemed to me to be full of four-foot wood.

We picked ourselves up—a good deal shaken. Our wood ship had struck the outside rocks, and leaped high and dry upon them, and the lake for about a quarter of a mile below was covered with sticks of wood, sliding in all directions. The mast and sail lay fully a hundred feet from the platform.

That was a dry shipwreck, but nonetheless a disastrous one. The two forward sleds were crushed to splinters, and the platform split and broken.

It took us and our troop of Canadians all the next forenoon to repair the damage and pick up the scattered wood; yet that load of wood went down to market the next afternoon. But after that experience we gave Sabbatus's Nose a wider berth.

For nearly three weeks no snow fell so as to remain on the ice, and the wind blew violently more than half of the time. During these days we shipped nearly all our remaining three hundred cords of wood, carrying them mostly on our wood ship. The weather afterwards became warmer, and nearly a foot of damp snow fell. The wood ship was laid up, and single loads had now to be drawn by teams as before.

Near March 7 there came a thaw, which was followed by sharp weather. The lake was again in a condition to be navigated by our wood ship.

There were about fifty "extra" cords of wood left to draw, and on the first windy day we hauled out our "ship," hoping to dispatch the wood to its destination in short order. The Canadians soon piled ten cords on the platform, and we got underway bright and early.

Halstead, as usual, took the steering lever in his own hands, but one of the Frenchmen, named Marc Clefeu, was stationed on the load to hold the sheet. I followed with the horses.

Towards spring, ice is not so strong and tough, in proportion to its thickness, as in December.

The load sailed off briskly, and soon left me far behind. It went on without accident for the first five miles, till it was passing opposite where a small river, called Ford's Stream, enters the lake. Probably the outsetting current of the stream had worn away and weakened the ice from beneath.

I was about a mile and a half behind, and was watching the load as it bowled swiftly on. Suddenly it sank down and vanished from sight.

Greatly astonished, I rubbed my eyes and looked again. A second after, a frightful crash, which shook the very ice under the horses' feet, resounded along the woody shores.

Springing on one of the horses, I started at a gallop for the scene of the accident. Before I reached the spot, Halstead had drawn himself out of the water by use of his picks and was trying to rescue the French boy. As much as a half-acre of ice was broken up! The water was full of wood and ice cakes, all dancing upon its surface together.

One of Marc's arms could be seen clinging round a long log, but the wood and ice held him down. We both ran out to him on the ice, jumping from cake to cake, and succeeded in pulling the poor fellow out, though we both fell in ourselves.

Marc was about exhausted and thoroughly chilled, for the wind blew piercingly, and the water was icy cold. He could not have got out without our help.

Halse said the ice broke all at once, without even a warning crack. They were going very swiftly, and he was about to call to Marc to slacken sail, when, with a noise like thunder, the whole load went down under them. He sprang off, went into the water up to his waist, but, catching his arms on one of the great cakes of ice, clambered out. Clefeu, however, went down with the load, head and ears under water.

That was the last trip with the ice ship, yet it had served us well, helping us complete our contract with the Old Squire, and demonstrating the thoughtfulness and energy Halstead was capable of, when given a task for which he was suited.

24

A Strange Legacy

WHEN NEWS IS SCARCE CERTAIN COUNTRY NEWS-
papers are accustomed to print a column of "old news" under the cap-
tion, "Hearken Back to the Past." In it they republish accounts of what
happened during the corresponding week years and years before. Often
the old accounts are amusing and for readers whose memory goes back
so far have all the charm of intimate reminiscence.

Recently our county newspaper ran such a column for a while,
selecting the items from the issues of thirty years before. The youth,
then eighteen years old, who reported those oldtime happenings afterwards won a national reputation as a humorist. There was plenty of fun
in him then if we may judge from his items, of which we give three
examples.

"Lew Fickett, Henry Wright, and Jim Cousins went deer hunting
to the lakes last week. They didn't get a deer, but contrived to shoot Jim
in the calf of his leg and had to lug him out to the settlement on the
door of an old logging camp. Fortunately, the bullet flew low and
selected a spot free from the vital organs—or so at least Dr. Hanbury
remarked after extracting it."

"The widow Hannah Hobbs, who lives alone in the northern part
of this township, has been terrorized by a tramp who pretended to be a
pack peddler. Hannah fled her domicile by the back door and raised the
neighbors *viva voce*. But when the assembled manpower of the vicinity
finally reached the place the pseudo-peddler had departed. Nothing

was missing except a loaf of brown bread and a ball of butter. About all the description the widow could give of her visitor was that he wore an old yellow cap and had a boil on one side of his nose. If anyone sees a vagrant thus becapped and afflicted, Deputy Sheriff Coulsen would like to have a word with him."

"Squire Stevens's grandson Addison has fallen heir to a trunkful of Bibles. That old hermit who lived up in the Great Woods so long has recently died; two hunters found him dead in his hut. Very few people ever went near him, for he didn't encourage calling. But Addison used to go to see him once in a while and sometimes befriended the old chap. His only asset besides his hut was a little old leather trunk, and tied to one of the handles they found a letter stating that the trunk was to be given to Addison. It was locked up hard and fast with a particularly self-willed lock, and they couldn't find the key. But when they finally got it open they saw that it was chock full of Bibles. Addison, we understand, isn't saying much about it, but when his friends meet him they put on a serious look and say, 'Search the Scriptures, Ad.'"

That last item, you may be sure, liberated a flood of memories! The old hermit was a strange character. While he lived we thought him a pathetic figure, and we continued to think so for a while after he died. No one ever really found out much about him. He did not leave a scrap of paper that threw the least light on his identity. He never said a word about his past life. Addison described him as the "remains" of a highly educated man who had Greek, Latin, and Hebrew at his tongue's end. He added that he had once said with a wink that his name was Solomon Solus. Every two or three months he visited the general store at the Corners to buy groceries, for which he always paid cash. His hut seemed to be a kind of workshop, for it contained numerous bottles of inks and chemicals and a little bench with stamps and dies. Some persons whispered the word counterfeiter, but they had no real evidence on which to base the charge.

We did know, however, that he occasionally slipped away at night from his hut in the woods and made trips no one knew where or why. Once he had been recognized at a railway station twenty miles distant. On that occasion he was clean shaven and neatly dressed in black—not at all like the stubbly bearded, shabbily dressed old fellow whom hunters and trappers were wont to see at his hut.

Addison used to go visit the man and talk with him once in a while. Sometimes in the fall he would carry him a peck of apples or plums and, once or twice, a bag of potatoes. I think that Addison rather enjoyed calling on the old fellow, though the walk was so long that he did not go often.

When the hermit died in September 1871, Addison was at Cambridge, where he was taking a scientific course. Theodora was attending school at Kents Hill Seminary thirty-three miles from the old farm and came home only once a week. And Ellen and I were trying to manage the farm. None of us were present at the fellow's funeral. He was buried at a little cemetery near our place, and afterwards the trunk, still locked, was brought down to the Old Squire's and left there. We wrote to Addison about his legacy, but he did not come home until Thanksgiving, two weeks later. He had no curiosity about the trunk; he would have laughed had anyone suggested that it held anything valuable.

When Addison came home for the holiday he brought with him a fellow student named Hyatt. They arrived the evening before Thanksgiving. After supper, when we were all gathered before the fire in the sitting room, the Old Squire brought the trunk from his bedroom and set it on the table in front of the fireplace.

"Here's your legacy, my boy," he said to Addison. "This paper is apparently a will and probably a legal one, for I see that the old recluse took the precaution to have it witnessed by two woodcutters who came to his hut."

We all gathered curiously round while Addison tried first one old trunk key and then another in the lock. But none fitted the ancient foreign lock. Finally, taking a hammer and a chisel, he cut off two rivets of the catch and raised the lid. The trunk was full of musty old books of various sizes, bound in moldy antique leather. One by one Addison took them out and put them on the table. They smelled as old as they looked, and the pages were yellow with age and otherwise discolored. Most of them were either in Greek or in Latin, but six or seven were in English. Several of the volumes had lost half a cover and many pages; some were without both cover and the title page and were tied together with strings. Not until we had laid out the entire collection on the table did we discover that every book in it was either a Bible or a part of a Bible. Hyatt, who was looking over the English Bibles, suddenly became interested. He pointed out that some of the books were not separated into chapters and numbered verses as they are in the King James Bible. "As I understand it," he said, "English translations of the Scriptures first began to be divided into chapters and verses as early as the middle of the sixteenth century. If that is so, you have a real find here."

Addison and he then began to examine the volumes more attentively, carefully separating the pages that age or dampness had stuck together. Between two leaves in the first English copy they looked at, they found a slip of paper on which was written, "This is a genuine copy of the so-called Unrighteous Bible, printed in the seventeenth century, which makes 1 Corinthians vi, 9, read, 'Know ye not that the unrighteous shall inherit the Kingdom of God!'" Addison hurriedly turned to Corinthians and found that the verse actually did read as the slip of paper said.

Over the title page of the next one that he and Hyatt looked at was pasted a slip of white paper on which was written, "This is one of the famous 'Bug Bibles,' printed in 1551, in which Psalm xci, 5, is translated, 'Thou shalt not be afraid of bugs by night.'"

On the title page of another of the English Bibles Addison discovered an inscription saying that it was a "Printers' Bible," published as early as 1702 and so called because a misprint makes the psalmist complain that "Printers (Princes) have persecuted me without a cause."

That set the Old Squire laughing; for the old gentleman was thinking of a book a friend of his had written for boys and of the incredible blunders the printers in Portland had made.

"Well, I hope you will not find any more such stuff in the Bible!" exclaimed Grandmother Ruth in a scandalized tone.

But Hyatt had already puzzled out a marginal note in another copy that he had been examining. That Bible had been printed in 1717 and, because Luke 20 is headed the Parable of the Vinegar instead of the Parable of the Vineyard, is known as the "Vinegar Bible."

"Never mind, Grandma," Addison remarked with a grin. "That's nothing to get sour over."

"And here is something to sweeten it with," Hyatt cried triumphantly, holding up another of the old volumes. "This is the celebrated 'Treacle Bible' of 1568, in which the word *balm* is translated *treacle!*"

The binding, the covers, and nearly half the text of the last of the English Bibles were missing; what remained was held together with a leather thong. It purported to be one of the tragic "Tyndale Bibles" that William Tyndale translated and printed at Marburg about 1530. Tyndale, who had become a convert to what was then termed the Reformed Church, tried to publish a "true" version of the Scriptures. Such efforts were perilous in those days. Tyndale was seized and strangled, and his body was burned in a prison yard near Brussels.

The quaint, faded old copies in Latin and Greek gave us more trouble and a good deal less diversion. We puzzled over them till late that night and, as a matter of fact, most of the next day.

According to custom, our Thanksgiving dinner was at eleven thirty in the forenoon. After dinner Theodora and I drove to Norway to bring back two friends from our Academy days, Bronson Chaplin and Lucia Scribner, who were to spend the afternoon with us and remain overnight. When we returned at three o'clock Addison and Hyatt were still in the sitting room, poring over the Bibles. The Old Squire and Ellen were also there with them, and, to judge from the sound of their voices, all were considerably excited. Ellen rushed out to meet Lucia and Bronson but hardly waited to greet them before she exclaimed, "What do you think that Addison and Mr. Hyatt have found among those old books? Some sort of Algerine Bible!"

"A what?" Theodora cried.

"Well, it sounded like that," Ellen said. "Anyhow, it is something very ancient; Gramp says he has read that the last one that was found was sold in London a few years ago for two thousand pounds, and that, you know, is almost ten thousand dollars!"

We all hurried to the sitting room. Addison, Hyatt, and the Old Squire were bending over an old volume beside the trunk on the table. Grandmother Ruth, standing back with her hands crossed, was looking on with a disturbed expression. Addison looked up long enough to nod and say, "Good afternoon!" and "How d'ye do!" to Lucia and Bronson and then turned eagerly back to the book.

"What's this Algerine Bible I hear you've found?" Bronson asked. "Tell us about it."

"'Algerine Bible?'" repeated Addison. "Oh, no; it's a 'Mazarin Bible'—so named because a copy was found in the library of Cardinal Mazarin in Paris. Some say it was the first book ever printed with movable metal types."

"Well, I don't care!" Ellen exclaimed in confusion. "It sounded like Algerine."

Meanwhile Theodora found an opportunity to introduce Hyatt to Lucia, and that reminded Addison to introduce him to Bronson. Then we all crowded round to see the dilapidated old book. To one of the last flyleaves at the back they had found pasted a much discolored sheet of paper on which was written, "This is a copy of the Holy Scriptures, presented to George Altemas by Cardinal Rizzio for the Mazarin Bibliotheque in return for three *pocula* of gold for the Cardinal's communion service."

You could see that Addison was greatly interested. He did not say much, but there was an unusual light in his eyes. The Old Squire, too, went and came that day like one whose mind is engrossed. Hyatt and Addison had begun going more carefully through all the other old Bibles, particularly the volumes in Greek and Latin; they looked between every pair of leaves. The idea had now taken possession of them that those musty old books might be of great value after all.

"Maybe you have a fortune here," Hyatt said. "Where do you suppose that old chap got all those Bibles? It looks as if he were an ancient Bible collector and had made a life job of it. My uncle collected violins," he added, laughing. "I know the kind."

Addison and he were going back to Cambridge the next morning and would have to make an early start to catch the train at the village station. Before going to bed Addison packed all the old volumes in the trunk and got it ready to take with him. He had decided to go to the Harvard University Library and seek the opinions of the librarians and of others who were familiar with old books. I think he had high hopes that his legacy might make him rich, or that it would at least defray the expenses of his education.

We did not hear from him for a month or more; he was never a punctual letter writer. Finally, he wrote from Cambridge to the Old Squire, and I still remember certain paragraphs of the letter, or at least the substance of them.

"I have had all those old Bibles examined both here and over in the city," he wrote. "You will be surprised, sir, and I dare say disgusted (at least I was) to learn that they are all forgeries, or rather that they are old Bibles, cunningly altered and doctored to simulate far older or very rare Bibles such as command high prices. They were examined very carefully, and the evidences of fraud are, the experts tell me, conclusive. They are curiosities of imposture, and I have sold the whole lot for a couple of hundred dollars, which will help me out a little next year.

"Of course the only inference is that our old hermit friend was a counterfeiter of old Bibles, and that he sallied forth into the world at intervals to dispose of one or more of the products of his 'industry' to dealers in old books or to libraries. I was assured that if those Bibles had been genuine the contents of the old trunk would have been worth more than fifty thousand dollars. It is lucky I had Hyatt with me, or someone might have suspected that I myself was the forger.

"What I surmise is that old Solomon Solus, as he called himself, imagined that I might be able to sell those volumes as he had done, and, feeling well disposed toward me, endowed me with that bonanza of fraud! In other words, he thought it was all right to pass his crookedness on to me. The old chap must have been far gone in the depths of moral obliquity, and I am thankful to be out of it. Hyatt stood by me loyally, but he has to have a joke about it. 'Well, how's the Bible counterfeiter feeling this morning!' he says to me once in a while, laughing."

25

At Anticosti

Part 1

SEEMS AS IF WE WERE A THOUSAND MILES FROM NO-where, doesn't it?" Willis Murch said, and Addison, Bronson Chaplin, and I rather gloomily agreed with him.

It was after ten o'clock at night, yet the twilight still lingered over the wild, somber woods on the island of Anticosti. In front of our camp washed and swashed the unquiet waters of the Gulf of St. Lawrence, lighted by a fitful red streak from our campfire. Along the beach to the left the bows and broken bowsprit of a wrecked brig loomed black in the failing light. To the right long ricks of lumber, which strewed the beach, told of other vessels that had foundered off the island.

From inland came the confused low cackle of hundreds of wild geese, a peculiar, drowsy sound that changed suddenly to loud outcries.

"Old ganders floggin' off a bear!" muttered Cain, the captain of the tug that had brought us to Anticosti. The uproar was prodigious, but before long it died away, and the captain chuckled. "They've run him off," he said. "And they'd run a man off, too. I'd go into a lion's den jest as soon as into one of them goose swamps."

"Great place for bears here, I've heard," remarked one of the crew of the tug.

The talk round the campfire was interesting, but Addison, Willis, Bronson, and I had been woefully seasick all the preceding night on the trip over from the mainland, and we soon crept to the shelter of a shed of boards that we had set up.

How we four, with the skipper of a tug and his crew, happened to be camping on that lonely island so far from the old farm in Maine came about in this way:

My cousin Addison had been studying in Cambridge under the celebrated Professor Louis Agassiz, who was then at the height of his fame as a naturalist. It was Professor Agassiz's custom to send his students out to collect specimens for museums, and the summer before he had sent Addison, with four other young men, to the islands of the Gulf of St. Lawrence, with special instructions to visit Anticosti, of which next to nothing was then known.

The boys spent almost six weeks in cruising round the gulf in a fishing schooner, and stopping at the various islands; they were successful in getting some specimens of unusual interest. When Addison came home for a day or two at Thanksgiving that fall, he had much to tell us about Anticosti.

Of course we had heard of the island, but we were astounded when Addison told us that it was actually 140 miles long and from 30 to 40 miles wide; moreover, he said that it was teeming with bears, deer, and moose and abounding in small creeks where the fishing was good for salmon and trout.

"And you should taste the 'baked apples'!" Addison said. "They're simply delicious!"

"What!" the Old Squire exclaimed. "Don't you tell me there are orchards on Anticosti!"

"Oh, no, sir! Not apple trees!" replied Addison, laughing. "It's a kind of plum, or rather berry, that grows on the peat bogs a little back from the shore; they're so plentiful that I've gathered a large bucketful in fifteen minutes. By the way, sir," he added, after a short pause, "do you suppose that you could get permission from the provincial government to go there and salvage what's on the beach?"

"Why, I think it likely," the old gentleman replied, a little puzzled. "What did you find?"

"Lumber," said Addison.

At the word *lumber* the Old Squire looked interested. At that time he was in the lumber business at Three Rivers with a Canadian named McCall, who lived in Montreal and attended to the details of the business.

"But I remember McCall's telling me," the old gentleman said, "that the growth on Anticosti is worthless for lumber."

"Oh, this lumber didn't grow there!" Addison exclaimed. "It is from lumber vessels that have been wrecked there."

"I have heard it is a bad place for wrecks," said the Old Squire. "Only a year ago a bark that loaded at Three Rivers was cast away there. In fact, there have been some ugly stories that a gang of wreckers are living on the island, but I don't suppose that's so."

"Well, sir, a good many ships must have gone down off Anticosti," Addison said. "On the beach there are piles of good pine boards, spruce deals, clapboards, and square timber."

"Why hasn't anyone salvaged it before?"

"I asked our skipper that, and he said that the ledges offshore are so treacherous that it isn't safe for a schooner or lighter to approach the island."

"But hasn't the lumber weathered badly, and isn't it broken up?" the Old Squire asked.

"No, sir! Good Canada West pine like that lasts for years. It lies there just as the breakers piled it up. In one place I saw about eight thousand bunches of clapboards that had not even broken apart. And you ought to see the great square dimension timbers of clear old pine, spruce, and tamarack."

The Old Squire was plainly interested in Addison's account.

"But if a schooner can't approach the place," he said, "how do you plan to salvage the stuff?"

"Raft the lumber and tow it off at high tide," Addison replied promptly. "The tide rises ten or eleven feet there. We could tow the rafts over to Gaspe Bay and there load them on vessels."

"Well, that sounds possible," the Old Squire said. "I'll think it over."

A day or two later Addison went back to Cambridge. But the Old Squire did not intend to let the matter drop, and the first time he went up to Three Rivers, he mentioned it to his partner. Mister McCall was greatly attracted to the scheme. He was of the opinion that if the reports were accurate it might be possible by hiring a tug and a crew of five or six men to clear up twenty thousand dollars or more. In January 1873, while the provincial parliament was in session at Quebec, Mister McCall applied to the government for permission to salvage the lumber on the beach of Anticosti. Two or three months later he received a letter from the lieutenant governor of the province, or his secretary, which, although it was not exactly a formal permit, said that the government would raise no objection to the applicant's picking up stranded lumber on Anticosti if he could find means to do so. Mister McCall sent this letter down to the Old Squire, and they both decided that it was sufficient authorization for them to go ahead with the project.

We hurried farmwork that spring, and as soon as Addison came home from Cambridge we made ready to start. There were to be five in the expedition: Addison and I; Willis Murch, one of our young neighbors, whom we had hired to go with us; Bronson Chaplin, a former classmate at the academy, to whom I had written of the projected trip, and who, having means to travel as he pleased, had asked to be allowed to join the party, and Mister McCall. We were to meet Mister McCall at Rimouski, where the tug, with its captain and crew of four men, was waiting for us.

We journeyed to Quebec, and from there to Rimouski. But when we reached the inn at which we were to meet Mister McCall we found a telegram from him, saying that the day before, while helping to load a brig with lumber at Three Rivers, he had fallen through a hatch into the hold and broken his leg. At first we thought of giving up the trip, but another telegram from him, two hours later, advised us to go on, since the tug was already hired and the contract signed.

At that time of year the voyage presented no unusual dangers. Neither the captain nor any of the crew had ever landed on Anticosti; however; seafaring men usually gave the place a wide berth.

After a hasty consultation we decided to go on. So we went down to the waterfront, found our tug, and at one o'clock that afternoon steamed out from Rimouski.

We soon encountered a heavy swell, and the tug pitched unpleasantly. As the hours passed and night came on, the weather got still rougher; cooped up in the little, bad-smelling cabin, we boys were pretty sick.

Toward morning fog came in. About three o'clock the captain sighted what he felt sure was the Admiralty light at the southwest point of Anticosti Island, but the fog soon obscured it. An hour later he saw for a few minutes through the fog another light off the port quarter, which he was certain could not be the light he had seen before. Puzzled and very much frightened, he stood offshore until daylight. The appearance of the mysterious light troubled the captain and the crew a good deal.

At daybreak the fog lifted a little, and we steamed along the coast a little way until we were perhaps twenty miles southeast of Lighthouse Point. Addison remembered having seen a great deal of lumber on that part of the beach, and so we decided to land. After some search we found a little creek that emptied into the gulf; it offered not only a good landing place but also a safe harbor for the tug. By night we had got our camping stuff ashore and had built a little shed of the lumber on the beach.

We got a good rest that night, and the next morning we felt entirely recovered from the effects of the rough voyage. After breakfast we set out to explore the beach.

We soon saw why little or no effort had been made to salvage the cargoes lost there. The coast of Anticosti consists of several benches or shelves of limestone and sandstone formation. The topmost, which lies just above high water, rises to a height of from ten to thirty feet, and in some places it overhangs the water. To the seaward of that line of crags and just under water at low tide, there is another shelf of ledges, which extends out to sea for three or four hundred yards before deep water begins. At high tide a vessel could sail over those submerged ledges; at low tide the water over them is often not more than three feet deep.

We went along the shore for several miles in either direction from our camp. Some of the lumber had lain there for years and of course was much weathered, but a good deal of the wreckage had been cast up not long before. One ship that had gone to pieces on the ledges had been laden with grindstones. At low tide we saw lying in the water enough grindstones to sharpen all the dull tools in Canada!

Some of the wreckage consisted of sawed timber of all sizes, apparently intended for house frames, but the larger part of the pine and spruce lumber was in boards of one-inch thickness, and in two- and three-inch deals. During the forenoon we found the eight thousand or more bunches of clapboards of which Addison had told us. They lay so high on the shore ledges that it would be an easy matter to salvage them. Near our camp we found a great number of crates, each of which contained from sixty to a hundred wooden bowls that had been turned out on lathes from some sort of hardwood. At another place a mile or more farther along the shore there were hundreds, yes, thousands, of ash handles for spades, shovels, and hoes, all corded up in bundles.

At one point within a little curve of the shore lay a vast quantity of laths for lath and plasterwork in houses, and farther on was a rick more than a thousand feet long of cedar shingles in bunches. A part of the hull of the schooner that had carried the shingles was still pounding on the ledges. Several miles from that place we found another rick of shingles—nine thousand bunches of them, according to a hasty estimate that Willis and Addison made.

The number of ships that must have gone down here was truly appalling. There was something so sinister in the appearance of that wreck-strewn beach that the cheerful spirit with which we had set out on our tour of exploration left us. We could not forget the stories we had heard that the wrecks off Anticosti were not caused by storms or sunken ledges, but by false beacons, and that set us to thinking again of the mysterious light we had seen when we were approaching the island.

When we neared the campfire, we noticed a strong odor of something scorching. Two of the crew were broiling lobsters on the coals. They had been lobstering out on the flats, and had caught fifty or more, some of which were huge fellows that must have weighed fifteen pounds! The men said that the waters round the outer line of reefs were swarming with lobsters. The feast that we had of them that night somewhat raised our spirits.

After talking the situation over with the captain—although he seemed to take no great interest in the affair—we agreed that the only way to salvage the lumber would be to get it into rafts as Addison had suggested, and to tow the rafts off at high tide in calm weather. One

day of good weather would be enough to tow a large raft over to Gaspe Harbor. Many practical difficulties presented themselves, but we thought that if fortune favored us we could surmount them.

After supper we strolled along the beach to look at some of the lumber again. Near one of the old hulks we found a mark cut on a stick of timber—three X's and "A.C." Rather disturbed, we walked on, talking the matter over. About half a mile farther on, we found the same mark cut on another stick. The marks seemed fairly fresh.

"Now, who do you suppose did that?" Willis said. "Looks to me as if someone else had been here looking this lumber over."

"Maybe," Addison said, "but we have a permit to get it; that makes it all right for us."

We had taken with us the letter that Mister McCall had sent down to the Old Squire. When we got back to camp, we read it again. Although it seemed conclusive as to our rights, those benchmarks made us a little uneasy.

Part 2

THE NEXT DAY we got to work at overhauling the ricks of lumber. We began with the cedar shingles. Addison thought, and so did I, that, with the tug costing us thirty dollars a day, we ought to waste no time in getting something done to show for the Old Squire's money.

The shingles were in bunches, which lay scattered along the shore for half a mile or so, where the storm waves had flung them up. For the most part they were dry, and the bunches were not too heavy for us to shoulder and to carry along the beach. We began to collect the best of them at a place where it seemed practicable to make a raft.

By eleven o'clock we had brought together almost nine hundred bunches. The day was hot, however, and the work by no means light, for the beach was rough and rocky. Addison, Willis, and I did not greatly mind it, but Bronson, who was not inured to work, looked wilted. After a while Addison, who was keeping an eye on him, said: "We ought to have some of those 'baked apples' for dinner. Bronson is nimble with his fingers, and he has brought his guns and fishing tackle; I move we elect him berry picker, hunter, and fisherman for the party."

Willis and I began to see what Addison was driving at, and heartily voted, "Aye"; for as Bronson was our guest, it did not seem right to make him work as hard as we should have to work.

"Well, then," Addison said, "we want some of those 'baked apples,' Bronson, and we want them in the course of an hour. So get a bucket and hurry up! There's sure to be plenty on the flats behind the beach. But take your gun. You may run into a bear or a moose almost anywhere behind the beach here."

About an hour had passed, when we heard Bronson "Soho!" at the camp. He had got back on time, but had less than a quart of "baked apples."

"Didn't find many," he said. "But, fellows, I came upon a mighty queer contrivance back there in the woods. I couldn't make it out."

"What was it?" Willis asked.

"It looks like a barrel, but it's iron," Bronson said. "It is on a support of logs, and has had a fire in it, but it doesn't look to me as if it were meant for cooking food."

"How far away?" Addison asked.

"Oh, not more than ten minutes' walk from here. It's at a ledgy place just before you come to the peat flats."

Just then Captain Cain and the four sailors, who had been working with us on the beach, came up. They were very grumpy, for they had expected to do nothing except navigate the tug and to have an easy time at Anticosti for a fortnight or so, but Addison had told them plainly that morning that the rate at which they were being paid included their labor in rafting the lumber. At last, with a good deal of grumbling, they had set to work.

The prospect of dinner cheered them up a little, and as we ate together they grew a little more genial. When we had finished, Addison proposed going to have a look at Bronson's find.

The place proved to be scarcely half a mile from the beach, at a point where an outcrop of the limestone ledges rose slightly above the surrounding level; the spruce and fir growth there was rather scattered and low. On a rise in the ground a structure of rough logs ten or twelve feet high had been built cob-house fashion; it narrowed toward the top, and was covered with a platform. On the platform stood what can best be described as an iron barrel, since it was much the shape of one, and of about the same size as an ordinary flour barrel. We easily climbed the rude pyramid and at the top found room on the platform for ten or twelve persons. Standing up there, we could look out to sea over the tops of the low trees.

We examined the queer barrel, and saw, as Bronson had said, that someone had built a fire in it within a few days. Charred brands and a foot or more of ashes lay at the bottom.

"Know what this is and where it came from?" said Captain Cain, tapping the iron barrel.

"I confess I don't," Addison admitted.

"That's an old crow's nest!" the captain exclaimed. "The lookout's barrel from the masthead of a whaler."

"I suppose some hunters found it on the beach and used it to build their campfire in," Willis said.

"But why should hunters want to have their fire up here?" Bronson exclaimed.

"Wal, the kind of hunters that built that fire wanted it there!" Cain growled, with a hearty execration. "Don't you see what this is for? Look round. Look out to sea!"

"A false beacon, of course!" Addison exclaimed.

"Sure as fate!" said Cain. "This is probably the light we saw when we were standing off the island. Someone ought to swing for it. I make no doubt that thing has sent more than one poor fellow to his death!"

The captain had all a mariner's natural hatred for a false beacon. "We must make our affidavits to this thing," he said. "There's evidence enough here to convict the scoundrels—if they can only be caught I dassay there's a gang of them not far away, like's not a whole settlement of 'em, with women and young ones, somewhere in the woods back of these peat flats."

"Yes, there's a big back country where no one is supposed to live," Addison said. "It is all of thirty miles across the island from where we stand."

"Oh, there's room enough for any number of 'em!" Cain exclaimed impatiently. "Officers might search for months and not find 'em! No doubt they keep spies on the lookout; they may be watching us this minute. But we'll take this old crow's nest with the ashes in it and put it where it'll be safe. It may be wanted as evidence."

"I wish he would let it alone!" Willis muttered to me, and somehow I felt that way about it myself. But Captain Cain handed the barrel down to the sailors.

"Don't spill the ashes out of it," he cautioned them. "We must keep those brands and ashes in it, to show how it has been used."

The four sailors carried the barrel right side up, first to camp and then, after further talk, to the tug in the mouth of the creek two or three hundred yards farther on, and stowed it away in the coal bunker. Cain said he would take it to Rimouski, when we returned, and afterwards forward it to the Canadian authorities at Quebec.

We then went to work again on our shingles, and continued until after four o'clock, when we began to notice a disagreeable odor. The wind had suddenly shifted from north to southeast; the odor came from that quarter and increased as the wind freshened.

"That's a dead whale!" Cain said.

"If it gets much worse, we'll have to move our camp!" Bronson exclaimed.

The captain and the sailors laughed. "You wouldn't do to go on a whaler," Cain said.

"Bronson, you are the hunter, you know," Addison said, at last. "I think it is your duty to go and investigate this."

"Aye, sir," Bronson responded, but as he started for the camp, Addison nodded to me to go with him. The discovery of the iron barrel had disturbed him more than he cared to show. Bronson had brought two guns with him—a double-barreled shotgun and a carbine; we took both pieces. As the tide was out, we crossed the creek on the bar at the mouth, and started along the beach to the southeast.

"I don't see how any earthly thing can give off so much odor!" Bronson said. "There must be cubic miles of it!"

We pushed on and finally, after we had gone far beyond where we had stopped on the preceding day, we turned a craggy point of the shore, and came in sight of a vast flock of sea birds, hundreds, yes, thousands of them, circling, settling, hovering over one spot. We were still nearly half a mile away, but we could see that the center of attraction was a long black-and-yellow object that lay in a pool among the exposed reefs.

There could be no doubt that it was a dead whale in an advanced stage of decomposition. We started to walk round to windward and approach nearer. At last we reached a place among the crags within two hundred yards of the pool in which the carcass lay. It was a large whale, at least seventy feet long.

At times the cloud of birds actually obscured the carcass from view, and their eager yet plaintive cries added a touch of strangeness to the wild surroundings. But the birds were not the only feasters present. Suddenly there popped forth from some cavity of the huge carcass a black animal, which looked small to us at first sight, but which we perceived was a bear.

"Let's get him!" Bronson exclaimed.

"Shoot away, then," said I. "You have the carbine."

Resting the gun across a rock, Bronson took aim and pulled the trigger. He missed the bear, but I think he hit the whale, for almost instantly two other bears popped out, followed by yet another, and then by one more. The last was really an enormous beast.

Bronson fired again, and then twice more, but such a prodigious rumble and roar of wings had begun—as the hundreds of screaming birds rose at once—that I do not think that the bears heard the shots. But they knew that something had happened, and, with the big one leading the way, all five of them started for the cover of the forest. As we were between them and the woods, they were heading straight for us.

Jumping up, I fired both barrels of the shotgun, but duck shot is not ammunition for bears. The animals did not pause an instant. Turning, Bronson and I started to run along the rocks out of their way. We covered a hundred yards in good time. When we looked round, the bears had taken to the woods, and judging by the noise in the brush, they were still going at a great pace.

We watched the birds for a few minutes longer, and then, since it was beginning to rain, we started back. Although we made haste, it had grown quite dark when at last we caught the glimmer of the campfire. They were broiling more lobsters, and the sailors were chanting a quaint French song.

As we ate, we reported concerning the whale, but we did not say a great deal about the bears, for we realized that we had not distinguished ourselves as bear hunters.

What with carrying shingles and walking so far, we had found it a tiring day. Addison suggested that we take turns standing watch that night, but the others thought that with nine of us sleeping there together, there was no danger. Pretty soon after supper we turned in.

I soon dropped into a restless sleep, from which I kept starting up. Too much lobster! Once I waked, thinking that someone stood looking into the shed, but I decided that I must have been dreaming. The others were snoring, and I soon drowsed off. By and by an odd noise waked me again. It sounded as if someone had dropped an iron bucket on the stones not far off. Addison had waked, too, and was sitting up.

"What was that?" he whispered, hearing me stir.

"Out there by the tug, wasn't it?"

The tide had come in, and we thought that the sound was made by a chain rattling as the tug lifted. We both lay down again, but a moment later we plainly heard someone treading on pebbles and loose stones.

"Someone's out there by the tug," Addison whispered, and, fumbling in his coat pocket, struck a match. We glanced round the shed. "Thought Captain Cain might have got up, but there he lies—snoring."

Reaching for Bronson's carbine, he pointed it out to sea and fired. Instantly we heard the sound of someone running away. The captain, Willis, and the others had started up.

"What's the matter?" they exclaimed.

"Someone's prowling round the tug," Addison answered.

Lighting a lantern, we set off down the beach toward the tug. We had not gone far when we came upon the crow's nest lying upset among the stones. Someone had ferreted it out in the coal bunker and had tried to carry it off!

"Shows one thing!" Bronson said, as we stood there listening. "Someone's got a bad conscience about this old barrel!"

"Shows another thing!" Captain Cain muttered. "Some of those chaps was a-watchin' us when we hid it. They knowed jest where to come for it! But they don't get it!" he exclaimed, with an oath. "Here, Pierre, and you, Lotte, pick that up and take it to camp! I'll keep my eye on it after this!"

The sailors lugged the barrel to the shed and, under Cain's directions, stowed it behind the bunk.

"There!" the captain exclaimed. "If anyone else comes for it, he will have to explain his business to me!"

The next morning we got together more shingles and about a thousand bunches of clapboards. When we returned to camp at noon, we found that someone had again tried to make off with the crow's nest. It was lying on its side at some distance from the shed. The marauder had moved the boards of the slant roof aside, and rolled it out; evidently our return had frightened him away.

"You see how bad they want it!" Cain cried. "It's my duty to report this thing at Quebec, right off, too, and have this gang of wreckers broken up before they do any more mischief."

He was much excited, and declared he would start as soon as the tide came in. Addison and I demurred, however, on account of the expense and loss of time.

"If you go off and leave us like that, you'll have to pay your own coal bill and lose your time," Addison told him.

Cain thought otherwise, and we had a hot discussion. At last Addison suggested that, as the weather was fine, we should make up a small raft and have the captain tow it down to Gaspe; there he could report the incident of the false beacon by telegraph to Quebec. An experimental trip seemed worthwhile, for it would show us whether we could really salvage the lumber. Cain rather surlily agreed to this plan.

Accordingly, we set to work that afternoon, and brought together timber and deals for a raft of about twenty thousand feet of lumber. It was heavy, hot work, and even lobsters failed to keep me awake that night. The few hours of darkness passed quietly, and we heard nothing further from the wreckers.

The next morning at ebb tide we laid the raft. We pinned the timbers together with cross sticks and secured them further with rope lashings before we piled on the deals and boards. On top of all we loaded five hundred bunches of cedar shingles.

The tide was not high enough to float the raft until after eight o'clock that evening. Then Cain, after getting the crow's nest aboard, worked the tug out of the creek and, making a circuit found the now submerged ledges, backed slowly inshore. He put one of the sailors on the raft, to give him the line and fend off. At last he got things to suit him, and pulled out to sea. As he went he gave us three long farewell toots of the whistle.

Part 3

WE STOOD THERE for some time in the deepening twilight and watched the tug, with the raft in tow, steam away southward. The gloom of night was already settling on the somber forest of spruce and fir that lined the beach. A few gulls passing on wavering wing sent down their peevish cries; there was no other sound.

Without a word we made our way back to camp; Willis began to throw broken clapboards on the fire.

"Well," Addison said, breaking the silence at last, "Cain ought to be back by day after tomorrow."

"We don't know when he will come back," Bronson declared. "He's gone off mad as a hatter. He will take his time. Like as not he will go to Rimouski, or Quebec, instead of Gaspe."

"Oh, no!" said Addison, laughing. "He knows he would forfeit his pay if he did that. He'll be back, all right, if the weather holds good, and tonight it looks fine."

I could see that Addison wanted to hearten us up a bit.

"Let's get our supper," he said. "Tomorrow we'll rest up and go fishing. We've been working pretty hard."

After supper we sat in front of the shed until the long twilight had quite faded out in the north, which, at that time of year and in the latitude of Anticosti, was not until about eleven o'clock.

"Now, I am going to keep awake awhile." Addison said, at last. "The rest of you can go to sleep. Along about two o'clock I'll speak to one of you, to take my place."

The hard work had been fatiguing, and before very long I fell asleep; so did Bronson and Willis.

Sometime later, Addison shook me gently.

"Is it my turn?" I whispered sleepily.

"No," said he. "But give Willis a shake. There's a fire off here."

I waked Willis and Bronson. Addison was standing in front of the shed, looking off along the shore. Although our campfire had smouldered out, I could see his face plainly—it seemed to be faintly lighted. Rushing out, we saw, a long way off to the east, a great fire.

"It's a forest fire!" I cried.

"No, it's on the beach," Addison said. "Looks to me as if it were just about where we came to that big rick of shingles."

"That's just what it is!" Bronson exclaimed. "But how could they have got afire?"

"Someone's campfire, maybe," Willis said. "Fishermen perhaps. Too bad! There were more than ten thousand bunches of cedar shingles there. Seven or eight thousand dollars' worth!"

"Isn't that a wicked shame!" cried Bronson.

We stood and watched the fire for some time. It appeared to be burning fiercely, and to be extending for some distance along the shore. Willis proposed that we go to put it out, or at least to stop it from spreading farther, but as it was several miles, Addison thought we had better not go so far by night.

I took my turn as watchman, and Addison lay down for a nap. Bronson and Willis presently fell asleep again. Fog was beginning to rise, as it did nearly every night, and after a while I crept into the shed and sat at the foot of the bunk; warm as the day had been, the air was now damp and chilly.

An hour or more passed; I was very sleepy, but suddenly I became wide awake, for I was quite sure that I heard footsteps behind the shed. After listening a moment I crept out on hands and knees and peered round the rear corner of the shack. Nothing stirred for some time, but then I made out the dark outline of a man moving slowly up toward the shed. A stone grated under his foot. I had little doubt that it was someone spying round in hope of finding the crow's nest. My first impulse was to fire the carbine, but then I had a whimsical notion.

"Your fire barrel has gone to Quebec," I said in low, distinct tones. "It is not here. You had better clear out, and pretty quick!"

The fellow had left on the run before I finished speaking. The boys came running out.

"Who are you talking to?" Addison exclaimed.

"To a fellow who came after the old crow's nest," I replied.

"What! You talked with him!" Bronson cried.

"Yes, I told him that his barrel had gone and that it was useless to come here after it," I said.

Addison and Bronson laughed.

"Well, I think that was a good thing to do," Willis declared. "I don't want them to suppose that their blessed old barrel is here."

The early dawn had begun to blanch the fog. We agreed to call it morning, and rekindled our campfire. As the sun rose the mist cleared away.

"Cain ought to have covered the sixty miles to Gaspe by this time," Addison remarked, as we were getting breakfast. "It will take him all day to look out for the raft there, but I think we may look for him back here by four tomorrow afternoon at the latest."

A great column of smoke was rising from the place where we had seen the fire in the night. It appeared to be at least three miles away. After breakfast Bronson got out his fishing tackle, and we went up the creek. Addison took the carbine and I the shotgun, to be prepared for defense if we should meet the wreckers.

Half a mile inland we came to a place where the creek fell over lime-stone ledges, and found the pool below so full of salmon that their backs were out of the water. The pool was literally packed with them. The creek was falling, and they could not get up the ledges. No need to cast a hook there. Willis cut a forked pole and pitched out all we needed. We could have thrown them out by the cartload!

Farther up the creek there were speckled trout so plentiful and so hungry that it was really no sport to catch them. Still farther inland the creek meanders through half-open lowlands of scattered gray tamarack, fir, and swamp bush, and there at last we came upon "baked apples" in abundance. This fruit grows on low bushes that creep along the ground like running raspberries. It is juicy, with a slight flavor of strawberry and blackberry combined. Many of the berries we gathered were as large as the end of your thumb, pinkish on one side and of a pale apple green on the other. We found them very palatable when eaten with the dry pilot biscuit, and later that day we learned that they make a fine salad with lobster, salmon, or trout.

About noon we returned to camp well laden with the spoils of the island. We had seen nothing of the wreckers, but while we were prepar-ing a feast of salmon a flat stone, with something white attached to it, fell close beside the table. Willis grabbed the shotgun and ran round behind the shed to see whether anyone was in sight, but the stone must have been flung from the edge of the fir thickets twenty or thirty yards away, for he found no one. Meanwhile Addison had picked up the missile.

"A *billet-douz*," he said, laughing, as he pulled off the string and unfolded a piece of crumpled paper. "And such a *billet-douz!*" he mut-tered angrily, after a short glance at it.

On the paper were scrawled the words: "You leve here. You clere out. You are goin' to git hurt ef you don't."

Underneath them someone else had written:
"*Allez vous en! Debarrassez nous de vous!*"

"Notice to quit," Bronson commented. "In two languages! What do you think of that? Looks as if they didn't like our company."

"We had mistrusted as much before," said Willis. "But they seem bashful about delivering their notice."

Addison walked to the edge of the firs. "What is it you want of us?" he shouted. "Come out in sight! Let's see you. We have not come here to disturb you!"

But there was no response.

"Well, they have served papers on us," he said, laughing. "Evidently want to scare us off."

After we had finished eating we hid our food supplies under a heap of seaweed in a cleft in the shore ledges a little distance from the shed. Then we set off along the beach to see what had burned in the night; for smoke was still rising in the east.

As Addison had suspected, it proved to be the long rick of cedar shingles from the wreck of a schooner. It had wholly burned, and the fire had run from the shingles to other lumber for five or six hundred yards along the beach.

We stayed there for a little while and then started back to camp. We had not gone far when Willis, happening to glance back, saw another column of smoke rising from the beach several miles back. That confirmed what we had begun to fear—that our enemies were purposely burning the lumber to annoy us or to drive us away. We were not a little discouraged. To have so much good lumber destroyed was calamitous.

The calm weather held. I never saw a lovelier sunset than the one that came while we were on our way back to the shed. An odd thing about it was that just before touching the horizon the sun assumed first an octagonal shape and a moment or two later appeared perfectly square; we could not account for the phenomenon.

No one had disturbed our cache of provisions, and we prepared a good meal of broiled trout and lobsters. When the night fog began to rise we turned in—all except Addison, who said that he would watch till two o'clock again. But he waked us suddenly a little after midnight.

"Get up quick!" he said. "Those scamps have set our lumber afire!"

We jumped up. Through the darkness we saw a red glow, just about at the spot where we had so laboriously brought together the piles of shingles, clapboards, and deals. Although the place was a quarter of a mile away, we could hear a crackling. Catching up two buckets, Addison gave me one of them. He ordered Willis to take the carbine and go ahead of us, and told Bronson to stay behind and guard the shed.

With Willis ahead, we ran along the beach. Right in the midst of the long tiers of shingles a blaze was shooting up ten feet high. Willis and I began to throw water on the flames. We had to fill our buckets more than twenty times before we had put out the fire. While we worked, menacing shouts were hurled at us from the woods, and before Addison could dissuade him, Willis let go a shot that echoed loudly across the dark forest.

"I guess I wouldn't try to hit anyone, Willis," Addison said.

"Confound them!" Willis replied angrily. "Trying to burn up this lumber we have worked so hard to collect! I'd like to riddle them!"

The shouts and hooting continued. There seemed to be several voices, but we could not make out what they said.

"It was a mistake speaking to them!" Willis exclaimed. "It has made them bolder. They think now that we won't do anything except talk."

"I'm afraid you're right," Addison said. "But I was in hopes we could pacify them somehow and stop the row."

When we came back to the shed we found Bronson standing on guard, shotgun in hand.

"Some of them are out back here in the woods," he said. "I guess they thought we had all gone to the fire, and came round here to smash things. When I yelled 'Clear out!' they fled."

While we stood in front of the shed another fire started up a mile or so down the beach, and soon afterwards we saw a third fire, burning furiously, still farther away. We were almost frantic with anger and disappointment. The worst of it was that we could think of no way by which to prevent the rogues from sneaking up and firing lumber in the night. Fifty thousand dollars' worth of lumber was lying along the shore, and we were helpless to save it!

When day dawned, Addison and Bronson went cautiously back into the woods. Addison still hoped that he could get speech with the prowlers; he thought that if he could find out what their grievance was he might be able to appease them and stop their mischief.

While Addison and Bronson were gone, Willis and I got breakfast. The others returned presently, with no important news. They had seen at a distance an oddly dressed fellow, but he ran away from them. When they shouted at him he turned and shook his fist at them. He carried what appeared to be a long gun.

While we were at breakfast Willis proposed that, in order to save the lumber that we had already collected for rafting, we move our camp out to the pile of shingles and clapboards and mount guard over it.

That we did during the forenoon, and in the afternoon we dragged more timber and deals together for another raft. The fire had done little damage there. There were 370 bunches of shingles, 4,000 bunches of clapboards. and a long pile of boards and planks.

"We can at least save that much from the firebugs," Addison said.

Through the night we took turns watching, but no one disturbed us. That day, as we worked on the proposed raft, we kept an eye out for the tug, as we had the day before, but again night drew on with no signs of it.

"What if Cain took a notion not to return at all?" Bronson said. "What would we do? Would we ever be able to get away from here?"

But Addison declared that we had no need to worry about that. "Something has detained him," he said. "But Cain will come back, of course, or send someone."

Above the cries of the gulls that evening we heard the distant hollow cries of several loons from some pond or lake back in the interior of the island.

"That," Willis remarked, "means change of weather with wind— when loons holler."

Part 4

OUR CAMP by the lumber pile was on the side next to the beach. It was merely a rough "tilt" to keep off fog or rain, with the shingle pile at our backs. During the evening dark clouds had risen in the northeast; now and then distant flashes of lightning glowed faintly against them. We turned in early—all except Willis, who was to watch until two o'clock. He sat at the foot of the bunk, brushing away an occasional mosquito and listening sleepily to the lap of the waves on the beach.

Suddenly—as suddenly as a thunderclap—several guns were discharged directly behind the lumber pile. Willis sprang up, with his carbine ready for use. Before the rest of us were fairly awake a shower of stones fell on the roof of boards over our heads; they made such a tremendous racket that we thought the roof was about to fall on us. We leaped out into the open, but the stones were falling so thick and fast that we hastily took refuge under the roof again. The whole gang of wreckers apparently was showering us from the thickets behind the lumber. In the midst of the bombardment several more gunshots rang out.

"Keep cool," Addison kept saying. "They're doing this to scare us. Don't get excited."

"Let's jump out and give them some shots!" Willis cried. "Let's scatter 'em!"

"Wouldn't do it, Willis," Addison replied.

"But who wants to lie here and be stoned? Let's give 'em Hail Columby!"

"No, lie low and let them work," Addison said. "Of course if they come round in front with their guns, or if they get on the lumber pile and try to pull off the roof, we'll defend ourselves. Till they do, let them go to it!"

But for some time he could barely keep Willis and Bronson from shooting back.

Presently there came a lull, but it was followed suddenly by more stones, two or three gunshots, and an outburst of yells. The racket sounded close behind the lumber pile.

"They're going to rush us!" Bronson muttered excitedly.

We all thought so for a few moments; we crouched there, listening and keeping our eyes on the beach both ways. We could see little, however, for the sky was now very dark with clouds. A few scattered drops of rain had begun to fall, and presently a smart shower was in progress. That seemed to dampen the ardor of our assailants. They threw a few more stones, hooted a while, and then took themselves off.

I have little doubt that the whole noisy performance was intended to frighten us, and that Addison had been right to keep us from firing. The wreckers knew that we had guns; our reluctance to fire probably impressed them all the more with the danger of coming round in front.

The attitude of the islanders puzzled us a good deal. We should have supposed that the wreckers, knowing that we had informed against them and that we had sent their fire barrel to the authorities, would seek vengeance against us. Yet from the first their acts seemed plainly to suggest that they were merely trying to frighten us off the island rather than trying maliciously to do us harm. Addison even suggested that perhaps we had been wrong in believing them to be wreckers. Yet there was the evidence of the false beacon against them.

We were altogether too excited to get any more sleep that night. At last morning dawned, cloudy and wet, with the wind in the east and a heavy surf rising. It was so cold that we built a windbreak of shingle bunches on the beach side of the shed. If Cain should arrive during the gale, he would not be able to land. The captain had carried off on the tug the larger share of the provisions. We had not much left except pilot bread and cheese, and the thought that the storm might last several days was not very comforting. What with the bad prospect about the lumber and the likelihood of our having more trouble with the islanders, we felt pretty blue and homesick that morning.

The tide was going out, and presently Bronson took the pole and went to get some lobsters, but he found the waves coming in so high that he got only one. While he was walking along the brink of the ledges, where they fell off into deep water, he caught sight, as a wave receded, of a square object down underwater in a chasm of the rocks. He at last made it out to be a large brass-bound chest, overgrown with barnacles and smaller shells.

"I've found some old captain's sea chest," he told us when he returned. "It's five or six feet under water, but who knows what treasures it may contain?"

After we had eaten breakfast, we went down with Bronson to have a look at his find. When the waves rolled back, we could see it plainly. We were eager to see what it contained, and so set to work at once to get it up. With a light stick of timber and a rope, we at last got hold of the chest and hauled it out, although not without trouble, for it was very heavy.

It proved to be almost five feet long, two and a half feet wide, and about two feet high. A very strong lock still held the lid fast, but Willis brought an ax from camp and knocked it open. What was our disappointment to see, instead of the store of golden ducats and priceless jewels that we had all secretly hoped to find, nothing except fragments of rock! The chest was crammed full of them.

"Nothing but ballast, I guess," Bronson said in disgust, as we turned the chunks of rock out on the ledge. "Just a chest of ballast for a yawl."

But Addison had begun to examine the pieces of rock more carefully. He broke one of them with the poll of the ax.

"Something besides ballast," he said, at last. "See those little yellow particles scattered through it. Boys, that's gold. This is a chestful of sample rock from a gold mine."

He broke up some more rock; each piece had a distinct yellow tint. "I shouldn't be surprised if those samples would assay a thousand dollars to the ton," he said. "It's rich. Wish I knew where they came from!"

"Not likely from here on Anticosti," Bronson remarked.

"Oh, no, that chest was probably onboard a vessel that was wrecked here," Addison said. "These specimens are most likely from the far west. Someone was taking them abroad, to England perhaps, with a view to selling a mine."

"Do you imagine the mine has ever been found and worked since?" Willis asked.

But that, of course, was a matter of mere conjecture. In Addison's opinion the samples had some money value, and so we put the specimens back into the chest and dragged it to the shed, where we hid it. We agreed that we had better not tell Cain or the crew about the chest when they returned; when we were ready to leave the island we could smuggle it aboard the tug.

The day passed without further incident. It rained fitfully at times, and by noon a heavy storm set in. Toward night we went up the creek to the first pool for more salmon; Addison and Willis scouted ahead with the guns, while Bronson and I threw out fish enough for several days.

The storm now had increased to a gale with driving gusts of rain. We piled more bunches of shingles on the beach side of the shed and, by battening the roof with more boards, made ourselves comfortable. Nothing disturbed our sleep that night, and we were thankful enough, for all of us were dead tired.

Another dull day of storm followed. Our only diversion during the forenoon was a passing steamer, which pitched very noticeably over the big billows. In the afternoon a pair of black finback whales appeared off the reefs; at intervals they dived and came up to blow noisily. Addison thought that they were feeding on the giant squid that are plentiful just off the outer line of reefs.

We had seen nothing of the islanders since they had made their night attack; they apparently thought they had frightened us enough for their purpose. There was no sign of the tug, and I began to take some stock in Bronson's gloomy prediction that Captain Cain had no intention of returning.

During the night the rain and wind abated, but a thick fog came in the next morning. At last, about three o'clock in the afternoon, we heard the tug whistling offshore; Addison fired a gun in response.

The fog hung so low that the captain did not dare to come in until nearly seven o'clock, although we fired numerous shots and at last hailed him from both sides of the creek mouth, in order to give him his bearings. Finally he crept in, and laid the tug up at its former berth inside the bar.

When the captain and the crew came ashore, we were almost sorry they had returned. All were in an ugly, surly humor, and I fully expected that we should have trouble with them. When Addison inquired why, he had stayed away so long, Cain asked with an oath whether we expected him to come back to such a coast in a gale.

"You should have been back two days before the storm," Addison retorted.

"Did I make any promises when I'd come back?" the captain cried hotly.

"No, you didn't," Addison said, keeping pretty calm. "But just remember that you are under contact, and that if you want your money you'll have to live up to that contract."

Cain seemed a little abashed, and muttered something about having had to wait for two of his crew, who had got drunk in Gaspe, to sober up. As a matter of fact, the captain's face showed that he had been drinking excessively himself, and he reported so indefinitely as to what he had done with the raft of lumber at Gaspe that we were afraid that it might prove a loss.

The only definite thing we could get out of him about his trip was that he had reported the matter of the false beacon to the Canadian authorities at Quebec. In token of it, he presented us a bill of three dollars, which he said he had paid at the telegraph office. He had also sent the old crow's nest to Quebec by steamer.

"Our best way will be to get all the lumber we have left here into another raft and go down there with it on the tug," Addison said to Willis and me.

While at Gaspe the tug's crew had allowed the provisions onboard to get wet; most of them were spoiled, and now the men were complaining about their food. Fortunately, we had some lobsters and salmon in camp, and we managed to feed them. Afterwards we watched, by turn, while they slept off the effects of alcohol; we knew that we should have to keep an eye on them from now on.

They were still in an ugly mood the next morning; when Addison asked them to work with us at rafting the lumber, the captain shouted, "I didn't come here to work like a dog!"

Addison flared up. "Captain," he cried, "you'll have to work a whole lot harder for us than you have in the past if you want to get paid! You've already wasted five days of our time in a drunken debauch. You need not deny it, for it's written right there in your face."

At that Cain flew into a passion and, with the sailors bunched behind him, moved threateningly toward us. We thought we were in for a lively fight, and quickly closed up together. Either because he saw that we were standing our ground or because he managed to control his anger, Cain stopped, and mumbled a sort of apology for his show of temper.

"We've put up with your grumbling about long enough," Addison said, looking him squarely in the eye. "Now, bring your men down to the beach and lend us a hand."

Addison's firm stand had evidently cowed the captain somewhat, for he led his men down to the beach and set to work. He dropped a remark, however, that worried us not a little.

"There's one thing about it," he said surlily, after we had been at work for an hour, "you won't do much more here!"

"What do you mean by that?" Addison asked.

Cain would not reply. The only explanation we could think of was that he heard something about our project at Gaspe. We thought of the bench marks that we had seen on some of the lumber, and wondered whether they could have any connection with his remark.

There was lumber for a very much larger raft than we had made before, and as we could lay the timber and deals for the bed of it only at ebb tide, we lost considerable time in placing it. Afterwards we had to pin and lash it. We did not complete the making of the raft until noon of the following day. The next thing that we had to do was to load the shingles and clapboards.

We hoped to get the raft offshore at flood tide that night, and Willis, Addison, and I exerted ourselves to the utmost. Bronson, too, worked like a beaver. If Cain and his men had worked as well, we should have bidden Anticosti good-bye that night, for the weather was fine and the sea smooth, but before we had finished loading the last of the shingles the ebb had begun.

The water on the bar at the mouth of the creek shoaled so much that the captain could not bring the tug out. The tide would not be at full before eight o'clock the next morning.

Part 5

AS WE WERE SITTING by the fire after supper that evening, planning the details of floating the raft the next morning, we heard the whistle of a steamer. No craft was in sight but the vessel was evidently coming along the coast from the west, and judging from the sound of the whistle, it was nearer inshore than steamships usually travel when passing Anticosti. Soon we heard the whistle again—this time three toots, as if the ship had been signaling, or trying to attract attention from shore.

"I believe that fellow wants to make a landing," Bronson said.

A few minutes later the vessel came in sight round a point a mile to the west of us. It was a small steamer like those that ply between Quebec and Isle Orleans, or Ste. Anne de Beaupre. Seeing our campfire, they whistled again, whereupon Bronson fired a shot in response. Apparently they wished to communicate with us, for the craft slowed down and immediately a boat with six or seven persons in it made for the mouth of the creek. Addison and I went along the beach to see what they wanted, and the others followed. It was still almost as light as day.

A young man of good appearance in a smart blue suit sprang ashore, followed by three older men who wore a sort of uniform. Addison bade them good evening.

The young man returned the greeting civilly, but followed it with a somewhat abrupt question.

"May I inquire what your business is here?" he said.

"Certainly you may," Addison replied pleasantly. "But first tell me why you wish to know that and whom I have the pleasure of addressing?"

The newcomer looked us over for a moment.

"My name is Bramhall," he said, "Eccles Bramhall. I am agent for the Anticosti Company, which has recently bought the island of Anticosti with the purpose of developing its resources. Our grant entitles us to everything here."

"But we have a permit from the provincial government to salvage lumber," Addison rejoined, and told Bramhall whom we represented. He also gave him our names.

"So?" said he. "Do you chance to have this permit with you?"

"Surely," Addison replied and produced the lieutenant governor's letter from his pocketbook.

Bramhall read it and looked at the signature. "This is merely a letter," he said. "Our title is under seal and sign of the dominion government."

"But Anticosti is in the province of Quebec."

"Yes, but the province executed a waiver of its rights in our favor. We paid a large sum—a million dollars—for the island. Our title was validated both by the province and by the general government at Ottawa."

"But when?" Addison asked.

"Two months since."

"Our permit dates back to the session of the provincial parliament of last winter," Addison declared. "That gives us rights ahead of yours."

"I don't think that it does. Our title covers everything from date of issue. Your permit is merely by letter and not in legal form."

"You don't doubt that it's genuine!" Addison exclaimed.

"Certainly not," Bramhall answered. "I think you've been acting in good faith, but I imagine that the letter you have was written without much consideration of the matter, and afterwards forgotten."

"But that wouldn't make it invalid!"

"You'll have to settle that with the provincial government. You can bring suit and see."

"But meanwhile what of the hard work we have done here?" Addison said. "What of the money we have spent? What of this raft of lumber that ought to be got offshore at once?"

"I shall have to forbid you to take anything away from this island!" Bramhall exclaimed.

"But we have already towed a raft to Gaspe," said Addison. "What of that?"

"I claim it as the property of the Anticosti Company. I was here a month ago and put our marks on the lumber."

A strained silence followed.

"Do you think this fair or just to us?" Addison asked at last.

"I admit I think it's pretty hard on you," Bramhall answered. "I do, indeed. But no other course is open to me. You can see that, acting for my company, I can't permit property to be taken away from the island."

There this rather painful interview—painful for us—ended, except for some questions about the supposed wreckers that the men with Bramhall asked us. They were a deputy sheriff and two constables from Quebec, and none of them seemed very desirous to search the dark woods that ran back from the beach. They were proceeding, they told us, to an inlet twenty or thirty miles farther along the coast, where the Jupiter River—the largest river of the island—enters the gulf. After a few minutes Bramhall and the men put off in the boat, and presently the steamer went on its way eastward.

"Well, this seems to be the end of our enterprise up here," Addison said gloomily, as we went back to the sled. "Too bad! There's six hundred dollars to pay for the tug. Wonder what the Old Squire will think?"

We did not sleep much that night, at least Addison and I did not. Willis and Bronson, too, felt nearly as bad as we did. Cain, however, did not show any signs of sympathy.

After breakfast the next morning he asked us what we were going to do. "The tide is in," he said. "Are you going to haul that raft offshore?"

"Would you advise that?" Bronson asked, to see what he would say.

"Sartin," Cain replied. "That's what they think you'll do. That's what they've gone off and left ye for—to give ye a chance to get away with it. Can't ye take a hint? You can turn that lumber into money down at Gaspe. They won't foller ye, but you was a loony to tell them about that other raft and where you took it to."

"Thanks for your advice, captain," Addison said. "We don't do business that way."

"Wal, all I care for is my own pay out of it," Cain retorted.

"You didn't need to tell us that," Bronson declared, and we all joined in a laugh that sent Cain stamping sulkily down the beach.

We were in a quandary what we should do.

"No use to go to Gaspe if those fellows claim the raft that's down there," Willis said. "And no use to stay here."

"Looks that way," Addison admitted, "but I do hate to quit and leave everything we have done."

We loafed nearly all that day, trying to reach a decision. Toward evening we again sighted Bramhall's steamer; it was returning along the coast, from Jupiter Inlet. They saw us, or the smoke from our fire, and saluted us with the whistle, but we were in no mood to fire a shot in response. They stopped off the mouth of the creek, and Bramhall and the deputy sheriff, whose name was McKittrick, with two rowers, put ashore again.

"So you are still here!" Bramhall cried, coming along the beach to our camp.

"Why, yes," Addison replied. "You've put us in such a hole that we hardly know what to do."

The agent laughed. "I think, myself, it's hard on you," he said, not without a certain kindliness. "But I'm absolutely helpless in the matter." He glanced at his companion. "McKittrick, here, thought we shouldn't find you. He made a wager with me that you would haul off your raft and go."

"We aren't sneak thieves," Addison replied. "We came here to do an honest business."

There was silence for a moment, and then Addison said, "What about this raft? It will soon break up and like as not go out to sea. You had better tow it down to Gaspe yourself, rather than have it a loss."

"We aren't fixed for towing a heavy raft like that," Bramhall replied. "We haven't tow lines, or power enough."

He and McKittrick went to the raft, climbed on it, and looked it over. After a while they came back to where we stood.

"Look here," Bramhall said. "I may be blamed for it, but I'm going to stretch a point and tell you to tow this raft down to Gaspe. We'll go along with you."

"You can hardly expect us to burn coal to transport lumber down there for nothing," Addison said. "We have lost too much already."

"But hear me out," Bramhall said. "When we get to Gaspe, I'll telegraph my company, state all the facts, tell them what you have done and ask to have some arrangement made that will be fair to you. I cannot guarantee anything—I haven't authority, but I think that they'll make a fair settlement."

We were afraid that this did not promise much for us, but, on the other hand, if we refused the offer, we should get nothing whatever. I thought that we had better do it, and Addison did, too; so after some further talk we reached an agreement with Bramhall.

That evening they brought their little steamer over the bar into the creek, and passed the night with us. Bramhall was a good fellow—genial and companionable; it was clear that he wanted to do what he could for us. Indeed, when Addison told him about the chest of sample rock, Bramhall raised no objection to our taking it off with us. Of course the amount of gold in the rock could not be great—perhaps not more than a hundred dollars' worth.

McKittrick inquired more about the wreckers, and went up to the place where we had found the fire barrel. For several days the bellicose islanders had not bothered us.

The tide was at flood about nine o'clock the next morning, and as soon as the raft floated clear we started. We had been at Anticosti sixteen days—days so full of stirring incidents that they seemed as many weeks. The tug slowly hauled the heavy raft out to sea, and the low black shore receded. Bramhall and the deputy followed us in their little steamer.

By four o'clock that afternoon we were well across the South Channel, between Anticosti and the New Brunswick coast, and slowly doubled Cape Rosier into Gaspe Bay. Nine o'clock that evening saw the raft in Gaspe Basin, the town harbor.

The little seaport of Gaspe is beautifully situated between two rivers near the head of the bay. The business of the place was then largely in the hands of a wealthy firm of good repute, known as Le Boutilliers. There was a homely little inn, called the Gulf House, where we all stayed for two days while Bramhall communicated with his company, the new owners of Anticosti.

Meanwhile, we telegraphed an account of what had occurred to McCall, who was still on his back with a broken leg at Three Rivers. His disability, however, did not prevent him from making brisk representations by wire to Quebec, in behalf of our interests. Vigorous claims and counterclaims were put forward, to the embarrassment of the government. It was, in truth, a very pretty tangle of claims.

The net result of all the negotiations was that the two rafts that we had taken to Gaspe were put into the hands of Le Boutilliers to dispose of; that firm eventually made a return of $2,960. Of that the new Anti-

costi Company executed a quitclaim for the sum of $1,000, leaving us, on the whole, a pretty fair settlement.

The third day after our arrival at Gaspe with the raft, we bade Bramhall good-bye and left for Rimouski on the tug. At Rimouski we settled with Cain in full, paying him $610, which McCall sent us there by mail for that purpose. We were glad to be quit of the fellow, although I will say that when we paid him he seemed a little ashamed of the way he had treated us. From Rimouski we went home by rail.

The entire expenses of the trip, including Willis's wages came to nearly $80. Thus, with the $80 that we got for the sample rock in the chest that we had found, we cleared about $250. It was not a big haul—vastly less than we had hoped for—yet it was enough to make us feel that our hard work had not been wasted.

"Well, boys, that is better than nothing," was the Old Squire's cheery comment. "It shows what you might have done if things had worked well. It was a twenty-thousand-dollar prospect."

We never found out definitely whether the islanders who had attacked us were really wreckers. Addison and I were inclined to believe that they were not, and that they had used the mysterious beacon, not to lure vessels onto the rocks, but to guide their own fishing vessels to a safe harbor. Their hostility to us could easily be explained by their fear that we had come to molest them, as our seizing the crow's nest could have very easily led them to suppose.

The Anticosti Company, which had put an end to our enterprise, was not successful in developing the resources of the island, and in 1895 Anticosti passed into the possession of Henri Menier, a French millionaire. In his efforts to colonize the island he came into conflict with a colony of rough, ignorant settlers, who, declaring that they had lived there for four generations, resisted his authority. He took the case to court, and in the subsequent proceedings the settlers were charged with being, not peaceful fishermen, but wreckers, who, by means of false beacons, had lured many vessels onto the rocks of Anticosti. Although the charges were not sustained, the settlers were expelled from the island.

Whether they were the same people, or descendants of them, who had made things hot for us during our stay on Anticosti, and whether they had really used the old crow's nest for any sinister purposes, we shall never know.

26

Wintering in a Dugout

THE CLIMATE OF MAINE IS GENERALLY CONSIDERED healthy. Nonetheless, has the population been decimated by "fevers" which at times assumed epidemic proportions.

There was the "Illinois fever" which depleted whole neighborhoods, the "Wisconsin fever" which came later, the "California fever," also called the "gold fever," which alone carried off twelve thousand young and middle-aged, and this was presently followed by the "Oregon fever" which swept away family after family and depopulated several entire school districts, with not a parent or pupil left to tell the tale.

During the late great war in Europe, when a soldier was killed or died of disease, his comrades said of him plaintively that he had "gone west." This was what happened to those who left us on account of the "fevers" alluded to: they went west.

In fact, it is measurably due to these feverish migrations that the population of the Pine Tree State has increased so slowly—our folks "went west." A large part, perhaps the best, most enterprising of our Maine people have migrated to Iowa, to Kansas, to Nebraska, to Illinois, to Wisconsin, to Ohio, and later to California, Oregon, and Washington State. Whoever travels there will find Maine people everywhere and will generally find them doing well. Therefore that very entertaining and usually very accurate author, Mr. Rudyard Kipling, was wrong when he expatiated on the decadence of the English race in New England. It has neither decayed nor died out.

It has gone west and is there now, contributing to make the west prosperous.

Indeed, "Dakota fever" took its toll on those of us at the Old Squire's farm. Theodora left to run a mission school, and Ellen and her husband soon followed to become wheat farmers. But perhaps our strangest loss was that of "Aunt" Olive Witham, a spinster lady who often helped Gram with her domestic work.

She was sixty-three years old, tall, austere, not wholly attractive, but of upright character and undaunted courage. Much of her life had been spent attending to her brother, the Elder Witham, who had been invalided during the last years of his life. And after his death she received $350 from his small estate.

Looking about her, with this small sum in her pocket, for a better opportunity in life, she thought of Ellen's letters about "homesteading" in the Dakota territories and began to contemplate an exploit of this sort. She had good health and strength, liked out-of-door life, and was not afraid of domestic animals under ordinary circumstances.

One day she broached the subject to her friend Helen Verrill, an unusually attractive young woman in her early twenties who had for several years been boarding with Aunt Olive while supporting herself by teaching country school. She too knew what it is to pinch and to plan with painful closeness since her annual income from this source was only about sixty dollars—twenty weeks of school, at three dollars a week. She contrived to live and dress quite neatly on this income, but seized upon the opportunity for economic expections as well as romance.

They planned it all out in advance, of course. They expected to work hard and endure privations for three or four years, but in the end, when their fine wheat farm was equipped, they fancied that they should reside on it only from April to October, and during the winters they should live in some large city.

They talked it over until they had convinced themselves that they could do it, and then they gathered together their small means and started for Dakota after selling Olive's house, a pretty good one, for another three hundred dollars. They began their journey on the last day of April 1877.

They settled a short distance from what is now the line between the two new states of North and South Dakota.

They spent a week making inquiries as to land, probable town sites, future railroads, highways, and so forth, and at last selected a surveyed quarter-section of land, along one side of which there once had been a little belt of timber. This wood had all been cut off by settlers at a distance, except eight shaggy oaks and two cottonwoods.

These ten trees were really what attracted them to the claim. It was farther from other settlers than they liked to be, but the land agent assured them that they should have plenty of neighbors before the close of the season. The trees, he remarked, would furnish logs for a house, and fuel for one winter, at least.

But Olive and Helen had other uses for the trees. They had resolved to preserve them all for shade.

They were assured that either a log cabin or a dugout was the proper sort of dwelling to start with, but they disliked the idea of a sod house, and at a cost of fifty dollars had a thousand feet of rough lumber delivered to them. Carpenters were scarce, but they succeeded in hiring one for a single day for seven dollars. His name was Andrew Phillister; he was a young man, and had recently preempted a claim two miles from theirs.

In one day Mr. Phillister built them a house, ten feet by twelve, put in two windows consisting of a pane of glass each, hung the door, cut a hole for the stovepipe, and put up a shelf-dresser, and with some two hundred feet of lumber which were left he constructed a cow shed and a chicken pen, and then with his ax trimmed up their grove, and built a cow yard of the brush. They had never seen a man work so rapidly. He had everything complete by five o'clock, and had found time all day to chat with Helen more than Olive approved of.

They bought a cow and twenty hens, and begged a cat, and, rather too late, they hired a man and team to break two acres of land for them, the most of which they planted to corn with their own hands, but the greater part of this corn was soaked out by a heavy rain early in June.

A garden plot a hundred feet square near their house, which they had spaded up earlier, did better. Olive had brought good seed from home, and they worked very hard in that garden. Nature smiled kindly on their efforts; it is quite astonishing what a crop they raised from it.

The sun browned their skins, and Helen complained of the hard work at times, but on the whole they were very happy all summer long. They had four hens, setting on about a dozen eggs each at one time, and later their yard swarmed with chickens; nor did they lose one chick from hawks, foxes, or coyotes.

During the whole summer they were not troubled by wild beasts, or by ill-disposed human beings. In fact, nobody came near them. Two or three times Olive or Helen walked to their Scandinavian neighbors, three miles away, and asked the husband—who spoke very little English—to bring them what they needed when he went to the "store," ten miles distant. Having produced their eggs, milk, butter, and garden crop, their food cost them surprisingly little. They had more milk than they could use, and had to throw some of it away.

The weather was delightful. They were well all the time, and Olive says she can but laugh now when she thinks how much they played— actually played! And at her age, too! But throughout her whole life she had never played half enough, and had had a great deal to make up for.

They sent for scythe, rake, and hay fork, and put up a stack of hay for winter. Their first efforts with the scythe were, Olive said, extremely funny.

Three thunder squalls, accompanied once by hail, and always by vivid lightning and wind, were about the only exciting incidents of the summer.

As I said above, they had never before been so happy, but thus far they had seen only the sunny side of pioneering.

September and October were busy times with them. They were preparing for a crop the following year. Olive had still a little money left, and they realized a little more from the sale of chickens and eggs. Six acres were prepared for wheat, although the man who plowed for them charged five dollars a day for himself and team.

They had raised enough garden vegetables, potatoes, and corn, for winter. To store their vegetables safe from frost, they dug laboriously a hole five feet square beneath their house floor. It was much like a squirrel's store. They spent a great many hours gathering dry stuff for fuel from the scattered brush and timber at a distance from their cabin. Where trees had been cut the year before they gathered bushels of dry chips, till they made a considerable woodpile beside their door.

With sods and earth they banked up the cow shed to the eaves, and they also built a chicken house adjoining it fifteen feet by ten, with walls of soil and a thatched roof of dry grass and poles.

Their house they also banked up to a height of three feet outside, carefully caulking all the cracks, and papering the inside with the newspapers which they received occasionally from home friends. A water supply was the requisite most difficult to manage. Thus far they had brought water from a slough two hundred yards or more away, and they did not feel able as yet to dig a well.

In October came what was the first touch of adversity and unhappiness. No one had called on them during the summer, but one day in October, as they were fetching chips in a blanket, they saw a man approaching across the prairie. Even before he had come within a quarter of a mile Helen exclaimed, "It's that Andrew Phillister!"

"What can he want?" Olive said. "We paid him his seven dollars." Helen laughed, although there did not appear to be anything especially ludicrous in his coming to call on them.

He bade them good morning very cordially, and looked about approvingly on their preparations for winter. He seemed somewhat embarrassed.

He told them that, after working at his trade for other settlers till September—during which time he had built thirteen houses, and an even greater number of barns—he had returned to his claim, and erected a house for himself.

His claim was just out of their view, over a swell of the prairie, and he seemed quite solicitous that they should come to see his new home. He offered several times to do any job of carpenter work that they might need that fall free of charge. In short, he made himself very agreeable, and remained with them two hours.

"Helen," Olive said, when at length Andrew had taken leave, "that fellow is coming here after you! He wants you for his new home. And you will desert me and go there!"

Two evenings afterward, Andrew called again and remained three hours. And to make what was not a very long story shorter still, five weeks later, Helen told Olive that Andrew had asked her to marry him—and—would she ever forgive her, and so forth, and so forth.

Olive, being a good Christian woman, uttered no reproaches, having already settled it in her mind, after a long struggle with herself. She foresaw, however, that thenceforward her life would be a solitary one.

Those were bitter days for Olive, but she summoned courage to go on alone. The sorrow she felt at Helen's desertion of her was even keener because she had come to love her like a sister.

With the first snow in November came Andrew with a horse and sleigh, and carried them both to the nearest town, thirteen miles distant, where the marriage ceremony was performed by a magistrate.

Next day they all returned to the couple's new home—a very comfortable little house, with a pretty set of furniture, and even a small cabinet organ—and Olive visited with them for an hour or two. They had very kindly planned to have her pass the cold season with them, but she declined—a little grimly, Andrew feared—and returning to her cold cabin, her cat, her cow, and her poultry, she settled herself to pass the long winter.

There was a period of good sleighing in December, and every day while it lasted Helen and Andrew rode over to call on Olive. They were so happy that she knew she ought to be glad for them.

The day after Christmas there came what was, for Dakota, a prodigious snowfall. There were several inches of it, and the prairie was covered with white drifts. The wind blew fiercely. Olive had difficulty in reaching the door of her cow shed, and for two weeks she was forced to melt snow for water. Blizzard weather was upon them, and she felt glad that Andrew did not attempt to come over to her cabin.

The fourth night after the storm, the wind blew a fearful gale. The gusts waked her, a little after midnight. The snow was sifting sharply against her little windowpanes.

Suddenly she heard a wild, loud, cracking noise, followed, an instant later, by a frightful crash upon her cabin. The roof broke down, letting in an avalanche of snow.

Fragments of split boards and brush fell upon her bed. She was slightly bruised, and held partly down by the weight of what had fallen.

One of the cottonwoods, dried up by the removal of the timber around it, had blown down, and the top of it had crushed her cabin.

She was greatly terrified. Extricating herself, she tried to dress, but it was so cold that she feared she should be frozen, and crept back beneath her blankets. She covered up her head and ears, and lay still and let the snow which fell in almost bury her. In the morning, having dressed literally in a snowdrift, she found her ax and began the cold task of clearing away the top of the tree, along with the wreck of her house.

The cabin was wholly shattered, and she now perceived how narrow her escape had been from being crushed to death. For the first time she felt thankful that Helen was in better quarters. She knew that Helen was not robust enough to endure what followed.

Olive's stovepipe and stove had been knocked down, and lay amidst the shattered boards. She had no means of making a fire, or preparing warm food. She saw that her cabin would have to be entirely rebuilt. She stood knee deep in snow and wept.

When her feet grew so numb that she knew they must be freezing, she went into her cow shed and warmed them on Spot, the cow. Ah, how comfortable the good creature seemed to her! Then she sallied forth, and with ax and shovel fell to work.

All that day she worked desperately. Not only did she clear away the wreck of the cabin and treetop, but she took up the floor, and with a shovel, enlarged her cellar from a hole five feet square to the full size of the cabin. In short, she transformed her cabin to a "dugout," and carrying up a wall of earth and turf to a height of three feet above ground, roofed it over, laid a floor, and lined the earthen sides with the cabin boards.

This may seem like a very large achievement, but to work hard was the only means by which she could keep from freezing, away from the cow. The cow, too, supplied her with milk.

She dug an incline, and set up the doorframe and door, but did not trouble about windows that day. Then she got her stove together and the pipe out through the roof and kindled a fire.

She said she did not think that the temperature had been higher than ten degrees below zero that day. And if any poor woman ever did a harder day's work, I pity her.

All her vegetables and potatoes chilled in spite of the bedclothes which she spread over them. Nearly all her dishes were smashed, and poor kitty had been crushed to death beneath a joist.

She put on a teakettle full of snow to melt, and made a basin of hot porridge for herself. Then she shook the snow out of her bedclothing, made up her bed, and sitting up in it began to drink her porridge. She passed the night miserably. Rising and dressing, she once more kindled a fire in her stove. She then found that the "dugout" held the heat much better than the cabin. In fact, the snow had drifted entirely over it, and the reason why her stove had been so slow in heating, was probably because the pipe was partly choked with snow.

As soon as her cow smelled the smoke of Olive's fire, she began to low plaintively to her for water. Olive could hear Spot's calls faintly through the snow canopy beneath which she sat. She had been unable to give her drink the previous day.

Opening her outside door, Olive filled her kettle with snow, to melt. Then she made coffee, baked potatoes, and prepared herself a good breakfast. She also made warm dough, well peppered, for her poultry, and as soon as it was light, she dug through into the cow shed and chicken house, where she found the fowls very stupid from cold.

The weather continued bitterly cold, and the wind blew almost constantly. It seemed that no living creature could exist abroad on the prairie, but at about ten o'clock on the third night after the accident to her cabin, she heard the wild yelping and howling of timber wolves, close at hand.

After listening awhile, she opened her door a crack and peeped out, and then distinctly heard the famished creatures digging furiously at the frozen sod walls of her cow shed and poultry house.

Fearing that they might break in and throttle her cow, she opened her stove, and first allowing the ends of two sticks of wood to get well afire and blazing, she ran suddenly out and threw them at the wolves.

She then adds that she ran in and fastened her door quite as quickly, for she was afraid of the hungry beasts.

The sight and smell of the fire frightened them away for the time, but they returned twice, and she spent the most of the night listening at the door, and preparing brands to throw at them. It was so dark outside that she did not obtain a good view of the wolves, but she thought that there were four of them.

The snowdrift in front of her dugout was now nearly five feet in depth, and next day she shoveled out a trench, in place of her path, from her door around to the door of the cow shed, down to the ground. She then covered this trench over, first with cottonwood brush, then with cakes of snow to a depth of three feet, thus making a covered way about thirty feet long.

This she did to defend her premises from wolves. It proved a great convenience throughout the remainder of the winter. She could now visit her animals without wallowing in snow, or facing the cold wind. But there were far more dangerous foes than the wolves abroad that winter.

The weather moderated a little at New Year's, and three days after the wolves had attempted to dig into her cow shed, Andrew came to see how she was faring.

He surveyed her premises for some time, so he said afterward, without being able to "make head or tail" of them. He might have supposed that her cabin had blown away if he had not seen the smoke issuing from the top of the stovepipe.

Then he walked upon her roof, and called to her. The creak of his snowshoes overhead was the first intimation which she had of his presence. Then she recognized his voice.

Olive had felt a lingering resentment against him, but the sound of a human voice that she knew fell so sweetly on her ear, that she found herself singing as she dug a hole up out of her covered way to admit him.

He took off his snowshoes, let himself down, and came into her dugout, and then he looked around and laughed heartily, until she grew quite indignant. When she told him of the tree fall and the wolves, he became grave.

"I oughtn't to have let you stay here alone!" he exclaimed. "And now you are going home with me and Helen."

This offer Olive peremptorily declined. He threatened to carry her by main force, but seeing at last that she was wholly in earnest, he dropped the subject, unwillingly.

I suppose she had not fully realized how lonesome she had been; for it seemed indescribably pleasant to her to hear a voice, and see someone sitting in Helen's chair on the other side of the stove. She prepared dinner, and Andrew remained nearly three hours, telling her all about his plans, and what a good time he and Helen were having; how she sang and played, and how they read stories aloud together in the evening. Olive was hungry to hear it all.

When he went away, she put her head up through the hole in her covered passage and watched him out of sight, and then had to go inside and have a good, long cry before she was fit to clear up the table and resume her solitary life.

Another storm was at hand. The gray and dreary night shut down over the lonely wastes of snow. "Well, another fortnight!" she murmured to herself, and proceeded to stop up the breach in the covered way.

A little later she was surprised at hearing Andrew shout to her from outside, and she made haste to open the breach again.

"Is Helen sick?" she exclaimed.

"Oh no," he replied. "I've come back to bring you some novelettes which we have read, and my carbine—if those wolves should come round again, you know."

"Oh dear!" said she. "Firebrands are better for me, I think. I never fired a gun in my life, and I don't believe I should like it. I would not know how to shoot."

"It's as easy as pumping water," said Andrew, confidently. "Just see how I do it. All you have to do is to tuck these cartridges in here—one, two, or seven of them. Then take hold of this lever, so—open it now, then replace it, see? The gun's all loaded. Now I will rest it out through the hole, and shoot at that tree trunk over there. Watch me raise the hammer, so. Take aim—so."

He discharged the piece, and planted the bullet in the tree.

"Now, see how I throw out the empty shell," he continued, "and raise in another cartridge—so. It's loaded again. Now you fire it, at the same tree. Don't be afraid. It doesn't kick. It will not hurt you a bit."

Olive took aim and fired, in some little trepidation. Andrew said that she hit the tree. Her eyes were shut. I do not think that he thought the piece "kicked"; nevertheless, it made a lump on her shoulder, although she did not let him know it.

She cannot say that she really wanted him to leave the gun with her, but he had determined to do so, and after some further explanation of the mechanism of a breechloader, he gave it to her with two dozen cartridges. When he had gone she placed it safely behind her vegetable bin. She had not the slightest intention to touch it again, for he had, he told her, left four cartridges in it.

As much as six inches more of snow came during that night and the next day, and again the wind blew, and the cold was intense.

She kept quite comfortable, however. The snow no longer troubled her, for she was completely snowed under. She took care of her stock, and to pass the time read novelettes. She sincerely wished for better books. The trashy stories were far from satisfactory, and she resolved that week—a resolution still kept—to begin a Chautauqua course of study.

The sixth night after Andrew had called last, Olive heard snowshoes creaking once more, and had no doubt that he had come over to look in upon her again, although it occurred to her that it was late for him to call.

She was on the point of crying out, "I hear you!" when she perceived from the sound that there was more than one person. "Is it possible that Helen has walked over with him?" she thought.

The sounds ceased for a moment, and she heard men's voices speaking in very low tones. Then something—a staff or a gunstock—was thrust down through the snow against the boards of the roof.

A sense of sudden fear possessed her. Then it occurred to her that they were probably a party of hunters in search of shelter. If they were decent persons and in distress, she might feed them and allow them to sleep in her cow shed.

All this passed through her mind in a moment, and again she heard the staff or gunstock thrust down through the snow.

Mustering her courage she called out, "Who's there, and what do you want?"

A moment of silence followed her hail; then again she heard low words, and a voice called down to her, "Say, old gal, is yer husband at home?"

Something in the tone of the speaker's voice gave her a thrill of repulsion. She felt instinctively that the men were ruffians of the worst sort, and a desperate determination to fight to the death rather than let them in, took possession of her.

Almost before she knew what she was doing, she had Andrew's gun in her hands, and was bent on fighting. At the same instant an idea occurred to her; she changed her tone to the deepest bass which she could summon from her throat, and in imitation of a man's voice, croaked out, "Who are you? What's your business here?"

Olive's ruse did not work. A roar of derisive laughter followed her effort, and a voice cried, "Too thin, old lady! We want to come in and get warm. We're travelin' missionaries, we are, an' we've got some tracts for ye! You may as well show us in. Where's yer door, anyway?"

"You can't come in!" she said, in as firm a voice as she could muster. "I warn you to go away!"

They laughed brutally. "We'll see about that!" one exclaimed. They begun to thrust down heavily through the snow again.

She knew that it was useless to utter another word. A feeling of desperation nerved her. She pulled back the hammer of the carbine, and holding the piece out at arm's length, and with the barrel pointing upwards toward the roof, discharged it.

It jumped downward from her hands, and the stock struck the floor. She was nearly deafened.

The cabin was filled with powder smoke. The bullet no doubt passed through the board and the snow, but how closely it passed to their bodies she did not know.

They withdrew hastily from the roof. At a little distance they stopped and relieved their feelings by an outburst of shouting.

Olive pulled open the door into the covered way, worked the lever of the carbine as Andrew had shown her, and then pushing the barrel out through the snow, in the direction from which the shouts came, discharged it again. It recoiled violently, possibly from snow getting in the muzzle, but she worked it, and fired again and again.

She knew then how soldiers feel in battle; it is a savage spirit that seems to rouse like a wild beast in its lair. She ran back and thrust more cartridges into the magazine, filled it full, and then stood at the door and listened. She expected that they would attack her, and she meant to shoot in the direction of any sound she heard.

But she heard nothing further from them. She now noticed that her wrists were covered with blood where, from the recoil of the carbine, the piece of iron around the trigger had scraped the skin from her hands. It was not till toward morning that she became calm enough to retire and fall asleep.

"Aunt" Olive was somewhat amazed at her own performance, and to tell the truth, a little ashamed of it. It did not seem to her that she had made a very brave or womanly defense, and yet, as it turned out, she no doubt did the best thing possible.

Toward evening the following day she again heard snowshoes, and this time Andrew called, in haste and excitement, to get his gun.

A sheriff and party of eight men had reached his home, and summoned him to accompany them in pursuit of four train robbers who had boarded an express car, fifty miles to the southeastward, killing the messenger and a brakeman. The sheriff was tracking them.

"And they passed right close by your cabin here!" Andrew continued.

"Yes," said Olive. They called, or tried to call, on me."

She pointed to the powder-blackened boards of her ceiling. "I made free use of your gun, Andrew, and you will find your cartridges four short," she said.

"Well, well!" he exclaimed, in astonishment. "Did you hit any of them?

"I don't suppose I did. I hope not," she replied.

"Hope not!" he cried. "If only you had stopped all four of them, it would have been the best job of the winter. I'll bring the gun back to you soon," he added, climbing out to set off.

"But what about Helen?" she called. "What will she do while you are gone?"

"Oh, I shall not be gone more than thirty-six hours," he said. "I wanted her to come over here, but the snow is too deep. So she is going to stay at our house."

Olive was anxious for Helen's sake all that night, the next day, and the next, for she could imagine how Helen would count the slow hours. If she did not hear from Helen that evening, she resolved to go to Andrew's cabin somehow the following forenoon, if she had to crawl over the drifts.

But toward sunset of the second day Andrew came back to leave his gun with her. He appeared greatly exhausted, and she noticed that his face had a gray, pinched expression.

"Bad luck," said he, wearily. "No luck at all. We ought never to have started with only ten men."

Olive made him come in for a few minutes while she prepared a cup of coffee for him, and he told her that the posse had found the robbers entrenched within a log hut in the valley of a creek.

"It will take a hundred men to get them out of it," he continued. "In their first volley at us they broke the sheriff's arm, and killed another of our party in his tracks. They laughed at us, and called out that they wouldn't fire again, we looked so cold and hungry! We were glad to take them at their word, and get away. They were so well fortified that we couldn't touch them. They gave us all sorts of chaff, and one of them shouted, 'Tell that wild woman back your way that we will see her later!'

"That was you, I suppose," Andrew added. "But you needn't be afraid. Our fellows have gone back to raise a big party and get soldiers, if need be. We will have them yet!"

She bade him go home to Helen, and tell her to give him a thorough sweat that evening, for she saw that he had taken a severe cold.

Olive kept the carbine loaded and at hand, and when, toward evening of the second day after, she heard a faint noise on the snow outside, she seized it promptly. She feared the train robbers might make good their threat to take vengeance on her.

But instead of robbers it was Helen. A moment after, she heard Helen call to her, and ran to show her the entrance into the covered way.

"You dear girl!" She cried. "What is the matter?"

"Oh, Olive!" she faltered. "Andrew is quite sick. Do you suppose we can get a doctor?"

"I'll go back with you, and we will see what we can do," said Olive. She drew the snowy, tired little woman inside while she fed the cow, and made hasty preparations to leave.

"He is feverish and badly pressed for breath," Helen told her. "Do you suppose it is pneumonia?"

Olive had no medicines save a bottle of ipecac and a box of mustard. They took those and set off at once. Helen had tried to walk on Andrew's snowshoes, but after many mishaps with them, had stood them up in the snow, and come on in the snowshoe tracks which Andrew had made while going to and from Olive's place. They did not break through these old tracks as badly as one might have supposed, but got on quite rapidly, and picking up the rejected snowshoes, reached Helen's cabin in the dusk.

Andrew was sitting up by the stove, and Olive found that he had been much opposed to Helen's going for her. "Why, it is only a bad cold," he said to Olive. "I didn't mean that she should go, but she slipped out before I knew it.

"I'm going after those robbers again tomorrow, when the big party comes along," he continued.

Olive noticed that his flesh was very hot, that his breath came rapidly, and that he frequently coughed in a particularly abrupt, harsh manner. She resolved, if he continued to get worse, to make an effort to send, or else go herself, for a physician the following morning.

At any rate they could probably reach their Norwegian friends on snowshoes—the distance was only about three miles—and induce the man to make the trip for them.

Whether or not the physician could be prevailed on to come out to them was a little uncertain, but Olive hoped that he would come, if the weather held fair.

They induced Andrew to put his feet in a pail of very warm water, with mustard in it, and they prepared a mustard draught for his chest. He was presently sent to bed, buried under blankets, and tucked in with three hot flatirons and two hot-water bottles.

But he could not lie down. At first they thought it obstinacy, for he laughed at them a little, but Olive soon saw that he could not breathe while lying down. So they let him sit up in bed, bolstered with pillows, and covered him in as best they could with the clothes.

Olive noticed that an asthmatic, wheezing sound issued from his throat or lungs. Still, neither Helen nor she realized that he was dangerously ill. About eleven o'clock, while Helen had gone out of the room for a moment, Andrew said to her: "Now 'Auntie', if anything should happen to me when I'm off with the party after those scamps, I want you and Helen to live together, just as you did before I came, and have my things here between you. 'Twas too bad of me ever to separate you from her. I knew it all the time. You'll never forgive me for it in this world."

Olive protested that she had already forgiven him.

"No, you never will," said he, absently.

Olive cannot narrate the sad scenes which followed that night. Nothing which Helen or she could do availed to help the unfortunate husband. He sank rapidly and fainted, and the breath did not return to his lungs.

Helen could not comprehend it. Olive had to take her hands and tell her the crushing truth: "Helen, he is dead!"

The pioneer, in the presence of death, is not surrounded by friends whose sympathy is in some measure a consolation. The calamity must often be faced alone.

There was no one nearer than the distant Norwegian settler to whom Helen and she could look for aid. They were alone with the dead, confronted with solemn duties which Helen scarcely knew how to perform. Olive had these things to think of as she strove to calm and comfort her heartbroken companion during those strangely silent hours of the waning night after Andrew's death.

Never did a colder, grayer, more desolate morning dawn. The sternest necessities of life seemed to be closing in around them.

Toward noon a large party of armed men passed the house at a little distance on snowshoes. They were the avengers, in pursuit of the train robbers.

One of them came down to the door and rapped loudly—a stern-visaged frontiersman, girt about with cartridge belt and revolvers, and with a carbine in his hand.

"Where's Phillister? Is he ready to go?" he asked, when Olive opened the door.

"No," she replied, with downcast head. "He cannot go with you."

"But he must! He's pledged!" exclaimed the man, with a trace of excitement in his voice.

"Come in and see," she said.

He followed her briskly in. She opened the door of the little inner room, and pointed silently to the bed. The man started, gazed fixedly for an instant, and then, with a movement that appeared to be wholly instinctive, pulled off his cap, and turned his face toward Helen and her with a glance of genuine compassion.

"That's hard on you two womenfolk," he said, briefly. Then after a moment's thought, he added, "Hadn't I better carry him out for ye? There's only one thing that we can do in such a case out here. We have to put the dead in the snow until we can get a coffin."

"Oh no, no, no!" sobbed Helen.

"Well, I wish I could help ye," said the man, compassionately. "If we come back this way, and I'm alive, I'll look in and do all I can for ye."

With a short "Good day!" He went out and hurried on after his fellow regulators.

It was a cold, bright afternoon, and after attending to the wants of the horse, the cow, and the poultry in the little stable, Olive took Helen with her, and went back to her home to look after her animals. The walk in the fresh, cold air was good for Helen. Her mind rallied somewhat from the paralyzing weight of her grief as they walked over the frozen snow.

They prepared supper at Olive's dugout, and remained till evening, intending to return by the light of a nearly full moon which had risen, and shone brightly on the snow.

But as they were setting out, they heard the howling of wolves, and not daring to face them, the women retreated indoors. The hungry creatures came about the place, yelping wildly as they dug once more at the frozen walls of Olive's little stable. She frightened them away by discharging the carbine.

As they sat beside Olive's little stove that evening, they took their circumstances under calmer consideration. Olive wrote a letter to Andrew's parents, who lived in West Virginia, telling them of his death, and of the wish which he had expressed during the last few hours of his life, that Helen should have what he possessed in the way of property.

As soon as they had returned to Helen's house the following forenoon, and had attended to the animals, Olive put on Andrew's snowshoes, and taking a part of her money, set off to walk to the cabin of the Norwegian settlers. She had but one thought—to make arrangements for a proper and seemly funeral.

It was her first experience upon snowshoes. The tracks which she made would probably have disqualified her, *prima facie*, for admission to any Good Templars' association. She had left Helen silently weeping, but months afterward Helen confessed to her that, as she watched Olive's surprising antics, she had difficulty in refraining from laughing outright.

The Norse husband, whose name was Bjornson, had great difficulty in understanding what Olive wanted, but finally she made him comprehend, as she thought, and concluded a bargain with him to take her letter to the next town, and ask the clergyman who resided there to come to Andrew's cabin if possible.

She entrusted ten dollars to Bjornson with which to purchase a coffin, and then returned to Helen.

They waited in much distress for two days and three nights before Bjornson came to them. Then, in his broken English, he endeavored to tell them that he had been to the town and posted Olive's letter, but that the clergyman was absent from home, and that, worse still, some rascally fellows who he met there had lured him into a building and robbed him of the money.

Probably Bjornson told them the truth for certainly he posted the letter. During the following June Helen received a reply from Andrew's old mother, in West Virginia, expressing a mother's grief for her boy, and declaring that she wished that his property should go, as he desired, to his wife, whom she would like dearly to see.

Compelled by necessity, Olive took down a part of one of the partitions inside of Helen's house, and with Andrew's tools constructed a coffin. In a secure place outside the house they left Andrew's remains to the care of the kindly frost until spring, and then they buried them in a shady spot under one of the oaks near Olive's cabin.

The exigencies of the pioneer's rude life again reclaimed their sway over them. The winter was snowy and cold beyond all precedent in Dakota. The snowdrifts were so deep that Olive could not drive her cow to Helen's cabin, or Helen's horse and cow to hers. In midwinter, therefore, they had to care for two claims, separated by two miles of well-nigh impassable walking.

Every day a trip had to be made from one place to the other, although sometimes, during storms, the poor animals went without water for two or three days. The women left water in tubs where the animals could reach it, but often the water froze. It was easy to place sufficient fodder from the stacks where they could eat their fill, but this, too, was attended by much waste.

Olive and Helen tried to make the trip every day, when the weather permitted, and for a long time they passed alternate nights at each place. One forenoon during the first fortnight they were caught out in a furious snow squall—almost a blizzard—and were so near to losing their way that they were greatly frightened. To obviate this danger in part they cut bundles of sticks and branches, which they carried along their beaten path and struck in the snow at distances of about forty feet apart, to guide them in case of sudden storms.

These constant trips added greatly to their hardships, but both Helen and Olive's health continued good, though they became somewhat weatherbeaten from facing the winds so much.

The frontiersman who had promised to look in upon them, on his return, never appeared. They learned afterward that the robbers were pursued in the direction of the Montana line, and that two men were killed and several wounded. The man who called on them may have been one of these victims.

Another source of anxiety and excitement with them was Nero, Andrew's horse, a young animal which had never been well broken either to halter or harness. Their attempts to care for him were attended by stirring episodes.

The poor creature tired of his stall, and Olive, fearing that some harm would come to him from inaction, often attempted to lead him out. She quite expected that he would disable her before spring, and still wonders that he did not. He bit her arm one day, through her dress sleeve, in a most painful manner. In fact, it was the last of a long series of bites which he had habitually given her.

February and the greater part of March passed by, the weather continuing steadily cold for the most part. Then came a great rainstorm and general thaw of the snow. During this downpour, equipped in rubber boots which they had been careful to bring with them, they made the trip from Helen's house to Olive's dugout, where they passed the night.

It rained all night. Next morning they found that Olive's covered way had fallen in, and that the snow had settled surprisingly and grown very soft. Olive's roof leaked badly, and as her dugout had not been constructed with a view to the careful exclusion of water, a puddle had gathered beneath the boards of the floor.

Still the rain fell in floods. It seemed useless to attempt to return to Helen's. Toward evening, however, the water came into Olive's dugout to such a depth that they began to wish they had done so. With much difficulty they hoisted the floor, and placed blocks beneath it.

Olive's head now touched the low roof. As much as two feet of water had collected in the hole beneath the floor.

By daylight next morning they were literally drowned out; not more than four feet of space was left between the submerged floor and the roof. They escaped out of doors, from their damp bed, with some difficulty.

Fortunately the weather continued warm, and the rain had now ceased. The clouds were breaking away, and the ground was bare in spots. The air was very refreshing.

They hurriedly fed old Spot and the fowls, and leaving the doors of the shed and the poultry house open, set off for Helen's.

Olive had remained behind for a moment, but as she emerged from the oaks, following their now icy old path, she saw that Helen had stopped short.

"Just look at the water!" Helen exclaimed to her. "How are we ever to get across?"

Down in the hollow beyond, the little creek, previously mentioned, was swollen to a veritable river, which roared as it rushed along.

They went slowly forward and gazed upon it in great perplexity. Where two days before they had crossed on the snow, with scarcely a thought of water beneath, there was now a yellow, snow-clogged torrent fully sixty feet in width.

For a mile or more they ascended the hither bank, looking in vain, for some narrower place, where possibly the ice still spanned it, but nowhere did they find a passable spot. There was little prospect that the waters would subside for several days, and yet they must cross it.

Olive set at work to build a raft. She cut two logs, each about eight feet in length, from the fallen cottonwood tree, and these they dragged down to the creek with Olive's clothesline.

The logs were green and heavy, but they served as frame for the floor of the raft, which the women laid on them, using the boards and joists of the floor of Olive's dugout, which was now afloat.

At last they completed a float which Olive was sure would sustain their weight. Then, providing themselves with two narrow strips of board, each about ten feet in length, to use as paddles, they put off.

The raft moved without difficulty, and they soon gained the middle of the creek. There the current proved too strong for them. Helen, growing frightened, sat down suddenly, and clutched the sides.

Olive was dizzy herself; for the raft revolved two or three times, and was carried swiftly downstream. Something—either the rotary movement, or the sight of the banks and bushes, gliding past them—rendered them both actually seasick.

Olive thinks they were carried down a hundred yards or more, still turning around. Recovering her head a little, she then made a vigorous effort to pole the raft ashore, and so far succeeded that she ran it upon a bunch of submerged brush, ten or a dozen feet from the bank, on the side of the stream toward Helen's claim.

Then the raft canted suddenly over with a very tipsy movement, and spilled them both off into the icy water. Olive says it is quite likely that they screamed, for although the water was not more than three feet deep there, it was terribly cold. Olive seized Helen, and they scrambled to land, gasping for breath.

Helen declared that she would "never go on that horrid thing again." But Olive still had hopes of it, and as she was as wet already as she could be, she again waded in, drew the raft ashore, and secured it.

They had crossed the creek, although not wholly in the manner that they had anticipated, and with chattering teeth they now ran to Helen's house, where they hastened to change their clothes, kindle a fire, and prepare a warm breakfast.

Olive feared that they had taken severe colds, but neither of them experienced any ill effects from the adventure. Hardships had inured them to such exposures.

Later in the day, after Olive had recovered her courage a little, she went back to the creek, tied a stone to the end of her line, and threw it across the stream several times, until she succeeded in lodging it amidst the brush on the other bank. Then, making the hither end of the line fast, she pulled the raft across the creek by aid of the line. Thus she established a sort of rude rope ferry, which answered their purpose very well. They crossed and recrossed by it twenty times during the next two weeks.

Spring had now returned. Olive's "winter in a dugout" had ended. Much more might be told of the ladies' subsequent experiences as homesteaders, but by far the worst of their troubles were over.

The season which followed was a very favorable one, and Olive and Helen did well with their poultry, their dairy products, and their garden.

However, the wheat crop which they raised from twelve acres of land returned scarcely ten dollars above the expenses of cultivation, and so they realized that they could not make money in raising wheat on such a tiny scale.

But the fever to possess a large wheat farm still possessed them. Not only did they resolve to retain both their claims, under the Homestead Law, they each also took steps to preempt a quarter-section of the land which lay between these claims.

Availing themselves still further of the generous lumber laws of our country, they each entered a claim, under the Timber Culture Act, and thus obtained possession of all the available land lying between their two original claims, uniting the whole tract into one farm.

It turned out, three years were required, just as they had thought, to make a beginning in wheat. Fortunately for them, their first wheat crop, on a larger scale, was a good one. It set them on their feet.

When I dropped by last year, on my trip to see Theodora, they had three hundred acres in wheat. They have hired several laborers, and I can truly say they are doing well and have realized the plans and the hopes which led them to seek a new home in the Dakotas. Helen and Robert, her new husband, run the farm while Aunt Olive—still energetic—looks after their three children and cooks. They are very comfortable, with many settlers about them, and a railroad and post office near.

27

What the Man in the Moon Saw

IN 1879 THE OLD SQUIRE RETIRED TO WORK ON A cyclopedia of knowledge: *The Book for Boys.* So it was his last year of lumbering up in the Flagstaff region. The winter's cut of spruce had gone down Dead River to the Kennebec, and the old gentleman had driven up from home to pay off the river drivers and had taken me with him—for this was after Addison, Halstead, and the girls had left the farm, and the old gentleman was there alone again, except for such assistance as the present writer—then about twenty-seven—could give him.

There was a crew of twenty-eight rivermen, and it is doing them no injustice to say they were rough fellows, noisy, sometimes quarrelsome, especially so after they were paid off for their season's work and, as was often the case, some sneaking bootlegger had taken possession of the little tavern where we had put up while adjusting their accounts, and after supper that night they were "celebrating" after their own fashion. The hubbub was prodigious. Some were roaring forth songs, some crowing like roosters, others dancing jigs, the caulks of their driver's boots splintering the floor. The crockery at the supper table suffered. Two chairs had crashed. High words rose at intervals, and there had been several scuffles.

To be out of the noise, the Old Squire walked out to the road which passed the tavern door. "It's their way of having a good time, I suppose," he said. "But crazy men couldn't behave worse. It's the same every year when they come off the drive. I'm afraid we shall get no sleep here."

Dusk was falling. But for the uproar in the tavern behind us, the night was very calm—the stillness of the northern wilderness when its burden of winter snow first goes off. At a distance the swollen river sent its low, hoarse murmur across the forest. A few frogs, after their long, cold slumbers, were raising tiny voices, hailing each other in the twilight, and afar, a little saw-whet owl began its measured crake. Then came a louder outburst of howls from the exhilarated crew inside the open tavern door. The Old Squire turned to listen.

"My son, what say to driving home tonight instead of stopping here?" he said suddenly. "'Tis thirty-eight miles, but the night isn't cold. The moon will be up in a little while. Our horse has been standing all day. And I'd like to think about my book." The suggestion pleased me immensely. "Well, then," the Old Squire cried, "you run and hitch up Whistle (our driving horse). I will go indoors, settle our bill and get our coats."

We had bought half a dozen bushel baskets that afternoon from an Indian basket maker who lived near the tavern—baskets woven from ash strip. After hitching up, I set the baskets together and lashed them on behind the buckboard seat. The Old Squire came out, and we set off, glad to get away into the restful quiet of the spring night.

"You may drive," he said. "Perhaps your eyes are sharper than mine." And then for some minutes he sat silent beside me as I guided Whistle along the narrow, dark road, which, indeed, was little better than a trail. "Oh, well, I suppose we must never allow ourselves to be discouraged about the human race," he said at length, and I knew he was thinking of the noisy crew we had just left at the tavern. "But improvement comes slow, painfully slow, and sometimes we grow disheartened because we fail to witness in one short lifetime that progress which only comes in the course of centuries. Patience is what we need to cultivate, patience and faith. I hardly hope to live long enough to see intoxicants abolished," he added. "But that will come in time."

A silvery radiance began to show above the eastern horizon, and ere long the full moon slowly poked up its round, ruddy face over the black tops of the spruce woods, preternaturally big and strangely like a human countenance. The Old Squire laughed. "The man in the moon is looking at us," said he. "Looks jolly, tonight, as if out for a frolic." He laughed again. "A full moon like that always makes me feel cattish, as if I would like to play hide-and-seek. When I was a boy, the young folks played hide-and-seek a good deal by moonlight. Hide-and-coop, we called it then, for when the one who 'blinded' had counted a hundred he shouted, 'Ready,' and all who had hidden cried, 'Coop.' Then the search for the hidden ones began, in the barns and about the corncribs and haystacks. There is something in moonlight that makes us feel antic."

Whistle trotted rapidly on; he had been homesick and was glad to get away from the wild uproar at the tavern. As we drew near Duck Pond, six miles on our way, voices were heard ahead, and the glare of a fire came in view. Pulling up at the long bridge over a brook that flowed into the pond, we saw torches along the brook bed. A party of young fellows were there, spearing suckers who had returned to deposit their spawn. By waiting till about an hour after dark and then obstructing the channel near the pond great numbers of these fish can often be speared.

The birch bark torches lit up the water; the fishers, each with his torch in one hand and his four-pronged spear in the other, were leaping briskly to and fro, and the thud of the iron points among the stones rang out sharply. On both sides, the banks were already "aflop" with the impaled fish.

As we sat watching the scene, one of the young torchbearers approached so near that Whistle snorted at the sputter of the blazing bark. "Don't you want some suckers?" the youngster shouted to us. "They're big."

Big ones they were, and for a twenty-five-cent piece he filled one of our bushel baskets from the squirming heaps on the bank. Numbers of these suckers would have weighed three pounds apiece. Then for two hours or more Whistle trotted on, the moon mounting higher, frogs peeping, and now and again an owl hooting in the forest depths. Twice our horse stopped short as if fearing to go on, and we surmised there was a bear not far away. Presently we heard one give its quite human-sounding outcry at a distance. Once as two porcupines scuttled across the road a lynx, evidently in pursuit of them, uttered its raspy screech from a nearby thicket. All the wild denizens of the forest were astir, seeking their prey or the companionship of their kind.

A hour later we emerged to a settlement along the intervales of Wild Stream, where there were five farms and a sawmill, a neighborhood quaintly known as "Jericho." At the first of these habitations the good people were apparently abed and asleep; not a light glimmered from a window. And now a roguish idea, inspired by the moon, perhaps, occurred to the Old Squire.

"What if we leave them a mess of suckers?" he said laughing. "We can put them in one of these new baskets and set it by the house door. When they find that basket and suckers in the morning, they will wonder where in the world they came from! When they quiz their neighbors about the basket, and find it doesn't belong to any of them, they will wonder still more! It will be a mystery in Jericho."

So we pulled up, put a half-dozen of the suckers in one of the new bushel baskets, which I deposited gently on the doorstep, then stole back to the buckboard.

For some reason, the humor of this prank appealed to the Old Squire that night. "Let's not show partiality in Jericho," he said. "It's rather expensive in bushel baskets. But never mind. We can get more. Let's leave a mess of suckers at every house here."

Accordingly we pulled up at the next farm. Here, too, all was dark and still, and, counting out six more suckers in another basket, I left it on the doorstep, and we walked Whistle on to the next place. It was there the sawmill was located. We knew the name of the folks there, having once called on our way up to the lumber camps. It was Kilburn. The man was a prosperous farmer and millman, with a large family of girls. The sawmill was on the stream just across the road from the farm. The latter consisted of a house and long ell, at the far end of which were a shed and a large barn. The mill was on the west side of the highway, and the farm on the east side. About the mill were numerous piles

of freshly sawn lumber, slabs, and edgings, all showing quite clearly in
the moonlight. Water was pouring through the sluiceway of the dam.
Otherwise all seemed quiet. On passing the house, however, we saw
that here the people were astir. Late as was the hour, two front windows of the ell were brilliantly alight.

"We must be cautious here," the Old Squire whispered, and what
we did was to pass the house for two or three hundred yards, before
stopping. I was of the opinion that the old gentleman had better remain
at the buckboard and hold Whistle while I went softly back, but I did
not like to tell him so, and he kept with me. He appeared to be renew-
ing his youth, that night! Accordingly, we tied Whistle to a tree by the
roadside at the edge of the woods, then went back with our basket. The
curtains of the two lighted windows were not drawn, and on approaching the door we could hardly help seeing what was going on inside.
The Kilburn girls must have had the company of their neighbors, that
night, for there was a party of eight young ladies there, sitting about a
long table, all busily engaged cutting and weaving strips of gay-colored
paper into some sort of airy fabrics, and, as this was about the first of
May, we guessed at once that their ornate creations were May baskets,
for use at May night frolics.

Afterward, I had little doubt that those Jericho girls were gathered
there, and sitting up late, in expectation of May night calls.

After a single hasty glance inside, I stole forward to deposit our
basket of fish on the doorstep, the Old Squire remaining a few steps
behind. The glare from the windows was in our eyes, and in setting the
large basket on the stone step I inadvertently jarred a tin pail that had
been left, bottom up, at one end of it. I think those girls must have been
listening. Slight as was the sound, they apparently heard it; yet even so,
how eight girls contrived to rush forth so quickly is still a mystery! We
had scarcely taken three strides before the door flew open and they
were out, laughing, shouting, and chasing us—for it is a part of the old
Mayday game to catch the fellow that hangs a May basket.

We were badly taken by surprise. Our plan hadn't provided for this.
I durst not speak aloud to the Old Squire, nor he to me. Aware, perhaps, that his legs were not quite what they once were, the old gentle-

man dodged round the corner of the house, then hooked it across the road to the cover of a lumber pile beside it, and from that, slid down a great heap of sawdust at the lower end of the mill and hid beneath the mill floor. But I had sprinted straight away down the road, to reach our team, and, though hotly pursued by three of the girls who ran like veritable Atalanta, I succeeded in casting off Whistle's halter, jumping on the buckboard and escaping, though not without a poignant sense of anxiety as to what was happening to the Old Squire, who had disappeared, I hardly knew how or where. One of those sharp-eyed girls had caught a glimpse of him, however, as he crossed the road, and five of them were after him among the board piles, but he got to cover beneath the mill floor and, scrambling over still greater heaps of the dry sawdust that lay under it, dug himself in, so to speak, far back and to considerable depth, then lay still. But of this, of course, I knew nothing.

My pursuers did not follow far, after I reached the buckboard. "Oh, we know you, Jim Brown!" one of them called out several times. "We know you, even if you have got on a new cap! Had to come with your horse, didn't you? Didn't dare to trust your own legs!" another cried, mockingly. Evidently I was mistaken for someone they knew well.

As soon as I was sure they had turned back, I pulled up, hitched Whistle again, and followed them softly, keeping to the shadows of the trees beside the road. I was consumed by anxiety about the Old Squire. I guessed now that he had run to the sawmill, for I heard the girls calling out to one another there, and I was afraid he might have tried to cross the stream on the mill dam and fallen in. At that season of the year the water was high. I stole nearer, through alder clumps, till I came within easy hearing distance, then listened intently. Judging from the voices, all eight of the girls were now at the mill, searching diligently. "Oh, we know you are hid here, somewheres, Mark Jordan!" one cried. "You may as well come out. You haven't fooled us by wearing that long coat and big hat!" another cried, laughing. "Emma saw you scud across the road. She knew you."

For some time longer the search went on, in and out among the piles of lumber and slabs, and in every dark nook and corner of the mill. Then they crept down the bank and looked under the mill floor, among the wheels and sawdust heaps. "If you've buried yourself up here, you had better come out," I heard one of them cry, and then they got sticks of edging and appeared to be prodding the heaps.

Where or in what plight the Old Squire was, I couldn't imagine. Apparently those girls believed he was Mark Jordan and was hidden somewhere thereabouts. At length two of them crossed over on the dam and searched the log piles and bushes on the other side of the stream. Afterward, they all stood around a long while in the moonlight, shouting occasional exhortations to the supposed Mark to come forth and show himself.

What to do, I hardly knew. If the Old Squire was safe, it was best, of course, for both of us to keep still, but I was dreadfully afraid something had befallen him. For a man of seventy-nine, he was active, but of course seventy-nine isn't twenty. I began to be afraid he might have had a bad fall among the logs below the dam or slipped off them into rapid water.

It seemed to me those girls would never go back indoors! Two of them stood on top of a board pile, watching the mill and everything about it. I began to fear they would remain there till morning! At last it occurred to me that the Old Squire might have reached the woods on the far side of the stream and made a circuit around to the road below, where we had left our team. In that case he would be waiting for me there, and upon that, I hastened back where I had last hitched Whistle. But he was not there, and again I stole back up the road toward the mill. I was now really alarmed, and my resolution was as good as taken to hail the girls, reveal our identity, and ask them to aid me in looking the Old Squire up. Before I came in sight of the mill, however, I saw someone stealing down the road in the shadow of the woods, and was vastly relieved a moment later to hear the old gentleman speak. The girls, it appeared, had at last given up the hunt and gone into the house. He was laughing, and he looked very dusty in the moonlight.

"Well, they didn't catch us, did they?" were his first words—with the grin of a boy eighteen, and as I brushed him off a bit he told me of his predicament under the mill. "I thought they would never give up!" he said. "They stuck sticks down all around me. Once they hit my leg, and one of them crept clean over me, pawing in the heap with her hands. I was nearly smothered. They were bent on capturing Mark Jordan."

We drove on—the moon riding at its full height in the heavens—and owing to our escapade in Jericho we did not reach home till nearly seven in the morning.

"It may be just as well not to say too much about this," the Old Squire remarked, with a droll glance at my face, as we drove up the lane. "Your grandmother, you know, has rather strict ideas about the behavior of old people. She might think this much worse than it really was."

I fully agreed with him, but we came near exposure at the start. Breakfast was ready on the table, and after putting up Whistle we went directly in, Grandmother greeting the Old Squire with a caress, as usual, after such absences from home. But something about his hair and his raiment instantly attracted her attention.

"Why, Joseph, your hair is full of something that looks like sawdust!" she exclaimed. "Your clothes, too, are all covered with it! And, my sakes! Both pockets of your coat are full of it. Where have you been?"

"Well, Ruth, the fact is we were rather busy for an hour or two at a sawmill up the country," the Old Squire replied with an all-wise glance across at me.

"I should say 'busy'!" the old lady cried, brushing at his sleeves. "You must have worked awfully hard! And at your age, too, Joe! Do come to the wood box while I empty your pockets." She added, "What could you have been thinking of?"

"Actually, I was thinking of my book," he said. "And of how I should write it for girls too, for they're far more curious than boys."

The dear old lady looked a little puzzled and, in fact, not wholly satisfied. But the choking sounds I made distracted her attention just then, and we were able to scrape by. Barely.

28

The Old Squire's Book

THE BOOK IS OUT OF PRINT NOW, AND I DO NOT KNOW
where a copy of it could be picked up. I have been to the old bookshops
in Boston and in Portland, also to the public libraries, and have advertised in a literary journal, but I have not come across a single copy of it.

That is not so very strange after all, for the book was not published
to sell. If I remember correctly, only seven hundred copies were printed,
and the Old Squire gave no copies to editors, reviewers, or libraries. As
long ago as 1888, he had given away his last copy to a boy who asked
for one; for that was what he had the book printed for—to give to boys.

When he was a lad of twelve, one of the old-time schoolmasters of
Maine gave him a little book called *Facts of Useful Knowledge*—a curious
volume that contained a miscellaneous collection of reading matter,
beginning with Eclipses and Comets, going on to the Atmosphere, the
Months of the Year, the Sources of the Mississippi, Insect Life, Washington's Personal Habits, the Grain Fields of the West, Remarkable
Books in Chinese, Latin and Labor, Educate Yourself, and so on for
fully two hundred different topics.

There were not many books in great-grandfather's pioneer cabin.
The Bible, the Catechism, the hymn book, and *The Farmer's Almanac*
were almost the only volumes to which, when a lad, the Old Squire had
access. So this little volume of useful facts was a bonanza to him. He
pored over it until he nearly knew it by heart, and he often said, in later
years, that this quaint little book had done more to foster his tastes and

to stimulate his ambition to learn than any textbook he studied subsequently at Hebron Academy. The book came to him at a time when his boyish mind was eager for information.

Remembering what good that little volume had done him, the Old Squire, who was rising eighty, determined to write a similar but more comprehensive book, and to give it to boys who did not have many advantages at home.

He retired from the lumber business, gave up the care of the farm to me, and set to work on that book. From week to week his interest in it grew. He went walking round the house and the farm, his face alight with the new ideas for the book that kept coming to his mind. He sent off for works on a great variety of subjects, thumbed through our encyclopedia set, and borrowed books from his friends in Portland. He had, I am sure, a tremendously good time with that book, for he was firm in his faith that it would accomplish a great work.

The old gentleman was a year or more in compiling it. At first he had planned a volume of about two hundred pages: but more and more things suggested themselves to him as he proceeded, and he added page after page, until the final volume contained 450 pages of fine, nonpareil type. He started the book with an account of the sun, the earth, the moon, the planets, the Milky Way, the fixed stars, the constellations, and the signs of the zodiac. Then came a description of the world. He explained the causes of earthquakes and volcanoes, and described some of the historic catastrophes and eruptions. He told how coal, petroleum, and fossils came to exist, and he wrote extensively about metals—gold, silver, copper, iron, and so forth—also about insect life, trees, flowers, reptiles, fishes, and mammals.

After that he described the different races of mankind. He gave an account of the Indians of America, and related ten lively stories of Indian war times. He also told of the Aztecs of Mexico and of the Incas of Peru, and described the conquest of those countries by Cortes and Pizarro. Much of this the old gentleman condensed and wrote out himself—a task in which he showed not a little skill in selecting the points of greatest interest.

Afterwards came accounts of the four great empires of antiquity, the Babylonian, the Persian, the Macedonian, and the Roman, with brief biographies of Nebuchadnezzar, Cyrus, Alexander the Great, and the Caesars. The history of Egypt and Greece and the wars of Rome and Carthage made thirty pages. Mythology came next and, following that, the great religions of mankind, what each taught, with sketches of their founders—Mohammed, Buddha, Confucius, and Jesus. He added selections from the Bible, the Koran, and the Vedas, and pointed out how Christianity differed from other creeds.

Then came a hundred pages of ancient literature, beginning with the Roman, Greek, and Hebrew alphabets. He included examples of Greek from Xenophon's *Anabasis* and Homer's *Iliad*, and of Latin from Caesar's *Commentaries on the Gallic War* and from Virgil, in order that boys might see how these languages looked and be stimulated to study them further. Translations from other classic authors followed.

He next took up modern literature, English, French, Italian, German, and Spanish; he gave citations from the most celebrated authors, and suggested what was most worth reading.

Finally came what was really the most wonderful part of the book: 210 pages of a truly wonderful miscellany; a veritable thesaurus of everything the Old Squire had ever seen that interested him or piqued his fancy. Where he had gathered all the facts, I cannot imagine. This miscellany included accounts of remarkable epochs, episodes, and crises of history, dates of all great achievements and inventions, and of birthdays of historic characters, wise sayings, last words of the departing great, quotations from famous speeches, and the Constitution of the United States. There followed a brief history of the Revolutionary War, the War of 1812, and the Civil War, with accounts of the great battles on land and sea, and also accounts of certain other great battles of the world.

That was not all, or the half, or the quarter of what was compressed into those 450 pages. I do not believe that anything equaling it was ever done before, or has been done since. It contained an education in itself.

I forgot to say that among all those different topics were sandwiched short anecdotes and stories, generally pertaining to the subject last treated. In short, from start to finish, it was what Horace Greeley would have called "mighty interesting reading."

The Old Squire had planned to have illustrations made for the book, but because of the difficulty of getting good pictures, he finally decided to use only a few portraits of famous personages. If set up in ordinary long primer type, the book would have made nine or ten hundred pages; that was why he chose nonpareil, for he wished to make it a book that a boy could carry in his pocket.

At the village, six miles from the old farm, there was a printer named Drake, who published the county paper, and a bookbinder named Noyes. To them the Old Squire applied, and after many conferences he contracted for the printing and binding of seven hundred copies of *The Book for Boys and Girls.*

He had really intended the book for boys, but he wished to be liberal and, on reflection, determined that girls should be included in the title. He dedicated his book, I remember, "To all the Boys and Girls whom I know."

After further discussions at the printing office, they agreed on a book six inches long and four inches wide, with margins of the pages cut narrow; the paper selected was thin but of good quality. Mister Noyes contracted to bind the book well and strongly in firm cloth—a binding that would stand hard usage.

I have forgotten the exact sum that the book cost, but it was so large that Grandmother Ruth murmured against the great expense.

"If you must give away books to boys, you had better give them Bibles," the old lady argued. "That would do them some good and make better men of them!"

The Old Squire did not at all resent the reflection on the character of his literary effort. "Yes, Bibles are good," he replied, and his faded blue eyes twinkled. "Suppose you give them the Bibles, Ruth. You've got quite a lot of money laid away."

Grandmother answered that she had never had any idea of bestowing books on all creation, and there the argument hung fire.

Setting the type and printing and binding the book took nearly seven months, and in the course of the work the rural compositors suffered much distress of mind. The Old Squire read and corrected the proof sheets himself. For hours and days he sat by the sitting room window with his spectacles far down on his nose, his pencil between thumb and forefinger, carefully and painstakingly going over each page and referring now and then to the dictionary. In spite of his scrutiny, however, a good many typographical errors escaped him. Proofreading is exacting work for a man wholly unaccustomed to it. But he toiled through it conscientiously, and afterwards, when the book was printed, he went over each copy and corrected the mistakes with pen and ink.

I feel sure that he drove to the village fifty times before the book was finally published. When it was done, and the books had lain four weeks under pressure for the binding to "set," the old gentleman went after them himself with the farm wagon and drew the three heavy boxes home. I helped him to unload them and to put them away in his room.

Grandmother said nothing; she was far from pleased.

For years afterwards, whenever the Old Squire drove out, he carried one of those books in his pocket. If he met a boy on the road, he always invited him to get in and ride. That, in fact, had always been his custom. He knew most of the boys in our rural town and a good many in adjoining towns. He liked to talk with boys and to find out what they were interested in. If a lad appeared fairly intelligent, the old gentleman would say when they came to part: "Oh, I've got a book here that perhaps you'd like to read. It tells a lot about the things we've been talking of. If you will read it, I'll give it to you, and next time we happen to meet you can tell me how you like it."

He was six or seven years in giving those books away. Most of them went to boys, but now and then he offered one to a girl if she seemed to have a taste for reading and study. He had intended to keep three copies at home, but he finally gave those away—the last one to a lame boy who was very eager to have it.

Years passed, and the book appeared to be entirely forgotten. The Old Squire lived for sixteen years after he had the book printed, reaching the advanced age of ninety-eight years and five months, but it was not till after he died that the work his book had done began to show.

It now seems that his effort to interest young people in acquiring useful knowledge and to stimulate them to get an education had been steadily and silently at work all that time. Within the past year we have heard of the book more than a score of times from men now prominent in business or professional life. The Old Squire's book, they declare, first started them on their way upward.

Only last year a man from the Pacific Coast, now a member of Congress, wrote to inquire whether we could get him another copy.

"I lost my first one, the one the Old Squire gave me, in a fire that burned my house two years ago," he wrote. "I felt worse about losing that book than losing anything else that burned; seeing the Greek alphabet in it, and reading those extracts from Xenophon's *Anabasis*, led me to fit for college.

"My folks lived in Maine then, and we possessed very few books. One June morning, when I was about eleven, I started to walk three miles to the store to buy firecrackers for the Fourth of July. On the way the Old Squire overtook me and asked me to ride. I told him where I was going and what for. He inquired whether I knew where firecrackers were made, and then told me about China and the Chinese. I suppose I looked interested, for when we came to the store he gave me that book. I used to spend hours reading it, but I don't believe I ever thought to come and thank him for it. Two years after that my folks moved west.

"I suppose the Old Squire can hardly be living at this time, but if he is, I shall be much inclined to travel to Maine on purpose to see him and thank him for that book. I want to take his hand and look into his kind face and tell him how much I owe to him."

A Friends of C. A. Stephens Society exists, hosting, among other things, an annual convention. Interested parties should write:

The Friends of Charles A. Stephens
219 Summit Hill Road
Harrison, ME 04040